PENGUIN BOOKS

COLLECTED SHORT STORIES

Robert Graves was born in 1895 in Wimbledon, son of Alfred Percival Graves, the Irish writer, and Amalia von Ranke. He went from school to the First World War, where he became a captain in the Royal Welch Fusiliers. His principal calling was poetry, and his *Selected Poems* have been published in the Penguin Poets. Apart from a year as Professor of English Literature at Cairo University in 1926, he earned his living by writing, mostly historical novels which include: *I, Claudius*; *Claudius the God*; *Sergeant Lamb of the Ninth*; *Count Belisarius*; *Wife to Mr Milton* (all published as Penguins); *Proceed, Sergeant Lamb*; *The Golden Fleece*; *They Hanged My Saintly Billy*; and *The Isles of Unwisdom*. He wrote his autobiography, *Goodbye to All That*, in 1929 and it rapidly established itself as a modern classic. *The Times Literary Supplement* acclaimed it as 'one of the most candid self-portraits of a poet, warts and all, ever painted', as well as being of exceptional value as a war document. His two most discussed non-fiction books are *The White Goddess*, which presents a new view of the poetic impulse, and *The Nazarine Gospel Restored* (with Joshua Podro), a re-examination of primitive Christianity. He translated Apuleius, Lucan, and Suetonius for the Penguin Classics, and compiled the first modern dictionary of Greek mythology, *The Greek Myths*. His translation of *The Rubáiyát of Omar Khayyám* (with Omar Ali-Shah) is also published in Penguins. He was elected Professor of Poetry at Oxford in 1961, and made an Honorary Fellow of St John's College, Oxford, in 1971.

Robert Graves died on 7 December 1985 in Majorca, his home since 1929. On his death *The Times* wrote of him, 'He will be remembered for his achievements as a prose stylist, historical novelist and memorist, but above all as the great paradigm of the dedicated poet, "the greatest love poet in English since Donne".'

ROBERT GRAVES

Collected Short Stories

*

PENGUIN BOOKS

PENGUIN BOOKS

Published by the Penguin Group
27 Wrights Lane, London W8 5TZ, England
Viking Penguin Inc., 40 West 23rd Street, New York, New York 10010, USA
Penguin Books Australia Ltd, Ringwood, Victoria, Australia
Penguin Books Canada Ltd, 2801 John Street, Markham, Ontario, Canada L3R 1B4
Penguin Books (NZ) Ltd, 182–190 Wairau Road, Auckland 10, New Zealand

Penguin Books Ltd, Registered Offices: Harmondsworth, Middlesex, England

First published in the United States of America by Doubleday & Company, Inc. 1964
First published in Great Britain by Cassell 1965
Published in Penguin Books as *Collected Short Stories* 1968
Reprinted as *The Shout and Other Stories* 1978
Reprinted under the present title 1984
5 7 9 10 8 6 4

Most of the stories in this volume have appeared in magazines. These
publications include *Punch*, the *New Statesman*, *Sports Illustrated*,
Gentleman's Quarterly, *Lilliput*, *Playboy*, and *Encounter*, More precise
acknowledgement is due to the *Saturday Evening Post* for 'Christmas
Truce', which was originally published as 'Wave No Banners' (copyright
© 1962 The Curtis Publishing Company); *Holiday*, for an early version of
'The Apartment House', published as 'An Imperial Tale' (copyright ©
1960 The Curtis Publishing Company), and the *New Strand* for the later
version of the same story, which they published as 'The Tenement: A
Vision of Imperial Rome' (copyright © 1962 International Authors N.V.);
and the *New Yorker*, in whose pages first appeared 'A Bicycle in Majorca',
'Evidence of Affluence', 'A Toast to Ava Gardner' and 'She Landed
Yesterday'.

Printed and bound in Great Britain by
Cox & Wyman Ltd, Reading
Set in Linotype Granjon

CONTENTS

Contents

MAJORCAN STORIES

INTRODUCTION

THE first of these stories, *The Shout*, was written in 1924; and the last, *Christmas Truce*, in 1962. Most of them, including such improbable ones as *Kill Them! Kill Them!*, *The Whitaker Negroes*, *Old Papa Johnson* and *A Toast to Ava Gardner*, are true, though occasional names and references have been altered. Nor can I claim to have invented the factual details even of *She Landed Yesterday*, or *An Appointment for Candlemas*. In fact, a correspondent who read *She Landed Yesterday* reproached me for not mentioning the two French copper coins found in the coffin-doll's pocket; and *An Appointment for Candlemas* brought members of the revived British witch cult to my door in search of information about flying ointments and such like. Pure fiction is beyond my imaginative range; I fetched back the main elements of *The Shout* from a cricket-match at Littlemore Asylum, Oxford.

All but two stories have been serialized on one side of the Atlantic or the other: in the *New Yorker*, *Punch*, the *Saturday Evening Post*, *Encounter*, *Playboy*, *Lilliput*, *Sports Illustrated*, the *New Satesman*, *Holiday* and elsewhere. The *New Yorker* demands particular acknowledgement of *She Landed Yesterday*, *Evidence of Affluence*, *A Bicycle in Majorca* and *A Toast to Ava Gardner*.

R.G.

Deyá,
Majorca,
Spain

ENGLISH STORIES

THE SHOUT

WHEN we arrived with our bags at the Asylum cricket ground, the chief medical officer, whom I had met at the house where I was staying, came up to shake hands. I told him that I was only scoring for the Lampton team today (I had broken a finger the week before, keeping wicket on a bumpy pitch). He said: 'Oh, then you'll have an interesting companion.'

'The other scoresman?' I asked.

'Crossley is the most intelligent man in the asylum,' answered the doctor, 'a wide reader, a first-class chess-player, and so on. He seems to have travelled all over the world. He's been sent here for delusions. His most serious delusion is that he's a murderer, and his story is that he killed two men and a woman at Sydney, Australia. The other delusion, which is more humorous, is that his soul is split in pieces – whatever that means. He edits our monthly magazine, he stage manages our Christmas theatricals, and he gave a most original conjuring performance the other day. You'll like him.'

He introduced me. Crossley, a big man of forty or fifty, had a queer, not unpleasant, face. But I felt a little uncomfortable, sitting next to him in the scoring box, his black-whiskered hands so close to mine. I had no fear of physical violence, only the sense of being in the presence of a man of unusual force, even perhaps, it somehow came to me, of occult powers.

It was hot in the scoring box in spite of the wide window. 'Thunderstorm weather,' said Crossley, who spoke in what country people call a 'college voice', though I could not identify the college. 'Thunderstorm weather makes us patients behave even more irregularly than usual.'

I asked whether any patients were playing.

'Two of them, this first wicket partnership. The tall one, B. C. Brown, played for Hants three years ago, and the other is a good club player. Pat Slingsby usually turns out for us too – the Australian fast bowler, you know – but we are dropping him today. In weather like this he is apt to bowl at the batsman's head. He is not insane in the usual sense, merely magnificently ill-tempered. The doctors can do nothing with him. He wants shooting, really.' Crossley began talking about the doctor. 'A good-hearted fellow and, for a mental-hospital physician, technically well advanced. He actually studies morbid psychology and is fairly well-read, up to about the day before yesterday. I have a good deal of fun with him. He reads neither German nor French, so I keep a stage or two ahead in psychological fashions; he has to wait for the English translations. I invent significant dreams for him to interpret; I find he likes me to put in snakes and apple pies, so I usually do. He is convinced that my mental trouble is due to the good old "antipaternal fixation" – I wish it were as simple as that.'

Then Crossley asked me whether I could score and listen to a story at the same time. I said that I could. It was slow cricket.

'My story is true,' he said, 'every word of it. Or, when I say that my story is "true", I mean at least that I am telling it in a new way. It is always the same story, but I sometimes vary the climax and even recast the characters. Variation keeps it fresh and therefore true. If I were always to use the same formula, it would soon drag and become false. I am interested in keeping it alive, and it is a true story, every word of it. I know the people in it personally. They are Lampton people.'

We decided that I should keep score of the runs and extras and that he should keep the bowling analysis, and at the fall of every wicket we should copy from each other. This made story-telling possible.

Richard awoke one morning saying to Rachel: 'But what an unusual dream.'

'Tell me, my dear,' she said, 'and hurry, because I want to tell you mine.'

'I was having a conversation,' he said, 'with a person (or persons, because he changed his appearance so often) of great intelligence, and I can clearly remember the argument. Yet this is the first time I have ever been able to remember any argument that came to me in sleep. Usually my dreams are so different from waking that I can only describe them if I say: "It is as though

I were living and thinking as a tree, or a bell, or middle C, or a five-pound note; as though I had never been human." Life there is sometimes rich for me and sometimes poor, but I repeat, in every case so different, that if I were to say: "I had a conversation," or "I was in love," or "I hear music," or "I was angry," it would be as far from the fact as if I tried to explain a problem of philosophy, as Rabelais's Panurge did to Thaumast, merely by grimacing with my eyes and lips.'

'It is much the same with me,' she said. 'I think that when I am asleep I become, perhaps, a stone with all the natural appetites and convictions of a stone. "Senseless as a stone" is a proverb, but there may be more sense in a stone, more sensibility, more sensitivity, more sentiment, more sensibleness, than in many men and women. And no less sensuality,' she added thoughtfully.

It was Sunday morning, so that they could lie in bed, their arms about each other, without troubling about the time; and they were childless, so breakfast could wait. He told her that in his dream he was walking in the sand hills with this person or persons, who said to him: 'These sand hills are a part neither of the sea before us nor of the grass links behind us, and are not related to the mountains beyond the links. They are of themselves. A man walking on the sand hills soon knows this by the tang of the air, and if he were to refrain from eating and drinking, from sleeping and speaking, from thinking and desiring, he could continue among them for ever without change. There is no life and no death in the sand hills. Anything might happen in the sand hills.'

Rachel said that this was nonsense, and asked: 'But what was the argument? Hurry up!'

He said it was about the whereabouts of the soul, but that now she had put it out of his head by hurrying him. All that he remembered was that the man was first a Japanese, then an Italian, and finally a kangaroo.

In return she eagerly told her dream, gabbling over the words. 'I was walking in the sand hills; there were rabbits there, too; how does that tally with what he said of life and death? I saw the man and you walking arm in arm towards me, and I ran

from you both and I noticed that he had a black silk handkerchief; he ran after me and my shoe buckle came off and I could
not wait to pick it up. I left it lying, and he stooped and put it
into his pocket.'

'How do you know that it was the same man?' he asked.

'Because,' she said, laughing, 'he had a black face and wore a
blue coat like that picture of Captain Cook. And because it was
in the sand hills.'

He said, kissing her neck: 'We not only live together and talk
together and sleep together, but it seems we now even dream
together.'

So they laughed.

Then he got up and brought her breakfast.

At about half past eleven, she said: 'Go out now for a walk,
my dear, and bring home something for me to think about: and
be back in time for dinner at one o'clock.'

It was a hot morning in the middle of May, and he went out
through the wood and struck the coast road, which after half a
mile led into Lampton.

('Do you know Lampton well?' asked Crossley. 'No,' I said,
'I am only here for the holidays, staying with friends.')

He went a hundred yards along the coast road, but then turned
off and went across the links: thinking of Rachel and watching
the blue butterflies and looking at the heath roses and thyme,
and thinking of her again, and how strange it was that they
could be so near to each other; and then taking a pinch of gorse
flower and smelling it, and considering the smell and thinking,
'If she should die, what would become of me?' and taking a slate
from the low wall and skimming it across the pond and thinking, 'I am a clumsy fellow to be her husband'; and walking
towards the sand hills, and then edging away again, perhaps
half in fear of meeting the person of their dream, and at last
making a half circle towards the old church beyond Lampton,
at the foot of the mountain.

The morning service was over and the people were out by the
cromlechs behind the church, walking in twos and threes, as
the custom was, on the smooth turf. The squire was talking in a
loud voice about King Charles, the Martyr: 'A great man, a very

great man, but betrayed by those he loved best,' and the doctor was arguing about organ music with the rector. There was a group of children playing ball. 'Throw it here, Elsie! No, to me, Elsie, Elsie, Elsie!' Then the rector appeared and pocketed the ball and said that it was Sunday; they should have remembered. When he was gone they made faces after him.

Presently a stranger came up and asked permission to sit down beside Richard; they began to talk. The stranger had been to the church service and wished to discuss the sermon. The text had been the immortality of the soul: the last of a series of sermons that had begun at Easter. He said that he could not grant the preacher's premiss that *the soul is continually resident in the body*. Why should this be so? What duty did the soul perform in the daily routine task of the body? The soul was neither the brain, nor the lungs, nor the stomach, nor the heart, nor the mind, nor the imagination. Surely it was a thing apart? Was it not indeed less likely to be resident in the body than outside the body? He had no proof one way or the other, but he would say: Birth and death are so odd a mystery that the principle of life may well lie outside the body which is the visible evidence of living. 'We cannot,' he said, 'even tell to a nicety what are the moments of birth and death. Why, in Japan, where I have travelled, they reckon a man to be already one year old when he is born; and lately in Italy a dead man – but come and walk on the sand hills and let me tell you my conclusions. I find it easier to talk when I am walking.'

Richard was frightened to hear this, and to see the man wipe his forehead with a black silk handkerchief. He stuttered out something. At this moment the children, who had crept up behind the cromlech, suddenly, at an agreed signal, shouted loud in the ears of the two men; and stood laughing. The stranger was startled into anger; he opened his mouth as if he were about to curse them, and bared his teeth to the gums. Three of the children screamed and ran off. But the one whom they called Elsie fell down in her fright and lay sobbing. The doctor, who was near, tried to comfort her. 'He has a face like a devil,' they heard the child say.

The stranger smiled good-naturedly: 'And a devil I was not

so very long ago. That was in Northern Australia, where I lived with the black fellows for twenty years. "Devil" is the nearest English word for the position that they gave me in their tribe; and they also gave me an eighteenth-century British naval uniform to wear as my ceremonial dress. Come and walk with me in the sand hills and let me tell you the whole story. I have a passion for walking in the sand hills: that is why I came to this town ... My name is Charles.'

Richard said: 'Thank you, but I must hurry home to my dinner.'

'Nonsense,' said Charles, 'dinner can wait. Or, if you wish, I can come to dinner with you. By the way, I have had nothing to eat since Friday. I am without money.'

Richard felt uneasy. He was afraid of Charles, and did not wish to bring him home to dinner because of the dream and the sand hills and the handkerchief: yet on the other hand the man was intelligent and quiet and decently dressed and had eaten nothing since Friday; if Rachel knew that he had refused him a meal, she would renew her taunts. When Rachel was out of sorts, her favourite complaint was that he was overcareful about money; though when she was at peace with him, she owned that he was the most generous man she knew, and that she did not mean what she said; when she was angry with him again, out came the taunt of stinginess: 'Tenpence-halfpenny,' she would say, 'tenpence-halfpenny and threepence of that in stamps'; his ears would burn and he would want to hit her. So he said now: 'By all means come along to dinner, but that little girl is still sobbing for fear of you. You ought to do something about it.'

Charles beckoned her to him and said a single soft word; it was an Australian magic word, he afterwards told Richard, meaning *Milk*: immediately Elsie was comforted and came to sit on Charles' knee and played with the buttons of his waistcoat for awhile until Charles sent her away.

'You have strange powers, Mr Charles,' Richard said.

Charles answered: 'I am fond of children, but the shout startled me; I am pleased that I did not do what, for a moment, I was tempted to do.'

'What was that?' asked Richard.

'I might have shouted myself,' said Charles.

'Why,' said Richard, 'they would have liked that better. It would have been a great game for them. They probably expected it of you.'

'If I had shouted,' said Charles, 'my shout would have either killed them outright or sent them mad. Probably it would have killed them, for they were standing close.'

Richard smiled a little foolishly. He did not know whether or not he was expected to laugh, for Charles spoke so gravely and carefully. So he said: 'Indeed, what sort of shout would that be? Let me hear you shout.'

'It is not only children who would be hurt by my shout,' Charles said. 'Men can be sent raving mad by it; the strongest, even, would be flung to the ground. It is a magic shout that I learned from the chief devil of the Northern Territory. I took eighteen years to perfect it, and yet I have used it, in all, no more than five times.'

Richard was so confused in his mind with the dream and the handkerchief and the word spoken to Elsie that he did not know what to say, so he muttered: 'I'll give you fifty pounds now to clear the cromlechs with a shout.'

'I see that you do not believe me,' Charles said. 'Perhaps you have never before heard of the terror shout?'

Richard considered and said: 'Well, I have read of the hero shout which the ancient Irish warriors used, that would drive armies backwards; and did not Hector, the Trojan, have a terrible shout? And there were sudden shouts in the woods of Greece. They were ascribed to the god Pan and would infect men with a madness of fear; from this legend indeed the word "panic" has come into the English language. And I remember another shout in the *Mabinogion*, in the story of Lludd and Llevelys. It was a shriek that was heard on every May Eve and went through all hearts and so scared them that the men lost their hue and their strength and the women their children, and the youths and maidens their senses, and the animals and trees, the earth and the waters were left barren. But it was caused by a dragon.'

'It must have been a British magician of the dragon clan,' said Charles. 'I belonged to the Kangaroos. Yes, that tallies. The effect is not exactly given, but near enough.'

They reached the house at one o'clock, and Rachel was at the door, the dinner ready. 'Rachel,' said Richard, 'here is Mr Charles to dinner; Mr Charles is a great traveller.'

Rachel passed her hand over her eyes as if to dispel a cloud, but it may have been the sudden sunlight. Charles took her hand and kissed it, which surprised her. Rachel was graceful, small, with eyes unusually blue for the blackness of her hair, delicate in her movements, and with a voice rather low-pitched; she had a freakish sense of humour.

('You would like Rachel,' said Crossley, 'she visits me here sometimes.')

Of Charles it would be difficult to say one thing or another: he was of middle age, and tall; his hair grey; his face never still for a moment; his eyes large and bright, sometimes yellow, sometimes brown, sometimes grey; his voice changed its tone and accent with the subject; his hands were brown and hairy at the back, his nails well cared for. Of Richard it is enough to say that he was a musician, not a strong man but a lucky one. Luck was his strength.

After dinner Charles and Richard washed the dishes together, and Richard suddenly asked Charles if he would let him hear the shout: for he thought that he could not have peace of mind until he had heard it. So horrible a thing was, surely, worse to think about than to hear: for now he believed in the shout.

Charles stopped washing up; mop in hand. 'As you wish,' said he, 'but I have warned you what a shout it is. And if I shout it must be in a lonely place where nobody else can hear; and I shall not shout in the second degree, the degree which kills certainly, but in the first, which terrifies only, and when you want me to stop put your hands to your ears.'

'Agreed,' said Richard.

'I have never yet shouted to satisfy an idle curiosity,' said Charles, 'but only when in danger of my life from enemies, black or white, and once when I was alone in the desert without food or drink. Then I was forced to shout, for food.'

Richard thought: 'Well, at least I am a lucky man, and my luck will be good enough even for this.'

'I am not afraid,' he told Charles.

'We will walk out on the sand hills tomorrow early,' Charles said, 'when nobody is stirring; and I will shout. You say you are not afraid.'

But Richard was very much afraid, and what made his fear worse was that somehow he could not talk to Rachel and tell her of it: he knew that if he told her she would either forbid him to go or she would come with him. If she forbade him to go, the fear of the shout and the sense of cowardice would hang over him ever afterwards; but if she came with him, either the shout would be nothing and she would have a new taunt for his credulity and Charles would laugh with her, or if it were something, she might well be driven mad. So he said nothing.

Charles was invited to sleep at the cottage for the night, and they stayed up late talking.

Rachel told Richard when they were in bed that she liked Charles and that he certainly was a man who had seen many things, though a fool and a big baby. Then Rachel talked a great deal of nonsense, for she had had two glasses of wine, which she seldom drank, and she said: 'Oh, my dearest, I forgot to tell you. When I put on my buckled shoes this morning while you were away I found a buckle missing. I must have noticed that it was lost before I went to sleep last night and yet not fixed the loss firmly in my mind, so that it came out as a discovery in my dream; but I have a feeling, in fact I am certain, that Mr Charles has that buckle in his pocket; and I am sure that he is the man whom we met in our dream. But I don't care, not I.'

Richard grew more and more afraid, and he dared not tell of the black silk handkerchief, or of Charles' invitations to him to walk in the sand hills. And what was worse, Charles had used only a white handkerchief while he was in the house, so that he could not be sure whether he had seen it after all. Turning his head away, he said lamely: 'Well, Charles knows a lot of things. I am going for a walk with him early tomorrow if you don't mind; an early walk is what I need.'

'Oh, I'll come too,' she said.

Richard could not think how to refuse her; he knew that he had made a mistake in telling her of the walk. But he said: 'Charles will be very glad. At six o'clock then.'

At six o'clock he got up, but Rachel after the wine was too sleepy to come with them. She kissed him goodbye and off he went with Charles.

Richard had had a bad night. In his dreams nothing was in human terms, but confused and fearful, and he had felt himself more distant from Rachel than he had ever felt since their marriage, and the fear of the shout was gnawing at him. He was also hungry and cold. There was a stiff wind blowing towards the sea from the mountains and a few splashes of rain. Charles spoke hardly a word, but chewed a stalk of grass and walked fast.

Richard felt giddy, and said to Charles: 'Wait a moment, I have a stitch in my side.' So they stopped, and Richard asked, gasping: 'What sort of shout is it? Is it loud, or shrill? How is it produced? How can it madden a man?'

Charles was silent, so Richard went on with a foolish smile: 'Sound, though, is a curious thing. I remember once, when I was at Cambridge, that a King's College man had his turn of reading the evening lesson. He had not spoken ten words before there was a groaning and ringing and creaking, and pieces of wood and dust fell from the roof; for his voice was exactly attuned to that of the building, so that he had to stop, else the roof might have fallen; as you can break a wine glass by playing its note on a violin.'

Charles consented to answer: 'My shout is not a matter of tone or vibration but something not to be explained. It is a shout of pure evil, and there is no fixed place for it on the scale. It may take any note. It is pure terror, and if it were not for a certain intention of mine, which I need not tell you, I would refuse to shout for you.'

Richard had a great gift of fear, and this new account of the shout disturbed him more and more; he wished himself at home in bed, and Charles two continents away. But he was fascinated. They were crossing the links now and going through the bent grass that pricked through his stockings and soaked them.

Now they were on the bare sand hills. From the highest of them Charles looked about him; he could see the beach stretched out for two miles and more. There was no one in sight. Then Richard saw Charles take something out of his pocket and begin carelessly to juggle with it as he stood, tossing it from finger tip to finger tip and spinning it up with finger and thumb to catch it on the back of his hand. It was Rachel's buckle.

Richard's breath came in gasps, his heart beat violently and he nearly vomited. He was shivering with cold, and yet sweating. Soon they came to an open place among the sand hills near the sea. There was a raised bank with sea holly growing on it and a little sickly grass; stones were strewn all around, brought there, it seemed, by the sea years before. Though the place lay behind the first rampart of sand hills, there was a gap in the line through which a high tide might have broken, and the winds that continually swept through the gap kept them uncovered of sand. Richard had his hands in his trouser pockets for warmth and was nervously twisting a soft piece of wax around his right forefinger – a candle end that was in his pocket from the night before when he had gone downstairs to lock the door.

'Are you ready?' asked Charles.

Richard nodded.

A gull dipped over the crest of the sand hills and rose again screaming when it saw them. 'Stand by the sea holly,' said Richard, with a dry mouth, 'and I'll be here among the stones, not too near. When I raise my hand, shout! When I put my fingers to my ears, stop at once.'

So Charles walked twenty steps towards the holly. Richard saw his broad back and black silk handkerchief sticking from his pocket. He remembered the dream, and the shoe buckle and Elsie's fear. His resolution broke: he hurriedly pulled the piece of wax in two, and sealed his ears. Charles did not see him.

He turned, and Richard gave the signal with his hand.

Charles leaned forward oddly, his chin thrust out, his teeth bared, and never before had Richard seen such a look of fear on a man's face. He had not been prepared for that. Charles' face, that was usually soft and changing, uncertain as a cloud, now hardened to a rough stone mask, dead white at first, and then flushing outwards from the cheek bones red and redder, and at last as black, as if he were about to choke. His mouth then slowly opened to the full, and Richard fell on his face, his hands to his ears, in a faint.

When he came to himself he was lying alone among the stones. He sat up, wondering numbly whether he had been there long. He felt very weak and sick, with a chill on his heart that was worse than the chill of his body. He could not think. He put his hand down to lift himself up and it rested on a stone, a larger one than most of the others. He picked it up and felt its surface, absently. His mind wandered. He began to think about shoemaking, a trade of which he had known nothing, but now every trick was familiar to him. 'I must be a shoemaker,' he said aloud.

Then he corrected himself: 'No, I am a musician. Am I going mad?' He threw the stone from him; it struck against another and bounced off.

He asked himself: 'Now why did I say that I was a shoe-maker? It seemed a moment ago that I knew all there was to be known about shoemaking and now I know nothing at all about it. I must get home to Rachel. Why did I ever come out?'

Then he saw Charles on a sand hill a hundred yards away, gazing out to sea. He remembered his fear and made sure that the wax was in his ears: he stumbled to his feet. He saw a flurry on the sand and there was a rabbit lying on its side, twitching in a convulsion. As Richard moved towards it, the flurry ended: the rabbit was dead. Richard crept behind a sand hill out of Charles' sight and then struck homeward, running awkwardly in the soft sand. He had not gone twenty paces before he came upon the gull. It was standing stupidly on the sand and did not rise at his approach, but fell over dead.

How Richard reached home he did not know, but there he was opening the back door and crawling upstairs on his hands and knees. He unsealed his ears.

Rachel was sitting up in bed, pale and trembling. 'Thank God you're back,' she said. 'I have had a nightmare, the worst of all my life. It was frightful. I was in my dream, in the deepest dream of all, like the one of which I told you. I was like a stone, and I was aware of you near me; you were you, quite plain, though I was a stone, and you were in great fear and I could do nothing to help you, and you were waiting for something and the terrible thing did not happen to you, but it happened to me. I can't tell you what it was, but it was as though all my nerves cried out in pain at once, and I was pierced through and through with a beam of some intense evil light and twisted inside out. I woke up and my heart was beating so fast that I had to gasp for breath. Do you think I had a heart attack and my heart missed a beat? They say it feels like that. Where have you been, dearest? Where is Mr Charles?'

Richard sat on the bed and held her hand. 'I have had a bad experience too,' he said. 'I was out with Charles by the sea and as he went ahead to climb on the highest sand hill I felt very faint and fell down among a patch of stones, and when I came to myself I was in a desperate sweat of fear and had to hurry home. So I came back running alone. It happened perhaps half an hour ago,' he said.

He did not tell her more. He asked, could he come back to bed and would she get breakfast? That was a thing she had not done all the years they were married.

'I am as ill as you,' said she. It was understood between them always that when Rachel was ill, Richard must be well.

'You are not,' said he, and fainted again.

She helped him to bed ungraciously and dressed herself and went slowly downstairs. A smell of coffee and bacon rose to meet her and there was Charles, who had lit the fire, putting two breakfasts on a tray. She was so relieved at not having to get breakfast and so confused by her experience that she thanked him and called him a darling, and he kissed her hand gravely and pressed it. He had made the breakfast exactly to her liking: the coffee was strong and the eggs fried on both sides.

Rachel fell in love with Charles. She had often fallen in love with men before and since her marriage, but it was her habit to tell Richard when this happened, as he agreed to tell her when it happened to him: so that the suffocation of passion was given a

vent and there was no jealousy, for she used to say (and he had
the liberty of saying) 'Yes, I am *in love* with so-and-so, but I
only *love* you.'

That was as far as it had ever gone. But this was different.
Somehow, she did not know why, she could not own to being
in love with Charles: for she no longer loved Richard. She
hated him for being ill, and said that he was lazy, and a sham.
So about noon he got up, but went groaning around the bedroom until she sent him back to bed to groan.

Charles helped her with the housework, doing all the cooking,
but he did not go up to see Richard, since he had not been asked
to do so. Rachel was ashamed, and apologized to Charles for
Richard's rudeness in running away from him. But Charles said
mildly that he took it as no insult; he had felt queer himself that
morning; it was as though something evil was astir in the air as
they reached the sand hills. She told him that she too had had
the same queer feeling.

Later she found all Lampton talking of it. The doctor main-
tained that it was an earth tremor, but the country people said
that it had been the Devil passing by. He had come to fetch the
black soul of Solomon Jones, the gamekeeper, found dead that
morning in his cottage by the sand hills.

When Richard could go downstairs and walk about a little
without groaning, Rachel sent him to the cobbler's to get a new
buckle for her shoe. She came with him to the bottom of the
garden. The path ran beside a steep bank. Richard looked ill
and groaned slightly as he walked, so Rachel, half in anger,
half in fun, pushed him down the bank, where he fell sprawl-
ing among the nettles and old iron. Then she ran back into the
house laughing loudly.

Richard sighed, tried to share the joke against himself with
Rachel – but she had gone – heaved himself up, picked the
shoes from among the nettles, and after a while walked slowly
up the bank, out of the gate, and down the lane in the unaccustomed glare of the sun.

When he reached the cobbler's he sat down heavily. The cobbler was glad to talk to him. 'You are looking bad,' said the
cobbler.

Richard said: 'Yes, on Friday morning I had a bit of a turn; I am only now recovering from it.'

'Good God,' burst out the cobbler, 'if you had a bit of a turn, what did I not have? It was as if someone handled me raw, without my skin. It was as if someone seized my very soul and juggled with it, as you might juggle with a stone, and hurled me away. I shall never forget last Friday morning.'

A strange notion came to Richard that it was the cobbler's soul which he had handled in the form of a stone. 'It may be,' he thought, 'that the souls of every man and woman and child in Lampton are lying there.' But he said nothing about this, asked for a buckle, and went home.

Rachel was ready with a kiss and a joke; he might have kept silent, for his silence always made Rachel ashamed. 'But,' he thought, 'why make her ashamed? From shame she goes to self-justification and picks a quarrel over something else and it's ten times worse. I'll be cheerful and accept the joke.'

He was unhappy. And Charles was established in the house: gentle-voiced, hard-working, and continually taking Richard's part against Rachel's scoffing. This was galling, because Rachel did not resent it.

('The next part of the story,' said Crossley, 'is the comic relief, an account of how Richard went again to the sand hills, to the heap of stones, and identified the souls of the doctor and rector – the doctor's because it was shaped like a whiskey bottle and the rector's because it was as black as original sin – and how he proved to himself that the notion was not fanciful. But I will skip that and come to the point where Rachel two days later suddenly became affectionate and loved Richard, she said, more than ever before.')

The reason was that Charles had gone away, nobody knows where, and had relaxed the buckle magic for the time, because he was confident that he could renew it on his return. So in a day or two Richard was well again and everything was as it had been, until one afternoon the door opened, and there stood Charles.

He entered without a word of greeting and hung his hat upon a peg. He sat down by the fire and asked: 'When is supper ready?'

Richard looked at Rachel, his eyebrows raised, but Rachel seemed fascinated by the man.

She answered: 'Eight o'clock,' in her low voice, and stooping down, drew off Charles' muddy boots and found him a pair of Richard's slippers.

Charles said: 'Good. It is now seven o'clock. In another hour, supper. At nine o'clock the boy will bring the evening paper. At ten o'clock, Rachel, you and I sleep together.'

Richard thought that Charles must have gone suddenly mad. But Rachel answered quietly: 'Why, of course, my dear.' Then she turned viciously to Richard: 'And you run away, little man!' she said, and slapped his cheek with all her strength.

Richard stood puzzled, nursing his cheek. Since he could not believe that Rachel and Charles had both gone mad together, he must be mad himself. At all events, Rachel knew her mind, and they had a secret compact that if either of them ever wished to break the marriage promise, the other should not stand in the way. They had made this compact because they wished to feel themselves bound by love rather than by ceremony. So he said as calmly as he could: 'Very well, Rachel. I shall leave you two together.'

Charles flung a boot at him, saying: 'If you put your nose inside the door between now and breakfast time, I'll shout the ears off your head.'

Richard went out this time not afraid, but cold inside and quite clear-headed. He went through the gate, down the lane, and across the links. It wanted three hours yet until sunset. He joked with the boys playing stump cricket on the school field. He skimmed stones. He thought of Rachel and tears started to his eyes. Then he sang to comfort himself. 'Oh, I'm certainly mad,' he said, 'and what in the world has happened to my luck?'

At last he came to the stones. 'Now,' he said, 'I shall find my soul in this heap and I shall crack it into a hundred pieces with this hammer' – he had picked up the hammer in the coal shed as he came out.

Then he began looking for his soul. Now, one may recognize the soul of another man or woman, but one can never recognize one's own. Richard could not find his. But by chance he came upon Rachel's soul and recognized it (a slim green stone with glints of quartz in it) because she was estranged from him at the time. Against it lay another stone, an ugly misshapen flint of a mottled brown. He swore: 'I'll destroy this. It must be the soul of Charles.'

He kissed the soul of Rachel; it was like kissing her lips. Then he took the soul of Charles and poised his hammer. 'I'll knock you into fifty fragments!'

He paused. Richard had scruples. He knew that Rachel loved Charles better than himself, and he was bound to respect the compact. A third stone (his own, it must be) was lying the other side of Charles' stone; it was of smooth grey granite, about the size of a cricket ball. He said to himself: 'I will break my own soul in pieces and that will be the end of me.' The world grew black, his eyes ceased to focus, and he all but fainted. But he recovered himself, and with a great cry brought down the coal hammer crack, and crack again, on the grey stone.

It split in four pieces, exuding a smell like gunpowder: and when Richard found that he was still alive and whole, he began to laugh and laugh. Oh, he was mad, quite mad! He flung the hammer away, lay down exhausted, and fell asleep.

He awoke as the sun was setting. He went home in confusion, thinking: 'This is a very bad dream and Rachel will help me out of it.'

When he came to the edge of the town he found a group of men talking excitedly under a lamppost. One said: 'About eight o'clock it happened, didn't it?' The other said: 'Yes.' A third said: 'Ay, mad as a hatter. "Touch me," he says, "and I'll shout. I'll shout you into a fit, the whole blasted police force of you. I'll shout you mad." And the inspector says: "Now, Crossley, put your hands up, we've got you cornered at last." "One last chance," says he. "Go and leave me or I'll shout you stiff and dead."'

Richard had stopped to listen. 'And what happened to Crossley then?' he said. 'And what did the woman say?'

'"For Christ's sake," she said to the inspector, "go away or he'll kill you."'

'And did he shout?'

'He didn't shout. He screwed up his face for a moment and drew in his breath. A'mighty, I've never seen such a ghastly looking face in my life. I had to take three or four brandies afterwards. And the inspector he drops the revolver and it goes off; but nobody hit. Then suddenly a change comes over this man Crossley. He claps his hands to his side and again to his heart, and his face goes smooth and dead again. Then he begins to laugh and dance and cut capers. And the woman stares and can't believe her eyes and the police lead him off. If he was mad before, he was just harmless dotty now; and they had no trouble with him. He's been taken off in the ambulance to the Royal West County Asylum.'

So Richard went home to Rachel and told her everything and she told him everything, though there was not much to tell. She had not fallen in love with Charles, she said; she was only teasing Richard and she had never said anything or heard Charles say anything in the least like what he told her; it was part of his dream. She loved him always and only him, for all his faults; which she went through – his stinginess, his talkativeness, his untidiness. Charles and she had eaten a quiet supper, and she did think it had been bad of Richard to rush off without a word of explanation, and stay away for three hours like that. Charles might have murdered her. He did start pulling her about a bit, in fun, wanting her to dance with him, and then the knock came on the door, and the inspector shouted: 'Walter Charles Crossley, in the name of the King, I arrest you for the murder of George Grant, Harry Grant, and Ada Coleman at Sydney, Australia.' Then Charles had gone absolutely mad. He had pulled out a shoe buckle and said to it: 'Hold her for me.' And then he had told the police to go away or he'd shout them dead. After that he made a dreadful face at them and went to pieces altogether. 'He was rather a nice man; I liked his face so much and feel so sorry for him.'

'Did you like that story?' asked Crossley.

'Yes,' said I, busy scoring, 'a Milesian tale of the best. Lucius Apuleius, I congratulate you.'

Crossley turned to me with a troubled face and hands clenched trembling. 'Every word of it is true,' he said. 'Crossley's soul was cracked in four pieces and I'm a madman. Oh, I don't blame Richard and Rachel. They are a pleasant, loving pair of fools and I've never wished them harm; they often visit me here. In any case, now that my soul lies broken in pieces, my powers are gone. Only one thing remains to me,' he said, 'and that is the shout.'

I had been so busy scoring and listening to the story at the same time that I had not noticed the immense bank of black cloud that swam up until it spread across the sun and darkened the whole sky. Warm drops of rain fell: a flash of lightning dazzled us and with it came a smashing clap of thunder.

In a moment all was confusion. Down came a drenching rain, the cricketers dashed for cover, the lunatics began to scream, bellow, and fight. One tall young man, the same B. C. Brown who had once played for Hants, pulled all his clothes off and ran about stark naked. Outside the scoring box an old man with a beard began to pray to the thunder: 'Bah! Bah! Bah!'

Crossley's eyes twitched proudly. 'Yes,' said he, pointing to the sky, 'that's the sort of shout it is; that's the effect it has; but I can do better than that.' Then his face fell suddenly and became childishly unhappy and anxious. 'Oh dear God,' he said, 'he'll shout at me again, Crossley will. He'll freeze my marrow.'

The rain was rattling on the tin roof so that I could hardly hear him. Another flash, another clap of thunder even louder than the first. 'But that's only the second degree,' he shouted in my ear; 'it's the first that kills.'

'Oh,' he said. 'Don't you understand?' He smiled foolishly. 'I'm Richard now, and Crossley will kill me.'

The naked man was running about brandishing a cricket stump in either hand and screaming: an ugly sight. 'Bah! Bah! Bah!' prayed the old man, the rain spouting down his back from his uptilted hat.

'Nonsense,' said I, 'be a man, remember you're Crossley. You're a match for a dozen Richards. You played a game and lost, because Richard had the luck; but you still have the shout.'

I was feeling rather mad myself. Then the Asylum doctor rushed into the scoring box, his flannels streaming wet, still wearing pads and batting gloves, his glasses gone; he had heard our voices raised, and tore Crossley's hands from mine. 'To your dormitory at once, Crossley !' he ordered.

'I'll not go,' said Crossley, proud again, 'you miserable Snake and Apple Pie Man !'

The doctor seized him by his coat and tried to hustle him out. Crossley flung him off, his eyes blazing with madness. 'Get out,' he said, 'and leave me alone here or I'll shout. Do you hear? I'll shout. I'll kill the whole damn lot of you. I'll shout the Asylum down. I'll wither the grass. I'll shout.' His face was distorted in terror. A red spot appeared on either cheek bone and spread over his face.

I put my fingers to my ears and ran out of the scoring box. I had run perhaps twenty yards, when an indescribable pang of fire spun me about and left me dazed and numbed. I escaped death somehow; I suppose that I am lucky, like the Richard of the story. But the lightning struck Crossley and the doctor dead.

Crossley's body was found rigid, the doctor's was crouched in a corner, his hands to his ears. Nobody could understand this because death had been instantaneous, and the doctor was not a man to stop his ears against thunder.

It makes a rather unsatisfactory end to the story to say that Rachel and Richard were the friends with whom I was staying – Crossley had described them most accurately – but that when I told them that a man called Charles Crossley had been struck at the same time as their friend the doctor, they seemed to take Crossley's death casually by comparison with his. Richard looked blank; Rachel said: 'Crossley? I think that was the man who called himself the Australian Illusionist and gave that wonderful conjuring show the other day. He had practically no apparatus but a black silk handkerchief. I liked his face so much. Oh, and Richard didn't like it at all.'

'No, I couldn't stand the way he looked at you all the time,' Richard said.

OLD PAPA JOHNSON

I N July 1916 I was in hospital with one Captain H. H. Johnson of the Army Service Corps, who had a habit of referring to himself in the third person as 'Old Papa Johnson'. I was in with a lung wound, and he with a badly fractured pelvis. 'Of all the inappropriate happenings!' he said. 'Imagine, Old Papa Johnson, of all people, being laid out by the kick of an Army mule in the middle of a European war!' He added, to remove any misunderstanding: 'No, the A.S.C. isn't my corps, except just now for convenience. I'm cavalry, really – did fifteen years off and on in the Lancers. I was with them at Le Cateau and got wounded. And then rejoined them at Ypres and got it again. This time it was shell, not bullet, and the medical board gave me "Permanently unfit for Combatant Service". So I transferred to the A.S.C. – yes, I know you fire-eating young infantry officers look down on that worthy corps – and I hadn't any great passion for acting as baker's boy and butcher's delivery man myself. Still, it was better than being in England. But now that ridiculous mule ...'

Papa Johnson was about forty-five years old; very broad shoulders, medium height, I judged (but it is difficult to judge the vertical height of a man whom one sees only in a horizontal position), and a comedian's face. I only once saw it as anything but a comedian's face, and that was when a hospital orderly was impertinent. Then it set hard as stone, and his voice, which was ordinarily a comedian's voice, too, rasped like a drill instructor's; the orderly was terrified. Papa Johnson talked the most idiotic patter half the time and kept the nurses in hysterics. I had to ask him once to stop it, because it was bad for my wound to laugh like that; it might start a haemorrhage again. He had a small make-up box with a mirror and grease paints, and an assortment of beards and moustaches. While Sister Morgan was taking his temperature he would get under the blankets with a pocket torch – the thermometer in his mouth – and when the two minutes were up he would emerge in some new, startling

character. A handkerchief and a towel were his only other
stage properties. Sister Morgan would take the thermometer
from him gravely, and he would say: 'Hello, boys and girls,
I'm Queen Victoria as a young wife and mother!' or 'Beware,
you wicked old men, I'm the Widow Twankey,' or 'Give ear, O
Benjamin, I am Saul the son of Kish in search of his father's
asses,' and she couldn't help laughing. And he would insist on
talking in character until breakfast came up. Biblical parts were
his speciality.

One day I was watching him at work on a complicated paper-
cutting trick. He folded a sheet of newspaper this way and that,
snipping it carefully here and there with a pair of nail scissors;
he had told me that when it opened out it was going to be what
he called 'Bogey-Bogey Ceremony in Sumatra'. He was full of
tricks of this sort. I quoted a verse of the Psalms at him about it
– I forget which it was – and he said, shaking his head at me
sorrowfully. 'No, no, little Gravy-spoons, you've got that all
awry. Never misquote the Psalms of David to Old Papa Johnson, because he knows them all off by heart.' And so he did, as I
found when I challenged him, and Proverbs, too, and St Mark's
Gospel ('it's the one that reads truest to me,' he said, 'the others
seem to me to have been played about with by someone who
wanted to prove something'), and most of Isaiah and the whole
of Job. Also Shakespeare's *Sonnets*. I was astonished. 'Where on
earth did you come to learn all that?' I asked. 'At a Jesuit
College as a punishment for independence of character?'

'No, no, no; bethink yourself, child! Do Jesuits use the
Sonnets as a textbook? I learned most of my stuff in the Antarc-
tic – I was on two expeditions there – while we were snowed up.
Some of it in the Arctic. But I learned most when I was Crown
Agent on Desolation Island.'

'Where's that? Is that one of the Fiji group?'

'No, no, no, child. That's in the Antarctic, too. It's the most
southerly land under the British flag. The appointment is made
yearly – it's well paid, you would say – but others wouldn't
agree – £1,000 a year and everything found. Usually a Scot
takes it on. The Scots don't mind living entirely alone in a howling wilderness as much as we English do; they are a very, very

sane people. But my Scottish predecessor stuck it only for nine months, and I stuck it for two years: you see Old Papa Johnson is just a little bit insane. Always was so from a child. So he didn't come to any harm there. Besides, he had company for the last ten months.'

'If the island's a wilderness, what's the sense of keeping an agent there and wasting all that money on him? It is just to keep the British claim from lapsing? Mineral deposits waiting for development?'

Johnson carefully laid down his 'Bogey-Bogey' business before answering. It was, by the way, a birthday present for Sister Morgan. Johnson went out of his way to be friendly with Sister Morgan, though I couldn't understand why. She was a V.A.D. nurse, middle-aged, incompetent, and always trying to play the great lady among the other nurses; they detested her. But with Johnson she behaved very well after a time and I came to like her, though when I was in another ward I had thought her impossible.

'As Crown Agent, I would have you understand, Captain Graves, I had to supervise His Majesty's customs, and keep a record of imports and exports, and act as Postmaster-General and Clerk of Works, and be solely responsible for maintaining the Pax Britannica in Antarctic regions – if necessary with a rope or a revolver.'

I never knew when Papa Johnson was joking, so I said: 'Yes, your Excellency, and I suppose the penguins and reindeer needed a lot of looking after; and what with their sending each other so many picture postcards and all, you must have had your hands full at the office.'

'Hignorance!' snapped Papa Johnson, in the idiotic tones that he used for the Widow Twankey, 'Reindeers hindeed! Hain't no sich hanimals hin hall Hant-harctica. Them dratted reindeers honly hinhabitates *Harctic* hareas. Which there wasn't no penguins neither, not a penguin hon hall that hisland. There was prions, and seahawks, and sea helephants come a-visting; but they wasn't no trouble, not they.' Then he continued in his usual voice. 'The gross value of imports and exports in the two years I was there amounted to ... guess, child!' I refused to guess, so he told me that the correct answer was something over one million seven hundred thousand pounds sterling.

'For I should have told you, little Gravy-spoons, that Desolation island has a harbour which is more or less ice-free for a month or two round Christmas every year. The whalers put in there then. It isn't every ship that can deal, like the *Larssen* can, with an unlimited quantity of whale; so when the smaller ships have more oil than they can manage comfortably and don't want to go back to Norway yet – half the world away – they dump it in barrels on Desolation Island, in care of the Crown Agent, and get a chit from him for it. There are big store caves blasted out of the rock. The oil tankers come to collect the stuff. Also, a Norwegian company had put a blubber-boiling plant on the island for the convenience of its smaller boats – three great metal cauldrons, each about twice the size of this room, and weighing I don't know how many hundred tons. They must have been landed in sections and welded together on the spot; but that was before my time.

'When those fellows came ashore to boil down their blubber, I always had a busy time. I had to watch that they didn't pinch Government property or the oil belonging to other ships that I had in bond, or raid my house when my back was turned. I carried my revolver loose and loaded and hardly had time to sleep. But I was the sole representative of His Majesty, and he had given me unlimited power to make laws for the entire period of my stay, and to see that they were kept. After my first experience with a blubber party, which ended in a death and a fire, I issued an edict that henceforth Desolation Island was to be the driest as well as the coldest of His Majesty's possessions. I couldn't stop the brutes from boozing themselves silly aboard their own vessels in the harbour, but I saw to it that not a drop was landed on British soil. (Tough! you wouldn't believe how tough these Norwegian whalingmen were. But their ships' officers were tougher still and kept them under.)

'One day a tanker put in and two unexpected visitors came off her. One of them, a tall fellow with a Guards' Brigade moustache (here Papa Johnson made one up to show me, from his make-up box) and a quarrelsome sort of face (here Papa Johnson made the sort of face he meant) came up to me and said in superior tones (here Papa Johnson imitated them): "Mr Henry Johnson, the British Crown Agent, I believe? My name's Morgan, Major Anthony Morgan of the Indian Army. I have come to live here with you. This is Professor Durnsford, who is on the staff of the New York Museum of Natural History," and he pulled forward a harmless-looking little fellow with a snub nose and the expression of a Pekinese. "We intend to do research work here." He handed me an introductory letter from the Government of New Zealand. I was too busy with customs business to read it, so I put it into my pocket – you see I disliked the man at first sight and didn't like having his company forced on me without a please or thank you – and I said: "Well, I can't refuse you, I suppose, if you have decided to dwell among me. There's my house; it's the only one on the island. Make yourselves at home while I attend to these papers. I'll send your stuff ashore when I've examined it."

'Morgan flared up. "You will certainly do no such thing as to tamper with my personal luggage."

'I shrugged my shoulders and said: "It's my job; I'm Customs here. Give me your keys."

'He saw that I was serious, and realized that the tanker was still in the harbour and able to take him off; I could refuse to put him up at my house and so he would have to go back in her. He threw me the keys with very bad grace, and Durnsford politely handed me his. They were numbered keys, so I had no trouble finding the right boxes for them.

'That evening I cooked the supper and Morgan got a mess kit out of his tin trunk to eat it in. The man Morgan actually tried to old-soldier Papa Johnson with his row of ribbons. And do you know what they were? Child, one was the Coronation ribbon and one was the Durbar ribbon and one was the Osmanieh, which one gets almost as a matter of routine if one is seconded to the Egyptian Army, and the fourth and last was the M.V.O. of the Third Class. So, pretending to be dazzled, I went off with the frying pan in my hand and changed into my old campaigning tunic, which sported Ashanti, Egypt, China, King's and Queen's medals South Africa, and North-West Frontier. Not a routine ribbon among them; they made his display look pretty sick. But I had only two stars up, so he tried to high-hat me with his crown.

'Believe me, child, there was the devil to pay about my embargo on wines and spirits; he had brought out twenty cases of Scotch. At first he didn't realize that Scotch was not drunk on Desolation Island. He said that in his opinion it would have been courteous of me, perhaps, to have put a bottle of my own stuff on the table, since I had not taken off any of his with the first boatload. But when I explained how it was, he went up in the air and bellowed at me as though he was in his Orderly Room and I was a poor devil of a Sudanese recruit. I won't repeat what he said, child, because a nurse might come in and catch a word or two and misunderstand. I was pleasant but firm; reminding him that I was Lord Chief Justice and Lord High Executioner and everything else on the island and that what I said went. Professor Durnsford had been a witness to his threats, I said, and I would subpoena him, if necessary, for the trial. And I quoted *Alice in Wonderland*: "I'll be the judge, I'll be jury," said cunning old Fury, "I'll try the whole cause and condemn you to death."

' "You can't prevent me bringing it ashore," he said at last.
' "Can't I?" I said, in nasty tones, showing my Colt.

'He broke into worse language than ever and the only true things he said about me were that I must be a little insane and that I had a face like Dan Leno on one of his off-nights. He ended: "Remember these words, for they are the last I shall address to you while I remain on this island." I answered, improving on poor Dan Leno: "Ha, Comma, Ha, among the trumpets. I'm Job's war horse, and I scent the battle from afar."

'Morgan kept it up throughout the meal. If he wanted the salt or beans or mustard when they happened to be right close to my plate, he would ask Durnsford, who sat between us, to pass them to him. I had decided to ship Morgan back home with his whiskey the very next day, but when he started this baby game of sending me to Coventry, I was so pleased that I decided to keep him with me. As you know, child, I love baby games. It was a nice game, because Morgan and I held the cards and Durnsford was pool for the winner to take. Not that I cared much about Durnsford then, but he seemed a decent little Pekinese of a man, too good to go coupled with an ill-tempered great mastiff like Morgan. They had arranged to come on this expedition together, by letter, before actually meeting. Morgan had written that he could get permission from the New Zealand Government for them both to put up at my house; and Pekey Durnsford was glad of a companion. Neither of them had been in the Antarctic before.

'Durnsford was the best possible "kitty" for our game of nap; he tried to be so neutral. Of course, I didn't go out of my way to make myself pleasant to him; that would have been no sort of game – an auction with the bidding in sugar plums and the prize to go to the men who bid highest. No, no, no! I answered his questions civilly, though not always pertinently, I supplied him with necessaries, and saw that he didn't run into danger: but I allowed him no loose conversation. Little Pekey Durnsford felt ever so uncomfortable (and even, I believe, went so far as to ask Morgan to apologize to me), but I felt perfectly happy. You see, child, having got accustomed to the deathly silence of Desolation Island when I was by myself for months at a time, I thoroughly enjoyed the very lively silence of the man Morgan. Often he was on the point of asking me something important about the island which only I could tell him, but then his haughty pride choked back the question. And so next day the question would come innocently enough through Durnsford. I would put on my "Schoolgirls we" voice and say: "Darling, that's a *great* secret. But if you promise *on your honour* never to tell anyone else in the world about it, I'll whisper it to you." Durnsford would smile unhappily, and Morgan would scowl.

'There were several rooms in my shack, but mostly store-rooms, and only one big stove. Morgan made a show of moving his belongings into another room; but he got too cold and had to sneak back. It was a log-built shack, by the way, with steel doors and steel window shutters. It had an airtight lining and it was anchored to the rock with four great steel cables that went right across the roof. Understand, child, that in the Antarctic we keep a special and unique sort of blizzard, so these were necessary precautions.

'Well! The oil tanker had steamed off and the whalers had come and dumped their barrels and had their blubber parties and said good-bye; so unless there came a chance call from a vessel that was built pretty sturdy against the ice, like the one my predecessor went away in – he'd been killing himself with Scotch and couldn't lay off it because nobody was at hand to tell him not to make a beast of himself – unless a chance vessel called, you see, there we were together for another nine or ten solid months. I had a wireless apparatus, but it hadn't much of a range, and it was rarely I picked up a passing ship except in the season.

'For five solid months the man Morgan kept it up' (here Papa Johnson resumed the moustache, which had fallen off). ' "Durnsford, old fellow, do you think that you could prevail on that comedian friend of yours to disencumber the case he's sitting on? It happens to contain the photographic plates. He has apparently taken a three-year lease on it, with the option of renewal. Haw! Haw! Haw!" Durnsford looked at me apologetically. I didn't get off the packing case, of course ... I never asked Durnsford to relay a message to Morgan. I pretended he didn't exist, and if he had been sitting on the packing case and I had wanted anything inside it, I should simply have opened it with him on it. He was afraid of me and careful not to start a rough-house.

'They didn't get on too well with their natural-history studies, because they didn't know where to look. I knew my island well and there's a surprising amount of life on it, if you look in the right places, besides the prions and the other creatures I mentioned before, which don't take much finding, and a few ratlike animals that spend most of their life hibernating, and even a few honest-to-God birds. In the interior are fresh-water pools with all sorts of little bugs living in the ice. Heaven knows how they keep alive, but when you thaw them out they wriggle nicely. Durnsford didn't know that I knew and I didn't let on; his big friend took him round to see the sights, but he wasn't by any means so good a guide as Old Papa Johnson would have been.

'One day, it was twelve noon on Midsummer Eve with the thermometer forty-five below and the stars shining very prettily – you have heard of our beautiful long Polar night, I expect, that goes on month after month without a spot of daylight to help it out? Well, one day – or night, if you prefer – after breakfast – or after supper if you like – the man Morgan puts on his snow-shoes and says to Durnsford: "Coming out for a shuffle, professor?" "All right, major," Durnsford answers, putting down his book and reaching for his snowshoes.

' "Durnsford," I said, "don't go out!" He asked: "Why?" in a surprised voice, so I said: "Look at the barometer!" Morgan interrupted, saying to Durnsford: "Your imbecile acquaintance has no understanding of barometers. This one has been rock-steady for the last twenty-four hours."

' "Durnsford," I said again, "don't go out!"

'Morgan haw-hawed: "Oh, don't listen to it; come along for a bit of exercise. Leave old Red Nose with his string of sausages and his red-hot poker; he's not in his best vein these days."

'Durnsford hesitated, with one snowshoe already on. He hesitated quite a long time. Finally he took it off again. "Thank you, Mr Johnson," he said. "I'll take your advice. I don't know what you mean about the barometer, but you must certainly understand conditions here better than Major Morgan."

'That was good to hear; I had won my game of nap with the man Morgan at last and scooped the kitty. And it wasn't bluff: the unnatural steadiness of the barometer meant trouble. I had made sure that the shutters were fast some hours before.

'So Morgan went alone, whistling "Oh, it's my delight on a starry night in the season of the year," and two minutes later a creaking and groaning and humming began. Durnsford looked puzzled and thought I was playing a trick. "No," I said, "it's only the house moving about a little and the cables taking the strain. A capful of wind. But have a look at that rock-steady barometer."

'He went over to it, and behold! the creature had gone quite off its chump and was hopping about like a pea in a saucepan.

Durnsford was silent for a minute or two and then he said: "Johnson, I know that the major has behaved abominably to you. But don't you think –?"

'"No, dearie," I said, "your poor old granny is very, very sleepy at the moment, and simply hasn't got it in her to think thoughts about troublesome majors and the likes of them."

'"Oh, stop your jokes for once!" he shouted, "I'm going out to look for him."

'He grabbed his shoes again. So I spoke to him severely and showed him my gun. I said that I didn't mind his slaying himself if he felt so inclined, but that I drew the line at his killing Old Papa Johnson too. They were double doors; the outer one was steel and the inner one solid two-inch oak planking, with an airlock between them. The moment he unbolted the outer door the wind would get into the air-lock and blow the inner one in and then tear the shack to pieces in three seconds.

'"But the major?" he gasped. "Won't he get frozen to death?"

' " Your intelligent friend was killed by the first gust of wind a few seconds after leaving the shack," I said.

'That blizzard blew without stopping for seventy-two hours; any moment I expected the cables to go. I set myself to learn the Book of Ruth to keep my mind from dwelling on our imminent fate. Then it stopped as suddenly as it began. We found the body only fifty yards from the shack, wedged between two rocks. And you wouldn't believe it, but that blizzard had got inside one of those big metal cauldrons – twice the size of this room, I'm telling you – and blown it clean into the harbour! As local registrar of births, deaths, and marriages I reported all these occurrences to a distant whaler, a month or two later, and when the tanker eventually turned up, it came with a letter from the man Morgan's sister, asking me to put her brother's remains in the lead coffin which she enclosed. So I had to dig them up again, though I had said the burial service over them and left nothing out.

'As for Pekey Durnsford, he was so full of gratitude to me for saving his life that he slobbered all over me. And soon I found that he liked silly games, just like I did. It was he who first taught Old Papa Johnson how to do this paper-folding business, though Papa's improved on Pekey's methods a lot since. And in return Papa showed him where to scare up all the living creatures in our kingdom. Pekey found one quite new species of fresh-water cheese mite which he called Something-or-other Papa-johnsonensis. And you should have seen the letter of thanks that I got from the New York Museum of Natural History!

'Morgan's sister – now child, for goodness' sake don't remind her who H. H. Johnson is – I recognized her handwriting when she put my name on the fever chart – is not a bad woman in spite of her airs, though it's taken me three weeks and a lot of patience to coax her to be my playmate. And do you know, little Gravy-spoons? if it hadn't been for that whiskey business I verily believe that Old Papa Johnson could even in time have made a playmate of her ill-tempered brother.'

TREACLE TART

THE news travelled from group to group along the platform of Victoria Station, impressing our parents and kid-sisters almost as much as ourselves. A lord was coming to our prep school. A real lord. A new boy, only eight years old. Youngest son of the Duke of Downshire. A new boy, yet a lord. Lord Julius Bloodstock. Same name! Crikey!

Excitement strong enough to check the rebellious tears of home-lovers, and make our last good-byes all but casual. None of us having had any contact with the peerage, it was argued by some, as we settled in our reserved Pullman carriage, that on the analogy of policemen there couldn't be boy-lords. However, Mr Lees, the Latin Master (declined: *Lees, Lees, Lem, Lei, Lei, Lee*) confirmed the report. The lord was being driven to school that morning in the ducal Rolls-Royce. Crikey, again! *Cricko, Crickere, Crikey, Crictum!*

Should we be expected to call him 'your Grace', or 'Sire', or something? Would he keep a coronet in his tuck-box? Would the masters dare cane him if he broke school rules or didn't know his prep?

Billington Secundus told us that his father (the famous Q.C.) had called Thos a 'tuft-hunting toad-eater', as meaning that he was awfully proud of knowing important people, such as bishops and Q.C.s and lords, To this Mr Lees turned a deaf ear, though making ready to crack down on any further disrespectful remarks about the Rev. Thomas Pearce, our Headmaster. None came. Most of us were scared stiff of Thos; besides, everyone but Billington Secundus considered pride in knowing important people an innocent enough emotion.

Presently Mr Lees folded his newspaper and said: 'Bloodstock, as you will learn to call him, is a perfectly normal little chap, though he happens to have been born into the purple – if anyone present catches the allusion. Accord him neither kisses nor cuffs (*nec oscula, nec verbera*, both neuter) and all will be well. By the way, this is to be his first experience of school life.

The Duke has hitherto kept him at the Castle under private tutors.'

At the Castle, under private tutors! Crikey! *Crikey, Crikius, Crikissime!*

We arrived at the Cedars just in time for school dinner. Thos, rather self-consciously, led a small, pale, fair-haired boy into the dining-hall, and showed him his seat at the end of the table among the other nine new-comers. 'This is Lord Julius Bloodstock, boys,' he boomed. 'You will just call him Bloodstock. No titles or other honorifics here.'

'Then I prefer to be called Julius.' His first memorable words.

'We happen to use only surnames at Brown Friars,' chuckled Thos; then he said Grace.

None of Julius's table-mates called him anything at all, to begin with, being either too miserable or too shy even to say 'Pass the salt, please.' But after the soup, and half-way through the shepherd's pie (for once not made of left-overs) Billington Tertius, to win a bet, leant boldly across the table and asked: 'Lord, why didn't you come by train, same as the rest of us?'

Julius did not answer at first, but when his neighbours nudged him, he said: 'The name is Julius, and my father was afraid of finding newspaper photographers on the platform. They can be such a nuisance. Two of them were waiting for us at the school gates, and my father sent the chauffeur to smash both their cameras.'

This information had hardly sunk in before the third course appeared: treacle tart. Today was Monday: onion soup, shepherd's pie and carrots, treacle tart. Always had been. Even when Mr Lees-Lees-Lem had been a boy here and won top scholarship to Winchester. 'Treacle. From the Greek *theriace*, though the Greeks did not, of course ...' With this, Mr Lees, who sat at the very end of the table, religiously eating treacle tart, looked up to see whether anyone were listening; and noticed that Julius had pushed away his plate, leaving the oblong of tough burned pastry untouched.

'Eat it, boy!' said Mr Lees. 'Not allowed to leave anything here for Mr Good Manners. School rule.'

'I never eat treacle tart,' explained Julius with a little sigh.

'You are expected to address me as "sir",' said Mr Lees.

Julius seemed surprised. 'I thought we didn't use titles here, or other honorifics,' he said, 'but only surnames?'

'Call me "sir",' insisted Mr Lees, not quite certain whether this were innocence or impertinence.

'Sir,' said Julius, shrugging faintly.

'Eat your tart,' snapped Mr Lees.

'But I never eat treacle tart – sir!'

'It's my duty to see that you do so, every Monday.'

Julius smiled. 'What a queer duty!' he said incredulously.

Titters, cranings of necks. Then Thos called jovially down the table: 'Well, Lees, what's the news from your end? Are the summer holidays reported to have been wearisomely long?'

'No, Headmaster. But I cannot persuade an impertinent boy to sample our traditional treacle tart.'

'Send him up here,' said Thos in his most portentous voice. 'Send him up here, plate and all! Oliver Twist asking for less, eh?'

When Thos recognized Julius, his face changed and he swallowed a couple of times, but having apparently lectured the staff on making not the least difference between duke's son and shopkeeper's son, he had to put his foot down. 'My dear boy,' he said, 'let me see you eat that excellent piece of food without further demur; and no nonsense.'

'I never eat treacle tart, Headmaster.'

Thos started as though he had been struck in the face. He said slowly: 'You mean perhaps: "I have lost my appetite, sir." Very well, but your appetite will return at supper time, you mark my words – and so will the treacle tart.'

The sycophantic laughter which greeted this prime Thossism surprised Julius but did not shake his poise. Walking to the buttery-table, he laid down the plate, turned on his heel, and walked calmly back to his seat.

Thos at once rose and said Grace in a challenging voice.

'Cocky ass, I'd like to punch his lordly head for him,' growled Billington Secundus later that afternoon.

'You'd have to punch mine first,' I said. 'He's a ... the thing we did in Gray's *Elegy* – a village Hampden. Standing up to

Lees and Thos in mute inglorious protest against that foul treacle tart.'

'You're a tuft-hunting toad-eater.'

'I may be. But I'd rather eat toads than Thos's treacle tart.'

A bell rang for supper, or high tea. The rule was that tuck-box cakes were put under Matron's charge and distributed among all fifty of us while they lasted. 'Democracy', Thos called it (I can't think why); and the Matron, to cheer up the always dismal first evening, had set the largest cake she could find on the table: Julius's. Straight from the ducal kitchens, plastered with crystallized fruit, sugar icing and marzipan, stuffed with raisins, cherries and nuts.

'You will get your slice, my dear, when you have eaten your treacle tart,' Matron gently reminded Julius. *'Noblesse oblige.'*

'I never eat treacle tart, Matron.'

It must have been hard for him to see his cake devoured by strangers before his eyes, but he made no protest; just sipped a little tea and went supperless to bed. In the dormitory he told a ghost story, which is still, I hear, current in the school after all these years: about a Mr Gracie (why 'Gracie'?) who heard hollow groans in the night, rose to investigate and was grasped from behind by an invisible hand. He found that his braces had caught on the door knob; and, after other harrowing adventures, traced the groans to the bathroom, where Mrs Gracie ...

Lights out! Sleep. Bells for getting up; for prayers; for breakfast.

'I never eat treacle tart.' So Julius had no breakfast, but we pocketed slices of bread and potted meat (Tuesday) to slip him in the playground afterwards. The school porter intervened. His orders were to see that the young gentleman had no food given him.

Bell: Latin. Bell: Maths. Bell: long break. Bell: Scripture. Bell: wash hands for dinner.

'I never eat treacle tart,' said Julius, as a sort of response to Thos's Grace; and this time fainted.

Those sent a long urgent telegram to the Duke, explaining his predicament: school rule, discipline, couldn't make exceptions, and so forth.

The Duke wired back non-committally: 'Quite so. Stop. The lad never eats treacle tart. Stop. Regards. Downshire.'

Matron took Julius to the sickroom, where he was allowed milk and soup, but no solid food unless he chose to call for treacle tart. He remained firm and polite until the end, which came two days later, after a further exchange of telegrams.

We were playing kick-about near the Masters' Wing, when the Rolls-Royce pulled up. Presently Julius, in overcoat and bowler hat, descended the front steps, followed by the school porter carrying his tuck-box, football boots and hand-bag. Billington Secundus, now converted to the popular view, led our three cheers, which Julius acknowledged with a gracious tilt of his bowler. The car purred off; and thereupon, in token of our admiration for Julius, we all swore to strike against treacle tart the very next Monday, and none of us eat a single morsel, even if we liked it, which some of us did!

When it came to the point, of course, the boys sitting close to Thos took fright and ratted, one after the other. Even Billington Secundus and I, not being peers' sons or even village Hampdens, regretfully conformed.

THE FULL LENGTH

WILLIAM ('the Kid') Nicholson, my father-in-law, could never rid himself of the Victorian superstition that a thousand guineas were a thousand guineas; income tax seemed to him a barbarous joke which did not, and should not, apply to people like myself. He had a large family to support, and as a fashionable portrait painter was bound to keep up appearances which would justify his asking the same prices for a full length as his friends William Orpen and Philip de Laszlo. He excelled in still-lifes and, though complaining that flowers were restless sitters, would have liked to paint nothing else all day except an occasional landscape. But full-length commissions were what he needed. 'Portraits seldom bounce,' he told me.

When I asked him to explain, he said: 'I have been painting and selling, and painting and selling for so many years now that my early buyers are beginning to die off or go bankrupt. Forgotten W.N. masterpieces keep coming up for auction, and have to be bought in at an unfair price, five times as much as they originally earned, just to keep the W.N. market steady. Some of them are charming and make me wonder how I ever painted so well; but others plead to have their faces turned to the wall quick. Such as those!'

It had come to a crisis in Appletree Yard. The Inland Revenue people, he told me, had sent him a three-line whip to attend a financial debate; also, an inexpert collector of his early work had died suddenly and left no heirs, so that his agent had to buy in three or four paintings which should never have been sold. 'Be sure your sin will find you out,' the Kid muttered despondently. 'What I need now is no less than two thousand guineas in ready cash. Pray for a miracle, my boy!'

I prayed, and hardly two hours had elapsed, before a ring came at the studio door and in walked Mrs Mucklehose-Kerr escorted by one Fulton, a butler, both wearing deep mourning. The Kid had not even known of her existence hitherto, but she seemed solid enough and the name of Mucklehose-Kerr was synonymous with Glenlivet Whisky; so he was by no means discourteous.

The introductions over, Mrs Mucklehose-Kerr pressed the Kid's hand fervently, and said: 'Mr Nicholson, I know you will not fail me: you and you alone are destined to paint my daughter Alison.'

'Well,' said the Kid, blinking cautiously, 'I am pretty busy at this season, you know, Mrs Mucklehose-Kerr. And I've promised to take my family to Cannes in about three weeks' time. Still, if you make a point of it, perhaps the sittings can be fitted in before I leave Town.'

'There will be no sittings, Mr Nicholson. There *can* be no sittings.' She dabbed her eyes with a black lace handkerchief. 'My daughter passed over last week.'

It took the Kid a little while to digest this, but he mumbled condolences, and said gently: 'Then I fear that I shall have to work from photographs.'

Mrs Mucklehose-Kerr answered in broken tones: 'Alas, there *are* no photographs. Alison was so camera-shy. She used to say: "Mother, why do you want photographs? You will always have me to look at – me myself, not silly old photographs!" And now she has passed over, and not left me so much as a snapshot. On my brother's advice I went to Mr Orpen first and asked him what I am now asking you; but he answered that the task was beyond him. He said that you were the only painter in London who could help me, because you have a sixth sense.'

Orpen was right in a way. The Kid had one queer parlour trick. He would suddenly ask a casual acquaintance: 'How do you sign your name?' and when he answered: 'Herbert B. Banbury' (or whatever it was), would startle him by writing it down in his own unmistakable handwriting.

'Look, here is her signature; this is the cover of her history exercise book.'

As he hesitated, his eye caught sight of the bounced canvases, leaning against the table on which lay the Income Tax demand. 'It is a difficult commission, Mrs Mucklehose-Kerr,' he said.

'I am willing to pay two thousand guineas,' she answered, 'for a full length.'

'It is not the money . . .' he protested.

'But Fulton will tell you all about dear Alison,' pleaded Mrs Mucklehose-Kerr, weeping unrestrainedly. 'Miss Alison was a beautiful girl, Fulton, was she not?'

'Sweetly pretty,' Fulton agreed with fervour. 'Pretty as a picture, madam.'

'I *know* you will consent, Mr Nicholson, and of course I will choose one of her own dresses for her to wear. The one I liked best.'

There was nothing for it but to consent.

The Kid took Fulton to the Café Royal that evening and plied him with whisky and questions.

'Blue eyes?' – 'Bluish, sir, and a bit watery. But sweetly pretty.'

'Hair?' – 'Mousy, sir, like her nature, and worn in a bun.'

'Figure?' – 'So, so, Mr Nicholson, so, so! But she was a very sweet young lady, was Miss Alison.'

'Any physical peculiarities?' – 'None, sir, that leaped to the eye. But I fear I am not a good hand at descriptions.'

'Had she no friends who could sketch her from memory?' – 'None, Mr Nicholson. She lived a most retired life.'

So the Kid drew a blank with Fulton, and his parlour trick did not help at all because he lacked the complementary faculty (with which Mrs Mucklehose-Kerr credited him, but which, in his own phrase, was a different pair of socks altogether) of conjuring up a person from a signature. The next day, in despair, he consulted his brother-in-law, the painter James Pryde. 'Jimmy, what on earth am I to do now?'

Jimmy thought awhile and then, being a practical Scot, answered: 'Why not find out from Fulton whether the girl ever went to a dentist?'

Sir Rockaway Timms happened to be a fellow-member of the Savile, and the Kid hurried to Wimpole Street to consult him.

'Rocks, old boy, I'm in a fearful hole.'

'Not for the first time, Kid.'

'It's about a girl of eighteen called Alison Mucklehose-Kerr, one of your patients.'

'You should leave 'em alone until they reach the age of discretion. Oh, you artists!'

'I never set eyes on her. And now, it seems, she's dead.'

'Bad, bad! By her own hand?'

'I want to know what you know about her.'

'I can only show you the map of her mouth, if that's any morbid satisfaction to you. I have it in this cabinet. Wait a moment. M ... Mu ... Muck ... Here you are! Crowded incisors; one heavily and clumsily stopped rear molar; one ditto lightly and neatly stopped by me; malformed canines; wisdom teeth not yet through.'

'For Heaven's sake, Rocks, what did she *look* like? It's life or death to me.'

Sir Rockaway glanced at the Kid quizzically. 'What do I get out of this?' he asked.

'An enormous box of liqueur chocolates swathed in pink ribbon.'

'Accepted, on behalf of Edith. Well, this Alison whom you betrayed in the dark forest was a sallow, lumpish, frightened Scots lassie with a slight cast in the off eye – but, for all that, the spitting image of Lillian Gish!'

The Kid wrung Sir Rockaway's hand as violently as Mrs Mucklehose-Kerr had wrung his own at parting. Then he rushed out to his waiting taxi.

'Driver,' he shouted. '*The Birth of a Nation*, wherever it's showing, as fast as your wheels will carry us!'

Mrs Mucklehose-Kerr, summoned to Appletree Yard a week later, uttered a moan of delight the moment she entered the studio. 'It is Alison, it is my Alison to the life, Mr Nicholson!' she babbled. 'I knew your genius would not fail me. But oh! how well and happy she is looking since she passed over! ... Fulton, Fulton, tell Mr Nicholson how wonderful he is!'

'You have caught Miss Alison's expression, sir, to the dot!' pronounced Fulton, visibly impressed.

Mrs Mucklehose-Kerr insisted on buying two of the bounced and unworthy early Nicholsons which happened to be lying face-up on the floor. The Kid had been on the point of painting them over; and his obvious reluctance to sell made her offer twelve hundred guineas for the pair.

He weakly accepted; forgetting what a terrible retribution the Inland Revenue people would visit on him next year.

EARTH TO EARTH

Y ES, yes and yes! Don't get me wrong, for goodness' sake. I
am heart and soul with you. I agree that Man is wickedly de-
frauding the Earth-Mother of her ancient dues by not putting
back into the soil as much nourishment as he takes out. And
that modern plumbing is, if you like, a running sore in the body
politic. And that municipal incinerators are genocidal rather
than germicidal ... And that cremation should be made a
capital crime. And that dust bowls created by the greedy
plough ...

... Yes, yes and yes again. *But!*

Elsie and Roland Hedge — she a book-illustrator, he an architect with suspect lungs — had been warned against Dr Eugen
Steinpilz. 'He'll bring you no luck,' I told them. 'My little finger
says so decisively.'

'You too?' asked Elsie indignantly. (This was at Brixham,
South Devon, in March 1940.) 'I suppose you think that because
of his foreign accent and his beard he must be a spy?'

'No,' I said coldly, 'that point hadn't occurred to me. But I
won't contradict you.'

The very next day Elsie deliberately picked a friendship — I
don't like the phrase, but that's what she did — with the Doctor,
an Alsatian with an American passport, who described himself
as a *Naturphilosoph*; and both she and Roland were soon im-
mersed in Steinpilzerei up to the nostrils. It began when he invited them to lunch and gave them cold meat and two rival sets
of vegetable dishes — potatoes (baked), carrots (creamed), bought
from the local fruiterer; and potatoes (baked) and carrots
(creamed), grown on compost in his own garden.

The superiority of the latter over the former in appearance,
size and especially flavour came as an eye-opener to Elsie and
Roland. Yes, and yes, I know just how they felt. Why shouldn't
I? When I visit the market here in Palma, I always refuse La
Torre potatoes, because they are raised for the early English

market and therefore reek of imported chemical fertilizer. Instead I buy Son Sardina potatoes, which taste as good as the ones we used to get in England fifty years ago. The reason is that the Son Sardina farmers manure their fields with Palma kitchen-refuse, still available by the cart-load – this being too backward a city to afford effective modern methods of destroying it.

Thus Dr Steinpilz converted the childless and devoted couple to the Steinpilz method of composting. It did not, as a matter of fact, vary greatly from the methods you read about in the *Gardening Notes* of your favourite national newspaper, except that it was far more violent. Dr Steinpilz had invented a formula for producing extremely fierce bacteria, capable (Roland claimed) of breaking down an old boot or the family Bible or a torn woollen vest into beautiful black humus almost as you watched. The formula could not be bought, however, and might be communicated under oath of secrecy only to members of the Eugen Steinpilz Fellowship – which I refused to join. I won't pretend therefore to know the formula myself, but one night I overheard Elsie and Roland arguing in their garden as to whether the planetary influences were favourable; and they also mentioned a ram's horn in which, it seems, a complicated mixture of triturated animal and vegetable products – technically called 'the Mother' – was to be cooked up. I gather also that a bull's foot and a goat's pancreas were part of the works, because Mr Pook the butcher afterwards told me that he had been puzzled by Roland's request for these unusual cuts. Milkwort and penny-royal and bee-orchid and vetch certainly figured among the Mother's herbal ingredients; I recognized these one day in a gardening basket Elsie had left at the post office.

The Hedges soon had their first compost heap cooking away in the garden, which was about the size of a tennis court and consisted mostly of well-kept lawn. Dr Steinpilz, who supervised, now began to haunt the cottage like the smell of drains; I had to give up calling on them. Then, after the Fall of France, Brixham became a war-zone whence everyone but we British and our Free French or Free Belgian allies were extruded. Consequently Dr Steinpilz had to leave; which he did with very bad grace, and was killed in a Liverpool air-raid the day before he should have sailed back to New York. But that was far from closing the ledger. I think Elsie must have been in love with the Doctor, and certainly Roland had a hero-worship for him. They treasured a signed collection of all his esoteric books, each called after a different semi-precious stone, and used to read them out aloud to each other at meals, in turns. Then to show that this was a practical philosophy, not just a random assemblage of beautiful thoughts about Nature, they began composting in a deeper and even more religious way than before. The lawn had come up, of course; but they used the sods to sandwich layers of kitchen waste, which they mixed with the scrapings from an abandoned pigsty, two barrowfuls of sodden poplar leaves from the recreation ground, and a sack of rotten turnips. Looking over the hedge, I caught the fanatic gleam in Elsie's eye as she turned the hungry bacteria loose on the heap, and could not repress a premonitory shudder.

So far, not too bad, perhaps. But when serious bombing started and food became so scarce that housewives were fined for not making over their swill to the national pigs, Elsie and Roland grew worried. Having already abandoned their ordinary sanitary system and built an earth-closet in the garden, they now tried to convince neighbours of their duty to do the same, even at the risk of catching cold and getting spiders down the neck. Elsie also sent Roland after the slow-moving Red Devon cows as they lurched home along the lane at dusk, to rescue the precious droppings with a kitchen shovel; while she visited the local ash-dump with a packing case mounted on wheels, and collected whatever she found there of an organic nature – dead cats, old rags, withered flowers, cabbage stalks and such household waste as even a national wartime pig would have coughed at. She also saved every drop of their bath-water for sprinkling the heaps; because it contained, she said, valuable animal salts.

The test of a good compost heap, as every illuminate knows, is whether a certain revolting-looking, if beneficial, fungus sprouts from it. Elsie's heaps were grey with this crop, and so hot inside that they could be used for haybox cookery; which must have saved a deal of fuel. I call them 'Elsie's heaps', because she now considered herself Dr Steinpilz's earthly delegate; and loyal Roland did not dispute this claim.

A critical stage in the story came during the Blitz. It will be remembered that trainloads of Londoners, who had been evacuated to South Devon when war broke out, thereafter de-evacuated and re-evacuated and re-de-evacuated themselves, from time to time, in a most disorganized fashion. Elsie and Roland, as it happened, escaped having evacuees billeted on them, because they had no spare bedroom; but one night an old naval pensioner came knocking at their door and demanded lodging for the night. Having been burned out of Plymouth, where everything was chaos, he had found himself walking away and blundering along in a daze until he fetched up here, hungry and dead-beat. They gave him a meal and bedded him on the sofa; but when Elsie came down in the morning to fork over the heaps, she found him dead of heart-failure.

Roland broke a long silence by coming, in some embarrass-ment, to ask my advice. Elsie, he said, had decided that it would be wrong to trouble the police about the case; because the police were so busy these days, and the poor old fellow had claimed to possess neither kith nor kin. So they'd read the burial service over him and, after removing his belt-buckle, trouser buttons, metal spectacle-case and a bunch of keys, which were irreducible, had laid him reverently in the new compost heap. Its other contents, he added, were a cartload of waste from the cider-factory, salvaged cow-dung, and several basketfuls of hedge clippings. Had they done wrong?

'If you mean "will I report you to the Civil Authorities?" the answer is no,' I assured him. 'I wasn't looking over the hedge at the relevant hour, and what you tell me is only hearsay.' Roland shambled off satisfied.

The War went on. Not only did the Hedges convert the whole garden into serried rows of Eugen Steinpilz memorial heaps, leaving no room for planting the potatoes or carrots to which the compost had been prospectively devoted, but they scavenged the offal from the Brixham fish-market and salvaged the contents of the bin outside the surgical ward at the Cottage Hospital. Every spring, I remember, Elsie used to pick big bunches of primroses and put them straight on the compost, without even a last wistful sniff; virgin primroses were supposed to be particularly relished by the fierce bacteria.

Here the story becomes a little painful for members, say, of a family reading circle; I will soften it as much as possible. One morning a policeman called on the Hedges with a summons, and I happened to see Roland peep anxiously out of the bedroom window, but quickly pull his head in again. The policeman rang and knocked and waited, then tried the back door; and presently went away. The summons was for a blackout offence, but apparently the Hedges did not know this. Next morning he called again, and when nobody answered, forced the lock of the back door. They were found dead in bed together, having taken an overdose of sleeping tablets. A note on the coverlet ran simply:

Please lay our bodies on the heap nearest the pigsty. Flowers by request. Strew some on the bodies, mixed with a little kitchen waste, and then fork the earth lightly over. E.H.; R.H.

George Irks, the new tenant, proposed to grow potatoes and dig for victory. He hired a cart and began throwing the compost into the River Dart, 'not liking the look of them toadstools', as he subsequently explained. The five beautifully clean human skeletons which George unearthed in the process were still awaiting identification when the War ended.

PERIOD PIECE

I⊤ was one July in the reign of Edward the Good, *alias* Edward
the Peacemaker, and I went for the long week-end to Castle
Balch – fine place in Oxfordshire – my cousin Tom's roost. Tom
was a bit of a collector, not that I ever held that against Tom,
and Eva must take the principal blame, if any: meaning that
the people she invited for house-parties were excessively what
the Yankees call (or called) 'high-toned' – artist-fellows, M.P.s,
celebrities of all sorts, not easy to compete against. On this particular occasion, Eva had flung her net wide and made a
stupendous haul. To wit: Nixon-Blake, R.A., who had painted
the picture of the year – do they have pictures of the year nowadays? It's years since I visited Burlington House – and Ratface
Dingleby, who had taken his twenty-foot *Ruby* round the Horn
that same February. Saw his obituary in *The Times* a couple of
years ago: lived to ninety, not born to be drowned. And, what
the devil was his name? the elephant-hunter who won the V.C.
in the Transvaal? – Captain Scrymgeour, of course! He got
killed under Younghusband in Tibet a year or two later. And
Charlie Batta, the actor-manager. None of whom I could count
as cronies. *Homines novi*, in point of fact. Fortunately, Mungo
Montserrat was there; my year at Eton. And Doris, his spouse,
a bit stuffy, but a good sort: another cousin of mine. I teem with
cousins.

This being described as a tennis week-end, we had all brought
our flannels and rackets, prepared to emulate the Doherty
brothers, then all the go. Both Castle Balch courts played admir-
ably – gardener a magician with turf – but being July, of course
it rained and rained ceaselessly from Friday afternoon to Monday
afternoon and the tournament was literally washed out. We enjoyed pretty good sport none the less – Tom had a squash court
for fellows like Mungo and me who were too energetic to content
themselves with baccarat and billiards. And Charlie Batta sent
to Town for some pretty actresses who happened to be seasonally
unemployed, or unemployable. Furthermore, Eva invented a lot

of very humorous wheezes, as the current slang was, to embar-
rass us – some of them pretty close to the knuckle. But no tennis
tournament took place; though a beautiful silver rose-bowl was
waiting on the smoking-room mantelpiece to reward the winner.

Forgot to mention the Bishop of Bangalore, who had been invited in error. The fun never started until he had turned in, but
fortunately the bish loved his pillow even more than his neighbour. On Monday evening then, about 12.15 a.m. in mellow
lamp light, don't you know, when the ladies had retired to their
rest and the Bishop had joined them – no allegation intended –
Tom spoke up and said forthrightly: 'Gentlemen, I'm as deeply
grieved by this tennis fiasco as you are, and I don't want that
jerry knocking around the Castle for ever afterwards to remind
me of it. Tell you what: I'll present same to the fellow who
supplies the best answer to a question that Eva was too modest
to propound with her own lips: "What were the most thrilling
moments of your life?"'

We all drew numbers out of the Bishop's fascinatingly laced
top hat, and spun our yarns in the order assigned by fate. Apart
from Mungo and me, every personage present was a born
raconteur. I assure you: to hear Charlie Batta, who tee'd off, tell
us how he played *Hamlet* in dumb show to a cellarful of Corsi-
can bandits who were holding him for ransom, and how, waiv-
ing the three thousand sov.s at which he had been priced, they
afterwards escorted him in triumph to Ajaccio, firing *feux-de-
joie* all the way in tribute to his art – that was worth a gross of
silver bowls. And doughty Scrymgeour on safari in German
East, when he bagged the hippo and the rhino with a right and
left; my word, Scrymgeour held us! Next, the R.A. (told you his
name, forgotten it again – had a small red imperial, eyes like
ginger-ale, and claimed to have re-introduced the yellow hunting waistcoat, though that was an inexactitude). He recorded an
encounter with a gipsy girl in a forest near Budapest – the
exact physical type he had envisaged for his picture *The Sor-
ceress* – whom he persuaded with coins and Hunnish endearments to pose in the nude; after which he painted those Juno-
esque curves and contours, those delicate flesh tints – and so
forth, don't you know – with ecstatic inspiration and anatomic

exactitude, careless though her jealous lover had by this time entered the grotto and was covering him with an inlaid fowling piece. At last the murderous weapon clattered to the ground and he heard a strangled voice exclaim: 'Gorgio, I cannot shoot you. I bow before your genius! Keep the girl – leave me the picture – go!'

Finally poor old Mungo, who had drawn No. 13, was prevailed upon to take the floor. My heart went out to him, me having made a damned mess of my own effort. These were Mungo's exact words: 'Gentlemen, I'm a simple chappy, never had any exciting adventures like you chappies. Sorry. However. If you want to know. The most thrilling moments of my life were when I married Doris – you all know Doris – and, well, when she and I . . . (Pause) . . . They still are, in fact.'

Mungo brought the house down. Tom thrust the rose-bowl into his unwilling hands, treated him to the stiffest whisky and soda on which I have ever clapped eyes, and sent him crookedly upstairs to the bedroom; where Doris was being kept awake, not by the sounds of revelry from the smoke-room, but by the frightful snores of the Bishop next door.

'What *have* you got there, Mungo?' she asked crossly.

'Rose-bowl,' Mungo mumbled. 'Tom offered it to the chappy who could best answer Eva's question about the most thrilling moments in his life. They all told such capital stories that, when it was my turn, I got into a mortal funk. But we had drawn lots from the Bishop's hat, and this inspired me. I said: "When Doris and I kneel side by side in church giving thanks to Heaven for all the blessings that have been showered on us." And they gave me the prize!'

'How *could* you, Mungo! You know that was a dreadful lie. Oh, now I feel so ashamed! It's not as though prayers and Church are anything to joke about.' She enlarged on this aspect of the case for quite a while, and Mungo resignedly hung his head. Whisky always made him melancholy; I can't say why.

The next morning the party broke up: one and all were catching the 10.45 express to Town. Doris Montserrat noticed a lot of admiring or curious glances flung in her direction, and conscience pricked. She stood on the hall staircase and made a startling little speech.

'Gentlemen, I'm afraid that Mungo won that rose-bowl on false pretences last night. He has only done ... what he said he did ... three times. The first time was before we married; I made him. The second was when we married; he could hardly have avoided it. The third was after we married, and then he fell asleep in the middle...'

WEEK-END AT CWM TATWS

I SHOULDN'T bring the story up – there's nothing in it really, except the sequel – if it wasn't already current in a garbled form. What happens to me I prefer told my own way, or not at all. Point is: I fell for that girl at first sight. So much more than sympathetic, as well as being in the beauty queen class, that . . .

In spite of my looking such a fool, too.

And probably if she'd had a wooden leg, a boss eye and only one tooth . . . Not that I was particularly interested in teeth at the moment, or in any position to utter more than a faint ugh, or even to smile a welcome. But how considerate of her to attend to me before taking any steps to deal with the heavy object on my lap! Most girls would have gone off into hysteria. But *she* happened to be practical; didn't even pause to dial 999. Saw with half an eye that . . . Put first things first. Besides looking such a fool, I was a fool: to get toothache on a Saturday afternoon, in a place like Cwm Tatws. As I told myself continuously throughout that lost week-end.

The trouble was my being all alone: nobody to be anxious, nobody to send out a search party, nobody in the township who knew me from Adam. I had come to Cwm Tatws to fish, which is about the only reason why anyone ever comes there, unless he happens to be called Harry Parry or Owen Owens or Evan Evans or Reece Reece or . . . Which I'm not. Tooth had already stirred faintly on the Friday just after I registered at the Dolwreiddiog Arms; but I decided to diagnose neuralgia and kill it with aspirin. Saturday, I got up early to flog the lake, where two- and three-pounders had allegedly been rising in fair numbers, and brought along my bottle of aspirins and a villanous cold lunch.

No, to fish doesn't necessarily mean being a Hemingway fan; after all, there was Izaak Walton, whom I haven't read either.

By mid-afternoon Tooth woke up suddenly and began to jump about like . . . I hooked a couple of sizeables, though nothing as big as advertised; both broke away. My error was waiting for the lucky third. That, and forgetting that it was Saturday afternoon. It was only when I got back to Cwm Tatws, which has five pubs (some bad, some worse), a police station, a post office, a branch bank and so forth – largish place for that district – that I decided to seek out the town tooth-drawer, Mr Griffith Griffiths, whose brass plate I had noticed next to 'Capel Beulah 1861'.

Not what you thought. Mr Griffith Griffiths was at home all right, most cordial, and worked Saturday afternoons and evenings because that was the day when everyone ... But he had recently slipped on a wet rock in his haste to gaff a big one and chipped a corner off his left elbow. Gross bad luck : he was left-handed.

'Let's look at it,' he said. And he did. 'No hope in the world of saving that poor fellow. I must yank him out at once. Pity on him, now, that he's a hind molar, indeed !'

What should X do next? Mr Griffith-heard-you-the-first-time will be out of action for the next month. X could of course hire a motor-car and drive thirty miles over the hills to Denbigh, where maybe tomorrow ...

I pressed and pleaded. 'Is there nobody in the five-pub town capable of ... A blacksmith, for instance? Or a barber? Why not the vet? Under your direction?'

'Well now, indeed, considering the emergency, perhaps, as you say, Mr Rowland Rowlands the veterinarian might consent to practise on you that which he practises on the ewes.'

Unfortunately Mr Rowland-say-it-twice had driven off to Denbigh himself in the last 'bus-motorr' (as they call it in Cwm Tatws), to visit his whatever she was.

Mr Griffith Griffiths right-handedly stroked his stubby chin. He couldn't shave now and thought the barber saloon vulgar and low. Said : 'Well, well, now, I shouldn't wonder if dear old Mr Van der Pant might peradventure play the good Samaritan. He is English too, and was qualified dental surgeon in Cwm Tatws, not altogether fifteen years ago; for it was from Mr Van der Pant that I bought this practice. A nice old gentleman, though a confirmed recluse and cannot speak a single word of Welsh.'

Welshlessness being no particular disadvantage in the circumstances, I hurried off to Rhododendron Cottage, down a wet lane, and up an avenue of wetter rhododendrons. By this time my tooth was ...

You are wrong again. I found Mr Van der Pant also at home, and he had not even broken an arm. But took ten minutes to answer the bell, and then came out only by accident, having been too deaf to hear it.

Let us cut short the dumb-show farce: eventually I made him understand and consent to ...

The room was ... Macabre, isn't it? 'Only Adults Admitted.' Had been locked up since whenever, by the look ot it. Cobwebs like tropical creepers. Dental chair deep in dust. Shutters askew. No heating. Smell of mice. Presence of mice. Rusty expectoration bowl and instrument rack. Plaster fallen in heaps from the ceiling. Wallpaper peeled off. Fascinating, in a way.

I helped him screw in an electric light bulb, and said: 'No, please don't bother to light a fire !'

'Yes, it must come out,' he wheezed. 'Pity that it's a posterior molar. Even more of a pity that I am out of anaesthetics.'

Fortunately he discovered that the forceps had been put away with a thin coating of oil, easily wiped off with ... He eyed it lovingly. Might still be used.

Was used.

By this time the posterior molar ... Or do I repeat myself? It could hardly have been more unfortunate, he complained. That forceps was not at all the instrument he should have chosen. Mr Griffith Griffiths had bought his better pair along with the practice. Still, he'd do his best. Would I mind if he introduced a little appliance to fix my jaws apart, so that he could work more cosily? He was getting on in years, he said, and a little rusty.

And please would I keep still? Yes, yes, most unfortunate. He had cut the corner of my mouth, he was well aware, but that was because I had jerked.

Three minutes best unrecorded. Not even adults admitted.

Mr Van der Pant then feared that we were getting nowhere. That forceps !

Tooth was rotten and he had nipped off the crown. Now we

must go deeper, into the gum. It might hurt a little. And, please, would I keep still this time? I should experience only a momentary pain, and then ... Perhaps if I permitted him to lash me to the chair? His heart was none too good, and my struggles ...

Poor blighter! 'You can truss me up like an Aylesbury duckling, if you care, so long as you dig this ... tooth out,' I said. He couldn't hear, of course, but guessed, and went out to fetch yards and yards of electric light flex.

Trussed me up good and proper: sailor fashion. 'Had he ever been dentist in a man-of-war?' I asked. But he smiled deafly. It was now about six-thirty on Saturday evening, and curiously enough he had begun telling me of the famous murderer – one Crippen, before my time – who had been his fellow dental-student when ... His last words were: 'And I also had the privilege once of attending his wife and victim, Miss Belle Ellmore, an actress, you will remember. She had split an incisor while biting on an ...'

I wish people would finish their sentences.

So, as I say, *she* turned up, providentially, at about eleven-fifteen, Monday, Mr Van der Pant's grand-niece, on a surprise visit. Lovely girl, straight out of Bond Street, or a band-box.

And there I sat in that dank room, on that dusty dental chair, with a dead dentist across my knees; my jaws held apart by a little appliance, a chill, a ripening abscess, my arms and legs and trunk bound tightly with yards of flex; not to mention, of course ...

Yes, I like to tell it my own way, though there's not much in it. Might have happened to any other damned fool.

But the sequel! Now that really was ...

HE WENT OUT TO BUY A RHINE

'HE was a very quiet, very sensitive young gentleman,' concluded Mrs Tisser, 'and punctual to the hour with his rent. I am truly sorry that he took the coward's way out. My own opinion is that the balance of his mind was upset.'

'Witness is not being questioned for her medical opinion,' whispered the Coroner's clerk. 'She is being asked for facts.'

The Coroner said: 'Mrs Tisser, you are not being asked for your medical opinion. You are being questioned for facts. The jury wants to hear more about the demeanour of the late Angus Hamilton Tighe on the morning of his death.'

Mrs Tisser stuck to her guns: 'The young gentleman's demeanour, your Honour, suggested that the balance of his mind had been upset.'

'Enlarge on that, please,' ordered the Coroner, conceding the point.

'He behaved very strangely, your Honour. At breakfast he told me, as I set down the tray beside him on the sitting-room table: "Mrs Tisser, I've been doing it wrong all my life: I keep my mouth open instead of shut." Well, that was what I had been praying for weeks that he *would* say, because the poor gentleman snored as a pig grunts. So I said: "Well, Mr Tighe, I'm glad to hear you make that confession. You ought to get Dr Thorne to operate on your nose, so that you'd never do it again." "Oh, but I enjoy the sensation," he said, with a wild look in his eye. "It invigorates the whole system. And it's a cheap pleasure, like sitting in the sun, or combing one's hair, don't you agree?" '

We glanced gravely at one another, as Mrs Tisser continued: 'I told him that I didn't agree, and that I'd dearly knock a shilling a week off his rent, if he could break himself of the habit. He laughed in what I can only call a fiendish manner, and I left the room without another word. He had never before made mock of me. Not that I felt vexed exactly. But his demeanour was certainly most alarming.'

'That took place shortly after 8 a.m., you say, Mrs Tisser?
Did you see him again that morning, before the fatality
occurred?'

'I did, your Honour; about five minutes later. We met on the
stairs. He seemed to be in a state of suppressed excitement, and
told me that he was going out to buy an "eternity" and do the
job properly at last. "An eternity?" I asked, thinking that perhaps I had misheard. "A rhine, if you like, Mrs Tisser," he answered, grinning like a devil.'

'And then?'

'And then, your Honour, he was away between ten minutes
and a quarter of an hour, and at last came rushing upstairs like
a whirlwind. Half a minute went by, and then I heard an extraordinary sound : a sort of muffled explosion from the sitting-
room. And I saw him dash through the open door, across the
corridor, and into the bedroom where he flung himself headlong
at the balcony beyond. I screamed, and hurried downstairs.'

'Thank you, Mrs Tisser, that will be enough. You need not
repeat that part of your evidence; we have inspected the french
windows and the shattered woodwork of the balcony which bear
out your evidence. One more question. Do you know anything
about the dead man's emotional life?'

'If you mean, did he ever try to bring a young woman home,
he certainly did not, your Honour. He was a most exemplary
young man in that respect; his medical studies seem to have been
"both parent, child and wife" to him, as the saying goes. The
only thing I recall ...'

'Yes, Mrs Tisser?'

'One night he confided to me his love for a lady whom he had
never met; someone who had taken complete possession of his
heart. I thought at first that it must be a film actress, but he said
that he didn't even know what she looked like, and he couldn't
understand a word of what she said, either. It was then I first
began to question his sanity. Well, about a week ago, as I was
doing his room, I noticed a crumpled letter lying half-charred in
the grate. My eye caught the first line : "O my wonderful Yma."
But I was too honourable to read any further, and I hardly like
to mention it even now. She seems to have been his dream-lady :

because once he came back from a visit to London, and his eyes were shining as he said: "Oh, I am so happy, Mrs Tisser." I asked: "On account of the lady you mentioned?" and he answered: "I spent the whole afternoon with her, Mrs Tisser." "So you've met her at last?" I said. "I mean in spirit," he told me.'

More evidence was called as to the late Angus Hamilton Tighe's state of health, but it proved to be inconclusive. We could not even decide that he had been overworking, or had financial difficulties, or was being blackmailed. Dr Thorne had never treated him for anything more than a twisted ankle. He possessed no close friends among his fellow medical students, and no relatives nearer than Canada. So we retired.

Since it seemed unlikely that Mrs Tisser had pushed him over the balcony, we naturally wanted to spare the feelings of the Tighe family in Alberta, by adding 'while of unsound mind' to the obvious verdict of 'suicide'.

Only one juryman, Mr Pink, a retired chemist, dissented. He called for silence, and then spoke in grave, authoritative tones. 'I think, ladies and gentlemen, that we can improve on that verdict. To begin with, I cannot regard it as a symptom of insanity in myself that I too admire, nay adore, the celebrated Peruvian singer Yma Sumac, though I have never seen her, nor do I know one word of Spanish. Her voice, surely the most wonderful in the world, compasses five full octaves and is true as a bell in every register. Poor young Tighe! I own a rare set of Yma's early recordings which would doubtless have given him infinite pleasure, had I been aware that he shared my view of her genius.

'But I have another observation to make of even greater importance: it is that when we inspected the corpse I noticed a discoloured right nostril.'

We gaped at him as he went on: 'Which did not figure in the post-mortem report and was, in my view, caused by a "sternutatory", not an "eternity"; or by an "errhine", not "a rhine". In non-technical language, by tobacco snuff. If the Coroner permits us, we will send a policeman to visit the only tobacconist in this town who sells that old-fashioned commodity — Hackett of Cold Harbour Cottages. The officer will almost certainly find that the

late Tighe visited Hackett at about 8.15 a.m. The fatal sternutatory is probably contained in the pencil-box on his desk. Moreover, I noticed a familiar medical work on elementary
physiology lying on the breakfast table. Look up "sternutation"
in the Index, turn to the relevant page; and you will find, I think,
a sentence to this general effect:

STERNUTATION: an involuntary reflex respiratory act, caused
by irritation of the nerve terminals of the nasal mucous membrane,
or by severe luminary stimulation of the optic nerve. The sternutator,
after drawing a deep breath, compresses his lips; whereupon the
contents of the lungs are violently expelled through the nostrils.

'I remember well the impression that this passage made on me
years ago, while I was studying for my pharmaceutical degree. I
said to myself, in the very words of the deceased: "I have been
doing it wrong all my life; I keep my mouth open, instead of
shut." The next time that I felt a sneeze coming on, I duly
compressed my lips and, hey presto! found myself hurtling
across the room like a stone from a catapult; but fortunately did
not make for the french windows. In fact, I knocked myself out
on the corner of the mantelpiece. Let me therefore record my
opinion that the late Angus Hamilton Tighe died a martyr to
scientific experiment and was no more suicidal than I am.'

So we brought in 'Death by Misadventure', after all, with a
rider against experimental use of sternutatories; which, I fear,
didn't mean a thing to the general public.

KILL THEM! KILL THEM!

THE potteries were by this time a distant smudge on the horizon behind us and the map showed us close to the Welsh border. Jenny drove.

Wales reminded us both of David, who had done his battle training in this region. So presently I said, knowing that this must be Jenny's line of thought too: 'They would have given him the award posthumously, of course, if the ground he won had been held. Not that it would have meant much to anyone, except the Regimental historian. Anyhow, the Japs infiltrated, the Indian battalions on the flanks rectified their line (as the saying is), and the Regiment had to fight its way back. It's a rule that a reverse cancels all citations.'

'An R.A.F. man who was giving the Brigade air-support – I met him last year in Trans-Jordania – says the attack was suicidal and criminal.'

'It wasn't the C.-in-C.'s fault. He had orders from London to secure a tactical success in that area before the monsoon broke. And felt awful about it.'

'How do you know that, Father?'

'Warell wrote to me as soon as the War ended and brought up the subject himself. His G.H.Q. was a thousand miles away, and though, when he'd seen the plan of attack submitted, he felt strongly tempted to fly up and run the show in person, a C.-in-C. couldn't very well take over from a brigade commander. It just wasn't done. Or so he said in his letter. I've kept it for you.'

'According to my R.A.F. man, everyone was hopping mad at having to assault a scientifically entrenched position without proper artillery support – and just before the rain bogged everything down for the season. That sense of victimization must have been what sent David berserk. As you know, he was a confirmed pacifist, and had nothing against the Japs.'

We kept silent for a mile or two. Then I said: 'One thing that he did has always puzzled me. At Oxford, when he was four years old, we were driving up the High and a great pack of black-coated, dog-collared parsons debouched from Queen's College and swarmed across the street, making for Oriel. An Ecclesiastical Congress was on. David shouted excitedly: "Kill them! Kill them!" Did he hate the colour of their clothes, do you think? Or was he simply anticlerical?'

'Neither,' Jenny answered. 'I should say that it was the *unnaturalness* of the sight. Probably he always thought of clergymen in the singular, as I do. The vicar on the altar steps: singular. Like the mother beside the cradle: singular. Or the headmistress in her study: singular. Each aloof, self-sufficient, all-powerful and, in fact, singular. Don't all Mothers' Meetings, Ecclesiastical Congresses, and Headmistresses' or Headmasters' Conferences seem terribly artificial and awkward and dismal to you – I mean because of the loss of singularity? Whereas soldiers or sailors, or undergraduates, or schoolchildren, who go naturally into the plural ...'

'Clergymen do behave very awkwardly in a bunch, I agree, and David may have wanted to put them out of their misery by a sudden massacre. He had a kind heart.'

'Also,' said Jenny, 'Mothers' Meetings and Headmistresses' Conferences go with seed-cake. When David was twelve and I was thirteen and we got invited to parties, he used to wander round and inspect the food supply as soon as we arrived. If it passed muster, we stayed. Otherwise he'd nudge me and whisper: "Seed-cake, Jenny." And then we always sneaked out. He hated seed-cake. Seed-cake's impersonal, and David was a real person.'

Green Welsh hills and wild-eyed Welsh sheep and the syllable *Llan* appearing on every second fingerpost. Hereabouts David had commanded his platoon in aggressive tactical schemes; perhaps had sten-gunned the imaginary garrison of that farmhouse at the top of the slope. It was a splendid eighteenth-century building with a broad whitewashed front, generous windows and an irregular slate roof yellow with lichen; also a large midden, cocks and hens ot an old-fashioned, handsome, uneconomical breed, black cows, and bracken litter at the entrance to the byres. A sign read T E A S.

As we rounded a sharp corner we came on a glossy charabanc,

which had just disgorged its load of excursionists by the farm-house gate. They were all earnest, black-coated, dog-collared clergymen, and seemed profoundly ill at ease. Forty or fifty at least, and – this is a true story, not a joke, for neither Jenny nor I felt prepared for a joke – every one of them had a slice of impersonal seed-cake in his hand, out of which he had taken a single thoughtful bite.

I had a vision of a serious apple-cheeked little boy, sitting be-tween Jenny and me and shaking his fist in a fury.

'Kill them, kill them!' I shouted involuntarily; but Jenny, scared as she was, had the presence of mind to swerve and drive on.

THE FRENCH THING

'Who the deuce put this foul French thing on my surgery table?'

Bella Nightingale took the crumpled magazine from him and studied the photographs over her breakfast plate. 'Oh, Lord,' she giggled, delightedly. 'Aren't they *horrors*?'

'I didn't ask for your aesthetic criticism,' Dr Nightingale snapped. 'I just wanted to know how that foul thing got on my surgery table. It certainly wasn't there last night, and Nurse Parker hasn't arrived yet.'

'Even if Nurse Parker *had* arrived, darling, you surely don't think she'd have given you so highly unsuitable a present? I know she adores you, but I can't see her risking her professional reputation by trying to get your mind working along lines like these ... Oh, Harry, *do* look at this anatomical monstrosity of a female – and taken from such a queer angle, too!'

Dr Nightingale snatched the magazine back. 'For Heaven's sake, Bella, get a grip on yourself and answer my question!'

'Mrs Jelkes came early today – I don't suppose you noticed – because she's got a funeral at eleven o'clock. She dusted your surgery after first doing out the spare room. That oafish nephew of yours left it in a fearful mess the other morning when he scrambled back to Camp. My theory is that Mrs Jelkes found the passion-parade under his pillow and thought she ought to warn you what sort of a lad he really is.'

Dr Nightingale's anger passed. 'Oh, well,' he sighed, 'I suppose that must be the explanation. It's her way of saying: "Don't invite Master Nicholas here again, or I'll get another job and tell the neighbours why." A pity! I hate sacrificing Nicholas to Mrs Jelkes's non-conformist conscience; but she's irreplaceable, I'm afraid. Or, at least, she's in a position to make herself so by blackmailing us. It'll be a bit awkward when Nicholas comes for another flying visit; I'll have to send him off and explain why he's no longer *persona grata*.'

'It's his own stupid fault. I'm sorry for young soldiers as a rule, but your Nicholas is a lazy, careless young dog, and you know it.'

'Do I? I'm relieved, at any rate, to know that he's a healthy heterosexual – one never can tell these days, especially when they write verse. Now, please burn it in the stove.'

'Can't. Mrs Jelkes is in the kitchen, and I don't want to give her the satisfaction of sniffing contempt at me.'

'Well, then hide it somewhere until she goes.'

The door-bell rang loudly and insistently.

'Road accident, by the noise,' said Dr Nightingale.

He was right. A lorry-driver with a gashed head and a dangling arm stood on the porch, supported by his mate.

As Dr Nightingale beckoned the pair in, the lorry-driver's mate fainted dead away across the threshold. 'He could never stand the sight of blood,' said the lorry-driver scornfully, 'this silly mucker couldn't !'

Nurse Parker had not yet appeared, so Bella Nightingale gulped down her coffee, shoved the magazine among a pile of weeklies stacked on the radio, and hurried into action by her husband's side.

In the middle of the confusion Nurse Parker's aunt rang up. She was grieved to say that Nurse Parker couldn't come that morning. Her bus had been run smack into by a lorry, and she was back in bed. 'No, no bones broken, praise the Lord ! Only shock.'

It was lunch-time before the air cleared. Bella had taken Nurse Parker's place and, besides the familiar Saturday patients, a stream of walking wounded came in from the Summer Camp – sardine-tin cuts, infected midge-bites, and badly grazed knees.

'Where's that French thing, Bella?'

'I shoved it in among the magazines.'

'Oh, you did, did you? . . . Well, *now* we're in the soup right up to our necks !'

'Oh Lord, you don't mean that the Reverend Mrs Vicar . . .?'

'I darned well do mean it. I happened to see her through my window, tripping down the garden path with the whole stack of magazines under her arm. Had you forgotten Mrs Jelkes's orders to hand them over to her on the last Saturday of every month?'

Bella laughed hysterically and then began to cry. 'Darling, we're socially ruined, and it's all my stupid fault! Mrs Vicar can't fail to go through the pile and when she comes across Nicholas's Parisian popsies, God, how the teacups will rattle and the kettle hiss in this frightful village! Mrs Jelkes has a far stricter code of honour than Mrs Vicar. She won't breathe a word unless Nicholas comes to stay here again. But Mrs Vicar ...'

'You must rush across and get the thing back. Explain that an important paper got mixed up with the magazines.'

'She'd insist on finding it for me. No, our only hope is that she'll bang the whole lot along to the Cottage Hospital unread. Let's cross our fingers ... Once it gets to the Hospital, we're safe. The Lady Almoner will find it and carry it home as a cosy reminder of her dead past. According to Dr MacGillicuddy, she was a photographer's model herself once, and not for face and ankles only.'

'*That* old hag? It must have been a long time ago; and I wouldn't trust her an inch, anyhow.'

'Harry ... about your French thing ...'

'Don't call it *my* French thing! Any new developments?'

'None. I've met Mrs Vicar several times since Saturday, and her manner is absolutely unchanged ...'

'That's really very odd. You see ... Well, I knew MacGillicuddy was a sportsman; so I rang him up at once at the Hospital, told him the story in confidence, and asked would he please see that the magazines got sent to his office, unsorted, the moment they arrived – not to the Lady Almoner. And it wasn't there, he swears.'

'Maybe the Vicar ...'

'The Vicar was away last week-end.'

'Maybe his *locum*, the sandy-haired youth with pince-nez ...'

'Maybe. He certainly preached a very odd sermon the next day on Jezebel and the dogs ...'

'Maybe Dr MacGillicuddy himself ...'

'Maybe. He's a bachelor. Anyhow, let's forget the unpleasant subject.'

'Bella ... talking of that French thing. It occurs to me that possibly ...'

'And to me! You mean what Mrs Vicar was telling us about the sudden gratifying increase in Sunday School attendance?'

'Exactly. Not girls, only boys. Four in all, including Harold Jelkes – and our little Robin Lostwithiel, of all children. She said that the dear laddies are so keen on Sunday School that they turn up half-an-hour early and play with her lonely little Evangeline.'

'Never underestimate the power of a woman, even at six years old.'

'This is worse than ever. If we're right, Evangeline is sure to be caught with the foul thing before long, and then it'll be traced to us. She'll open her baby-blue eyes wide and say: "Oh, I didn't think there was any harm in it, Mummy! Mrs Nightingale sent it us with the *Picture Posts* and things." We simply *must* get it back somehow, by fair means or foul. It'll be somewhere hidden among her toys.'

'Harry, how on earth do you expect me to burgle Evangeline's playroom?'

'I don't know. But it was you who got us into this mess. So you'd better get us out again pretty quick. Or else ...'

Barbie Lostwithiel, extravagantly dressed and perfumed as usual, strolled in unannounced through the french windows and kissed both the Nightingales on either cheek, Continental fashion. Dr Nightingale rather liked this unconventional salute, especially as Bella didn't grudge it him.

'Chums,' Barbie said in a husky whisper, 'I do want your advice so badly. You know how I am with Robin, ever since I got sole custody. No lies, no secrets, no half-truths, all absolutely above-board between us twain. I know you don't approve altogether, but there it is! Well, a tiny little rift in the lute occurred last Sunday after lunch, when Robin cancelled our old-time ceremonial game of draughts and wanted to hurry off early to the

Rectory. Of course, I had thought it a bit odd when he said the week before that he wanted to try Sunday School; but I didn't care to oppose him if that was his idea of fun. So this time I asked: "Bobbie, are you in love with Evangeline by any chance?" "No, Barbie, of course not," he said with that engaging blush of his, "but she has some very interesting photographs of ladies in a magazine from Paris. Ladies don't wear any clothes in Paris, you see, and I feel sort of happy looking at them just as they really are underneath. But I'm not to tell anyone, not a soul – of course you don't count, Barbie darling – in case Evangeline gets in a row with the Vicar. She stole it from the Hospital magazine collection." '

The Nightingales said nothing, but their fingers clenched and unclenched nervously.

Barbie Lostwithiel went on: 'I've been wondering what to do about it all the week. I don't in the least mind Bobbie's admiring the undraped female figure, so long as it's not misbehaving itself too shockingly – as I gather it isn't in this case, apart from a bit of candid acrobatic posturing. But I *do* mind his getting involved in a dirty little, sniggering, hole-and-corner Rectory peep-show – that *Turn of the Screw* Evangeline's clever contribution to the Church's standing problem of how to fill empty pews. Unfortunately, I can't confide in Mrs Vicar. She hates my guts as it is, because I'm a *divorcée* – even if I'm billed as the innocent party. I mean: I couldn't tell her what's in the air without breaking Robin's confidence and spoiling his faith in my absolute discretion. Besides, I'd be getting him in bad with the Sunday School gang. Harry, can't you, as the local physician, have a man-to-man talk with the Vicar? Say that a boy's father has been complaining; which would let Robin out nicely. *Please!*'

'Barbie, dearly as I may be supposed to love you and yours, I can't and won't do anything of the kind! The Vicar would toss me through his study window if I accused his innocent little daughter of keeping a ... a *salon des voyeurs*, I suppose the official phrase would be. The Vicar played "lock" in the English Rugger pack only six years ago.'

So Bella Nightingale and Barbie Lostwithiel put their heads

together. Their main problem was how to administer the doped chocolate without suspicion. Barbie solved that one easily. She borrowed the Church key from the sexton, on the pretext of putting two vasefuls of Madonna lilies from her garden on the Communion table; and, as she went out, paused briefly at the Rectory pew. There she hid a chocolate under Evangeline's prayer book – wrapped in a small piece of grimy exercise paper marked: 'Love from Harold Jelkes X X X.'

Bella, a certified dispenser before she married, had calculated the dose nicely. Soon after Sunday lunch, Mrs Vicar rang up to say that Evangeline was down with a violent tummy-ache and would Dr Nightingale be good enough to come at once?

Dr Nightingale answered that surely a simple stomach-ache ...? He was just off with his wife for a picnic on the Downs. Still, since poor wee Evangeline ...

'Now's your heaven-sent chance, Bella,' he said, when Mrs Vicar had rung off.

'Oh, very well, if I must, I must,' said Bella. She had carefully not told him about the chocolate, because such a bad actor as he would be sure to give the game away. Besides, it was notoriously unethical for a doctor to charge fees for curing an ailment in the causing of which he had connived. Harry would certainly prefer not to know of her device.

They collected the picnic things and drove to the Rectory. Bella went into the house, too, to express sympathy, but waited outside in the playroom, while Mrs Vicar was closeted with Dr Nightingale in Evangeline's bedroom.

Bella unearthed the magazine, after a rapid search, from under the snakes-and-ladders board, which lay under an illustrated *Child's Wonder of Nature*, which lay under a row of Teddy Bears. She shoved it down the neck of her blouse, buttoned her coat, replaced the Teddy Bears, and sat down placidly to read *Sunday at Home*.

Meanwhile, Dr Nightingale was puzzled. As Bella had foreseen, Evangeline did not own up to eating sweets in Church, especially love gifts from vulgar little boys.

'Odd,' he told Bella as they drove off. 'I don't think that stomach-ache is due to a bug. The action is far more like colo-

cynth or some other vegetable alkaloid of the sort; yet she seems
to have eaten her usual breakfast and lunch, with nothing in
between but a glass of milk. Anyhow, I put her on a starvation
diet for a day or two, the little basket! Did you find the French
thing?'

'I did.'

'Good girl! Burn it!'

Bella showed the magazine to Barbie, as she had promised.
Barbie gave a little yelp. 'Oh, my poor darling Robin!' she said,
tragically throwing up her hands and eyes. 'To think that his
first introduction to the female form divine should have been a
set of five-franc cats like these!'

'Really, Barbie! Your language!'

'It's enough to upset his psychic balance for all time. I could
slap your Mrs Jelkes for starting this lark.'

'She's already suffered quite a lot, I'm glad to report,' said
Bella. 'Her poor Harold passed a terrible night with so-called
"hives" — tossing, turning, screaming, scratching, and keeping
the whole household awake until the small hours. Not a wink of
sleep did Mrs Jelkes get. When Harry called in the morning, he
found nothing wrong with the brat — except itching-powder in
his pyjamas. Evangeline's hit back for the stomach-ache, I suppose. I wonder how she worked it? Thank Goodness, she
doesn't suspect *us*!'

Barbie was left to burn the French thing in her garden in-
cinerator. When she got around to doing so, a week later, Robin
strolled up unexpectedly and asked what the funny smell was.

Barbie got flustered, and told him her first lie. 'I'm just burning a few bills, darling. So much easier than paying them, as
you'll find when you grow up.'

'I see ... But, Barbie darling!'

'Yes, my love?'

'We met Evangeline in the wood. She says the Vicar found
that Paris magazine and snatched it away from her. He was
awfully cross, she says, and gave her a terrible beating with a
knobbed stick — so bad that she had to be put to bed and Dr

Nightingale was sent for, to cure her with bandages and iodine. And after that the Vicar nearly starved her to death. And she told us that our fathers will give us all terrible whippings, too, and starve us nearly to death, if they hear we've looked at the undressed Paris ladies. (Lucky I haven't a father now, isn't it?). But she's promised to watch for someone to send another copy. She doesn't know whose pile the first one came from. She *thinks* it was the Nightingales'. But there's sure to be another, she says. And she'll find a safer hiding place next time.'

A MAN MAY NOT MARRY HIS...

YOUR correspondent, telephoning from 'The Twelve Commandments', a charming little public house not a hundred yards from the gates of Lambeth Palace, reports that deep concern has been caused in that edifice by an examination of the quarterly report of the Archbishops' Standing Committee on Matrimony. This highly technical and still secret report, signed by Prebendary Palk, D.D., the biggest troublemaker in the whole Anglican Confession, emphasizes certain deficiencies in the *Table of Kindred and Affinity*: a legal document which your correspondent in his childhood used to study attentively during sermon time as a relaxation from the ardours of the Litany, and on which he is still something of an expert.

Half an hour ago, the bald and booming Prebendary unbosomed himself to your correspondent, who had invited him to a double gin-and-lime in the discreet bar-parlour. 'The Church,' he said, 'has hitherto been content to accept *Genesis* i, 27: "male and female created he them" as definitive; to believe that every human being is predestined before birth to one sex or the other. Insufficient credit has been given, however, to the mystery and evolutionary wonder of the Divine Scheme, and the remarkable skill with which, ahem, Providence has been pleased to endow certain outstanding surgeons and physicians. It has now been proved that a man or woman, even after consummating his or her marriage by an act of procreation, may experience a partial change of sex which these physicians and surgeons are empowered to make total.'

Pressed tactfully by your correspondent, the Prebendary enlarged on this theme: 'The Standing Committee,' he allowed himself to be quoted as saying, 'are by no means satisfied that the prohibited degrees listed in the *Table of Kindred and Affinity* have been defined with sufficient exactitude to prevent what may seem – I must emphasize, *seem* – scandalous marriages from taking place: unions which are, *prima facie*, incestuous in spirit, if not in letter. It is, for instance, a law of almost platitudinous force that a man may not marry his deceased wife's grandmother, nor (as he may more readily be tempted to do, if his grandfather has married a young girl and left her all the family cash) his deceased grandfather's wife. Yet since a certificate, signed by two or three qualified doctors and approved by a magistrate, now enables a man legally to register himself at Somerset House as a woman, what – pray, tell me that? – prevents him, as the Law stands, from marrying his deceased wife's grandfather, or his own grandmother's husband who may well be in his vigorous sixties?'

'Provided always that there is no consanguinity, and the spouses evince a genuine desire for the procreation of children,' your correspondent put in, sympathetically but doubtfully, from behind a pink gin.

'Quite, quite,' agreed the Prebendary, who is, by the way, a confirmed bachelor. 'Though in a civil marriage, you know, the registrar does not insist on the moral safeguard you very properly mention. But the question arises: should such a marriage, even between Christians of the highest principles and the deepest devotion for each other, be solemnized in a church? What troubles us committee-men is that, if such a man, now legally a woman, has been christened as a man, and if, worse – or I should say "better", I suppose – he has solemnized a Church marriage and begotten children on his wife now deceased, he must necessarily remain a male in the Church's sight, since these sacraments cannot be annulled or disregarded, even if the subject becomes a declared renegade to the faith. This consideration implies that in accordance with I *Corinthians* xi, 4, he would be obliged to appear in church with his head uncovered, not covered as in verse 5.'

'Don't let a little thing like that trouble you, Prebendary. In these days of empty pews, parsons admit women bareheaded, bare-footed, and even in two-piece bathing suits. Besides, ritualistic changes of sex among physically normal women are already legalized in this country.'

'Ha! How's that?' he asked sharply.

'Well,' explained your ingenious correspondent. 'One Sunday, Jane Doe, a Bishop's daughter, greets the Queen with a low

curtsy when, as Head of the Church, she lays the foundation
stone of a new cathedral. On the following Sunday, the same
Jane Doe, a sergeant-major in the W.R.A.C., assists at a Church
Parade and salutes the Queen, as her Colonel-in-Chief. The
salute is, in theory, a removal of the hat, which Jane Doe per-
forms as an honorary man, but which would have been forbidden her, as a Bishop's daughter, on the previous Sunday.'

Here the Prebendary tried to argue the toss, but your correspondent reminded him that the symbolic removal of the hat is
emphasized by Queen's Regulations, which make it a punish-
able offence to salute bareheaded.

Prebendary Palk then grunted with less than conviction, and
returned to his marriage hypothesis: 'Granted that the Divine
Law, as starkly laid down in *Leviticus* xx, 13, prevents the
Church from recognizing a physical union between man and
man; yet if one partner in this union be physically a female, is
not the spirit of the Law observed? And would this spirit not
be flouted were the union one between a woman who was
legally and physically a man, and a man who had retained his
physical male nature?'

Your blushing correspondent was obliged to agree that, in his
opinion, flouting would have occurred.

'And, to take an extreme instance: what of a marriage solemnized in church between a man who has been physically and
legally, but not spiritually, changed to a woman, and a woman
who has been physically and legally, but not spiritually, changed
to a man? I can see no possible moral objection to a match of
this sort, because the spouses belong to opposite sexes whichever
way you look at it. But, if the ex-woman prove her intrinsic
masculinity by begetting children on the ex-man, and if the ex-
man proves his intrinsic femininity by bearing and suckling
these, to which of the two are the offspring to yield obedience as
the spiritual male authority (*Genesis* iii, 16) in the household?
And which of the two should be churched after the birth of
each legitimate offspring?'

'Search me,' replied your correspondent gravely, signing to
the tapster, who at once refilled the Prebendary's glass. 'Perhaps
the decision would be better left to the individual conscience?'

'These are indeed thorny problems,' declared Prebendary Palk, 'but they must be resolutely faced, and not only by the Protestant Churches. Heaven knows what the Vatican reaction will be, but only yesterday I was talking to a Greek Orthodox dignitary – the Lesbian Patriarch in point of fact ...'

'Off record,' interrupted your correspondent boldly, 'what counsel would you give to a legalized ex-man if he were to fall honourably in love with his deceased grandmother's husband and find his feelings tenderly reciprocated?'

'Strictly off record,' the Prebendary answered, venting a non-ecclesiastical chuckle, 'I should advise him to get on with it while the going is good, publish the banns in a remote parish, and not disclose the relationship to the officiating priest. It is, after all, as the Chief of Sinners pointed out, better to marry than to burn; and whatever legislation may be called for will not retrospectively illegitimize the offspring of such a union – we can promise your friend that.'

'I assure you, the case is quite hypothetical,' your correspondent stammered, meeting the Prebendary's shrewdly curious gaze with some embarrassment.

AN APPOINTMENT FOR CANDLEMAS

Have I the honour of addressing Mrs Hipkinson?

That's me! And what can I do for you, young man?

I have a verbal introduction from — from an officer of your organization. Robin of Barking Creek was the name he gave.

If that isn't just like Robin's cheek! The old buck hasn't even dropped me a Christmas card since the year sweets came off the ration, and now he sends me trouble.

Trouble, Mrs Hipkinson?

Trouble, I said. You're not one of us. Don't need to do no crystal gazing to see that. What's the game?

Robin of Barking Creek has been kind enough to suggest that you would be kind enough to ...

Cut it out. Got my shopping to finish.

If I might perhaps be allowed to carry your basket? It looks as if it were rather heavy.

O.K., you win. Take the damn thing. My corns are giving me gyp. Well, now, out with it!

The fact is, madam, I'm engaged in writing a D. Phil. thesis on Contemporary Magology ...

Eh? What's that? Talk straight, *if* you please!

Excuse me. I mean I'm a University graduate studying present-day witchcraft; as a means of taking my degree in Philosophy.

Now, that makes a bit more sense. If Robin answers for you, I don't see why we couldn't help – same as I got our Deanna up into O level with a bit of a spell I cast on the Modern School examiners. But don't trouble to speak in whispers. Them eighteenth-century Witchcraft Acts is obsolescent now, except as regards fortune-tellers; and we don't touch that lay, not professionally we don't. Course, I admit, we keep ourselves to ourselves, but so do the Masons and the Foresters and the Buffs, not to mention the Commies. And all are welcome to our little do's, what consent to be duly pricked in their finger-tips and take the oath and give that there comical kiss. The police don't interfere.

Got their work cut out to keep up with motoring offences and
juvenile crime, and cetera. Nor they don't believe in witches,
they say; only in fairies. They're real down on the poor fairies,
these days.

*Do you mean to say the police wouldn't break up one of your
Grand Sabbaths, if ...*

Half a mo'! Got to pop into the Home and Commercial for a
dozen rashers and a couple of hen-fruit. Bring the basket along,
ducks, if you please ...

As you were saying, Mrs Hipkinson?

Ah yes, about them Sabbaths ... Well, see, so's to keep on the
right side of the Law, on account we all have to appear starko,
naturally we hire the Nudists' Hall. Main festivals are quarter-
days and cross quarter-days; them's the obligatory ones, same as
in Lancashire and the Highlands and everywhere else. Can't
often spare the time in between. We run two covens here, used
to be three – mixed sexes, but us girls are in the big majority.
I'm Pucelle of Coven No. 1, and my boy-friend Arthur o'Bower
(radio-mechanic in private life), he's Chief Devil of both. My
husband plays the tabor and jew's-trump in Coven No. 2. Not
very well up in the book of words, but a willing performer,
that's Mr H.

*I hope I'm not being indiscreet, but how do you name your
God of the Witches?*

Well, we used different names in the old days, before this village became what's called a dormitory suburb. He was Mahew,
or Lug, or Herne, I seem to remember, according to the time of
the year. But the Rev. Jones, our last Chief Devil but two, he was
a bit of a scholar: always called the god 'Faunus', which is
Greek or Hebrew, I understand.

*But Faunus was a patron of flocks and forests. There aren't
many flocks or forests in North-Eastern London, surely?*

Too true, there aren't; but we perform our fertility rites in aid
of the allotments. We all feel that the allotments is a good cause
to be encouraged, remembering how short of food we went in
the War. Reminds me, got to stop at that fruit stall: horse-
radish and a cabbage lettuce and a few nice carrots. The horse-

radish is for my little old familiar; too strong for my own
taste.... Shopping's a lot easier since Arthur and me got rid of
that there Hitler ...

Please continue, Mrs Hipkinson.

Well, as I was saying, that Hitler caused us a lot of trouble.
We don't hold with politics as a rule, but them Natsies was just
too bad with their incendiaries and buzz-bombs. So Arthur and
I worked on him at a distance, using all the strongest enchant-
ments in the *Book of Moons* and out of it, not to mention a
couple of new ones I got out of them Free French Breton sailors.
But Mr Hitler was a difficult nut to crack. He was *protected*,
see? But Mr Hitler had given us fire, and fire we would give
Mr Hitler. First time, unfortunately, we got a couple o' words
wrong in the formula, and only blew his pants off him. Next
time, we didn't slip up; and we burned the little basket to a
cinder.... Reminds me of my great-grandmother, old Mrs Lou
Simmons of Wanstead. She got mad with the Emperor Napo-
leon Bonapart, and caused 'im a horrid belly-ache on the Field
of Waterloo. Done, at a distance again, with toad's venom –
you got to get a toad scared sick before he'll secrete the right
stuff. But old Lou, she scared her toad good and proper : showed
him a distorting looking-glass – clever act, eh? So Boney
couldn't keep his mind on the battle; it was those awful gripings
in his stomjack what gave the Duke of Wellington his opportunity. Must cross over to the chemist, if you don't mind ...

For flying ointment, by any chance?

Don't be potty! Think I'd ask that Mr Cadman for soot and
baby's fat and bat's blood and aconite and water-parsnip? The
old carcase would think I was pulling his leg. No, Long Jack of
Coven No. 2 makes up our flying ointment – Jack's assistant-
dispenser at the Children's Hospital down New Cut. Oh, but
look at that queue! I don't think I'll trouble this morning. An
aspirin will do me just as well as the panel medicine.

*Do you still use the old-style besom at your merrymakings,
Mrs Hipkinson?*

There's another difficulty you laid your finger on. Can't get a
decent besom hereabouts, not for love nor money. Painted white
wood and artificial bristles, that's what they offer you. We got to

send all the way to a bloke at Taunton for the real thing – ash
and birch with osier for the binding – and last time, believe it
or don't, the damned fool sent me a consignment bound in
nylon tape! Nylon tape, I ask you!

*Yes, I fear that modern technological conditions are not
favourable to a spread of the Old Religion.*

Can't grumble. We're up to strength at present, until one or
two of the older boys and girls drop off the hook. But TV isn't
doing us no good. Sometimes I got to do a bit of magic-making
before I can drag my coven away from that Children's Hour.

Could you tell me what sort of magic?

Oh, nothing much; just done with tallow dolls and a bit of
itching powder. I raise shingles on their sit-upons, that's the
principle. Main trouble is, there's not been a girl of school-age
joined us since my Deanna, which is quite a time. It's hell beating up recruits. Why, I know families where there's three generations of witches behind the kids, and can you guess what they
all say?

I should not like to venture a guess, Mrs Hipkinson.

They say it's *rude. Rude!* That's a good one, eh? Well now,
what about Candlemas? Falls on a Saturday this year. Come
along at dusk. Nudists' Hall, remember – first big building to
the left past the traffic lights. Just knock. And don't you worry
about the finger-pricking. I'll bring iodine and lint.

*This is very kind of you indeed, Mrs Hipkinson. I'll phone
Barking Creek tonight and tell Robin how helpful you have
been.*

Don't mention it, young man. Well, here's my dump. Can't
ask you in, I'm afraid, on account of my little old familiar
wouldn't probably take to you. But it's been a nice chat. O.K.,
then. On Candlemas Eve, look out for three green frogs in your
shaving mug; I'll send them as a reminder .... And mind, no
funny business, Mister Clever! We welcome good sports, speci-
ally the College type like yourself; but nosy-parkers has got to
watch their step, see? Last Lammas, Arthur and me caught a
reporter from the *North-Eastern Examiner* concealed about the
premises. *Hey presto!* and we transformed him into one of
them Australian yellow dog dingoes. Took him down to

Regent's Park in Arthur's van, we did, and let him loose on the grass. Made out he'd escaped from the Zoological Gardens; the keepers soon copped him. He's the only dingo in the pen with a kink in his tail; but you'd pick him out even without that, I dare say, by his hang-dog look. Yes, you can watch the dingoes free from the 'Scotsman's Zoo', meaning that nice walk along the Park railings. Well, cheerio for the present!

Good-bye, Mrs Hipkinson.

THE ABOMINABLE MR GUNN

ONE Monday morning in September 1910, the abominable Mr J. O. G. Gunn, master of the Third Form at Brown Friars, trod liverishly down the aisle between two rows of pitch-pine desks and grasped the short hairs just above my right ear. Mr Gunn, pale, muscular and broad-faced, kept his black hair plastered close to the scalp with a honey-scented oil. He announced to the form, as he lifted me up a few inches: 'And now Professor Graves will display his wondrous erudition by discoursing on the first Missionary Journey of St Paul.' (Laughter.)

I discoursed haltingly, my mind being as usual a couple of stages ahead of my tongue, so that my tongue said 'Peter' when I meant 'Paul', and 'B.C.' when I meant 'A.D.', and 'Crete' when I meant 'Cyprus'. It still plays this sort of trick, which often makes my conversation difficult to follow and is now read as a sign of incipient senility. In those days it did not endear me to Mr Gunn ...

After the disaster at Syracuse, one Athenian would often ask another: 'Tell me, friend, what has become of old So-and-so?' and the invariable answer came: 'If he is not dead, he is school-mastering.' I can wish no worse fate to Mr J. O. G. Gunn – father of all the numerous sons-of-guns who have since sneered at my 'erudition' and cruelly caught at my short hairs – than that he is still exercising his profession at the age of eighty-plus; and that each new Monday morning has found him a little uglier and a little more liverish than before.

Me erudite? I am not even decently well read. What reading I have done from time to time was never a passive and promiscuous self-exposure to the stream of literature, but always a search for particular facts to nourish, or to scotch, some obsessive maggot that had gained a lodgement in my skull. And now I shall reveal an embarrassing secret which I have kept from the world since those nightmare days.

One fine summer evening as I sat alone on the roller behind the cricket pavilion, with nothing much in my head, I received a sudden celestial illumination: it occurred to me that I knew everything. I remember letting my mind range rapidly over all its familiar subjects of knowledge; only to find that this was no foolish fancy. I did know everything. To be plain: though conscious of having come less than a third of the way along the path of formal education, and being weak in mathematics, shaky in Greek grammar, and hazy about English history, I nevertheless held the key of truth in my hand, and could use it to open any lock of any door. Mine was no religious or philosophical theory, but a simple method of looking sideways at disorderly facts so as to make perfect sense of them.

I slid down from the roller, wondering what to do with my embarrassing gift. Whom could I take into my confidence? Nobody. Even my best friends would say 'You're mad!' and either send me to Coventry or organize my general scragging, or both; and soon some favour-currier would sneak to Mr Gunn, which would be the end of everything. It occurred to me that perhaps I had better embody the formula in a brief world-message, circulated anonymously to the leading newspapers. In that case I should have to work under the bedclothes after dark, by the light of a flash-lamp, and use the cypher I had recently perfected. But I remembered my broken torch-light bulb, and the difficulty of replacing it until the next day. No: there was no immediate hurry. I had everything securely in my head. Again I experimented, trying the key on various obstinate locks; they all clicked and the doors opened smoothly. Then the school-bell rang from a distance, calling me to preparation and prayers.

Early the next day I awoke to find that I still had a fairly tight grasp of my secret; but a morning's lessons intervened, and when I then locked myself into the privy, and tried to record it on the back of an old exercise-book, my mind went too fast for my pen, and I began to cross out – a fatal mistake – and presently crumpled up the page and pulled the chain on it. That night I tried again under the bedclothes, but the magic had evaporated and I could get no further than the introductory sentence.

My vision of truth did not recur, though I went back a couple of times to sit hopefully on the roller; and before long, doubts tormented me, gloomy doubts about a great many hitherto stable concepts: such as the authenticity of the Gospels, the perfect-tibility of man and the absoluteness of the Protestant moral code. All that survived was an after-glow of the bright light in my head, and the certainty that it had been no delusion. This is still with me, for I now realize that what overcame me that evening was a sudden infantile awareness of the power of intuition, the supra-logic that cuts out all routine processes of thought and leaps straight from problem to answer.

How easily this power is blunted by hostile circumstances Mr Gunn demonstrated by his treatment of one F. F. Smilley, a new boy, who seems, coincidentally, to have had a vision ana-logous to mine, though of a more specialized sort. Smilley came late to Brown Friars; he had been educated at home until the age of eleven because of some illness or other. It happened on his first entry into the Third Form that Mr Gunn set us a prob-lem from Hilderbrand's *Arithmetic for Preparatory Schools*, which was to find the square root of the sum of two decimals, divided (just for cussedness) by the sum of two complicated vulgar fractions. Soon everyone was scribbling away except F. F. Smilley, who sat there abstractedly polishing his glasses and gazing out of the window.

Mr Gunn looked up for a moment from a letter he was writing, and asked nastily: 'Seeking inspiration from the dis-tant church spire, Smilley?'

'No, sir. Polishing my glasses.'

'And why, pray?'

'They had marmalade on them, sir.'

'Don't answer me back, boy! Why aren't you working out that sum?'

'I have already written down the answer, sir.'

'Bring your exercise-book here! ... Ah, yes, here is the answer, my very learned and ingenious friend Sir Isaac New-ton' – tweaking the short hairs – 'but where is it worked out?'

'Nowhere, sir; it just came to me.'

'Came to you, F. F. Smilley, my boy? You mean you hazarded a wild guess?'

'No, sir, I just looked at the problem and saw what the answer must be.'

'Ha! A strange physical phenomenon! But I must demand proof that you did not simply turn to the answer at the end of the book.'

'Well, I did do that afterwards, sir.'

'The truth now slowly leaks out.'

'But it was wrong, sir. The last two figures should be 35, not 53.'

'Curiouser and curiouser! Here's a Brown Friars' boy in the Third Form who knows better than Professor Hilderbrand, Cambridge's leading mathematician.'

'No, sir, I think it must be a misprint.'

'So you and Professor Hilderbrand are old friends? You seem very active in his defence.'

'No, sir, I have met him, but I didn't like him very much.'

F. F. Smilley was sent at once to the Headmaster with a note: 'Please cane bearer for idleness, lying, cheating and gross impertinence' – which the Headmaster, who had certain flaws in his character, was delighted to do. I cannot tell the rest of the story with much confidence, but my impression is that Mr Gunn won, as he had already won in his battle against J. X. Bestard-Montéry, whose Parisian accent when he was called upon to read '*Maître Corbeau, sur un arbre perché*' earned him the name of 'frog-eating mountebank', and a severe knuckling on the side of the head. Bestard was forced to put a hard Midland polish on his French.

Mr Gunn, in fact, gradually beat down F. F. Smilley's resistance by assiduous hair-tweakings, knucklings and impositions; and compelled him to record all mathematic argument in the laborious way laid down by Professor Hilderbrand. No more looking out of the window, no more guessing at the answer.

Whether the cure was permanent I cannot say, because shortly before the end of that school-year the Chief of County Police gave the Headmaster twenty-four hours to leave the country (the police were more gentlemanly in those Edwardian days), and Brown Friars broke up in confusion. I have never since heard of F. F. Smilley. Either he was killed in World War I, or else he is schoolmastering somewhere. Had he made his mark in higher mathematics, we should surely have heard of it. Unless, perhaps, he is so much a back-room boy, so much the arch-wizard of the mathematical-formula department on which Her Majesty's nuclear physicists depend for their bombs and piles, that the Security men have changed his name, disguised his features by plastic surgery, speech-trained him into alien immigrance, and suppressed his civic identity. I would not put it past them. But the mathematical probability is, as I say, that Gunn won.

HAROLD VESEY AT THE GATES OF HELL

THE dim old 'Pelican' sign had been wittily repainted by a modern poster artist. The once foul stable yard, frequented by hordes of sooty sparrows, had been converted into a car park. White muslin curtains graced the windows. An adjoining network of howling, stinking, typhoidal slum, where in my childhood policemen dared enter only four by four – truncheons drawn and whistles in their mouths – had utterly vanished; garaged residences now occupying the site were already well matured, their elms almost overtopping the roofs. The road-crossing which pale-faced street-Arabs with ragged trousers, bare feet and scanty brooms used to sweep clear of mud and horse-dung for us gentry to cross – 'Don't forget the sweeper, lady!' – had become a gleaming asphalt roundabout, and the rain-water gurgling down the gutters looked positively potable.

'There are the gates of Hell!', I nevertheless reminded myself, as I pushed open the door marked 'Saloon Bar'. Amelia, my nurse, had told me so when I was four years old, pointing across the road through the bathroom window. 'A man goes in at that door sober, industrious and God-fearing; he comes out a fiend in human guise, whether it's the beer or whether it's the gin.' She then dabbed her eyes with a handkerchief. 'I had a good home and husband once,' she said. 'I never thought as I should be forced to earn my living in domestic service at twenty pound a year. And look what's happened to that poor foolish Annie! The Pelican has been her downfall, too.' She was referring to our parlour-maid's fatal love for Harold, the barrel-man, a big red-faced ex-soldier with shoulder-of-mutton fists, green baize apron, and shiny black corduroys. Annie had stolen two of our silver entrée dishes to buy Harold a watch-chain for Christmas; and been dismissed without a character.

Mr Gotobed, Junior, the plump-faced innkeeper – probably 'Brassy' Gotobed's grandson – lounged alone behind the bar. He was youngish, with side-burns, Savile Row tailoring and an Old

Malthusian tie. I entered hesitantly and earned an easy though enigmatic smile.

On the walls hung three Baxter prints, two matched warming-pans, a cluster of knobkerries, an Indian Mutiny bundook, a dartboard, a large wooden spoon, a pair of indifferent French Impressionist paintings in art-gallery frames, and an iron hoop.

'With what may I have the pleasure of serving you, sir?'

'A double brandy,' I ordered, remembering the beer and the gin.

'Splash?'

'No, thanks; neat.' And I drank it at a blow.

'These were the gates of Hell, Mr Gotobed,' I remarked, putting down two half-crowns.

'Sir?'

'I used to live in that big house opposite.'

'You mean Rosemary Mansions?'

'I mean Rosemary House, before it became immansionized. That was when the Pelican's best beer still sold at twopence a pint; and was strong as the kick of a dray-horse. When tankards and curses flew along this ancient bar like bees on a summer's day. When soused lobsters went tumbling out into the inspissated muck, heels over busby, with almost boring regularity, propelled by the hobnailed boots of courageous Corporal Harold Vesey. These, I repeat, were the gates of Hell.'

'That will have been in what I might call pre-Reformation days, sir,' he said rather crossly. 'My clientele now consists almost entirely of City men. But we have a lot of quiet democratic fun here together. It amused us last year to form a Saloon Bar Darts Club and enter for the South-West London Championship. We won that wooden spoon fair and square; and my team treasure it like the apple of their corporate eye.'

But I refused to be sidetracked. 'It was the time,' I insisted, pointing to a handsome portrait of the Duke of Cornwall suspended behind the bar, 'of that boy's great-great-great-grandmother. I remember the old lady well, driving along High Street in an open barouche with a jingling escort of Lancers.'

He eyed me with awe. '*Three* greats?' he inquired, 'are you sure?'

'Rip van Winkle's the name,' I answered. 'I suppose it's no use asking you what happened to Corporal Harold Vesey? I'm sure of the surname because he sent our parlour-maid Annie a lace Valentine inscribed: "Yours respectably, Harold Vesey, Corporal, 1900"; that was after he came back gloriously wounded from the South African war. Harold was barrel-man; and porter at the Gates of Hell.'

'Rings a bell,' said Mr Gotobed meditatively. 'Hell's bells, if you like, ha, ha! 1900? Time of my grandfather?'

'If your grandfather was the bold hero in the purple waist-coat whom the boys nicknamed "Brassy" ', I said, and ordered another brandy.

He waved that one off. 'Funny,' he remarked, 'how we reckon time here in terms of war. South African. First World. Second World.'

'Harold Vesey had served at Tel-el-Kebir in 1882. He was a veteran when I knew him.'

'Indeed? Well, I never saw any service myself, and I'm not ashamed to tell you the story, now it's all over. If it had been a question of volunteering, I dare say I'd have gone along with all the other b. fools. But not under Conscription. We Malthusians have our pride. Between you and me I fooled the Board by a simple and quite ingenious wheeze. A fortnight beforehand I started eating sugar. Gradually worked up to two pounds a day. Ghastly treatment with ghastly symptoms. Ghastly expensive, too, with rationing in full blast. Naturally, just because of the rationing, the medicos never suspected a thing.'

'Naturally,' I agreed. 'Harold once fooled his M.O. too, to avoid being drafted somewhere on garrison duty. He chewed cordite, which sent up his temperature to 106. When duly crimed, he owned up; whereupon the Colonel drafted him to South Africa instead, which was what he wanted. And he sub-sequently had the pleasure of relieving Ladysmith. But that, of course, took place in the days before Conscription.'

'Good for him!' said Mr Gotobed without conviction and switched the topic again. 'By the way, see that iron hoop over

there? It's a curious relic of my grandfather's days. I bought it at
an antique shop for our Christmas celebration to use as a frame
for the wreath of holly and ivy over the door. The old merchant
told me that iron hoops were trundled here in the days of
gaseous street-lighting and horse-drawn traffic.'

'Harold Vesey gave me an iron hoop once,' I said, 'but unfortunately I wasn't allowed to use it. I was a little gentleman and
little gentlemen were supposed to use only wooden hoops. We
were also forbidden to whistle on our fingers or turn cartwheels,
because that was what the street-Arabs did. Thus you obscure
the relentless evolution of modern society, Mr Gotobed. The
street-Arab is forced by industrial progress to become a respectable citizen. His grandsons, if not his sons, are born little gentlemen; and therefore forbidden to whistle on their fingers or turn
cartwheels on the bemuddied crossing. And iron hoops, like peg-
tops with dangerous spikes (another ancient working-class distinction) are relegated to the antique shops. Harold Vesey would
have been surprised.'

I kept on the Harold Vesey track mercilessly, until the bell
rang again in Mr Gotobed's mind.

'Vesey? I've got it now. Yes, my grandfather employed one
H. Vesey at the Pelican. Comic story in its weird way. It seems
that soon after he sent that Valentine to your parlour-maid, an
aunt died and left him an Essex country cottage and a small
legacy – in recognition of his patriotic services. However, just
before Hitler's War, when he was in his late seventies, the
County Council condemned the cottage and transplanted him
to a brand-new Council-house: modern plumbing, well-
equipped kitchen, built-in cupboards, everything laid on. But
the obstinate old – well – basket didn't take to it. Sulked. Sat
out on a bench in the garden, all weathers, "just to spite them,"
he said – until he was carried off by pneumonia. The joke was
that they never got around to pulling down the cottage after all.
Its timbers were still sound and the premises served during the
War to accommodate evacuees. Recently my father bought the
place – that's how I happen to know the story. He spent four
or five thousand pounds on doing it up for a week-end hang-
out. But the Council wouldn't let us alter the façade or build

another storey, because by then – this is the real pay-off – the cottage had been scheduled as an ancient monument. What a country, eh?'

But at that moment jovial members of the City clientele came wandering in, and called for dry Martinis. I managed to retire without comment or attention.

CHRISTMAS TRUCE

Young Stan comes around yesterday about tea-time – you know my grandson Stan? He's a Polytechnic student, just turned twenty, as smart as his dad was at the same age. Stan's all out to be a commercial artist and do them big coloured posters for the hoardings. Doesn't answer to 'Stan', though – says it's 'common'; says he's either 'Stanley' or he's nothing.

Stan's got a bagful of big, noble ideas; all schemed out carefully, with what he calls 'captions' attached.

Well, I can't say nothing against big, noble ideas. I was a red-hot Labour-man myself for a time, forty years ago now, when the Kayser's war ended and the war-profiteers began treading us ex-heroes into the mud. But that's all over long ago – in fact, Labour's got a damn sight too respectable for my taste! Worse than Tories, most of their leaders is now – especially them that used to be the loudest in rendering 'We'll Keep the Red Flag Flying Still'. They're all Churchwardens now, or country gents, if they're not in the House of Lords.

Anyhow, yesterday Stan came around, about a big Ban-the-Bomb march all the way across England to Trafalgar Square. And couldn't I persuade a few of my old comrades to form a special squad with a banner marked 'First World War Veterans Protest Against the Bomb'? He wanted us to head the parade, ribbons, crutches, wheel-chairs and all.

I put my foot down pretty hard. 'No, Mr Stanley,' I said politely, 'I regret as I can't accept your kind invitation.'

'But why?' says he. 'You don't want another war, Grandfather, do you? You don't want mankind to be annihilated? This time it won't be just a few unlucky chaps killed, like Uncle Arthur in the First War, and Dad in the Second ... It will be all mankind.'

'Listen, young 'un,' I said. 'I don't trust nobody who talks about mankind – not parsons, not politicians, nor anyone else. There ain't no such thing as "mankind", not practically speaking there ain't.'

'Practically speaking, Grandfather,' says young Stan, 'there *is*. Mankind means all the different nations lumped together – us, the Russians, the Americans, the Germans, the French, and all the rest of them. If the bomb goes off, everyone's finished.'

'It's not going off,' I says.

'But it's gone off twice already – at Hiroshima and Nagasaki,' he argues, 'so why not again? The damage will be definitely final when it *does* go off.'

I wouldn't let Stan have the last word. 'In the crazy, old-fashioned war in which I lost my foot,' I said, a bit sternly, 'the Fritzes used poison gas. They thought it would help 'em to break through at Wipers. But somehow the line held, and soon our factories were churning out the same stinking stuff for us to use on them. All right, and now what about Hitler's war?'

'What about it?' Stan asks.

'Well,' I says, 'everyone in England was issued an expensive mask in a smart-looking case against poison-gas bombs dropped from the air – me, your Dad, your Ma, and yourself as a tiny tot. But how many poison-gas bombs were dropped on London, or on Berlin? Not a damned one! Both sides were scared stiff. Poison gas had got too deadly. No mask in the market could keep the new sorts out. So there's not going to be no atom bombs dropped neither, I tell you, Stanley my lad; not this side of the Hereafter! Everyone's scared stiff again.'

'Then why do both sides manufacture quantities of atom bombs and pile them up?' he asks.

'Search me,' I said, 'unless it's a clever way of keeping up full employment by making believe there's a war on. What with bombs and fall-out shelters, and radar equipment, and unsinkable aircraft-carriers, and satellites, and shooting rockets at the moon, and keeping up big armies – takes two thousand quid nowadays to maintain a soldier in the field, I read the other day – what with all that play-acting, there's full employment assured for everyone, and businessmen are rubbing their hands.'

'Your argument has a bad flaw, Grandfather. The Russians don't need to worry about full employment.'

'No,' said I, 'perhaps they don't. But their politicians and commissars have to keep up the notion of a wicked Capitalist

plot to wipe out the poor workers. And they have to show that
they're well ahead in the Arms Race. Forget it, lad, forget it!
Mankind, which is a term used by maiden ladies and bun-
punchers, ain't going to be annihilated by no atom bomb.'

Stan changed his tactics. 'Nevertheless, Grandfather,' he says,
'we British want to show the Russians that we're not engaged in
any such Capitalist plot. All men are brothers, and I for one
have nothing against my opposite number in Moscow, Ivan
Whoever-he-may-be ... This protest march is the only logical
way I can show him my dislike of organized propaganda.'

'But Ivan Orfalitch ain't here to watch you march; nor the
Russian telly ain't going to show him no picture of it. If Ivan
thinks you're a bleeding Capitalist, then he'll go on thinking
you're a bleeding Capitalist; and he won't be so far out, neither,
in my opinion. No, Stan, you can't fight organized propaganda
with amachoor propaganda.'

'Oh, can it, Grandfather!' says Stan. 'You're a professional
pessimist. And *you* didn't hate the Germans even when you were
fighting them – in spite of the newspapers. What about that
Christmas Truce?'

Well, I'd mentioned it to him one day, I own; but it seems he'd
drawn the wrong conclusions and didn't want to be put straight.
However, I'm a lucky bloke – always being saved by what other
blokes call 'coincidences', but which I don't; because they always
happen when I need 'em most. In the trenches we used to call
that 'being in God's pocket'. So, of course, we hear a knock at
the door and a shout, and in steps my old mucking-in chum
Dodger Green, formerly 301691, Pte Edward Green of the 1st
Batt., North Wessex Regiment – come to town by bus for a
Saturday night booze with me, every bit of twenty miles.

'You're here in the exact nick, Dodger,' says I, 'as once before.'
He'd nappooed a Fritz officer one day when I was lying with
one foot missing outside Delville Wood, and the Fritz was kindly
putting us wounded out of our misery with an automatic pistol.

'What's new, Fiddler?' he asks.

'Tell this lad about the *two* Christmas truces,' I said. 'He's trying to enlist us for a march to Moscow, or somewhere.'

'Well,' says Dodger, 'I don't see no connexion, not yet. And marching to Moscow ain't no worse nor marching to Berlin, same as you and me did – and never got more nor a few hundred yards forward in the three years we were at it. But, all right, I'll give him the facts, since you particularly ask me.'

Stan listened quietly while Dodger told his tale. I'd heard it often enough before, but Dodger's yarns improve with the telling. You see, I missed most of that first Christmas Truce, as I'll explain later. But I came in for the second; and saw a part of it what Dodger didn't. And the moral I wanted to impress on young Stan depended on there being *two* truces, not one: them two were a lot different from one another.

I brings a quart bottle of wallop from the kitchen, along with a couple of glasses – not three, because young Stan don't drink anything so 'common' as beer – and Dodger held forth. Got a golden tongue, has Dodger – I've seen him hold an audience spellbound at 'The Three Feathers' from opening-time to stop-tap, and his glass filled every ten minutes, free.

'Well,' he says, 'the first truce was in 1914, about four months after the Kayser's war began. They say that the old Pope suggested it, and that the Kayser agreed, but that Joffre, the French C.-in-C. wouldn't allow it. However, the Bavarians were sweating on a short spell of peace and good will, being Catholics, and sent word around that the Pope was going to get his way. Consequently, though we didn't have the Bavarians in front of us, there at Boy Greneer, not a shot was fired on our sector all Christmas Eve. In those days we hadn't been issued with Mills bombs, or trench-mortars, or Verey pistols, or steel helmets, or sand bags, or any of them later luxuries; and only two machine-guns to a battalion. The trenches were shallow and knee-deep in water, so that most of the time we had to crouch on the fire-step. God knows how we kept alive and smiling ... It wasn't no picnic, was it, Fiddler? – and the ground half-frozen, too!

'Christmas Eve, at 7.30 p.m., the enemy trenches suddenly lit up with a row of coloured Chinese lanterns, and a bonfire started in the village behind. We stood to arms, prepared for whatever happened. Ten minutes later the Fritzes began singing a Christmas carol called "Stilly Nucked". Our boys answered with "Good King Wencelas", which they'd learned the first verse of as Waits, collecting coppers from door to door. Unfortunately no one knew more than two verses, because Waits always either get a curse or a copper before they reach the third verse.

'Then a Fritz with a megaphone shouts "Merry Christmas, Wessex!"

'Captain Pomeroy was commanding us. Colonel Baggie had gone sick, second-in-command still on leave, and most of the other officers were young second-lieutenants straight from Sandhurst – we'd taken such a knock, end of October. The Captain was a real gentleman: father, grandfather, and great-grandfather all served in the Wessex. He shouts back: "Who are you?" And they say that they're Saxons, same as us, from a town called Hully in West Saxony.

' "Will your commanding officer meet me in No-man's land to arrange a Christmas truce?" the Captain shouts again. "We'll respect a white flag," he says.

'That was arranged, so Captain Pomeroy and the Fritz officer, whose name was Lieutenant Coburg, climbed out from their trenches and met half-way. They didn't shake hands, but they saluted, and each gave the other word of honour that his troops wouldn't fire a shot for another twenty-four hours. Lieutenant Coburg explained that his Colonel and all the senior officers were back taking it easy at Regimental H.Q. It seems they liked to keep their boots clean, and their hands warm: not like our officers.

'Captain Pomeroy came back pleased as Punch, and said: "The truce starts at dawn, Wessex; but meanwhile we stay in trenches. And if any man of you dares break the truce tomorrow," he says, "I'll shoot him myself, because I've given that German officer my word. All the same, watch out, and don't let go of your bundooks."

'That suited us; we'd be glad to get up from them damned fire-steps and stretch our legs. So that night we serenaded the Fritzes with all manner of songs, such as "I want to go Home!" and "The Top of the Dixie Lid", and the one about "Old Von Kluck, He Had a Lot of Men"; and they serenaded us with *Deutschland Uber Alles*, and songs to the concertina.

'We scraped the mud off our puttees and shined our brasses, to look a bit more regimental next morning. Captain Pomeroy, meanwhile, goes out again with a flashlight and arranges a Christmas football match – kick-off at 10.30 – to be followed at two o'clock by a burial service for all the corpses what hadn't been taken in because of lying too close to the other side's trenches.

' "Over the top with the best of luck!" shouts the Captain at 8 a.m., the same as if he was leading an attack. And over we went, a bit shy of course, and stood there waiting for the Fritzes. They advanced to meet us, shouting, and five minutes later, there we were ...

'Christmas was a peculiar sort of day, if ever I spent one. Hobnobbing with the Hun, so to speak: swapping fags and rum and buttons and badges for brandy, cigars and souvenirs. Lieutenant Coburg and several of the Fritzes talked English, but none of our blokes could sling a word of their bat.

'No-man's land had seemed ten miles across when we were crawling out on a night patrol; but now we found it no wider than the width of two football pitches. We provided the football, and set up stretchers as goal posts; and the Rev. Jolly, our Padre, acted as ref. They beat us 3–2, but the Padre had showed a bit too much Christian charity – their outside-left shot the deciding goal, but he was miles offside and admitted it soon as the whistle went. And we spectators were spread nearly two deep along the touch-lines with loaded rifles slung on our shoulders.

'We had Christmas dinner in our own trenches, and a German bugler obliged with the mess call – same tune as ours. Captain Pomeroy was invited across, but didn't think it proper to accept. Then one of our sentries, a farmer's son, sees a hare loping down the line between us. He gives a view halloo, and everyone rushes to the parapet and clambers out and runs forward to cut it off. So do the Fritzes. There ain't no such thing as harriers in Germany; they always use shot-guns on hares. But they weren't allowed to shoot this one, not with the truce; so they turned harriers same as us.

'Young Totty Fahy and a Saxon corporal both made a grab for the hare as it doubled back in their direction. Totty catches it

by the forelegs and the Corporal catches it by the hindlegs, and
they fall on top of it simultaneous.

'Captain Pomeroy looked a bit worried for fear of a shindy
about who caught that hare; but you'd have laughed your head
off to see young Totty and the Fritz both politely trying to force
the carcase on each other! So the Lieutenant and the Captain
gets together, and the Captain says: "Let them toss a coin for
it." But the Lieutenant says: "I regret that our men will not
perhaps understand. With us, we draw straws." So they picked
some withered stems of grass, and Totty drew the long one. He
was in our section, and we cooked the hare with spuds that night
in a big iron pot borrowed from Duck Farm; but Totty gave the
Fritz a couple of bully beef tins, and the skin. Best stoo I ever
ate!

'We called 'em "Fritzes" at that time. Afterwards they were
"Jerries", on account of their tin hats. Them helmets with
spikes called *Pickelhaubes* was still the issue in 1914, but only
for parade use. In the trenches caps were worn; like ours, but
grey, and no stiffening in the top. Our blokes wanted pickelhaubes badly to take their fiancées when they went home on
leave; but Lieutenant Coburg says, sorry, all pickelhaubes was in
store behind the lines. They had to be content with belt-buckles.

'General French commanded the B.E.F. at the time – decent
old stick. Said afterwards that if he'd been consulted about the
truce, he'd have agreed for chivalrous reasons. He must have
reckoned that whichever side beat, us or the Germans, a Christmas truce would help considerably in signing a decent peace at
the finish. But the Kayser's High Command were mostly Prussians, and Lieutenant Coburg told us that the Prussians were
against the Truce, which didn't agree with their "frightfulness"
notions; and though other battalions were fraternizing with the
Fritzes up and down the line that day – but we didn't know it
– the Prussians weren't having any. Nor were some English
regiments: such as the East Lancs on our right flank and the
Sherwood Foresters on the left – when the Fritzes came out with
white flags, they fired over their heads and waved 'em back. But
they didn't interfere with our party. It was worse in the French
line: them Frogs machine-gunned all the "Merry Christmas"

parties . . . Of course, the French go in for New Year celebrations more than Christmas.

'One surprise was the two barrels of beer that the Fritzes rolled over to us from the brewery just behind their lines. I don't fancy French beer; but at least this wasn't watered like what they sold us English troops in the estaminets. We broached them out in the open, and the Fritzes broached another two of their own.

'When it came to the toasts, the Captain said he wanted to keep politics out of it. So he offered them "Wives and Sweethearts!" which the Lieutenant accepted. Then the Lieutenant proposed "The King!" which the Captain accepted. There was a King of Saxony too, you see, in them days, besides a King of England; and no names were mentioned. The third toast was "A Speedy Peace!" and each side could take it to mean victory for themselves.

'After dinner came the burial service – the Fritzes buried their corpses on their side of the line; we buried ours on ours. But we dug the pits so close together that one service did for both. The Saxons had no Padre with them; but they were Protestants, so the Rev. Jolly read the Service, and a German Divinity Student translated for them. Captain Pomeroy sent for the Drummers and put us through that parade in proper regimental fashion: slow march, arms reversed, muffled drums, a union jack and all.

'An hour before dark, a funny-faced Fritz called Putzi came up with a trestle table. He talked English like a Yank. Said he'd been in Ringling's Circus over in the United States. Called us "youse guys", and put on a hell of a good gaff with conjuring tricks and juggling – had his face made up like a proper clown. Never heard such applause as we gave Herr Putzi!

'Then, of course, our bastard of a Brigadier, full of turkey and plum pudding and mince pies, decides to come and visit the trenches to wish us Merry Christmas! Captain Pomeroy got the warning from Fiddler here, who was away down on light duty at Battalion H.Q. Fiddler arrived in the nick, running split-arse across the open, and gasping out: "Captain, Sir, the Brigadier's here; but none of us hasn't let on about the Truce."

'Captain Pomeroy recalled us at once. "Imshi, Wessex!" he

shouted. Five minutes later the Brigadier came sloshing up the communication trench, keeping his head well down. The Captain tried to let Lieutenant Coburg know what was happening; but the Lieutenant had gone back to fetch him some warm gloves as a souvenir. The Captain couldn't speak German; what's more, the Fritzes were so busy watching Putzi that they wouldn't listen. So Captain Pomeroy shouts to me: "Private Green, run along the line and order the platoon commanders from me to fire three rounds rapid over the enemies' heads." Which I did; and by the time the Brigadier turns up, there wasn't a Fritz in sight.

'The Brigadier, whom we called "Old Horseflesh", shows a lot of Christmas jollity. "I was very glad," he says, "to hear that Wessex fusillade, Pomeroy. Rumours have come in of fraternization elsewhere along the line. Bad show! Disgraceful! Can't interrupt the war for freedom just because of Christmas! Have you anything to report?"

'Captain Pomeroy kept a straight face. He says: "Our sentries report that the enemy have put up a trestle table in No-man's land, Sir. A bit of a puzzle, Sir. Seems to have a bowl of goldfish on it." He kicked the Padre, and the Padre kept his mouth shut.

'Old Horseflesh removes his brass hat, takes his binoculars, and cautiously peeps over the parapet. "They *are* goldfish, by Gad!" he shouts. "I wonder what new devilish trick the Hun will invent next. Send out a patrol tonight to investigate." "Very good, Sir," says the Captain.

'Then Old Horseflesh spots something else: it's Lieutenant Coburg strolling across the open between his reserve and front lines; and he's carrying the warm gloves. "What impudence! Look at that swaggering German officer! Quick, here's your rifle, my lad! Shoot him down point-blank!" It seems Lieutenant Coburg must have thought that the fusillade came from the Foresters on our flank; but now he suddenly stopped short and looked at No-man's land, and wondered where everyone was gone.

'Old Horseflesh shoves the rifle into my hand. "Take a steady aim," he says. "Squeeze the trigger, don't pull!" I aimed well above the Lieutenant's head and fired three rounds rapid. He staggered and dived head-first into a handy shell-hole.

' "Congratulations," said Old Horseflesh, belching brandy in my face. "You can cut another notch in your rifle butt. But what effrontery! Thought himself safe on Christmas Day, I suppose! Ha, ha!" He hadn't brought Captain Pomeroy no gift of whisky or cigars, nor nothing else; stingy bastard, he was. At any rate, the Fritzes caught on, and their machine-guns began traversing tock-tock-tock, about three feet above our trenches. That sent the Brigadier hurrying home in such a hurry that he caught his foot in a loop of telephone wire and went face forward into the mud. It was his first and last visit to the front line.

'Half an hour later we put up an ALL CLEAR board. This time us and the Fritzes became a good deal chummier than before. But Lieutenant Coburg suggests it would be wise to keep quiet about the lark. The General Staff might get wind of it and kick up a row, he says. Captain Pomeroy agrees. Then the Lieutenant warns us that the Prussian Guards are due to relieve his Saxons the day after Boxing Day. "I suggest that we continue the Truce until then, but with no more fraternization," he says. Captain Pomeroy agrees again. He accepts the warm gloves and in return gives the Lieutenant a Shetland wool scarf. Then he asks whether, as a great favour, the Wessex might be permitted to capture the bowl of goldfish, for the Brigadier's sake. Herr Putzi wasn't too pleased, but Captain Pomeroy paid him for it with a gold sovereign and Putzi says: "Please, for Chrissake, don't forget to change their water!"

'God knows what the Intelligence made of them goldfish when they were sent back to Corps H.Q., which was a French luxury *shadow* . . . I expect someone decided the goldfish have some sort of use in trenches, like the canaries we take down the coal pits.

'Then Captain Pomeroy says to the Lieutenant: "From what I can see, Coburg, there'll be a stalemate on this front for a year or more. You can't crack our line, even with massed machine-guns; and we can't crack yours. Mark my words: our Wessex and your West Saxons will still be rotting here next Christmas — what's left of them."

'The Lieutenant didn't agree, but he didn't argue. He answered: "In that case, Pomeroy, I hope we both survive to meet again on that festive occasion; and that our troops show the same gentlemanly spirit as today."

' "I'll be very glad to do so," says the Captain, "if I'm not scuppered meanwhile." They shook hands on that, and the truce continued all Boxing Day. But nobody went out into No-man's land, except at night to strengthen the wire where it had got trampled by the festivities. And of course we couldn't prevent our gunners from shooting; and neither could the Saxons prevent theirs. When the Prussian Guards moved in, the war started again; fifty casualties we had in three days, including young Totty who lost an arm.

'In the meantime a funny thing had happened: the sparrows got wind of the truce and came flying into our trenches for biscuit crumbs. I counted more than fifty in a flock on Boxing Day.

'The only people who objected strongly to the truce, apart from the Brigadier and a few more like him, was the French girls. Wouldn't have nothing more to do with us for a time when we got back to billets. Said we were *no bon* and *boko camarade* with the *Allemans*.'

Stan had been listening to this tale with eyes like stars. 'Exactly,' he said. 'There wasn't any feeling of hate between the individuals composing the opposite armies. The hate was all whipped up by the newspapers. Last year, you remember, I attended the Nürnberg Youth Rally. Two other fellows whose fathers had been killed in the last war, like mine, shared the same tent with four German war-orphans. They weren't at all bad fellows.'

'Well, lad,' I said, taking up the yarn where Dodger left off, 'I didn't see much of that first Christmas Truce owing to a spent bullet what went into my shoulder and lodged under the skin: the Medico cut it out and kept me off duty until the wound healed. I couldn't wear a pack for a month, so, as Dodger told you, I got Light Duty down at Battalion H.Q., and missed the fun. But the second Christmas Truce, now that was another matter. By then I was Platoon Sergeant to about twenty men signed on for the Duration of the War – some of them good, some of 'em His Majesty's bad bargains.

'We'd learned a lot about trench life that year; such as how to drain trenches and build dug-outs. We had barbed wire entanglements in front of us, five yards thick, and periscopes, and listening posts out at sap-heads; also trench-mortars and rifle-grenades, and bombs, and steel-plates with loop-holes for sniping through.

'Now I'll tell you what happened, and Dodger here will tell you the same. Battalion orders went round to company H.Q. every night in trenches, and the C.O. was now Lieut.-Colonel Pomeroy – D.S.O. with bar. He'd won brevet rank for the job he did rallying the battalion when the big German mine blew C-company to bits and the Fritzes followed up with bombs and bayonets. However, when he sent round Orders two days before Christmas 1915, Colonel Pomeroy (accidentally on purpose) didn't tell the Adjutant to include the "Official Warning to All Troops" from General Sir Douglas Haig. Haig was our new Commander-in-Chief. You hear about him on Poppy Day – the poppies he sowed himself, most of 'em! He'd used his influence with King George, to get General French booted out and himself shoved into the job. His "Warning" was to the effect that any man attempting to fraternize with His Majesty's enemies on the poor excuse of Christmas would be court-martialled and shot. But Colonel Pomeroy never broke his word, not even if he swung for it; and here he was alongside the La Bassée Canal, and opposite us were none other than the same West Saxons from Hully!

'The Colonel knew who they were because we'd coshed and caught a prisoner in a patrol scrap two nights before, and after the Medico plastered his head, the bloke was brought to Battalion H.Q. under escort (which was me and another man). The Colonel questioned him through an interpreter about the geography of the German trenches: where they kept that damned minnywerfer, how and when the ration parties came up, and so on. But this Fritz wouldn't give away a thing; said he'd lost his memory when he'd got coshed. So at last the Colonel remarked in English: "Very well, that's all. By the way, is Lieutenant Coburg still alive?"

' "Oh, yeah," says the Fritz, surprised into talking English. "He's back again after a coupla wounds. He's a Major now, commanding our outfit."

'Then a sudden thought struck him. "For Chrissake," he says, "ain't you the Wessex officer who played Santa Claus last year and fixed that truce?"

' "I am," says the Colonel, "and you're Putzi Cohen the Conjurer, from whom I once bought a bowl of goldfish! It's a small war!"

'That's why, you see, the Colonel hadn't issued Haig's warning. About eighty or so of us old hands were still left, mostly snobs, bobbajers, drummers, transport men, or wounded blokes rejoined. The news went the rounds, and they all rushed Putzi and shook his hand and asked couldn't he put on another conjuring gaff for them? He says: "Ask Colonel Santa Claus! He's still feeding my goldfish."

'I was Putzi's escort, before I happened to have coshed him and brought him in; but I never recognized him without his grease paint – not until he started talking his funny Yank English.

'The Colonel sends for Putzi again, and says: "I don't think you're quite well enough to travel. I'm keeping you here as a hospital case until after Christmas."

'Putzi lived like a prize pig the next two days, and put on a show every evening – card tricks mostly, because he hadn't his accessories. Then came Christmas Eve, and a sergeant of the Holy Boys who lay on our right flank again, remarked to me it was a pity that "Stern-Endeavour" Haig had washed out our Christmas fun. "First I've heard about," says I, "and what's more, chum, I don't want to hear about it, see? Not officially, I don't."

'I'd hardly shut my mouth before them Saxons put out Chinese lanterns again and started singing "Stilly Nucked". They hadn't fired a shot, neither, all day.

'Soon word comes down the trench: "Colonel's orders: no firing as from now, without officer's permission."

'After stand-to next morning, soon as it was light, Colonel

Pomeroy he climbed out of the trench with a white hankerchief in his hand, picked his way through our wire entanglements and stopped half-way across No-man's land. "Merry Christmas, Saxons!" he shouted. But Major Coburg had already advanced towards him. They saluted each other and shook hands. The cheers that went up! "Keep in your trenches, Wessex!" the Colonel shouted over his shoulder. And the Major gave the same orders to his lot.

'After jabbering a bit they agreed that any bloke who'd attended the 1914 party would be allowed out of trenches, but not the rest – they could trust only us regular soldiers. Regulars, you see, know the rules of war and don't worry their heads about politics nor propaganda; them Duration blokes sickened us sometimes with their patriotism and their lofty skiting, and their hatred of "the Teuton foe" as one of 'em called the Fritzes.

'Twice more Saxons than Wessex came trooping out. We'd strict orders to discuss no military matters – not that any of our blokes had been studying German since the last party. Football was off, because of the overlapping shell holes and the barbed wire, but we got along again with signs and a bit of café French, and swapped fags and booze and buttons. But the Colonel wouldn't have us give away no badges. Can't say we were so chummy as before. Too many of ours and theirs had gone west that year and, besides, the trenches weren't flooded like the first time.

'We put on three boxing bouts: middle, welter and light; won the welter and light with k.o.s, lost the middle on points. Colonel Pomeroy took Putzi up on parole, and Putzi gave an even prettier show than before, because Major Coburg had sent back for his grease paints and accessories. He used a parrokeet this time instead of goldfish.

'After dinner we found we hadn't much more to tell the Fritzes or swap with them, and the officers decided to pack up before we all got into trouble. The Holy Boys had promised not to shoot, and the left flank was screened by the Canal bank. As them two was busy discussing how long the no-shooting truce should last, all of a sudden the Christmas spirit flared up again. We and the Fritzes found ourselves grabbing hands and forming a ring around the pair of them – Wessex and West Saxons all mixed anyhow and dancing from right to left to the tune of "Here We Go Round the Mulberry Bush", in and out of shell holes. Then our R.S.M. pointed to Major Coburg, and some of our blokes hoisted him on their shoulders and we all sang "For He's a Jolly Good Fellow". And the Fritzes hoisted our Colonel up on their shoulders too, and sang *Hock Solla Leeben*, or something ... Our Provost-sergeant took a photo of that; pity he got his before it was developed.

'Now here's something I heard from Lightning Collins, an old soldier in my platoon. He'd come close enough to overhear the Colonel and the Major's conversation during the middle-weight fight when they thought nobody was listening. The Colonel says: "I prophesied last year, Major, that we'd still be here this Christmas, what was left of us. And now I tell you again that we'll still be here *next* Christmas, *and* the Christmas after. If we're not scuppered; and that's a ten to one chance. What's more, next Christmas there won't be any more fun and games and fraternization. I'm doubtful whether I'll get away with this present act of insubordination; but I'm a man of my word, as you are, and we've both kept our engagement."

' "Oh, yes, Colonel," says the Major. "I too will be lucky if I am not court-martialled. Our orders were as severe as yours." So they laughed like crows together.

'Putzi was the most envied man in France that day: going back under safe escort to a prison camp in Blighty. And the Colonel told the Major: "I congratulate you on that soldier. He wouldn't give away a thing!"

'At four o'clock sharp we broke it off; but the two officers waited a bit longer to see that everyone got back. But no, young Stan, that's not the end of the story! I had a bloke in my platoon called Gipsy Smith, a dark-faced, dirty soldier, and a killer. He'd been watching the fun from the nearest sap-head, and no sooner had the Major turned his back than Gipsy aimed at his head and tumbled him over.

'The first I knew of it was a yell of rage from everyone all round me. I see Colonel Pomeroy run up to the Major, shouting for stretcher-bearers. Them Fritzes must have thought the job was premeditated, because when our stretcher-bearers popped out of the trench, they let 'em have it and hit one bloke in the leg. His pal popped back again.

'That left the Colonel alone in No-man's land. He strolled calmly towards the German trenches, his hands in his pockets — being too proud to raise them over his head. A couple of Fritzes fired at him, but both missed. He stopped at their wire and shouted: "West Saxons, my men had strict orders not to fire. Some coward has disobeyed. Please help me carry the Major's body back to your trenches! Then you can shoot me, if you like; because I pledged my word that there'd be no fighting."

'The Fritzes understood, and sent stretcher-bearers out. They took the Major's body back through a crooked lane in their wire, and Colonel Pomeroy followed them. A German officer bandaged the Colonel's eyes as soon as he got into the trench, and we waited without firing a shot to see what would happen next. That was about four o'clock, and nothing did happen until second watch. Then we see a flashlight signalling, and presently the Colonel comes back, quite his usual self.

'He tells us that, much to his relief, Gipsy's shot hadn't killed the Major but only furrowed his scalp and knocked him senseless. He'd come to after six hours, and when he saw the Colonel waiting there, he'd ordered his immediate release. They'd shaken hands again, and said: "Until after the war!", and the Major gives the Colonel his flashlight.

'Now the yarn's nearly over, Stan, but not quite. News of the truce got round, and General Haig ordered first an Inquiry and then a Court Martial on Colonel Pomeroy. He wasn't shot, of course; but he got a severe reprimand and lost five years' seniority. Not that it mattered, because he got shot between the eyes in the 1916 Delville Wood show where I lost my foot.

'As for Gipsy Smith, he said he'd been obeying Haig's strict orders not to fraternize, and also he'd felt bound to avenge a brother killed at Loos. "Blood for blood," he said, "is our gipsy motto." So we couldn't do nothing but show what we thought by treating him like the dirt he was. And he didn't last long. I sent Gipsy back with the ration party on Boxing Night. We were still keeping up our armed truce with the Saxons, but again their gunners weren't a party to it, and outside the Quarter-master's hut Gipsy got his backside removed by a piece of howitzer shell. Died on the hospital train, he did.

'Oh, I was forgetting to tell you that no sparrows came for biscuit crumbs that Christmas. The birds had all cleared off months before.

'Every year that war got worse and worse. Before it ended, nearly three years later, we'd have ten thousand officers and men pass through that one battalion, which was never at more than the strength of five hundred rifles. I'd had three wounds by 1916; some fellows got up to six before it finished. Only Dodger here came through without a scratch. That's how he got his name, dodging the bullet that had his name and number on it. The Armistice found us at Mons, where we started. There was talk of "Hanging the Kayser"; but they left him to chop wood in Holland instead. The rest of the Fritzes had their noses properly rubbed in the dirt by the Peace Treaty. But we let them rearm in time for a second war, Hitler's war, which is how your Dad got killed. And after Hitler's war there'd have been a third war, just about now, which would have caught you, Stanley my lad, if it weren't for that blessed bomb you're asking me to march against.

'Now, listen, lad: if two real old-fashioned gentlemen like Colonel Pomeroy and Major Coburg – never heard of him again, but I doubt if he survived, having the guts he had – if two real men like them two couldn't hope for a third Christmas Truce in the days when "mankind", as you call 'em, was still a little bit civilized, tell me, what can you hope for now?

'Only fear can keep the peace,' I said. 'The United Nations are a laugh, and you know it. So thank your lucky stars that the Russians have H-bombs and that the Yanks have H-bombs, stacks of 'em, enough to blow your "mankind" up a thousand times over; and that everyone's equally respectful of everyone else, though not on regular visiting terms.'

I stopped, out of breath, and Dodger takes Stan by the hand. 'You know what's right for *you*, lad,' he says. 'So don't listen to your Grand-dad. Don't be talked out of your beliefs! He's one of the Old and Bold, but maybe he's no wiser nor you and I.'

YOU WIN, HOUDINI!

Jenkins, Howell & Edwards,
Solicitors,
3, Victory Chambers,
Pontypool,
S. Wales.

July 24th, 1959

Dear Captain Graves,

You're unlikely to recall my name after so long a lapse, though we coincided at the Royal Welch Depôt a couple of times in 1916; but you can't have forgotten 'Houdini' Cashman. I had a mind to write you about him when I first read your autobiography, and there came across a mention of his abrupt departure from the regiment two or three months after the Armistice. You say:

... next day the senior lieutenant of the company which I was to have taken over went off with the cash-box, and I should have been legally responsible for the loss of £200. Before the war he used to give displays on Blackpool Pier as 'The Handcuff King'. He got away safely to the United States.

The subject nagged at me again when you reissued the book last year and, to cap it all, I had a letter from young Bob Stack – the bigger, taller brother of Dick Stack, who was in the 2nd Battalion with you; I don't think you knew Bob. He was one of the best, and did pretty well for himself when he emigrated to Australia and made a fortune in wool. He now has nine grandchildren, one of whom is named Daniel in my honour. We still write each other every so often and regularly exchange cards at Christmas. Anyhow, he sent me a Melbourne newspaper cutting about the death in prison of one Victor Cashman, formerly a professional conjuror. There can't be more than one Victor Cashman in the conjuring world: besides, the story makes good sense to anyone who knew Houdini. So, before it's too late, I'm going

to get the whole saga off my chest, and apologize in advance
for its inordinate length, hoping that you won't be bored.

I recall Houdini's arrival at the Depôt in June 1917, when the
Military Service Act was flooding the regiment with swarms of
skrim-shankers who had been winkled out of non-essential jobs
– scrapings from the bottom of a pretty foul barrel. Of course,
along with them came some red-hot lads just old enough to
qualify for the sausage-machine. As for the new officers, they
were – you remember – a thoroughly mixed lot, and caused
Colonel Jones-Williams a deal of trouble, what with affiliation
orders, bringing women into the Camp, complaints of dud
cheques from tradesmen, etc.

Houdini came wearing two Boer War ribbons. The Adjutant
didn't question them, but they made some of us very suspicious.
He claimed to have served in South Africa with the City Imperial Volunteers, but when Jock Wilson, who won a D.C.M.
with the same corps in 1900, cross-examined him about the
various engagements in which they'd taken part, and about their
officers, Houdini could remember nothing. He'd been kicked on
the head by a mule, he said, just before the Cease-Fire sounded,
and his war memories had faded completely from his mind. We
began to wonder how the hell Houdini had got a commission,
because he knew no more drill than he could have picked up
in the Boys' Brigade. And with what regiment, if any, had he
served since the war started? He claimed to have been a despatch
rider during the Retreat, and carried his left arm as though he'd
been wounded in the shoulder. I reckon that Houdini Cashman,
with his cissy manner, simpering through his ingrowing moustache, and sitting cross-legged like a Buddha on the floor of his
hut, was the queerest fish in the entire British Army.

Most of us felt some sympathy for true-blue Bible-punching
Conchies, who quoted the Sixth Commandment at the tribunals,
and damn well meant it – what we couldn't stand were dirty
yellow-bellied column-dodgers of the Cashman type, who banked
on being safer *in* the Army than *out*, if they played their cards
properly – and Houdini Cashman had his tunic sleeves stuffed
with aces. Literally, as well as in a manner of speaking, because
a deck of fake cards was his principal stock-in-trade. He'd

nearly dug himself in at the Depôt as Assistant Musketry
Officer, on the strength of his ribbons, having ingratiated himself with old Major Floods by his usual thimble-rigging tricks,
when Jock Wilson called on the Adjutant. 'Willie,' he said, 'that
Cashman fellow's a wrong 'un. You'd be wise to put him on
the next draft before worse befalls us. And in case the stinker
goes sick, as I think he will, be sure to warn the M.O. beforehand.'

So Houdini found himself at Rouen Base Camp soon afterwards, on the same draft as myself – ten officers and two
hundred men. You'll remember Captain Sassoon's lines:

> When I am old and bald and short of breath
> I'll live with scarlet Majors at the Base
> And speed glum heroes up the Line to Death:
> You'll see me with my puffy, petulant face
> Gulping and guzzling at the best hotels . . .

In my opinion, Houdini must have inspired that poem! At
Rouen, he followed much the same procedure as had nearly
proved successful at the Depôt. He gave a conjuring gaff in the
Y.M.C.A. hut – Magic Circle stuff, almost up to Maskelyne's
show at the Egyptian Hall, though he hadn't the requisite
mirrors and gear. Then he sucked up to the Commandant,
Major Charlie Short (Sir Wm Short's brother) by letting him
spot the right card every time where everyone else failed – and
by making a fool of Captain Hotson of the South Wales
Borderers, whom he knew Major Short disliked. In a mind-
reading and fortune-telling turn, Houdini told the audience:
'I've lost a photograph of Gigi, my French fiancée. The cards
inform me that someone present has it in his wallet.' Major
Short smilingly inquired whom the cards suspected. Houdini
tapped the knave of hearts. 'It's that Captain sitting in the
corner,' he said. So the Major asked Hotson if he would produce
his wallet and open it. Hotson said: 'Of course!' and pulled it
out. There he found a postcard of a great buxom French nude
with 'From Gigi to her darling Monsieur Victor!' scrawled
across the back in violet ink. You should have seen Hotson's
face when Houdini displayed the card to the front rows!

Invited to dine that night at H.Q. Mess, Houdini brought the conversation round to a party of deserters, said to be ensconced in a wood near the Camp, and living by armed raids on our transport. Four thousand of our chaps would be beating the wood next day, strung out at a few paces' interval, with Major Short in charge. Houdini remarked: 'I've no doubt that you'll catch those toughs, sir; but be careful with them afterwards. They're all old lags, so they'll probably be able to slide out of a pair of Army handcuffs in just one minute.'

'Nothing wrong with our handcuffs,' barked the Major. '*You* try and get out of a pair, my friend! I'll bet a hundred francs you can't do it in five minutes, let alone one.'

'If they're ordinary Army handcuffs, I'm willing to risk the bet,' says Houdini.

I happened to be invited too that night, having known Major Short, J.P., all my life. As the squire of Llanfihangel, my native village, he recommended me for my commission in September 1914. Let me confess that Houdini was using me as his confederate. One of my tasks had been to hold Hotson in conversation at the shower baths, just before dinner, while Houdini planted the postcard in his wallet. Half Houdini's tricks depended on a confederate, and I was the last person anyone would suspect of associating with such a crummy character. It beats me, in fact, why I ever took on the job!

When the port came round, Major Short sent for the Provost-sergeant, and said: 'A pair of handcuffs, Sergeant! I'm about to put one of the officers here under close arrest.' The Provost-sergeant saluted smartly and marched out again. I was watching whether he would let his eyes stray for a moment in Houdini's direction, but since he didn't, I don't know to this day whether he was in the know: I mean, whether what he brought back — perhaps just a little too promptly — were a pair of trick handcuffs, or the real thing.

Major Short led Houdini into the middle of the mess-room and announced: 'Gentlemen, this officer has cast grave doubts on the efficiency of our handcuffs. We've agreed that if he can't release himself within five minutes from this regulation pair, he'll wear them until reveille tomorrow.'

Houdini answered in his prissiest tones: 'Fair's fair, sir. But if I succeed, everyone here will see how it's done, and the news will soon get around. For the sake of good order and discipline, I suggest you put a screen around me.'

Major Short agreed and sent for the screen. Then he snapped the bracelets on Houdini's wrists from behind. 'Ready, now?'

'Ready, sir!'

I noticed a skylight above the screen, and quietly slipped out of the mess, set a handy fire-ladder against the wall, climbed on the roof and peeped down. Houdini was shaping to wriggle his fat bottom through his arms when he spotted me. 'Stop!' he squealed. 'There's a Peeping Tom up there!' I shinned down the ladder in double-quick time and stowed it back where I'd found it, before returning. 'That makes one minute, Mr Cashman,' said Major Short, as he studied his gold half-hunter, 'but I'll let you have an extra ten seconds because of the interruption.'

'Thank you sir, but I don't need it,' simpered Houdini, as he emerged smiling from behind the screen and presented the handcuffs to the Major.

'A hundred francs, wasn't it?' asked the Major glumly, taking out his wallet. Then his face went purple at finding the same nude lurking among the larger notes.

'No need to settle at once, sir. What about a double or quits? I'll handcuff Captain Hotson, or anyone else you care to name, and if he can slip the bracelets in five minutes no money changes hands.' Houdini didn't refer even obscurely to the postcard; which was tact, and not far short of blackmail.

Hotson declined the honour: 'I never did time in Parkhurst or Princetown, where one learns these things.'

To show he was a good sport, Houdini joined in the laughter against him and – would you believe it? – the next morning he came on parade mounted! The Commandant had made him Assistant Adjutant. And I'm damned if that same evening Houdini didn't read out the roll of officers and men due to entrain for the Line!

You win, Houdini! A very fine performance! No blood sports on Pilckem Ridge for you, no free-for-all tussles with Jerry in salubrious Langemarck, no mudlarking in the airy shell-craters of Passchendaele. Your job from now on is to 'speed glum heroes up the Line to Death'. *'Bonjour et bonne chance, cher Monsieur Victor!'*

When Winnie Churchill lost his job at Whitehall as a result of the Dardanelles mess, he volunteered for the trenches and for a while commanded the 6th Royal Scots Fusiliers. We relieved them once on the Somme. Then his friends at the War House, afraid that he might collect too much glory, broke up the battalion. Winnie reappeared in Parliament, and you may remember that debate on combing out more civilians from jobs which could be held by women and disabled ex-servicemen, because the Army needed cannon-fodder. Winnie made a speech saying that hundreds of thousands of able-bodied men already in the Forces were being kept behind the lines on useless jobs. He turned the Gospel verse 'Physician, heal thyself!' into 'Physician, comb thyself!' This had some effect. A few young, red-tabbed pimps from Army H.Q., for example, were moved up as far as Divisional H.Q.; also A.1 men were taken off road repair and replaced by B.1s; but that was about all. At Rouen, Houdini kept his charger and increased his hold on Major Charlie Short.

I got hit twice more, once at Langemarck in September 1917; and again in February 1918, while marching up the *pavé* towards Messines. Each time, when I rejoined the Battalion by way of Rouen, there was Houdini as large as life and a great deal uglier. He now wore a wound stripe, also three stars, which were more than I ever collected. Though several times in temporary command of a company – and once of the Battalion, when everyone else got knocked out – I was always superseded just before reaching acting rank. A subaltern I would die, that was clear! Nor did I collect any decorations.

Came the summer of 1918. It was 'Backs to the Wall!' Old Ludendorff had driven our gallant allies, the Pork-and-Beans, out of the Neuve-Chapelle sector, bust the line wide open, and forced Butcher Haig to evacuate the whole Ypres salient. Then he pushed the French off the Chemin des Dames, and if the Yanks hadn't come up just in time, and held him at

Château-Thierry, he'd have goose-stepped into Paris, and that would have been that !

At home, they raised the military age, and combed away for dear life. Down by the Somme, we waited at Stand-to every morning for the biggest, bloodiest Boche barrage ever, that would blast Ludendorff's way clear to Amiens. The wind was up, vertically, with a whiff of panic even in the bumph that the brass-hats circulated from their cosy *châteaux*. In fact, things must have looked pretty desperate down at Rouen because, one evening, who should stumble into our Company dug-out at Beaumont-Hamel, but Captain V. Cashman !

Jock Wilson was commanding 'B' Company; he'd lost three lunch-hooks and was full of odd pieces of metal, but still ticking. The dour old bird, by the way, had been engineer at the Blaenau-Ffestiniog slate quarries before the war, and spoke a glorious Merionethshire Welsh, which endeared him to the troops. He picked up the field telephone and at once rang Battalion, insisting that Houdini should take down two of his three stars (acting rank only). The Colonel saw the point. If Jock got scuppered, Houdini would be left in charge of the company, though not having hitherto muddied his boots in shell-hole or sump-pit, and knowing *cooch nay* about trench warfare.

Jock's own military value had sunk by this time. Scots are pretty good drinkers, born with two livers and a spare set of kidneys; but this one had reached the three-bottles-a-day stage. In point of fact, he was almost a passenger, and left the running of the company to me and young Stack. Jock needed a spot of leave to set him up again. He'd been sweating on that for months, but to no avail. His only hope now was another wound, preferably not either in the head or stomach.

A sequence of barrages had played hell with the Beaumont-Hamel trench system. But at least it wasn't yet a row of shell-craters sketchily joined together with a few hurried scrapes of an entrenching tool, as at Passchendaele and elsewhere. We 'B' officers even sat down to dinner that night at a small table, in an at least pip-squeak-proof dug-out, and each had a solid ammunition box under him. Young Stack was on duty, which left Jock, Houdini and me to eat our stew together.

Well, you know how it is with beasts when they're scared: most species have only one way of facing danger. Cats enhance themselves into great spitting furies; rabbits scud off; bulls lower their horns and charge; some insects and reptiles sham dead. Houdini was properly scared, but neither enhanced himself, nor scudded off, nor charged, nor shammed dead. Instead, he started on his usual stunts, in the pathetic hope, I suppose, of softening Jock's heart and wrangling himself a cushy job as Company Entertainments Officer. Psychologically very interesting, I suppose, if I'd happened to be a psychologist, which I wasn't.

He put a fist into his mouth and planked down on the table beside me a complete set of dentures, joined by a spring. As he removed his hand, they sprang open. Jock's face was as red as the side of a Cuinchy brick-stack, and his eyes bloodshot and unwinking. He'd seemed almost unaware of Houdini's presence, except that his jowls hung heavy with dislike; but now they stirred slightly. 'Take that damned animal away!' he growled.

Houdini pushed the set in his pocket, smiling feebly.

'Keep it there!' said Jock. 'And button up the flap!'

Since, a few seconds later, Houdini was munching away at ration-biscuits, I conclude either that the comic dentures had not originally come from his mouth, or that he hadn't really put them back in his pocket. Between mouthfuls, he palmed my knife and fork; produced an egg from my gas-mask case; wrapped a tumbler in a piece of newspaper and smashed it with a blow of his revolver – but the tumbler wasn't inside after all; and kept up the fun for about twenty minutes. Neither Jock nor I made a single comment. Maybe Houdini took this for a respectful hush of awe, but pausing at last and looking expectantly at Jock's face, he found it as impassive as a Jubilee statue of Queen Victoria. No flicker of interest. Suddenly Jock turned to me and said in Welsh: 'Dan bach, take this toad away before he does something clever with his bloody navel!' So I took Houdini along to relieve young Stack, whom we found at Left Post.

Left Post hung in the air; the Borderers had abandoned their suicidal front-line trenches and were holding a position parallel to us, fifty yards back. Young Stack gave Houdini his orders. 'You're to stay here until relieved. Keep the troops on their toes. Take an occasional tour of the company frontage. And don't use the telephone except in an emergency. "Emergency" means when Jerry's barrage drops.'

'You can forget about the telephone,' I interrupted. 'When the barrage drops, there'll be no need to announce the fact – it'll be audible in Calais, Dover and Whitehall. Besides, in two minutes we'll all be wiped out. Dead men don't phone.'

I couldn't see in the darkness how Houdini had reacted to this information. It was a quiet night. 'Suspiciously quiet,' said young Stack, taking his cue from me. 'That's typical of Ludendorff. He doesn't want to give his hand away, so he orders quiet. But these Jerries are too damned thorough. There should at least be normal activity if they want to pretend that this is a normal night, and not *the* night.'

Sergeant Foster, commanding No. 1 platoon, winked at me, and contributed his bit. 'Not a Verey Light for hours, sir. It's coming, for sure!'

Houdini had already squeezed into the Post cubby-hole, but we went on chatting outside.

'Good night, Sergeant,' I said. 'Look after Mr Cashman. He's an old soldier, but he's seen no action since Mafeking, and this isn't the sunny South African veldt.'

'Not "good night," sir! It's "good-bye"!'

On getting back to Company H.Q., I found myself in command. Jock hadn't been killed, wounded or even carried off by an attack of D.Ts. His leave had miraculously come through, and off he'd buzzed, in too much of a hurry even to finish his third bottle of whisky, which he'd just opened when the news arrived.

Twenty-four hours went by before I revisited Left Post. I had to keep close to the phone, and trips to either flank were pretty dangerous by daylight. Also, I'd lost young Stack – lent to 'C' Company, two of whose officers had been killed by the same shell. But he came home to us that night, when someone was sent to relieve him.

Dinner time, and no Houdini. 'I'm disappointed, Dan,' says young Stack. 'My batman tells me you had a buckshee conjuring show last night.'

'We can command a repeat performance,' I suggested.

Still no Houdini. Then a runner arrives with a verbal message from Sergeant Foster. 'Rum shortage: will the Company Commander be good enough to inspect Left Post as soon as convenient?'

I asked Ought-Three Davies, the runner: 'Where's the new officer, my lad?'

'Haven't seen a sign of the gentleman, sir.'

Young Stack took over the phone, while I went up to reconnoitre. 'If the C.O. wants to know where I am, say I'm investigating a report of trouble near Left Post.'

Sergeant Foster wore a grim look as he jerked his head towards the cubby-hole. 'The new officer's been out but once, sir, since you left; and then only for a certain purpose.'

'Right, Sergeant. Let's dislodge him!'

I squeezed in, and shone a pocket torch around. A two-gallon rum jar lay on its side in the middle of the floor. I handed it back to the Sergeant.

'Not a drop left, sir.'

Houdini huddled on some sandbags in the far corner, watching me. How queer he looked! Ingrowing moustache meeting two days of blue stubble, and his eyes like currants in a half-cooked suet pudding.

I could get nothing into Houdini, or out of him. He crouched there, making whining noises, for all the world like a puppy that's been caught misbehaving in the best parlour.

'Goddam that fellow! Turn your back, please, Sergeant, while I give him the pasting of his life. I don't want witnesses.' But when I came closer, Houdini squealed. It was a terrible noise that ran down my spine and churned my bowels.

I came out again, regretting that the rum jar was empty. 'He'll not get away with this lot,' I said. 'I'm going down to Battalion H.Q. Set a sentry on him, Sergeant!'

So I pushed off, stopping only to put young Stack in charge of the telephone. But soon I barged into Barney, our new

Medical Officer, who had graduated from Trinity College, Dublin, two months before, and still found the war a great joke.

'Begob! Ye look as though yer heart's throubled and sore,' he said in the exaggerated stage-Irish he used for our amusement.

I unloaded on him. 'Ah, so 'tis like that, is it?' says Barney. 'Let's be taking a sly peep at the poor divil.'

Back with Barney to Left Post. Barney put his head into the cubby-hole, then slowly shook it in wonder and admiration: 'Holy Mother of God, 'tis powerful drunk he is!'

But when I let myself go on the subject of Houdini in plain English, Welsh, and other languages, Barney got the point. 'Very well, Dan,' he said soberly, 'I'll go down to Battalion myself. Trust me to save awkward questions. It won't do anybody any good if you bring a charge against the bastard.'

Barney was right. The C.O. would appreciate my silence, and keep the case dark. What with young Howland, who had deserted off leave and barely escaped the firing squad, and Lance-corporal Peters, the one who murdered an estaminet-keeper, and the Sergeant Phillips scandal, we'd had more than our plateful of notoriety in recent months.

I let Barney have his way, and that was the last I ever saw of Houdini; for the Adjutant smuggled him down the line in an ambulance, without even informing me that he'd gone.

'You win, Houdini!' But the magnitude of his victory did not appear until Jock returned off leave. Jock had stopped at Rouen to replenish his whisky store, and whom should he meet in the main square but Houdini! Once more a captain, and in the saddle again. Houdini explained that he'd been invalided back as a food-poisoning case, and written to Major Short from No. 2 Red Cross Hospital. The Major, it seems, was delighted, because Houdini had been giving him lessons in trick shuffling and trick dealing — guaranteed to fascinate an indefatigable bridge-player who had once lost a packet to some sharpers on an Atlantic voyage.

Jock didn't know the facts of the story until he got them from Barney and me. And even if he'd known, what could he have done to upset Houdini's apple-cart? Officially, it *was* food-poisoning!

More posh dinners for you, Houdini, at the *Couronne* and the *Fleur de Lys*; but for Jock and young Stack and me the glories of the wading of the Ancre, and the hundred days from Albert to Maubeuge. Ludendorff had shot his bolt, and it was our turn again. Near Maubeuge, Jock succumbed at last to a spent machine-gun bullet that entered his temple – not very deeply, but deep enough – as we bivouacked in a plum orchard. He was asleep, and nobody knew a thing about it until next morning.

In November came the eerie Armistice; then a lot of square-pushing and shining up of brasses, and education courses, and other morale-raising employment.

The day after I got demobbed, I picked up the *Daily Mail*, and read:

OFFICER ABSCONDS WITH COMPANY CASH.
ARRESTED AT LIVERPOOL. AWARDED TWO
YEARS' HARD LABOUR.

But you write that Houdini got clear away to the States. He must have slipped his handcuffs; which makes me think that those he used at Rouen weren't trick ones.

I don't know how or when he went to Australia, or what his activities were in the long gap between 1919 and 1958; but I can tell you how he ended. While serving a ten-year stretch for fraud, he was made a 'trusty', and endeared himself to the Prison Governor 'by his remarkable talents as a conjurer'. The Governor, in fact, managed to get the last four years of his sentence remitted for good conduct. You win again, Houdini!

But this time his victory was short-lived. The day before he should have been freed, they found him in the Prison Library with his throat cut by the jagged edge of a dinner plate. R.I.P.

With good wishes and more apologies
for the length of this screed,
very sincerely yours,
Daniel Edwards
(late R.W.F.)

ROMAN STORIES

EPICS ARE OUT OF FASHION

PETRONIUS did his best. He wasn't a bad fellow at heart, though he had the foulest mind in Rome and drank like a camel. And he was such an expert in the art of modern living that the Emperor never dared buy a vase or a statue, or even sample an unfamiliar vintage, without his advice.

One evening Petronius dropped in to dinner at the Palace and was handed a really repulsive-looking sauce, of which herb-benjamin and garlic seemed to be the chief ingredients. Since the waiter actually expected him to pour it over a beautifully grilled sole, Petronius made Nero blush to the roots of his hair by asking in his silkiest tones: 'My dear Ceasar, can this be *exactly* what you meant?' Nero's eager, anxious glances, you see, made it quite obvious that he had invented the sauce himself; and if Petronius had been weak enough to approve, every noble table in Rome would soon have stunk with the stuff. Our hearts went out to him in gratitude.

My brother-in-law Lucan notoriously lacked Petronius' poise, and yet was far too pleased with himself. I had always regretted my sister's marriage: Lucan, the son of rich Spanish provincials, never ceased to be an outsider, although his uncle Seneca, Nero's tutor, had now risen to the rank of Consul and become the leading writer and dramatist of his day. Seneca doted on young Lucan, an infant prodigy who could talk Greek fluently at the age of four, knew the *Iliad* by heart at eight; and before he turned eleven had written an historical commentary on Xenophon's *Anabasis* and translated Ibycus into Ovidian elegiacs.

He was now twenty-five, two years older than Nero, who had taken him as his literary model. Lucan repaid this kindness with a wonderful speech of flattery at the *Neronia* festival. But when that same night Petronius visited our house – Lucan was staying with us at the time – on the pretext of congratulating him, I guessed that there was something else in the wind. So I dismissed the slaves, and out it came.

'Yes, Lucan, a most polished speech; and I am too discreet to inquire how sincerely you meant it. But ... well ... a rumour is about that you're working on an important historical poem.'

'Correct, friend Petronius,' Lucan answered complacently.

'For the love of Bacchus, you aren't after all writing your *Conquests of Alexander*, are you?'

'No, I scrapped that, except for a few fine passages.'

'Wise man. You might have inspired our Imperial patron to emulate the Macedonian by marching into Parthia. Despite his innate military genius, and so on, and so forth, I cannot be sure that the army would have proved quite equal to the task. Those Parthian archers, you know ...' He let his voice trail off.

'No, since you ask, the subject is the Civil Wars.'

Petronius threw up his hands. 'That's what I heard, and it alarmed me more than I can say, my dear boy! It's a desperately tricky subject, even after a hundred years. At least two-thirds of the surviving aristocratic families fought on the losing side. You may please the Emperor — I repeat *may* and underline it — but you'll be sure to tread on a multitude of corns. How long is the poem?'

'An epic in twelve books. Nine are already written ...'

'An *epic*, my very good sir?'

'An epic.'

'But epics are ridiculously out of fashion!'

'Mine won't be. I make my warriors use modern weapons; I rule out an absurd personal intervention of the gods; and I enliven the narrative with gruesome anecdotes, breath-taking metaphors, and every rhetorical trope in the bag. Like me to read a few lines?'

'If you insist.'

While Lucan is away fetching the scroll, Petronius plucks me by the sleeve. 'Argentarius, you must stop this nonsense somehow — anyhow! The Emperor has just coyly asked me: "What about those *Battle of Actium* verses I showed you the other night? Were you too drunk to take them in?" "No, Caesar," I assured him, "your remarkable hexameters sobered me up in a flash." "So you agree that I'm a better poet than Lucan?" To which I replied: "Heavens above, there's no comparison!" He must have taken this all right, because his next remark was:

"Good, because those lines form part of my great modern epic." '

Re-enter Lucan. Petronius breaks off the sentence dramatically and reaches for the scroll. Lucan watches him read. After an uncomfortable quarter of an hour Petronius lays the scroll down and pronounces: 'This will take a lot of polishing, Lucan. I don't say it's not good, but it must be far, far better before it can go to the copyists. Put it away in a drawer for another few years. In my opinion (which you cannot afford to despise) the modern epic is a form that only retired statesmen or young Emperors should attempt.'

Lucan turns white. 'What do you mean?' he asks.

'I have nothing to add to my statement,' replies Petronius, and waves his hand in farewell. Petronius was so drunk, by the way, that he almost seemed sober.

Lucan tried to cut Petronius in the Sacred Way early next morning; but found himself forcibly steered into the back room of a wine shop. 'Listen, imbecile,' Petronius said, 'nobody denies that you're the greatest poet in the world, *with one exception*; but that exception has got wind of your project, and he'll be very cross indeed if you presume to compete with him. For the love of Vulcan, light the furnace with that damned papyrus! Write a rhymed cookery-book instead – I'll be delighted to help you – or some more of your amatory epigrams about negresses with lascivious limbs and hair like the fleece of Zeus's black Laphystian ram; or what about a Pindaresque eulogy of the Emperor's skill as a charioteer? Anything in the world – but *not* an epic about the Civil Wars!'

'Nobody has a right to curb my Pegasus.'

'Those were Bellerophon's famous last words,' Petronius reminded him. 'The Thunderer then sent a gadfly which stung Pegasus under the tail, and Bellerophon fell a long way, and very hard.'

Lucan flared up. 'Who are you to talk about caution? You satirize Nero as Trimalchio in your satiric novel, don't you? Nobody could mistake the portrait: his flat jokes, his rambling nonsensical talk, his grossly vulgar taste, his heart-breaking self-pity. Oh, that squint-eyed, lecherous, illiterate, muddle-pated, megalomaniac, morbid, top-heavy mountain of flesh!'

Petronius rose. 'Really, Spaniard, I think this must be good-bye! There are certain things that cannot be decently said in *any* company.'

'But which I have nevertheless said, and will say again!'

It proved to be their last meeting. A month later Lucan invited a few friends to a private banquet where, after dessert, he declaimed the first two or three hundred lines of his epic. It started by describing the Civil Wars as the greatest disgrace Rome ever suffered, but none the less amply worth while, since they guaranteed Nero's eventual succession. Then it promised Nero that on his demise he'd go straight up to the stars, like the divine Augustus, and become even more of a god than he already was — with the choice, though, of deciding whether to become Jove and wield the Olympian sceptre, or Apollo and try out the celestial Sun-chariot.

This was all very well so far; but then came the pay-off. You must understand that Petronius had got away with the Trimalchio satire because he was an artist: careful not to pick on any actual blunder or vulgarity of Nero's that had gone the rounds, but burlesquing the sort of behaviour which (under our breaths of course) we called a Neronianism. Nero would never have recognized the *nouveau-riche* Trimalchio as himself; and, obviously, nobody would have dared enlighten him. But Lucan wasn't an artist. He soon let his mock-heroic eulogy degenerate into ham-handed caricature: he begged Nero when deified not to deprive Rome of his full radiance by planting himself in the Arctic regions of Heaven or in the tropical South, whence his fortunate beams would reach us only *squintingly*; and he was, please, not to lean *too heavily* on any particular part of the aether for fear his *divine weight* would tilt the heavenly axis off centre and throw the whole universe out of gear. And the idiot emphasized each point with a ghastly grimace — which caused such general embarrassment that the banquet broke up in confusion.

Nero, as it happened, heard only a vague rumour about the affair, but enough to make him ask Petronius whether Lucan had been warned not to trespass on the Imperial preserve. Petronius answered without hesitation: 'Yes, Ceasar. I explained that it would be ridiculous for him to compete with his master in literature.' So Nero sent a couple of Guards officers to Lucan's house with the curt message: 'You will write no more poetry until further notice!'

The sequel is well known. Lucan persuaded a few other hot-heads to join his plot for assassinating the Emperor in the name of artistic freedom. It miscarried. His friends were arrested; and Lucan had his veins opened by a surgeon in the usual warm bath, where he declaimed a tragic fragment from his *Conquests of Alexander*: about a Macedonian soldier dying for loss of blood.

Lucan's father naturally had to follow his dreary example, and so did old Seneca. (Rather hard on my poor sister, that!) Moreover Lucan had left a rude letter behind for the Emperor, if rude be a strong enough word, incidentally calling Petronius a coward for pulling his punches in the Trimalchio portrait. So Petronius was in for it too!

But I had run straight from the banquet down to Ostia — a good twelve miles — with all the gold I could cram into a satchel, and taken ship to Ephesus; where I dyed my hair, changed my name, and lay low for three or four years until Vespasian had been securely invested with the purple. Thank goodness I was stupid at school, and never felt any literary ambitions whatso-ever! But nobody in Rome could touch me as a long-distance man ...

THE TENEMENT: A VISION OF
IMPERIAL ROME

'GREETINGS, my lord! Red dawn and a clear sky,' says Sophron, as he gently opens the shutters of an unglazed window. I can see climbing plants on my balcony, and the similar balcony of a tenement house opposite. Throwing off blanket and quilt, I look about me at the familiar square room, unfurnished except for my bed, a bedside table, and a wooden chest painted with a spirited scene of cupids mounted on hares and hunting a weasel.

We Romans sleep in loincloth and tunic, so the old Syrian slave merely hands me my shoes and lifts the toga (a huge semi-circle of thick white woollen material) from its peg. He shakes his head sadly at last night's wine stain. 'Arrange the folds carefully, Sophron, and it won't show,' I say.

He drapes one toga-end over my left shoulder, letting it fall to the thigh; next, winds the straight edge round the back of my neck and under the right arm, then grabs the mass of material low down and throws the other toga-end past the first, so that it hangs behind me. Finally, he fixes the 'navel boss' at my mid-riff. That leaves me warmly swathed, except for the right shoulder, and provides a capacious pocket at chest level. Whenever possible, one wears only a tunic, supplemented by a rough, hooded poncho if the weather is bad; because togas are clumsy, burdensome, and difficult to keep clean in this filthy city, though required dress on all formal occasions. Into the pocket go my wax tablets and stilus, my handkerchief, and a small heap of money from the table. The coins are mainly those of the Emperors Augustus, Tiberius and Caligula; but here's the latest issue – a bright bronze piece with Claudius' head on one side, on the other an oak-wreath, commemorating his recent fantastic conquest of Britain.

'Hand me the goblet, Sophron!'

I rinse my mouth with water, spit out into the street, drink the rest. 'Send Alexander for the mule! And, while you are waiting, empty the chamber pot.'

I married three years ago. My maternal uncle arranged the match when he paid my debts. I did not love Arruntia, nor she me, but the creditors were savage as wolves, and her substantial dowry, inherited from a great-aunt, was tempting. Arruntius, my father-in-law, is armourer to the Imperial School of Gladiators on the Via Labicana, which this uncle runs. He lets me live, rent-free, in a first-storey apartment above his armoury, so long as I help him with the business. A terrible man, though! Sentenced to death ten years ago for the brutal murder of Arruntia's mother, pardoned on condition that he became a gladiator – gladiators are public slaves – took up the net-and-trident style of fighting and killed or maimed twenty-five opponents in his first two years. When he had brought the score to fifty, a vociferous Amphitheatre crowd demanded his release, and Caligula sent him the customary wooden foil; but also an insulting message: *'Rude rite donatur ignavus'* – 'The coward is duly granted freedom.' Arruntius angrily snapped the foil in two, and re-engaged. His score had crept up to seventy by the time of Caligula's assassination. When the crowd again demanded his release, Claudius, the new Emperor, sent him another wooden foil with the characteristic message: *'Desine: tridens tibi nimium placet'* – 'Fight no more; you take too much pleasure in your trident!' So he obeyed, was given back his forfeited possessions plus ten years' interest, and bought this six-storey tenement house near the Subura.

At Rome almost everyone lives in tenements like ours; the whole city of a million people can't contain more than a thousand private houses. Apartments are excessively hard to find; besides, Arruntius' ground floor has real running water, piped from a reservoir, which he puts at our disposal – the other tenants depend on the dirty goatskins of thievish water carriers. He also has an oven heated by the forge, and we may use this in the afternoons; otherwise we should have to get our joints and poultry roasted at the baker's two streets off.

Since I collect Arruntius' rents, I know that he makes a profit of over twenty per cent on his investment. The rooms are more and more crowded, the higher one climbs. Fifty-five poor wretches jammed in the attic – Cilicians, Syrians, Moors –

jointly pay almost the same rent as we first-floor tenants. They buy space by the square yard – just enough to put down a mattress and a small cooking-stove – and dispute possession with fleas, bedbugs and mice. Nor do they dare ask Arruntius to mend the hazardous roof.

'Any message for the Lady Arruntia, my lord, if she rises before your return?'

'Say that I'll ride straight home after my duty call.'

Sharp words, a blow and a whimper from next door indicate that the new slave girl is at work on Arruntia's tedious toilet. Arruntia always keeps up with the fashions. She has discarded the simple Republican coiffure (hair parted down the middle and coiled into a bun at the nape) for the latest style which piles her tresses high in curls and braids, supported by a good deal of false hair from the Orient, and held by gold pins and combs until it suggests the wall of a fortress. But first the slave girl slaps lotions and pomades on Arruntia's face and neck; applies chalk and white lead to her arms, eye-black to her eyes, rouges her cheeks with ochre, reddens her lips with wine-lees, dabs behind her ears ... Not being vulgarians, Arruntia and I occupy separate bedrooms, and I am forbidden to see her until she is wearing a load of rings, ear-rings, necklace, brooches, pendants, bangles, bracelets, and that long violet silk tunic, gathered at the waist by an embroidered belt, not to mention the Tyrian shawl.

'Allow me to pass a comb through your lordship's hair,' says Sophron.

Meanwhile Alexander, my younger slave, mutters a surly 'Good day!', unbars the apartment door, and pads out. Soon I follow him down the stairs and step inside the armoury. The master-smith has no time for chat. 'My lord Egnatius, excuse me! We're sadly short-handed since that prize-fool Hylas insulted his master.'

Sophron carries the chamber pot past me to the street corner. Tenement houses have no plumbing at all. Night soil is dumped on a midden at the dead end of the nearest alley. Chamber pots are emptied into a big tank outside the laundry; the laundrymen use its contents to clean woollens, with the help of potash and fuller's earth. They pay a City tax for this privilege.

I cross the street, and glance up. A bulge in the wall of our second storey worries me; so does the wide crack near our front window. It may be my imagination, but both seem more pronounced than in September when I last looked. Most modern houses in Rome are jerry-built, because the building contractor need not submit his plans to a municipal architect, and because only temples are erected for eternity. Still, Arruntius swears that the fabric is sound, and continues to live underneath us.

By now the last straggling cart has left the city. To end traffic jams once and for all, Julius Caesar prohibited all wheeled vehicles – with the exception of ceremonial chariots and wagons engaged in the building trade – from using the streets between sunrise and dusk. As a result, our nightly sleep is forever broken by rumbles, creaks, bumps, shouts and oaths as the carts pass. Rome's streets and alleys, none of them lit or marked with its name, run higgledy-piggledy in every direction. Carters often lose their bearings, and when two lines of traffic meet in an alley, argue half an hour as to which of them must back out again. Carts caught by police patrols after sunrise must stay empty and immobilized for the next twelve hours; so traffic quarrels grow more violent at first cock-crow.

Several stores have opened, and their stock is being piled on either side of the street, leaving only a narrow passage between – and a foul one at that. Near me, under an awning, a boys' school is already at work. No history, geography, literature, religion, or rhetoric taught here! It's reading, writing, arithmetic all the year round, from dawn to noon, without a break; except summer holidays, and one day off in eight. The schoolmaster, a ferocious wretch in a rickety chair, sits waggling his birch rod. Frightened pupils huddle together on benches. He distributes bead-frames among them, one to every group of three and, while I am waiting, sets them a problem. 'Add seventeen, two thousand, and one hundred and fifty-four. Hurry, villains! And no prompting!' Each boy moves beads along the wires for his third-share of the problem, and when everyone has finished, the tyrant checks results. There follow heavy blows of the rod,

dealt out by groups – he never bothers to find out which boy
has miscalculated.

Alexander leads up Bucephalus, harnessed. As I mount him
from a handy barrel, he backs into a pyramid of earthenware
pots. Several break. The shopkeeper explodes with rage, schoolchildren shout and cheer; the master rains blows on them in-
discriminately. 'Two sesterces will cover the damage,' I tell
Alexander, dipping into my pocket for the coins. 'Street vendors
display breakable goods at their own risk.'

My beard is so fair that I can get by with a shave every other
day. Oh, what a bore shaving can be, even though my rank
allows me to jump the queue! Our street barber happens to be
a patient, painless operator, who softens one's whiskers with
warm water, hones his iron razor frequently, and takes at least
half an hour over the job; but I'd rather be bored by his gossip
than trust myself to the assistant – a slap-dash fellow who shaves
four customers to his one, and never apologizes for a gash as he
stanches the blood with spiders' webs and vinegar.

I clatter off to pay my morning duty call on Lucius Vitellius.
Some years ago, I served as commissariat officer in Northern
Italy under his eldest son, recently Consul. Old Vitellius, a close
friend of the Emperor's, is a model patron. When Sophron got
wrongfully arrested this summer, after a brawl in the Fish Market, Vitellius sprung him at once and had the charge with-
drawn. At New Year, he always gives me a handsome present
of table silver, or a toga. Last time it was Bucephalus. I try to be
a model client, and frequently perform delicate missions for
him – sometimes with the help of two ex-gladiators, Arruntius'
cronies.

Having tethered Bucephalus outside Vitellius' mansion on
the Quirinal Hill, I enter the marble-walled lobby. Clients by
the hundred are assembled here, among them a dozen senators.
We are admitted in strict order of precedence to the hall, which
is flanked by ancestral statues. Old Vitellius has a nod or a joke
for each of us. He asks me: 'How's the mule, Spaniard?' 'Magnificently frisky, my lord.' 'Kicked anyone of importance today?' 'No, my lord, we met none of your enemies. He merely
pulverized a display of Sicilian glassware. The merchant is

claiming fifty denarii damages.' 'Then he'll accept twenty? Very well, my lad. Collect them and, in future, give your steed less food and more exercise.'

Noble Bucephalus! He's earned me nineteen denarii. I collect from the steward, who stands behind his master's ivory chair, and will soon be dealing out the daily food allowance – six sesterces per man – to all the poorer clients.

Back again. Since Arruntia is still inaccessible, I remove my toga and set off for the Fish Market with Sophron, who shoulders the baskets. Our women are not trusted to do the shopping; in theory, they sit at home and spin. (Imagine Arruntia handling a spindle!) I try Zeno's stall, and my luck is in: he offers large red mullets at only half a denarius the pound! We shall be six to dinner; no, seven with Arruntius. I buy accordingly. Thence to the poultry and vegetable markets. A sauce for grilled red mullet, Sophron says, demands rue, mint, green coriander, basil, lovage, fennel – all fresh; also Indian pepper, honey, oil and stock, which we have in the larder. Agreed. And after the fish, chicken? I insist on Fronto's recipe: pullets first browned and then braised with stock, oil, dill, leeks, savory and coriander. One each will be enough. I buy seven large pullets at the price of six. The dessert? Let us say pomegranates, quinces stewed in honey, and a couple of melons. At Oppian's fruit and vegetable stall I pick out all I need, bargain loudly for a while, and beat Oppian down to nine sesterces – he has asked twelve. 'Put these in the other basket, away from the fish, Sophron!'

I find Arruntia looking like Messalina, Caesar's naughty wife, or like some ruinously expensive Greek courtesan from Baiae; and tell her my morning's adventures. When she grows restless, wondering whether I have forgotten her birthday, I produce a square silver cosmetic-box engraved with the Judgement of Paris, and underneath: *'Formosissimae adjudicatur'* – 'The verdict goes to the most beautiful.' She kisses me tenderly. The fact is, I can't yet afford to divorce Arruntia, and her latest lover happens to be an aedile – one of the City magistrates responsible, among other things, for prosecuting breaches of the civil decencies, such as flagrant immorality, or betting (except on chariot races), or throwing filth into the street from windows. If I cross her, she may easily get him to frame me.

We breakfast together on bread, cheese and grapes. The bread is a tough, flat, wholemeal cake baked in a mould. We rub garlic on our slices and dip them in oil. Arruntia asks after the investments which I manage for her. 'Remind me about them in a month's time, and I'll have good news,' I smile. She need not know that I bought the silver box with a bribe given me by the owner of a tile factory: not to foreclose on her mortgage, but let him have another month to find the interest.

'What are you doing this morning, my beloved?' 'Oh,' she says, 'I have to attend a coming-of-age ceremony across the Tiber. Later, my friend Pyrrha will be taking me ... I forget the street – somewhere in the same district – at any rate, it's a recital of poems by that boring Marcus What's-his-name....' She invites me to join her there. I excuse myself: Arruntius needs me to examine the shields and weapons for tomorrow's gladiatorial fight, and make sure that they'll pass muster. Owing to the shortage of smiths he's including some second-hand stuff from the provinces.

Arruntia sends her slave girl round the corner to hire a 'senatorial' litter. Evidently she means to create an impression on someone. On whom? That Indian scent she's wearing was not intended merely to please me, and her aedile lover will be busy in Court all morning. Still, what do I care?

After checking the weapons with Arruntius, who is in a jovial temper, I stroll along the Subura towards the Forum; and have reached the Temple of Castor and Pollux when sudden shouts go up. 'Clear the way! Clear the way!' Lictors come swaggering down the street, six abreast, followed by the Imperial sedan and an escort of Praetorian Guards. Old Claudius reclines inside, head jerking, fingers trembling. The crowd cheer, and laugh. A young Gaul tosses Claudius a petition, which hits him in the face. He protests angrily: 'Is this the way to treat a fellow-citizen, my lord? You'll be throwing paving stones next, I shouldn't wonder!' 'Roses, only roses, never paving stones for the Conqueror of Britain!', the embarrassed Gaul cries. Claudius smiles indulgently, unrolls the petition, reads a few lines, and hands it to Secretary of State Pallas, who is riding beside him. 'Petition granted,' Claudius says. 'The man looks honest and can write a good clean Latin.'

I visit Sosius' publishing house, close by in the Forum, at the corner of the Tuscan quarter. The open patio holds some eighty desks, at each of which a scribe sits, bent over a long parchment scroll. A clear-voiced reader delivers the text which these slaves are copying: Claudius' own learned *History of the Etruscans*. He spells it out, letter by letter, warning them beforehand where each line ends; so that all copies will be uniform and mistakes easily checked. The book is to consist of twenty scrolls, at five denarii a scroll.*

At Sosius' I meet the very man I have been looking for: Afer, just up from Herculaneum, near Naples. 'Is it true, Afer, that you have a red-headed British slave named Utherus for sale?' 'Well, maybe ... if the price is right.' 'Then I'll be frank. One Glabrio, who wants to marry my sister, bought another of your Britons recently, but can't get him to work. The fellow spends most of his time weeping, and won't eat; and all because he's been separated from his brother Utherus. Glabrio is my neighbour, and I happen to need a porter. It would be a charity ...'

Afer considers. 'What would you pay?'

'Twelve hundred. The slave's strong and healthy?'

'I'll guarantee that.'

An hour later we settle for fourteen hundred denarii, and strike hands on the bargain before witnesses. Glabrio's slave, let me confess, is not really pining; but has casually told Sophron that Utherus was one of King Caractacus' most experienced swordsmiths, and that if I could find him a job.... I'm pretty sure I can sell Utherus to my father-in-law, and make a couple of thousand on the deal. Or, failing him, then to his rivals in the Via Impudica. This is a lucky day! I shall buy my pretty mistress Clyme a blue silk scarf.

Home to luncheon a little late. Arruntia is even later. Nobody excuses himself for not being on time in Rome, where only millionaires own water-clocks. We guess at the hours from sunrise

* About $30 for 150,000 words.

to noon, and then the official timekeeper at the Law Courts shouts: 'Midday, my lords!', and his cry is joyfully taken up and carried along all the streets and alleys. Tools are downed, shops shut, pleadings end: for no Romans work in the afternoon, apart from tavern keepers, barbers, policemen and public entertainers. And almost every other day, on one excuse or another, is a public holiday.

Questioned about Marcus What's-his-name's recital, Arruntia returns the vaguest possible answers; but I know where she's been, because I sent Alexander to tail her. Not content with the aedile, she's started a serious affair with Ascalus, the famous pantomime actor!

Luncheon consists of cold left-overs from last night: spiced Lucanian sausages and mock-achovy pâté. For want of anchovies, Sophron took fillets of sea-perch, grilled and minced them, simmered them in stock with eggs, added pepper and a little rue, laid a fresh jellyfish on top to cook in the steam. None of us guessed the ingredients.

While Arruntia takes her siesta, I slip out to give Clyme the new silk scarf. How generously she shows her gratitude!

Later in the afternoon I escort Arruntia to the Hot Baths of Agrippa, beyond the Forum; her slave girl carrying the silver cosmetic-box, Alexander carrying my gear in a leather satchel. Mixed bathing is the rule there. Only shy young virgins and sour matrons who have lost their figures attend the private establishments reserved for women. At Agrippa's, neither sex wears a stitch while in the water, but the aediles' police are present in force to discourage loose behaviour. Arruntia undresses in the women's quarters; I in the men's. Then, clad in short tunics, we skip off to the enormous exercise room. Arruntia and two girl cousins play triangle-catch; she has brought three small balls of kidskin stuffed with feathers. The object is not to drop any of them, while gradually increasing the pace. Experts use both hands and six balls instead of three. The most popular sport is bladder-ball: anyone may join in and try to keep the bladder off the floor. Personally, I prefer *harpastum*: you grab the heavy pigskin ball, full of sand, and carry it hither and thither until robbed – dodging, feinting, leaping, handing off. But first you oil yourself all over to get slippery. Tripping and low tackling are against the rules. Today I am in splendid form and twice break through a group of twenty players, running from wall to wall and back again, before someone jumps on my shoulders and down I go. By an extraordinary coincidence, both of Arruntia's lovers have joined the party. I flash Licianus the aedile a pleasant smile, and rob Ascalus of the ball after a long run. Licianus congratulates me on my play; so does Ascalus.

Presently we remove our tunics and go naked into a duck-boarded sweat-bath, which lies above the main furnace. Sweat flows in rivers, and soon we totter to the warm bathroom. There our slaves sponge us with hot water from the central cauldron, scrape us with silver *strigils*, and rub us down with towels. Clean as cupids, and some five pounds lighter, we make for the cool swimming pool, where we frisk about like dolphins.

Arruntia, mother-naked, swims up to the rope which divides the sexes. 'What shall we do?' she wails. 'Neither of my brothers can come to dinner, only my dreadful sisters-in-law!' 'They're not too bad,' I say, 'when on their own.' Then one of the gods – perhaps Vulcan the Cuckold – prompts me to add maliciously: 'I'll persuade two distinguished friends of mine to fill the vacant couches.'

'Do you know my wife Arruntia?' I ask the aedile as he swims by. 'This, my dear, is Licianus the Aedile, who has been playing a tough game of *harpastum* with me. May I invite him to dinner?' Ah, I do it all so innocently; and the aedile accepts so innocently; and Arruntia beams so innocently! To point the joke, my other guest must be Ascalus!

The day approaches its climax. Arruntia hurries away to get her face fixed up again – she has kept the elaborate tresses well out of the water – and then I take her home. She is unusually silent; and I unusually talkative. At nightfall the guests arrive. We recline around our expensive citrus-wood table. The red mullets are beautifully served, and Sophron has excelled himself with the braised pullets.

At first, Licianus and Ascalus address most of their conversation to the sisters-in-law or Arruntius, afraid of treating Arruntia too familiarly by mistake. And Arruntia is at pains to flatter me. Soon I produce a jar of the best Falernian. Licianus, our Master of Ceremonies, wearing his purple-bordered toga, insists on mixing it with as little water as is decently allowed – none but thieves and gladiators drink neat wine – and when the usual toping match begins, at dessert, shows his hand more boldly. He proposes toast after toast, always increasing the number of cups that must be downed for each: hoping, I suspect, to make us all dead drunk, keep a clear head himself, and end up in Arruntia's arms.

But the old Falernian is mischievous. I heave myself up from the couch and call for silence. 'Arruntia, dearest wife, listen to me! On my birthday gift which you admire so much, is engraved a Judgement of Paris. Prince Paris, Homer says, was ordered to present the loveliest of three goddesses with an apple – a choice that needed remarkable tact. Paris chose the Goddess of Love, and thereby won the favours of Helen. Now, here's a "Judgement of Helen" for you! Give this pomegranate to the handsomest of us three young men.... Pray, my dear, do not yield to self-interest as Paris did, but make an honest judgement. Consider neither the rank and eminence of Licianus, nor the fame of Ascalus, nor the wifely duty you owe Egnatius, your humble husband. Speak straight from the bottom of your truthful breast! I can count upon my equitable father-in-law to see fair play.'

Through her chalk and rouge Arruntia blushes a deep red. Licianus hides her aquiline nose in an agate wine-cup. Ascalus assumes a theatrical posture, like Ajax defying the lightning. But Arruntius bursts into a roar of drunken laughter and thumps me on the back. 'Egnatius,' he yells, 'you're a man after my own heart! Go on! Roast that she-ass for us on the public spit!' Both sisters-in-law giggle nervously. They hate Arruntia, but are scared of scenes, especially when Arruntius has been drinking. He never knows his own strength; and this, indeed, was his plea long ago when, suspecting Arruntia's mother of infidelity ...

'Choose, then, most beautiful of women, Rome's own Helen!' I insist, perfectly master of the situation. 'Choose!'

Arruntia cups her chin in deep thought. Will she? Won't she?

The dramatic hush is broken by a loud crash and horrified shrieks from somewhere high above us, followed almost immediately by an echoing boom and a still louder shriek. Fascinated, I watch the street wall slowly buckle and give. ... Then everything falls at once!

Did any of us survive? I doubt it. My next distinct memory is of being a child once more. Martial music sounds. Mother lifts me up to watch, through a well-glazed English nursery window, the decorated carriages and red-coated soldiers of Queen Victoria's Diamond Jubilee procession.

THE MYCONIAN

I

OUTSIDE the wineshop everyone was teasing the mild-mannered stranger who wore the grey cloak of a Greek philosopher. The usual run of philosophers are much-travelled, sharp as needles, knowing as vultures; but this one seemed ignorant and artless, a regular hick.

'In Hell's name, where do you spring from?' Scorpus asked. 'Anyone would think you'd been asleep a thousand years and just woken up!'

'From Myconos, the Aegean island. It's not very big, but quite famous. Why, the Giants who attacked Heaven are buried beneath our granite rocks, which the God Hercules threw at them. And we show the Tomb of Ajax, too – a Trojan War hero.'

The philosopher then began to quote Homer, but Scorpus cut him short. 'You're not a real Myconian,' he teased.

The philosopher blushed. 'How did you guess?'

'Look at your thatch! *"Myconi calva omnis juventas!"* – All Myconians are bald as pumpkins, even boys.'

'Yes,' he mumbled. 'My family, I confess, originated in Athens. Political refugees. This thick hair does make me somewhat conspicuous at home. But I have the most beautifully bald wife and children.'

He spoke in such earnest tones that we took to him in a big way. 'Ever travelled before?' I asked, when the laughter had subsided.

'Some years ago I attended a course in philosophy at Athens. From there I went to the Olympic Games: an unforgettable experience! As Homer says ...'

'Forget Homer! We're not buying Homer. Did you see good sport at Olympia?'

'Sir, it was fabulous! A score of events crammed into five days! First, the sacrifices and the classification of athletes; then a contest between trumpeters. Great Heavens, you should have

watched them puff out their cheeks until they looked like pigs'
bladders – veins swelling on foreheads, eyes bulging. A little
fellow from Sicily ought to have won, but the judges disquali-
fied him after an objection; it seems he had once served a prison
term at Syracuse for striking a priest. Only freeborn Greeks of
good character may compete at Olympia. But, by Jove, how he
blew – what sweet thunder! Next, to whet our appetite, the
boys' races! So two days glided by in the horseshoe Stadium.
No less than forty thousand visitors must have gathered there
from all over the Greek world! We put up tents and picnicked
beside the river. The third day, the day of champions. ... Two-
hundred-yard sprint, quarter-mile and two-mile footraces. Classical wrestling. A race between armed soldiers carrying shields
and spears; our Myconian champion came in third. Hard-
glove boxing. Free-style wrestling. Magnificent! The competi-
tors had trained for years.'

'*Footraces!*' scoffed Bufotilla, Scorpus' green-eyed girl friend,
blowing her nose daintily with thumb and fore-finger, and
wiping them on my cloak. 'Left, right; left, right; left, right –
elbows jogging, lungs whistling, eyes glazed – round and round
and round ... I can't imagine a drearier spectacle.'

'Ah, dear women!' sighed the philosopher, 'you're all alike –
pretending to despise the Games which you are forbidden, on
pain of death, to witness!'

Bufotilla stared at him. 'Forbidden – on pain of death? And
why, pray?'

'Because Olympic athletes wear no clothes, young lady,' replied the philosopher.

'By the Girdle of Venus, what's wrong with that? Don't you
have nude mixed bathing at public baths in Greece?'

This time it was the philosopher who stared at Bufotilla.

'Well, don't you?' she insisted, sharply.

Scorpus had heard vague talk, some place or other, about the
Olympic Games, and broke in: 'Big prizes, eh? Heavy
bonuses?'

'No, Sir. The same award serves all events: an olive-wreath,
cut with a golden sickle from the sacred tree.'

'Yes, yes, that's the token award, I don't doubt. But how

much cash does it mean? You can't tell me that these fellows train for years, then flock to Olympia from all over the Greek world, in the hope of winning only a wretched wreath, such as they could cut anywhere themselves?'

The philosopher smiled reprovingly. 'We are Greeks, not barbarians,' he said.

'So what? Doesn't anyone ever sell a race or match at Olympia?'

'They swear a solemn oath beforehand that they won't. At the altar of Olympian Zeus, in front of all the judges.'

'And if an athlete breaks his oath?'

'The judges fine him severely, and the city he represents is shamed. At Olympia, you can see rows of bronze images flanking the Temple steps. They were paid for with fines imposed on men who bribed their opponents to lose: long rows of images, worth I don't know how much.'

'Thanks, I knew that money came into it somehow,' said Scorpus. 'It always does.'

We burst out laughing, but the philosopher saw no joke. 'It's true,' he said, 'and on each image is engraved a warning that the Olympic Games were founded by Hercules as a contest in manliness, not in money; and that the Gods always discover cheats.'

'Oh, get on with your tale! Bufotilla's growing nervous; aren't you, my honey? We want to hear about the chariot race. That's the main draw at any Games.'

'Not at Olympia. When we talk of bygone Olympics, we always identify them by the name of whichever athlete won the sprint – our earliest and most important athletic event. The chariot-race winner may be a moribund old prince from Cadiz, or the Black Sea provinces, who never saw Greece before but happens to own a good stable. In the sprint, it is the *man* who wins, the *man* whom poets celebrate – not a team of dumb horses. Therefore we philosophers despise the chariot race: it infringes the Olympic rule that money is no substitute for manliness.'

'Haven't you forgotten the charioteer?' asked Scorpus gently, stroking his large nose. Any other member of Scorpus' profession would have knocked the philosopher down, instead, and jumped on him. But Scorpus could afford to be forbearing.

'Oh, yes,' the philosopher answered. 'Charioteers get the best out of their teams, I suppose; but at Olympia nobody pays them much attention. It is not a dangerous race: a driver who deliberately fouled an opponent's chariot, why, he would be disgraced for life!'

This drew fresh guffaws from our party, and Bufotilla cried: 'By all the Gods in Heaven and Hell, what a nation of sissies! No wonder our Roman legions went through you like string through cheese!'

Scorpus, controlling his mirth with a great effort, said: 'Go on about this most ethical chariot race. How many laps are run?'

'Laps? Just one – as in Homer's day.'

'Mention Homer again, and I'll *scream*!' screamed Bufotilla.

'And the length of the run?' Scorpus asked.

'Five hundred yards.'

'You call that *sport*?'

'Certainly!'

'Then you'd better watch a Roman race this afternoon, and improve your education. Take charge of him, Glabrio, will you? See he gets a seat with the Family.'

I said I would. Then along came a crowd of young noblemen, all wearing blue favours, caught sight of Scorpus, lifted him on their shoulders, cheering madly, and bore him off.

'With what paragon of men have I had the honour to converse?' exclaimed the philosopher.

'With Scorpus: our greatest charioteer for generations. He's turned the tide of fortune from the Green faction to the Blue – won us over eleven hundred victories since the Emperor's accession. Worth nearly two million in gold! If he'd slit your throat just now, when you talked of charioteers as though they were country carters, would any Roman have dared inform against him? Not one! So far as he's concerned, police and magistrates can go to Hell. He hobnobs with the Emperor Domitian himself. Senators' wives and daughters pant for him, but he brushes them off like flies.'

'This Scorpus comes of noble stock?'

'Noble? His father was a slave from York, employed in the Imperial stables. And if you want to know why he despises the Olympic chariot race no less than you philosophers do, it's because *his* course is seven times round the Great Circus, with bloody murder lurking at each post. Few charioteers escape a broken leg or arm for long. Ten races; twenty perhaps, if they're lucky: then, crash! ... Scorpus' luck has been phenomenal; only three serious accidents in five years. Everyone wonders why he doesn't retire on the winnings.'

'Why doesn't he?'

'Says he mustn't fail his public. But I don't think it's quite that. In his heart he despises the public; all experienced charioteers do. I guess he just gets a kick out of playing with death. Besides, if he retired, tell me some other job he could take and still feel a man – short of turning gladiator?'

A poster on the wineshop wall announced that one of Menander's comedies would be playing that afternoon in Pompey's Theatre. The philosopher wanted to see it. 'No,' I said, 'you're not going!'

'Why not?' he asked, rebelliously.

'For three good reasons. First, because it's in Latin translation; and you're short on Latin.'

'I'll risk that.'

'Second, because you'll find the Theatre's altogether too big. I've been around in Greece; I've seen plays acted there ... Audiences of two thousand at the most. Here, they're nearer sixty thousand! Against all that talking and coughing and shuffling, how can dialogue be followed, even with a wind blowing from the right quarter? And the back rows can't easily distinguish between the players. So prostitutes always wear yellow; old men wear white; the hero wears mixed colours; merchants, purple; beggars, red; etcetera ... And all you get of the comedy, besides madly expensive sets, are fragments of shouted dialogue, and theme songs. Theme songs played by the orchestra, sung by the choir, and danced by Paris.'

'Who may Paris be?'

'The leading man, whom our women dote on. As he cavorts across the stage he registers terror, anguish, obscene passion,

filial tenderness, corny humour, bestial cunning – the whole
works! Does it all with gestures. Menander would turn in his
grave to see what's happened to his lines; and I gather you respect Menander? Our actresses strip to the buff in aid of greater
realism. And no holds barred. It's a liberal education, sometimes
... Why, recently the Emperor let a convict be substituted for
the brigand chief in the last act of *Laureolus*, and actually be
crucified on-stage!'

'What is your third reason?'

'The most important one! It's that Scorpus expects you to
watch the chariot-racing in the Great Circus. See?'

We ate lunch – bread and black puddings – at another wineshop, near the Citadel. The big race wouldn't be run for another two hours; which left us plenty of time to visit the late
Emperor Titus' Amphitheatre, commonly called The Colosseum. I own a couple of good seats there, on the shady side; and
even if I forget my tickets, I can always get in as a member of
Scorpus' 'family'. I'm his saddle-master: the man solely responsible for his reins, traces and harness ...

We strolled past the Forum. A pretty girl in a violet silk
gown, wearing half a pound of bangles and necklaces, linked
the philosopher's arm endearingly in hers. 'Coming for a
walk, Socrates?' she inquired. 'I could ask you some tough
questions.'

I firmly unhooked them, and shooed her away.

'Why did you do that?' he bleated.

'I'd hate my friends to find me arm in arm with a philosopher *and* a prostitute ...'

'But I thought prostitutes always wore yellow?' he sighed.
What superb innocence! I must remember to tell Scorpus!

This being the noon interval, we found the Colosseum less
than half-full: a mere thirty thousand spectators. During the
interval, second-class entertainment is the rule – animal turns
or acrobatics; but I'm glad we went, because a 'No-reprieve'
show was put on. 'No-reprieve' is an amusing alternative to
crucifixion – and the criminals appreciate it: death comes quick,
and most of them get the pleasure of killing as well as the mis-
fortune of getting killed. Ten criminals were announced that

day: among them bandits, men convicted of incest or arson, and parricides. A villainous lot, except for one fine-looking Sicilian bandit, by name Julius Ferox. Every woman in the audience waved her scarf at him on hearing that, before his capture, he'd flattened three soldiers and their sergeant. Julius would appear third.

A roll of kettle-drums, and the parricide was led in, naked. He glanced wildly about: gates shut and barriers too high to scramble over. Then in strutted another criminal in full armour, with shield and sword – a mad Moor from Tangiers, who had burned down an apartment house, causing considerable loss of life. He caught his man after a long chase which ended rather tamely, because the desperate parricide took a leap at the barrier and knocked himself out. Then the Moor was himself disarmed by two guards, who gave his gear to Julius Ferox. The Moor had not run three paces before Julius thrust him through the lungs.

Poor sport; but now came Julius' turn to be disarmed, and a ruffian from the Sabine Hills had the chance to murder him. Julius showed no dismay. Though mother-naked, he met the rush, flung back his head and dealt a violent kick at the Sabine's wrist. Away flew the sword; Julius tackled low, got hold of the shield, and drove its sharp boss through his enemy's temple. He rose, walked up to the guards, and remarking carelessly: 'I'll fight without these,' handed over the arms. 'Next customer!'

The crowd cheered his bravado. He now confronted a tough cut-throat from Naples, cleverly working him round to face the midday sun; then, stooping, he threw a handful of sand in his eyes and took a running kick at his genitals. In no time at all he'd won a third victory.

'Next customer!'

Terrific applause; and the lady below me screamed at her husband: 'Oh, Tullius, if only you had that bandit's physique, what a happy woman I should be!'

'And if only I had his kick,' growled Tullius, 'I'd soon cure your itch!'

Julius had little trouble with the miserable Tuscan dandy,

convicted of raping his niece. No gladiator, this one! Julius went up, saying: 'Your sword, lad!', calmly borrowed it and cut off his head at a stroke.

'Next customer!'

His new opponent was a fellow-bandit, formerly his lieutenant, who'd betrayed him to the authorities in the vain hope of winning a pardon. While tussling for the sword, Julius was gashed and stabbed in three places; but then used it mercilessly, lopping off the traitor's ears, nose and hands before dispatching him. The crowd stood up, roaring delightedly, and appealed for pardon; but this was a 'No-reprieve' show. So Julius committed suicide. He didn't seem to mind, now that suitable vengeance had been taken.

'Congratulations!' I said to the philosopher. 'Beginner's luck. Best show this year; and in the Interval, too! The regular fights will seem flat after this ... Of course, if Hermes were on, that would be another kettle of fish! A wonderful gladiator; but he's in hospital just now – jabbed in the thigh by a net-and-trident expert. An all-round man is Hermes: trident, spear, sword, on horseback, or on foot. Fills all the tiers. Well, what about getting along? The next numbers will only be a negro tight-rope walker, a dwarf riding a goat over a row of obstacles, and a duel between two delinquent housewives armed with cleavers.'

The philosopher's face had turned green, and he'd shut his eyes tight so as not to see the remaining criminals done in.

I nudged him again: 'Coming?'

'Where can I vomit?' he gasped.

'You talk of manliness,' I said, leading him out, 'and yet you want to vomit! How was that for a display of manliness? If a bandit can prove himself a hero, what do you think the rest of us are like?'

He kept silent until we'd left the Colosseum and his nausea had passed. Then he answered: 'The heroism of a Sicilian bandit gives me no clue to the spirit of ordinary Roman citizens – wine-sellers, actors, or saddle-masters. Have you yourself taken part in a war? No? Or faced a storm at sea? No? Do you box, even with soft gloves?'

I shook my head.

'What are your sports?'

'None, now. At the Baths, I sometimes raise a sweat by joining in an aimless medicine-ball scrimmage. I used to wrestle, but not after I put my thumb out. And no self-respecting Roman boxes; we leave that to gladiators – cauliflower ears and broken noses have no attraction for pretty ladies. Gladiators don't care; they cheerfully used spiked knuckledusters. The other day I saw Hermes taking on an enormous black bear – killed it, too, with a left to the muzzle and a right to the jaw.'

'Then you expect slaves, criminals, and the desperately poor to display courage on your behalf?'

'Put it that way, if you like. I won't argue against a philosopher.'

'Is it true,' he asked, 'that at the Colosseum batches of Jewish mystics are daily thrown to hungry lions?'

'Yes, I believe so: in the early morning when the gates first open. They're let down in cages, by a crane. Few people attend, because there's nothing to bet on. And it's a pretty tame spectacle. These Christians, as they're called, show no fight when released from the cage; just kneel down, pray and sing. Curious, isn't it? But they can't be altogether Jewish: I hear they eat pork freely.'

As we mixed with the crowd streaming towards the Great Circus, a couple of policemen frog-marched a bedraggled fellow to the lock-up.

'Betting?' I asked.

They nodded and went on.

The philosopher exclaimed: 'Yet at the wineshop I heard one of those young noblemen openly backing Scorpus for ten thousand gold pieces to six! Is there one law for the poor, and another for the rich?'

'You've missed the point. The law forbids casual betting. If caught, you're fined four times the value of your stake, or else go to gaol. But everyone's encouraged to bet on the chariots and the gladiators. I'm sorry now that you missed seeing a Colosseum fight. We should have stayed. It can be great fun – if it's not rigged ... Say you bet on a targeteer who's meeting a gladiator with a large shield. Say you stake a month's wages; say they fight good and hard – without any need for the whipper to warm them up by lashing their legs. The crowd yells: "At him, the Blue!", "Murder him, the Green!" (We have Blue and Green factions here, too.) Soon it's: "Burn him, roast him, flay him, gut him, pickle him!" Or: "Hey, mind out, Green!" Then at last: "Good lad, that got him!" – and you watch the targeteer's sword sink up to the hilt in Green's belly ... You feel fine, see? It's as though you'd killed him yourself. The Blue targeteer's brought home your bacon. A grand instance of Roman sport – manliness and money, hand in hand.'

'Well,' said the philosopher, irritably twitching his grey cloak, 'you Romans have indeed mastered the art of making poor wretches commit mutual murder for your sakes! And do you have even one native Roman out of every ten soldiers enrolled in your legions – apart from senior officers?'

'I doubt it. That's what the poet Virgil, or maybe it was Cicero, calls being a master race,' I answered cheerfully.

2

As we walked towards the Great Circus, I pointed up at a gilt statuary group on a massive marble pedestal.

'The Sun-god?' The philosopher asked.

I grinned. 'Don't his nose and chin remind you of someone?'

'Yes, indeed! What a strange resemblance to your friend Scorpus!'

'It *is* Scorpus!'

The philosopher stopped dead. 'Once,' he said severely, 'it was considered a sin to honour even kings with statues. Yet to-day one may mistake the gilded statue of an ex-slave for a divine image!'

'Why not? The Blue faction set up that group to celebrate Scorpus' thousandth victory. If every god treated his worshippers as generously as Scorpus has treated the Blues, religion wouldn't be in such a poor way.'

He asked me to explain the factions in easy language. A difficult task for a professional like me ...

'Well,' I said, 'each faction is known by a colour, one of those that everyone's wearing – Green, Blue, White and Red. The four racing stables are managed by millionaire syndicates. Green has White as its partner; Blue has Red. You'll have noticed that Green and Blue favours predominate. But don't despise the minor colours: White and Red charioteers come in handy by opening up for their partners, or baulking the enemy.'

'Do these colours mean anything in particular?'

'Not that I've ever heard.'

'Yet I seem to be the only person here not wearing a favour!'

'It's quite a story,' I told him. 'A few generations back, we Romans fought one Civil War after another: all for political reasons. They lasted till the Republic broke down and Augustus made himself Emperor. Since then, discounting a spot of trouble at Nero's death, we've had continuous peace – and no politics! So Rome's grown incredibly rich. Rich in slaves, rich in trade. This is the "Good Life" of our ancestors' dreams. Free citizens need to work only till noon. What's more, they can take every other day off, buy all they need, and still have money to jingle. .... Here's a novel problem: How to spend their leisure time? Every blessed afternoon, every other morning as well! I'm fortunate to be in show business; keeps me occupied.'

'*I* should buy books,' said the philosopher eagerly.

'Books? But then you're Greek. We Romans don't read unless we're sick. Elsewhere, idle men finding themselves without jobs or money nurse political grievances; here they're denied even that comfort. And the Emperor can't set them all to work raising colossal pyramids – which, for all I know, may have been how the Pharaohs solved Egypt's leisure problem. He'd run a risk of assassination. Instead, he subsidizes free gladiator shows and chariot races, and lets faction politics replace party politics. Only a fool would want a change in government when the factions supply a simple means of turning his spare cash into a fortune.'

'How so?'

'By betting, of course! Anyone can join either the Blues or the Greens; and though both factions are equally crooked, the betting works well enough.'

'I should find it demoralizing to be a perpetual spectator !'

'There the Emperor agrees with you. He's just proclaimed a four-yearly "Roman Games" on the Olympic model; doubtless hoping that we'll all turn enthusiastic athletes. But even if the factions take over, which seems improbable, I can't see a future in athletics. Apart from popular music and dancing at the Theatre, Rome cares for little except sex, gladiators, racing and betting: we don't pretend to be Greek idealists.'

A cockfight announcement, posted on a building, caught the philosopher's eye – one of the entries was a Myconian bird. He insisted on going inside. Look-outs stood by the door of this miniature Colosseum, where one may bet only in hazel-nuts. The audience wore patched and dirty cloaks; yet the stakes were heavy. Neither the stink and vermin of the cockpit, nor its obscene wall-paintings troubled the philosopher. He forced me to sit through three fights until the Myconian cock was put in, for the main, by a bald compatriot of his.

Though a small bird, ye Gods !, what a game one ... The tall Tanagran, matched against him, mauled his head to a gory mess; but he kept his stubby crest erect and fought like Jove's eagle. Pretty soon he had the Tanagran guessing, and took his revenge. Up in the air he flew and, with a single backward thrust, too quick to follow, drove a sharp spur clean through his opponent's skull. 'Great Heavens, what timing !' exulted the philosopher. He made as much fuss of that cock as if it had saved all Greece from disaster !

I teased him: 'So you're a convert to the Roman view of sport? Just now you griped because we like watching gladiators commit mutual murder for our amusement.'

He had his answer ready: 'Who needs to train cocks at a gladiatorial school? Who forces them to fight desperately, like your doomed ruffians, by way of avoiding gaol or the galleys? Who stands behind them with a whip? Cocks battle to the death of their own free will, because such is their nature – and in the barnyard as readily as in the pit.'

'Don't under-estimate our gladiators,' said I. 'Hermes, for instance, leader of the Blue troop at the Colosseum: he's a born killer. Enjoys every minute of life, except when he's in hospital.'

We pushed our way into the Great Circus through Titus'
Arch, and found Opimus, the stout Blue faction-chief, fuming
outside his office. 'You're late, Glabrio!' he bellowed. 'Hurry off
and check the harness. Hurry! There's only a quarter of an
hour left.'

'Checked it before lunch, Sir. Scorpus was with me. Ask him!
Zeno's been keeping an eye on it meanwhile.'

'Zeno! What do I care about *him*?' Opimus stormed. 'How
can I tell he's not been got at? Zeno's a Red, and no employee
of mine. Don't you know that a million in gold hangs on this
race? Check everything again! And hurry, I say!'

I went to the Harness Room, a stable-guard at my side, un-
locked the door, and checked again. The gold-plated chariot, inlaid with lapis lazuli and turquoise, was not my concern – not
even the harness rings. But the traces, yes! I paid them out
slowly – thirty flawless yards of new bull's hide, tough and
supple, every inch of it; the splices sewn and oversewn with fox-
gut! Then the reins: also brand new. Harness: sound, though
too lavishly decorated. I hate seeing good leather spoiled by
plaques and jewels and amulets; however, if the crowd admires
that sort of nonsense. . . . Finally, the bronze bits. I'm expected to
wash these before each race, for fear someone may have doped
them, and to use water from a sealed jar. The stable-guard keeps
a beady eye on me.

'All correct, Sir!' I told Opimus.

The grooms wheeled out Scorpus' chariot, fastened the yoke,
and threw the harness over the waiting stallions. First the team,
a matched pair of Thessalian duns, on either side of the shaft.
Then the two bay tracers: this course is always taken counter-
sunwise, so the tracers are made fast to rail-rings on the off-side.
A posse of stable-guards watched sullenly. No one in the Circus
trusts anyone.

Now cock your ear for a stable secret! We Blues pamper our
stallions on barley mash doctored with raw, chopped horseflesh – which makes cannibals of them! Remember how King
Diomedes, whom Hercules slew, fed his mares on human flesh?

I once laughed at that as a poetic fable; now I know that horses are gluttons for meat. The Greens haven't yet discovered why Scorpus, apart from his wonderful driving, gets an extra half-length out of his team in every lap. They've tried most known stimulants on their beasts, even peppered oysters! But raw meat's the answer, either beef or horseflesh.

Scorpus emerges from his dressing-room – in a sky-blue silk tunic, with long strips of buckskin swathed around his legs, crash-helmet, dagger and whip. His nose and chin jut magisterially. 'All set?' he asks Opimus.

'All set, champion. How do you feel?'

'As I look.'

I prod the philosopher out of his dreams. 'Aren't you betting?'

'I never laid a bet in my life – not even on the cocks.'

'What? You're still a virgin? Lend me your luck, in Heaven's name: lay a maiden bet for me! I'll give you half the winnings, I swear.'

'It goes against my principles.'

'To the crows with your principles! Take this purse: there should be ninety-six gold pieces in it. Run across to the Greens at once, and put the lot on Scorpus! Lodge your bet at the corner bookmaker's. The Greens somehow fancy Thallus to win; so don't accept less than evens! A maiden bet, ye Gods! I've never once known a maiden bet go astray. If you won't help me, Myconian, I'll beat you till you sneeze!'

Most reluctantly, he took the purse and placed the bet, getting evens all right. I could have done better, probably, because Thallus and Scorpus were almost equally fancied, and five to one was being quoted against the field. Five to one may seem short odds, but think how many eager punters back the field!

There we sat, in marble seats, up front, beside the rest of Scorpus' 'family' – his trainer, chariot-master, head stable-lad, veterinary, and his green-eyed girl friend Bufotilla. It's 'First come, first get' here with all seats except the Imperial Enclosure and the rows reserved for Senators, Knights, and faction officials like ourselves. That's why thousands of sportsmen queue up, the evening before, to grab good seats when the gates open at daybreak. An hour later they'd find standing-room only. You never know whom you'll be next to; I first met my Syrian wife in a Circus queue . . .

Thallus' 'family' sat near us, across a gangway. The philosopher's grey cloak puzzled them. 'What business has Scorpus with philosophy?' they wondered. 'Philosophy's something that generals and statesmen take up in retirement. Can Scorpus be retiring?'

We let them wonder. Jokes and insults flew between the rival families.

The philosopher had been enormously impressed by the Colosseum audience; but at the Great Circus he doubted his eyes. 'How many! How many!' he groaned, gazing around him.

'Almost a full house,' I said. 'Above a quarter of a million people. Including the Emperor Domitian himself – over there in scarlet! With the purple cloak, the golden wreath, and his favourite dwarf.'

I remember the veterinary saying he felt worried. Something he'd heard in the crowd suggested that Blue had been got at.

We took him up on this at once. 'What do you mean "got at"? By whom? Let's have it! Together, we five are responsible for the whole turn-out – except for Scorpus. And that's Bufotilla's job. Got anything against Bufotilla?'

'He better hadn't!' said Bufotilla fiercely.

'No, no, don't talk that way,' protested the veterinary. 'It's just something in the air. Those Greens look so damnably cocksure.'

Trumpets blew and, amid tempestuous cheers, the four teams entered at a trot and lined up behind the starting-rope. The draw for places had been unfortunate. Scorpus got the outer berth; his Red partner got the inner; and between them Green and White – so that from inside to outside the colours ran Red, White, Green, Blue.

A beautiful, warm, windless day; the vast, tight-packed Circus; the fine yellow sand; the charioteers poised like gods, leaning back a little, with the reins wound fast about their waists;

the horses pawing, snorting, and flaunting coloured favours. Above them, on the long, narrow embankment around which the course ran, towered the immense obelisk brought by Augustus from Egypt; and on either side of it stood marble images of Neptune, Hercules and the Heavenly Twins. Also bronzes of deified Caesars: Augustus, Claudius and Vespasian – each of whom in his lifetime had generously patronized this Circus.

The Emperor waved his napkin to signal 'Begin!' Another trumpet flourish: the taut rope fell, four whips cracked as one, and the chariots were off, scattering clouds of sand.

Blue's partner, Red, having drawn the best berth, should have gone hell for leather to reach the turning-post first, then rounded it in a wide enough sweep to hold White and Green securely on his flank, while letting his partner, Blue, nip in behind and steal the turn. I've watched that manoeuvre often; but it needs judgement. On this occasion Red got away to a slow start, let White crowd him into the embankment, four lengths before the post, and thus open the inner berth for Thallus. Scorpus, counting on Red to reach the post unchallenged, hadn't let his team go full out; by the time he'd whisked around White at the turn, Green was well ahead. (These two posts, at either end of the embankment, are pillars of gilt bronze; seven huge wooden eggs rest on a frame above them. An Imperial slave takes one egg down as soon as the leading chariot has gone past; and another at each lap, until all seven eggs have disappeared. It saves charioteers and spectators the trouble of keeping count.)

A bad beginning. Thallus kept his lead of three lengths, and completed the first lap with so sharp a turn that I'd swear his wheel shaved the gilt off both sides of the bronze! After him shot Scorpus, now far enough away from White not to be worried by him; though plainly worried by the Green tunic in front. Later we heard that our near team-horse had not been in top condition.

Three very fast laps, no change in position, and towards the end of the fourth lap Scorpus challenged; he ran neck to neck with Green for a while, but failed to make that inner berth at the turn.

Four eggs down! Five eggs down!

Scorpus didn't challenge again; he waited, despite jeers, protests, whistles and encouraging yells. He waited patiently, until Red had lost a whole lap and was hugging the embankment, some lengths in the rear of White, with Green threatening to pass him at the post. *'Ag'ut primā debebas!'* Scorpus shouted – he lay a little behind and beyond Green – 'Do what you should have done at the first post!'

Red understood; he flogged blood and sweat out of his nags, and this time rounded the turn wide enough to carry Green with him. Scorpus, wheeling almost at right angles, nipped in behind so neatly that his off-tracer's shoulder grazed the Red chariot-tail: he'd beaten Green to the inner berth and won three lengths.

'Successit et vicet!' the Blues roared – 'He's gained the lead, and he'll keep it!'

Six eggs down!

Now White, just ahead of Scorpus, though still in the fifth lap, was weaving in and out to hamper him; Green ran a close third. Caught between his two rivals, Scorpus made a bold decision. He forced his tracers to take the last turn wide; whereupon White lost his whip, as well as his head. Mistaking Thallus' team for Scorpus' – the Green tracers being also bays – he baulked him at the critical moment. Thallus' wheel struck the post, square, the chariot broke up. In the nick of time he used his dagger to cut himself free from the reins. On rushed the horses, hauling the wreckage after them.

A thunderstorm of cheers and curses. It was Blue's race all right – Scorpus could have finished at a walk. But as he walloped his triumphant Thessalians at high speed down the stretch, a small, ragged-shirted figure leaped the barrier and ran across the sand, shaking his puny fists. There he stood – directly in the chariot's path! Expecting him to lose his nerve and dart back, Scorpus neither reined in nor swerved. The intruder sprang at the duns' heads, then fell with a scream under their iron hooves. The tracers, meanwhile, had shied and plunged, slewing the chariot around. Scorpus was thrown, and his helmet struck sickeningly against the marble embankment. He was dragged past the winning-post – one lap and five lengths ahead of White.

An indescribable hubbub. I heard the chariot-master's gasp of horror. In a nightmare, I heard my own groans, as if heaved from some other man's guts. Scorpus, our great Scorpus! Down at last with a smashed skull and broken neck! The long play had ended. We wept like orphan children.

Bufotilla fainted; the veterinary took charge of her. I was glad she'd fainted. We all thought the world of her. She and Scorpus were to have married in the New Year. One can find no words of comfort on such occasions . . .

Further hubbub. The judges were signalling a Blue victory. Someone tugged at my sleeve. 'You've won your ninety-six gold pieces!' said the philosopher. 'I renounce my share. It would be disgraceful to profit from a man's death.'

He was being illogical. Dead men don't win races, and the judges' decision clearly showed that Scorpus had been dragged alive past the mark. But why argue?

'What pain! What misery!' I mourned. 'Scorpus is gone! Those murderous Greens must have been counting on Ragged Shirt to save their bets. A suicidal wretch, who'd bet against Scorpus once too often? But I won't believe a man could have scrambled over that barrier without help!'

Just then the Imperial catapults opened up: a volley of metal vouchers scattering in showers among the seats. Some were for money, anything from a single gold piece to a hundred; some had even higher value, gifts of farms, houses, shops – properties confiscated by the Emperor from banished noblemen, or left him in wills.

'I can stand no more!' the philosopher exclaimed shrilly. 'To-morrow I shall return to Myconos, if the kind Gods will arrange my passage.' And that the Gods were kind, and very kind, a most curious coincidence proved. A voucher struck the head of some woman sitting behind us and bounced into the philosopher's lap. It entitled him to 'a fifty-ton merchant vessel, the *Good Fortune*, at present lying off Naples; warranted sound and well found'. How's that for maiden luck? And only five days later an Imperial Edict banished all philosophers from Rome!

*

Not since the Emperor Titus died have I seen a better attended funeral. The Spanish poet Martial wrote a graceful dirge: 'Let Victory sadly break her palm, *etcetera, etcetera...*' Also an epitaph: to the effect that an envious Fate having counted Scorpus' victories, decided that at twenty-seven years he'd won enough for a lifetime; then took up her shears and snipped his vital thread. I'm no judge of verse, but I admired the sentiment.

Thallus has succeeded to Scorpus' throne; and we Blues seldom win these days. Besides, racing isn't what it was: the Emperor, for inscrutable reasons of State, has formed two new factions – Purple and Gold. Our harassed bookmakers never know how to figure the odds.

And I'm sick of the Colosseum as well. Hermes, my favourite gladiator, left hospital too soon and got chopped in his first show. Talk of the Good Life! If things don't improve soon, and if I get any balder from worry, I'm half inclined to sail for Myconos myself and open a quiet little cockpit there.

MAJORCAN STORIES

THEY SAY ... THEY SAY

THIS is Saturday, listeners, and here I am standing beside the old recording van in a Spanish seaport town on the Costa Brava. The sun is pretty hot, even for this time of year: several scores of farmers and dealers, mainly from outlying districts, have taken possession of the Market Square cafés. Nice fellows, too. Not a knife, pistol or unkind thought in the whole crowd. That hoarse buzz you hear is their usual exchange of views on the price of tomatoes, olive futures, the effects of drought on the regional economy, and so on. The overtones are excited argument about the Grand Tour of Catalonia – on push-bike – and the fearful struggle of the local *futbol* team to avoid relegation to the Third Division of the League.

Now, suppose we bring the microphone over to a corner table and listen to what those two very relaxed-looking types are saying to each other over their coffee and *anis*. The melancholy-looking fellow in black corduroys, sporting a massive silver watch-chain, is Pep Prat. Pep breeds mules; and his rubicund *vis-à-vis* with the blue sash, by name Pancho Pons, grows carnations for the Barcelona market.

PANCHO: Well, Master Pep! Been along Conception Street lately?

PEP: And if not, have I missed much, Master Pancho?

PANCHO: Nothing, nothing, I was only making conversation.

PEP: Make some more by all means.

PANCHO: I went this morning to change a one-hundred-*duro* note at the Banco Futuristico.

PEP: Did they short-change you? Mistakes often happen on a Saturday.

PANCHO: No, indeed. Don Bernardo Bosch was in a very good humour. He now has an enchanting little office with three easy chairs, a mahogany desk and a window overlooking the street.

PEP: Of course ... Of course ... Ah, Master Pancho! That poor woman's face comes back to me so clearly!

PANCHO: What courage, eh! I should never have dared address him as she did.

PEP: It is now more than a year ago.

PANCHO: Yet the words still ring in my ears. I happened to be doing some business with the cheesemonger next door, and poor saintly Margalida never spoke in a low voice, even at the worst of times. On that occasion she might have been missionizing the heathen. She said: 'Don Bernardo, not another word! I have this shop on a hundred years lease, with eighty-six more to run and since (thanks be to God!) I am now only thirty years old and enjoy good health, it should last out my life. I am not selling, I do not need to sell, and though the shop may measure only twenty-five and a half square metres it suffices for my modest business.'

PEP: She had spirit.

PANCHO: And Don Bernardo answered: 'You are a blood-sucker, you are a negress, Margalida Mut, you are Jael and Sapphira rolled into one. I offer you fifteen hundred *duros* a square metre to surrender your lease and you dare refuse it!' And the poor creature answered: 'I am not selling, you gipsy! But if you and your colleagues think of selling the Banco Futuristico equally cheap, let me know — I may need it as a lumber room. *Adiós*!' That ended the comedy.

PEP: But tell me: exactly why would she not sell?

PANCHO: Ask me, rather, why she should sell. Should she sell just because the Banco Futuristico had bought up the rest of the site, and did not wish her rusty shutters and peeling sign to interrupt their beautiful marble façade in Conception Street? Margalida was a martyr to principle.

PEP: Nevertheless, principle puts no bacon in the stew. Her trade was beggarly. She called herself an antique-dealer but I have seen better stuff spread out on a sack in the Flea Market: nails, horseshoes, a broken sewing machine, three cracked dishes, books without covers, half a Salamonic bedrail.

PANCHO: Mind, I know nothing, but they say ... very unjustly no doubt ... that the excellent woman was a receiver of stolen goods, a usuress at compound interest, a blackmailer, a Protestant!

PEP: They say! Ah, the hypocrites! They said nothing like that at her funeral. What a display! A thousand people at least walked in it, besides priests and acolytes. And an epidemic of tall wax candles. Also columns in the *Heraldo* about her good works and devotion and saintliness. I recall how shocked Don Bernardo was when he heard the news. He hurried at once in his very pyjamas to condole with the deceased's afflicted sister Joana Mut.

PANCHO: It was well done, although Margalida had not been on speaking terms with either of the two sisters since their parents' death – some dispute about the inheritance, they say.

PEP: Yes, they say. And they say . . . But never mind.

PANCHO: An extraordinary end, eh? Altogether baffling. It happened, you will remember, at precisely seven o'clock, when all the shutters in the street were clanging down; and her protests, if any, must have been drowned in the noise. Nobody was aware that anything unusual had occurred until nine o'clock next morning when someone noticed the gap at the bottom of the shutter – which showed that she had not locked it as was her custom when she went home to her solitary flat. A pity, because it was then too late to telephone the station-police at Port Bou and have the passengers searched as they crossed the frontier. You may be sure that the assassin was French.

PEP: My brother-in-law at Police Headquarters disagrees.

PANCHO: No Catalan of the Costa Brava would murder even a supposed usuress for her money!

PEP: Certainly not! But no money was taken. A two-hundred-*duro* note was left untouched in the open cash-box. They say that the assassin was a married lady who wished to retrieve some compromising document from it. They say that a long strand of hair was found in poor Margalida's fingers . . .

PANCHO: Yes, they say! But they also say it was Margalida's own hair, torn out in the struggle.

PEP: Of the same colour and thickness, I admit. It certainly seemed to be Mut hair . . . What I cannot understand is why

my brother-in-law had orders from high up to post an armed
guard at either end of the street for a whole month; as if to
prevent a disturbance.

PANCHO: It is, of course, a theory that murderers revisit the
scene of their crimes. But what I should have liked to ask
your brother-in-law was, why he allowed that picture of poor
Isidoro Nuñez to appear in the *Heraldo* entitled: 'Wanted,
dead or alive, for the Conception crime!' Isidoro is not a bad
fellow. Once he got drunk and borrowed the mayor's bicycle
and ran it into a tree, so they jailed him for a couple of
months; but that was his one crime. Actually, it was well
known that he had gone off, two days before, to visit his
father in Galicia; and when he returned the police did not
even interrogate him. They say . . .

PEP: Oh yes, they say! They also say that it was a love tragedy,
that the poor woman was killed by an amorous and impulsive
youngster whom she had rejected.

PANCHO: Ka! Margalida was as ugly as a fisherman's boot.

PEP: Pancho, you must not speak disrespectfully of the dead..
Very well, let us suppose that the amorous youngster was
really after her money . . .

PANCHO: Good! And that he believed her to have already
closed the bargain with Don Bernardo. Tell me, by the way,
did her heirs sell the lease for those fifteen hundred *duros* the
square metre?

PEP: No. You see, Margalida had not been quite accurate: she
had the shop on a life tenure only. When she died it reverted
to the landlord. A pity, because under the Rent Restriction
Law the landlord could never have made the lessee pay more
than the price originally agreed on – a mere ten *duros* a
month. That law is a great protection to poor people.

PANCHO: Who was the landlord, by the way?

PEP: By a remarkable coincidence it was Joana Mut herself.
And since she had no aptitude for the family antique business,
she regretfully parted with the freehold. The Bank paid a
thousand *duros* a square metre, they say, but that may be an
exaggeration. The other sister got nothing except Margalida's
stock and personal effects, poor child!

PANCHO: Garlic and onions, Pep! Do you know what I think?

PEP: Tell me.

PANCHO: I think that the unfortunate angel pulled down the shutters and choked herself with her own hands in mortification for having turned down Don Bernardo's offer!

PEP: It is very possible. Indeed, they say ...

Well, listeners, I expect you have heard enough. But before I return you to the Studio let us cross the street and hear what that vigorous but charming-looking fishwife has to say for herself. The one with the spotted handkerchief round her hair. Well, well, what a coincidence! If she isn't Aina, the youngest of the three Mut sisters! I wish you could watch her now, knife in hand, ripping the tough brown skin off an ugly-looking stingray! My word, personally I shouldn't like ... And, look, if that isn't Don Bernardo himself buying prawns at the next stall! Good Heavens! Aina has recognized him! She has laid down the sting-ray ...

Oh! Oh! I'm glad you missed that, listeners! Garlic and onions!

DEAREST Aunt May,

You will never guess what happened to me yesterday, which was Ascension Day, besides being my birthday! I met our new postman at the front door and collected your 'Now you are 11' birthday card – thanks awfully! He was a young man with very long hair, and wanted to know what the card meant. So I told him. Then he asked if I was acquainted with the foreign family Esk. I said 'No, but show me the letters, please!' and they were all for Father, ten of them – 'William Smith, Esq' – the postman had had them for a week! So we were both very pleased. Then I mentioned that Señor Colom was taking me to the bullfight for a birthday treat, and his face lighted up like a Chinese lantern. I asked: 'Are they brave bulls?' and he said: 'Daughter, they are an escandal!' and I asked: 'How an escandal?' And he explained that Poblet, the senior matador, had written to his friend Don Ramon, who had a bull farm near Jerez and was supplying the six bulls for the fight, to send him under-weight ones, because he wasn't feeling very well after grippe and neither were the two other matadors, Calvo and Broncito; and he'd pay Don Ramon well and arrange things quietly with the Bull Ring Management. So everything was fixed; until the new Captain-General of Majorca, who's President of the Ring and very correct, went to see the bulls as they came ashore. He took one look and said: 'Weigh them!' So they put them on the scales and they weighed about half a ton less than the proper weight. So he said: 'Send them back at once and telephone for more.' The second lot had just arrived by steamer. The new postman told me that they were a disaster, and looked like very especial dangerous insects.

My friend Señor Colom is really a music critic, but that position is worth nothing, only a few pesetas a week; he gets his living from being a bull critic. A regular matador earns about two or three thousand pounds a fight, so his agent can afford to pay the critics well to say how much genius and valour he has, even if he hasn't. Señor Colom writes exactly what he really thinks about concerts, but bullfights are different; he makes the agent himself write the review, then reads it over for grammar-faults and puts in a few extra bits, and signs it. That is the custom.

Anyhow, Señor and Señora Colom and I went, and the U.S.A. fleet was in port and two American sailors sat next to us. It seems that the Captain-General had measured the bulls' horns himself and told the herdsman: 'When these beasts are dead I will measure their horns again. If they have been shortened and re-pointed, someone will go to prison.' Then he had checked the pics to see that they didn't have longer points than is allowed, and also sent a vet to see that nobody gave the bulls a laxative to make them weak. So it was going to be fun to watch.

The Captain-General was in the President's box and after the march-past he waved his handkerchief and the trumpets blew and the first bull was let loose. He was a great cathedral of a bull, and rushed out like the Angel of Death. But when the cape-men came out and began to cape him, there was a sudden growl and loud protests and everyone shouted *'Bizgo! Bizgo!'* which meant that the bull was squint-eyed and wouldn't answer to the cape. So the Captain-General sent the bull away, and Poblet, who should have fought it, gave a nasty grin, because there were no substitute bulls. One had got drowned when he slipped off the gangplank of the steamer, and another had got horned by a friend. The Captain-General looked furious.

The next bull was very fierce, and the cape-men ran for their lives behind the shelters. One of them couldn't quite get there, so he dashed for the wooden wall and shinned up and escaped into the passage behind. The bull jumped right over the wall after him and broke a news-photographer's camera and spec-tacles, and gave him an awful fright. The crowd laughed like anything. Then the trumpets blew again and 'in came the cavalry' as Señor Colom always calls the picadors. The bull went smack at the first horse, before the peon who led it had got it into position, and knocked all the wind out of its body. The picador was underneath kicking with his free boot at the bull's nose. One of the two American sailors fainted, and his friend had to carry him out. Four more American sailors fainted in different parts of the ring; they are a very sensitive class of people.

This bull was Broncito's.

Broncito is a gipsy and engaged to Calvo's sister. He is very superstitious, and that morning had met three nuns walking in a row, and told Calvo he wouldn't fight. Calvo said: 'Then you will never be my brother-in-law. Would you disgrace me before the public? Would you have me kill your bulls for you as well as my own? I don't like them any more than you do.' So Broncito promised to fight. Well, the picador wasn't hurt, they never are. The cape-men drew the bull away and the peons got the horse up again, and it seemed none the worse. And the picadors did their work well and so did the banderilleros. But Broncito was trembling. He made a few poor passes, standing as far away as he could, and then offered up a prayer to the Virgin of Safety, the one who saves matadors from death by drawing the bull away with a twitch of her blue cape. The bull happened to be in the right position, standing with his legs apart, so Broncito lunged and actually killed it in one. The public was furious because he hadn't played the bull at all, hardly, and the play is what they pay to see.

The third bull was Calvo's, and Calvo was terribly valiant because he was so ashamed of Broncito. He made dozens of beautiful passes, high and low, also veronicas and some butterfly passes which everyone but Señor Colom thought wonderful. He had known the great Marcial Lalanda who first perfected them and said that Calvo's were both jerky and ungenial; though, of course, he couldn't *write* that for his paper. Calvo killed after two tries and was rewarded with both ears. His chief peon cut off the tail too, and gave it to him, but the Captain-General had signalled only for the ears, so the peon got fined 500 pesetas for presumption.

After the interval, with monkey-nuts and mineral water, it was Poblet's turn again. His bull came wandering in very tranquilly, had a good look round and then lay down in the middle of the ring. After a lot of prodding and taunting of which he took no notice, they had to send for a team of white and black oxen, with bells, who came gambolling into the ring and coaxed him out again. Do you know the story of Ferdinand the Bull? It ends all wrong. Bulls like Ferdinand don't go back to the farm to eat daisies. I'm afraid they get shot outside the ring by the Civil Guard, like deserters in battles.

The public was getting impatient. It booed and cat-called like anything, but the fifth bull (Broncito's again) was a supercathedral; soap-coloured and with horns like an elephant's tusks. Broncito was sick with horror, and when both the horses had been knocked down before the picadors could use their pics, and only one banderillero had been tall enough to plant his pair of darts well, he went white as a sheet. He pretended to play the bull but it chased him all over the place and the crowd roared with laughter and made rude jokes. So he shook his fist at them and called for the red *muleta* and sword and then, guess what! He *murdered* the bull, with a sidepass into his lungs instead of properly between the shoulder-blades. There was an awful hush from the Spaniards, who couldn't believe their eyes – it was like shooting a fox; but tremendous cheers came from the American sailors who thought Broncito had been very clever. Then of course the cheers were drowned by a most frantic booing, and the Captain-General sprang to his feet and cursed terribly. The next thing was that two *guardias* arrested Broncito and marched him off to prison.

The last bull was easily the best of the six and Calvo was more anxious than ever to show off. He wanted both ears *and* the tail *and* the foot (which is almost never given) and when he came to play the bull he dedicated it to the public and did wonderful, wonderful, fantastic things. There's a sort of ledge running round the wooden wall which helps cape-men when they scramble to safety. He sat down on it, to allow himself no room to escape from a charge, and did his passes there. Afterwards he knelt and let the bull's horns graze the gold braid on his chest. And did several *estupendous* veronicas and then suddenly walked away, turning his back to the bull, which was left looking silly. Calvo had waved all his cape-men far away and the crowd went wild with joy. But some idiot threw his hat into the ring, which took the bull's attention from the *muleta*, and Calvo got horned in the upper leg and tossed up and thrown down. Then the bull tried to kill him. I don't know how many more sailors fainted; I was too busy to count.

Suddenly an *espontáneo* in grey uniform with long hair simply hurled himself into the ring and grabbed Calvo's sword and red *muleta* and drew the bull off. It was our sloppy new postman! And while the peons carried Calvo to the surgery, he played the bull very valiantly and got apotheosistical cheers, louder even than Calvo's, and the Captain-General himself applauded although the postman was committing a crime. Everyone expected Poblet to enter and finish off the bull, but Poblet had now also been arrested for insulting the Lieutenant of the Civil Guard for insulting Broncito; so there was no other proper matador left. But Calvo petitioned that the postman should be allowed to finish off the bull, for having saved his life. The Captain-General consented and, when I waved madly, the postman recognized my yellow frock and rededicated the bull to me – me, Aunt May! Because it was my birthday and because of the Esq. And though the poor boy was rustic and quite without art, as Señor Colom said (and wrote), he managed to kill his enemy at the second try.

Then, of course, he was arrested too. All *espontáneos* are.

But the Captain-General let him off with a caution and a big box of real Havana cigars.

Ever your loving niece,
Margaret

A BICYCLE IN MAJORCA

IT was not always so. Majorca used to be the most crime-free island in Europe. When I came back here with my family shortly after World War II, one could still hang one's purse on a tree and return three months later to find its contents still intact. Unless, of course, someone short of change had replaced the small bills with a larger bill of equal value.

I am wasting this morning in the draughty corridors of the Palma Law Courts, because of my son William's 'abstracted' bicycle. He lent it to his younger brother, Juan, a year ago, when Juan's own bicycle. . . . But forget Juan's bicycle for the moment and focus on William's. We imported both of them from England. The Spaniards certainly know how to ride bicycles; they are heroic racing cyclists, and the mortality among leaders of the profession is a good deal higher than among bull-fighters. A recess at the back of the Palma Cycling Club provides a shrine for one of its members killed on a mountain road during the Tour of Spain – his pedals and shoes hung up beneath a plaque of St Christopher, with candles perpetually burning. Other members, who have died in lesser contests, are not so commemorated. But we British at least know how to *make* bicycles. I hasten to say that I am not criticizing Spanish workmanship. The British just happen to be experts in this particular trade; they even export vast quantities of bicycles to the choosy United States. The Spanish government will not, of course, agree that anyone else in the world can make anything better than Spaniards do, and surely a government's business is to foster faith in the nation's industrial proficiency? This attitude, however, makes it difficult for a Spaniard or a foreign resident in Spain – here comes the point – to import a British bicycle, especially when Spanish sterling reserves are low. Such a person must fill out fifteen forms in quintuplicate, supplying all his own vital statistics, with those of his relations in at least the nearer degrees, and showing just cause why he should be allowed a British bicycle (despite the hundred-per-cent Spanish import duty) instead of a much better, locally manufactured machine, which can be bought at half the cost. When he has waited fifteen months for an answer, while sterling reserves continue to fall, the chances are that the answer will be: 'We lament to inform you that last year's bicycle import quota has already been satisfied; we therefore advise you to fill out the necessary forms in quintuplicate for the present year's quota' – the year which, as a matter of fact, ended three months before. The most painless, therefore, way to import a British bicycle, as I learned from a friendly clerk at the Town Hall, is to arrive with it at the frontier, prepared to pay the import duty in cash, and insist on entry.

'If you are accompanied by children,' said the friendly clerk, 'there should be no trouble. All Spaniards are sympathetic towards fatigued fathers of families who have taken long journeys by train.'

'And if, by ill luck, I hit on an exception?'

'Then try a frontier post farther up the Pyrenees. On occasion, the officials at remote posts have no information about the rate of payment due from residents of Spain for imported bicycles. If the traveller happens to be a fatigued father of a family, they may well advise him – this has, in fact, happened – to rub a little mud on the machine and so convert it into an old one. His son can then ride across the frontier as a summer tourist.'

It's a long story. . . . At any rate, we got William's bicycle to Majorca legally enough. That was in 1949, and no immediate trouble ensued. The British bicycle was much admired, for the solidity of its frame and for being the only one on the island with stainless-steel wheel rims and spokes, brakes that really braked, and an efficient three-speed gearshift. Then, around 1951, British, French, and American travellers accepted the fantasy of Majorca as the Isle of Love, the Isle of Tranquillity, the Paradise where the sun always shines and where one can live like a fighting cock on a dollar a day, drinks included. A tidal wave of prosperity struck these shores, and though statistics show that a mere three per cent of the Paradise-seekers return, there are always millions more where they come from. Which means, of course, that thieves, beggars, dope pedlars, confidence tricksters, gigolos, adventuresses, perverts, inverts, deverts, and circum-

verts come crowding in, too, from all over the world – of whom
no less than ninety-seven per cent stay. Their devious activities
place unreasonable burdens on the shoulders of the gentle Civil
Guards. Repeat 'gentle'. The Civil Guards are, by and large,
gentle, noble, correct, courageous, courteous, incorruptible, and
single-minded. They are probably the sole Spaniards without the
national inferiority complex about not being bullfighters, which
attacks even racing cyclists. You are earnestly advised to refrain
from laughing at the Civil Guards' curiously shaped patent-
leather helmets and calling them 'comic-opera'. This antique
headgear usually covers real men.

A Civil Guard barracks stands just around the corner from
our Palma apartment. Conditions inside are pretty austere, the
living quarters being not unlike those in the prison recently
demolished near Boston – what was it called? The one where
they had so many mutinies? I know two or three of the Guards
there, and my family has a standing invitation to their annual
show on March 1st (the Day of the Angel of the Guard), which
is really quite something. So when, one evening in 1952, William's bicycle was stolen from the entrance hall of our apartment
house – we live on the second floor – I went straight to a Guard,
whom I remembered as a fat and dirty baby back in 1929, and
asked him for immediate action. He called a plainclothes colleague, whose children had been at school with mine, and sent
him down to the gipsy camp by the gasworks. (One early sign
of Majorcan prosperity was an influx of undisciplined and
picturesquely filthy gipsies from the south of Spain.) The camp,
consisting of low, unmortared, doorless stone shelters, roofed
with driftwood, rags, and odd sheets of rusty metal, is where
one would normally search for stolen bicycles. On this occasion
a blank was drawn. But as the plainclothes Guard, trudging
back, came within sight of the barracks – its entrance inscribed,
'All for the Fatherland' – a bicycle shot across the road out of
control, brushed past him, and piled up against a lightpole. Its
rider, a half-witted young man from Minorca, was severely injured – and so was William's bicycle. Unaccustomed to a three-
speed gear, the poor fellow had changed down as he passed the
barracks, without ceasing to pedal, had broken a cog in the gear-

box, and thus lost his head, his balance, his consciousness, and his freedom. I had to sign a long charge against the Minorcan and also swear to the bicycle before being allowed to take it back. 'Mind you,' said the lieutenant, 'this machine must be produced in evidence when the criminal comes up for trial. Since we know you well, you may keep it temporarily, but look after it with care!'

The wave of prosperity had caused such a fearful bottleneck in judicial activity that the case is still on the waiting list. Prisoners are allowed bail, but the Minorcan could not even afford to pay for the damage done to William's bicycle, so if he has not succumbed to his injuries, I imagine some prison or other holds him yet. All I can say is that the local press keeps silence on the subject. A young English acquaintance of mine saw the wrong side of a Palma jail not long ago; he was charged with being drunk and in possession of a lethal weapon. When the Captain-General released him, in return for some obscure favour from the British Consul, I heard a lot about that jail. A prisoner could earn a day's remission of sentence for every full day of voluntary work (this meant plaiting the palm-leaf baskets, which have 'Souvenir of Majorca' and a few flowers stitched on in coloured raffia, for tourists), also two days' remission for overtime on Sundays and national holidays. The only other inmate, besides the Englishman, who refused to work was a Valencian pickpocket, found guilty of several delinquencies and sentenced to a stretch totalling a hundred and eighty years. From my friend's description, it seemed a very old-fashioned jail as regards bedding, plumbing, and social arrangements – 'pure eighteenth-century, a regular collectors' piece'. But card-playing, drink, unimproving (i.e., non-devotional) books, and American cigarettes were forbidden. No Majorcans figured among the eleven criminals with whom he shared the cell – they had to occupy the only three beds in four shifts – because Majorcans seldom commit crimes (unless smuggling be so regarded, which must remain an open question) and can always raise bail from near or distant relations.

Well, when the bicycle case comes up, perhaps even this year, and the Minorcan is given a ten-year sentence, he will already have cleared it off and be a free man again, with a trade at his fingers' tips, and money in his pocket – accumulated payment at one cent for each and every basket plaited, less deductions for an occasional coffee or shave. Meanwhile, we have repaired the bicycle, which had lost a pedal bar, and fitted it with a Spanish lamp and a Spanish front mudguard, the original ones having become casualties. The three-speed gear is hardly what it was, but the bicycle still runs, despite other accidents soon to be related.

Now, to speak of Juan's own bicycle, also legally imported – or very nearly so. We chose one of pillar-box red, for conspicuousness, because the wave of prosperity was mounting and we did not want it stolen. Being a perfectionist, Juan treasured that bicycle like the apple of his eye, treating it daily with oily rag, duster, and saddle soap. In an evil hour we entered him at – let us call it San Rococo – reputedly the best boys' school in Palma. Juan is a Protestant, and the worthy priests who run San Rococo hoped to steer him into the Catholic fold, as they had just steered in a little Dane, two little Germans, and another little Englishman. But Juan, who has inherited bitter black Protestant blood from both sides of his family, remained obdurate. The baffled priests withdrew their fatherly protection, and Juan was soon assaulted by a group of his classmates. It happened that England had just beaten Spain at association football, four goals to one, so these patriotic lads accused the English forwards, and Juan, of foul play. They kicked out two of his bicycle spokes, threw the top of his bell over a wall, wrecked his lighting dynamo, and made away with his pump. It should be explained that they were not Majorcans but sons of wave-of-prosperity Galicians, recently come to Palma, and that Spain's goalkeeper had been a Galician.

'Juvenile high spirits,' sighed Father Blas when I complained. 'It would be virtually impossible to discover the names of the culprits, because in San Rococo we do not encourage tale-bearing. Besides, your son's lack of cooperation in our Christian devotions ...'

So Juan's bicycle was repaired at our expense, but it was stolen, early one Monday morning, from the school lockup inside the building while he was at his studies. I went to protest that same night. Father Blas beamed, and would not take the matter seriously. He had no doubt but that one of his sportive pupils was playing an innocent joke on my son. The solution – please God! – would appear the next day, and I need hardly disquiet myself, since the lockup was under the charge of a reliable seminarist. 'If it does not turn up tomorrow,' I said, 'please report the matter to the Civil Guard without delay. My wife and I are flying to Madrid tonight and cannot attend to it ourselves. Juan's is a distinctive bicycle, and even if it were repainted –'

'Not another word, my dear sir! What you say is perfectly logical,' cried Father Blas.

Juan's pillar-box-red bicycle was not returned by any sportive pupil. On the following Monday another bicycle was stolen, and on the Monday after that five more – all non-Protestant machines. On my return from Madrid, I went to see Father Blas again, and asked for news. Father Blas admitted to having taken no practical steps in the matter as yet, since the school had been engaged in a severe course of spiritual exercises (this was a sideswipe at the uncooperative Juan), but tomorrow, without fail, the reliable seminarist would advise the Civil Guard of the mysterious disappearances.

I said firmly that unless Juan got back his legally imported British bicycle within the next ten days, I should expect San Rococo College to repay me its value, which amounted to two thousand pesetas, including duty – or, say, fifty dollars. Father Blas shook hands warmly on my departure; he would write to me at once after a deliberation with his reverend colleagues. His answer came just before the end of term, enclosed with the school bill: a terse note to the effect that in the considered opinion of the lawyers retained by San Rococo College, the said college incurred no responsibility for the disappearance of bicycles from its lockup, since no particular charge had been made to scholars for the privilege of keeping them there during school hours.

One soon learns in Majorca never to sue for anything so unimportant as a bicycle. An action, I knew, would cost far more than the bicycle's value, and a year or two must elapse before the case would come to court; besides, as my barber pointed out when I discussed the matter with him, the Church always wins – always has won, except during the iniquitous Liberal regimes of the early nineteenth century and under the equally iniquitous Republic. So I simply took Juan away, wrote Father Blas a courteous letter thanking him for the care he had lavished on my son's education, and omitted to pay the school fees. It cuts both ways: San Rococo would never sue me – an action would cost them far more than the value of the school fees, and my counter-claim for the bicycle would do the college no good, especially if our lawyer cited the six other thefts as evidence of negligence.

Since then, Juan has taken most of his lessons at home, but attends French classes at the *Alliance Française*. And William, now being educated in England, has lent him his bicycle during term-time. 'And if you ever forget to fasten it with a chain and padlock while I'm away, I'll kill you!'

This brings us to February 1957, when I gave some lectures in the States. My Majorcan friends were anxious about my voyage to that land of gangsters, neurotics, Red Indians, and sheriffs' posses, so familiar to them from the cinema; the more pious of them, I believe, burned candles on my behalf to their favourite saints. I had a clamourous welcome when I·returned home bearing my sheaves with me – candy, nylons, rock-'n'-roll records, Polaroid film, ballet slippers, a Panamanian shrunken head – and a respectful salutation in the local press. To my relief, I found William's bicycle safely chained and padlocked to the newel post at the bottom of our staircase.

At eight o'clock next morning, as I dressed unhurriedly for breakfast (to be followed by a revision of Juan's Latin exercises done in my absence), I was startled by a yell and a fearful crash. I assumed that Juan had been celebrating the shrunken head in a truly Indian orgy and had accidentally knocked over the crockery cupboard. 'Stop it!' I shouted.

Juan appeared, looking scared. 'It's outside,' he said. 'I think they must be fighting again.'

Two years ago, the staircase of our apartment house had been the scene of a sanguinary battle. A respectable Majorcan couple living on the fourth floor had objected to the constant flamenco singing of a servant girl employed by a non-Majorcan woman living below them. In Majorca, nobody sings or dances flamenco except gipsies and girls in the red-light district and occasional American lady tourists who buy castanets and attend (let us call it) Pascualita Pastis's School of Spanish Dancing to justify the shawls, tortoise-shell combs, and ear-rings they have bought in Seville. The Majorcan couple called the flamenco-singing girl by a bad name. She flew at them, bit the wife's hand to the bone, and broke the husband's ankle. Her employers, who hated the Majorcan couple – their old aunt's venerable sewing machine shook the ceiling above them far into the night, and their young child played at ninepins all day – did nothing by way of dissuasion. The incident gave our street quite a bad name.

But this can hardly be another fight, I thought, as I hurriedly put on my slippers. The flamenco singer and her mistress had moved away long ago, and the whole building was respectable again. We were the only non-Majorcans left, so far as I knew.

I ran out of the apartment and stood on the landing. As I touched the iron banisters, a drop of blood fell on my hand and I heard a gurgling noise overhead. I looked up. A young man with contorted features, glaring eyes, and a bleeding forehead stood poised on the banisters one floor above me. He was about to leap down the well for the second time. I shouted in Spanish: 'Get off from there, and behave in a Christian manner!' – but he screamed and jumped. I made a grab at him as he flashed past. His weight was too much; down he went to the bottom of the well, struck the bicycle with the same crashing noise that had startled me only a minute before, rolled over, and lay still.

This second attempt at suicide looked pretty successful; all I know about first aid is how to apply a tourniquet above a gunshot wound in a limb – I learned that during World War I – and how to administer morphia if anything worse has happened. So I ran downstairs, then out of the front hall and around the corner to the Civil Guard barracks. I reported, panting, to the Guard on duty: 'A man has just tried to kill himself outside my apartment door. Please fetch a doctor.'

'One moment, sir! Do you wish to make a charge? If so, you must wait until the office opens; the desk sergeant has not yet breakfasted.'

'No, no, man! He may be dying, and though I regret disturbing the sergeant's breakfast —'

'Is the individual personally known to you?'

'No.'

'Does he seem to be a foreigner?'

'I could not say. The important thing is to fetch a doctor.'

'I cannot take that upon myself. Who would pay him? Why not fetch a doctor yourself? Try the nursing home down the road. It would surely be quicker than waking the sergeant and asking him to wake the lieutenant.'

I saw the force of his argument, and hurried to the nursing home. By chance, a car labelled 'MEDICO' had just drawn up there. I buttonholed the driver as he got out: 'Please, Doctor, come at once to my house – no more than a hundred yards away. A man has jumped from the third floor and hit the paved floor.'

'Let me alarm the nuns,' he said. 'Myself, I am only an analyst. My surgical training lies many years behind me.'

I thanked him for his kindness. Well, I thought, we had better get the madman on a mattress and under a blanket, if he is still alive. Returning to the scene of the incident, I found a great crowd of jabbering neighbours – but no victim. It seems that he had recovered enough to crawl up two flights of stairs and start making a third gallant attempt at suicide from the landing, but that Juan had summoned the rest of my family, who held him until help arrived. Then the midwife who lives in our building, and has had no lack of experience with excitable husbands, took charge.

When all had quieted down again, a couple of Civil Guards turned up. Since the would-be suicide proved to be a respectable Majorcan grocer, who blamed his fall on a sudden blackout caused by an anti-catarrhal injection given him by a French doctor in Marseilles a few days previously, the sergeant was able to report the incident as a regrettable loss of balance overcoming Don Pedro Tal y Cual while he descended the stairs from a business visit to friends on the third floor. 'Any important damage done to your machine,' the sergeant said to me, 'will be paid, naturally, by the unfortunate man himself – against whom, it is hoped, you will bring no charge.'

'No, no,' I answered. 'After all, he is our neighbour and a Palma man – not by any means to be suspected of criminal intent.'

'They take a lot of punishment, these British bicycles,' said the blacksmith admiringly as he straightened the fork. 'If it had been one of ours, that grocer would not have bounced off the frame. By the way, how is the poor fellow?'

'Suffering from a headache, I am told, and a grazed elbow.'

'A miracle!'

'This is a very historic bike,' Juan told the blacksmith. 'It has sent one man to prison and saved another's life.'

A week had not passed before the bicycle was stolen from the lockup at the *Alliance Française* during one of Juan's evening classes. He went at once to the Civil Guard barracks and reported the loss. 'Run away, boy, you are too young to make a proper charge,' he was told. 'Besides, the charge office is closed until tomorrow morning. Ask your professor to come here at about ten o'clock.'

Juan trailed miserably home, late for supper. 'William's bike is stolen,' he managed to force out between sobs, 'and William said he'd kill me . . .'

'Wasn't it chained?'

'No, that's the worst of it. On the way to class, I remembered that I'd forgotten the chain and padlock, so I biked back, but then I couldn't remember what it was I'd forgotten, so I whizzed down to the class again and hoped it would be all right. But it wasn't!'

We gave Juan some sausage and coffee, and then hurried to the port. The night boat to Barcelona had not yet sailed. I asked the Civil Guard sergeant at the barrier whether an English-type bicycle had come through, by any chance. 'We have just had one stolen,' I explained. 'Sometimes, they say, thieves steal bicycles and hurry them aboard at the last minute, aware that official charges cannot be made at this late hour.'

'No, sir. No such bicycle had passed through this barrier. But you are misinformed. This being an era of prosperity, the Barcelona fences are now interested only in stolen motor bicycles.'

'We shall never see that historic bike again,' Juan mourned. 'I can't face William when he comes home at Easter.'

Since bicycles are occasionally borrowed for a joy ride and then abandoned, we went to the Lost Property Office at the Town Hall, where municipal policemen bring them in. No luck.

The man in charge advised us against reporting the loss to the Civil Guard. 'If they do find your bicycle, you may never get it back. It will be held in evidence until the case comes up in court.'

'Better that than never, surely?' I asked.

'A distinction without a difference, I fear, sir,' he answered gloomily.

I regret not taking his advice. Although by this time the Civil Guard had forgotten about the Minorcan prisoner, and associated the bicycle only with an attempted suicide, they made me put the loss on record. And the very next day Juan's best friend at the *Alliance Française* happened to spot the bicycle in a disreputable alley, some distance away, propped unattended against a wall. We celebrated the discovery with a chicken dinner. But a Civil Guard called soon afterwards to inquire whether the bicycle had been recovered. We reported that – God be praised! – it was in our possession once more.

'My friend Pepe found it in Oil Street,' said Juan.

'Who is this Pepe? What is his surname? Where does he live?'

Today I have been ordered to appear before the judge in the matter of 'a summary which instructs itself concerning the ninety-sixth bicycle abstraction of the current year; on the penalty of the prescribed fine'. It occurs to me that our new Captain-General may have started tightening things up and demanding vengeance on bicycle thieves, and that the lieutenant of the Civil Guard may suspect Juan's friend Pepe of abstracting the bicycle himself. I don't know whether the difference between abstracting and robbery is the same in the States as in Spain.

Here, if the lockup had been really locked, or if Juan had remembered to chain the bicycle, and if the thief had then used force to possess himself of it, why, that would have been robbery, and worth several more years in jail.

I don't see Pepe anywhere around, nor do I expect to see him marched up presently between a couple of Civil Guards. Though not a respectable Majorcan (which would exempt him from all suspicion), he happens to be even better placed: his father is the new Civil Guard captain at the other barracks, a fire-eater from Estremadura.

THE FIVE GODFATHERS

DEAR Auntie May,

About that christening. The baby's father, Don Onofre Tur y Tur, was a lawyer; but that doesn't mean much here in Majorca. Only a few lawyers have offices and clerks and things. The rest take law degrees because their fathers want to make gentlemen of them that way; though there isn't enough law work to go around among them all. And once they become gentlemen they are ashamed to sell melons in the market, or plough olive terraces with a mule-plough; so most of them waste their time in cafés, or make love to foreign lady-tourists who look lonely.

Onofre's father, Don Isidoro, had earned lots and lots by selling ice-cream outside the boys' colleges in the summer and doughnuts in the winter. Afterwards he bought a dance-house called 'The Blue Parrot' and a souvenir shop called 'Pensées de Majorque', and thus became immensely rich, like Charles Augustus Fortescue in the *Cautionary Tales*. But Onofre fell in love with Marujita, one of the taxi-girls at 'The Blue Parrot' and secretly married her. (The taxi-girls' job is to dance with the customers and make them buy gallons of expensive drink, and then sit in corners and cuddle them all night.) Don Isidoro was furious when he found out; he banished Onofre to Binijiny with an allowance of a hundred pesetas a day, telling him never to show his face in Palma again.

Of course, everyone at Binijiny knew the story; and the mayor's wife and the secretary's wife were awfully catty to Marujita. But Onofre said she mustn't pay any attention to these low people. He managed to be quite happy himself: he had a motor-bicycle, and an apparatus for spearing fish under water, and a gun for shooting rabbits, and a quail for decoying quail, and a net for netting thrushes. He also used to play poker every day with two American abstract painters and one New Zealand real painter. Marujita may have been a bit lonely, but she loved having a home of her own, after being a taxi-girl, and a hundred pesetas a day seemed like riches.

One day the rumour went round that Marujita was 'embarrassed and soon going to give light', meaning she expected a baby, and presently Onofre asked mother to arrange things with the midwife, a kind woman from Madrid who thinks Binijiny very rustic. So mother did. Marujita couldn't manage the housework towards the end, but the neighbours pretended to be too terribly busy to look in, and we live on the other side of the valley. So, because a Spanish man doesn't help in the house, especially if he's a gentleman like Onofre, Marujita cabled for her younger sister Sita. Don Isidoro had dismissed Sita from 'The Blue Parrot', where she was dancing too, for fear the men customers found out that she was his relative; he gave her a day's notice and her boat fare, third-class, to Valencia. Wasn't that mean? Well, Sita turned up in Binijiny a month before the baby was expected, and though she seemed scared of mother and us at first, as though we'd certainly be unkind to her, we liked her awfully. The two sisters were always crying over each other and kissing, and saying rosaries; and Sita knitted vests and socks all day.

Anyhow, the baby got safely born, and because it was a boy Onofre simply had to call it after the grandfather; that's a rule here, just as the second son has to be called after the other grandfather. Sita was splendid. She helped the midwife with Marujita, and didn't scream or run in circles like Binijiny women do; but she made the baby feel at home and washed it and changed it and sang it lovely Flamenco songs. She also cooked the meals and did all the other housework. Onofre had told her on the first day: 'Sister-in-law, you're a very good girl; you shall be godmother.' When the New Zealand painter was asked to be godfather he answered, 'Look here, I'm a Protestant.' But Onofre said, 'No matter, it's all the same. Priests are priests everywhere.'

Of course, Onofre had announced the birth to the grandparents, first with a respectful telegram, and then with a flowery letter, enclosing an invitation card to the christening. He never expected to get any answer; it was just to keep his allowance safe.

Well, on the day of the christening, Sita put on her Sunday dress and wiped off her make-up and arranged the drinks and cakes and biscuits and *tapas* for the baptismal party in the sitting-room. Then she wrapped the baby like a mummy in four or five thick shawls and Doña Isabel the midwife accompanied her because she had never been a godmother before. Marujita wasn't well enough to go, so she stayed in bed. Onofre had sent out a whole packet of invitations to the christening, but nobody else came at all except mother and father and me and Richard, and the two American abstract painters and the New Zealand real painter.

The priest was waiting at the church door but the acolytes hadn't arrived. We waited about for nearly an hour talking and joking, while the baby slept. At last the priest said he had other business to do and he must start without the acolytes, and perhaps Onofre would condescend to assist? So he did, to save time. Sita already had the lighted candle in her hand, which every godmother carries, when a large, splendid car drew up in the Plaza, and Don Isidoro and Doña Tecla entered. Onofre turned pale, and the beastly old man said at once: '*I* am godfather here and no one else, understand, Onofre? What's more, this immodest women is not going to be godmother by my side. Unless she goes away I'll cut off your allowance and the child will starve.' Onofre turned paler still, but Sita kept calm. She said to the priest: 'Father, I renounce my rights. Nobody will ever say that I prejudiced the good fortune of this precious infant.' Then she handed the candle to Doña Isabel and went home to tell Marujita. The New Zealand painter also gave up, of course, so the priest started; but as soon as he turned his back and bowed to the altar Doña Tecla seized the baby from Doña Isabel, and said '*I* am godmother here, woman, and no one else, understand?'

But Doña Isabel hung on to the candle, and told the grandparents in a loud whisper that Sita was worth forty basketfuls of *canaille* like them. Doña Tecla screeched back at her, cackling like an old hen, which made the priest lose his place in the book and start reading prayers for missionaries in foreign parts. He had just found out his mistake and said 'Caramba, what a folly!' when in ran the acolytes without their surplices and laughing fit to burst. The manager of the hotel had sent them to fetch Doña Isabel at once, because two Belgian ladies insisted on sunbathing naked by the fishermen's huts, and if the Guardias caught them *he'd* be fined two hundred and fifty pesetas for each woman, because they were guests in his hotel, and that is the law. Doña Isabel asked 'Why me?' And they answered 'Because you are accustomed to deal with undressed women.' So Doña Isabel said 'Patience, in a moment!'

The priest took the baby and put the usual salt in its mouth to drive out the Devil, but for some reason or other it didn't cry. Perhaps it liked the taste. So Don Isidoro said 'Put in more, man; the Devil's still inside!' and Doña Tecla reached forward under the shawls and pinched the poor little baby on purpose to make it yell. Onofre noticed that and said in a loud voice 'Mother, you may insult my sister-in-law, and the certificated midwife of this village; these are women's affairs in which I don't meddle. But you will *not* pinch my son's bottom.'

The priest hurriedly made the sign of the cross on the baby's forehead, and called it Onofre, by mistake for Isidoro. Then Onofre took it from him and gave it to mother, who hurried it out of church before worse could happen. Doña Isabel went with her, still holding the candle.

Naturally Don Isidoro disowned Onofre, and Doña Tecla slapped his face before they stamped out of the church and drove off in their large splendid car. The rest of us trailed along to the baptismal party. Onofre did his best to be cheerful, and said 'Come along, friends, and help me drink up the brandy, because tomorrow we're all beggars.'

Sita was there when we arrived, rocking the baby and looking very pretty and pale without her make-up. Everyone began at once to drink and dance. Our family went away early because Richard had eaten too much cake and drunk half a glass of *anís*; but presently another guest invited himself in, an officer of the Spanish Blue Division whom the Russians had just let out of prison after fourteen years. He had no friends left and wanted to celebrate his return. Doña Isabel also came. She had frightened the Belgian women into putting on their clothes and then gone back to the church, where she found that Doña Tecla hadn't signed the register as the baby's godmother. So she signed it herself; because, after all, she'd held the candle. And the name would be Onofre, she said, not Isidoro, and that was God's will.

Just before midnight Onofre beat his head with his fist and shouted 'I had almost forgotten; my beast of a father did not sign the book either. Quick, gentlemen, to the Rectory, before the clock strikes twelve and the day becomes extinct!' So the Blue Division prisoner and the two abstract painters, and the real one, all trooped up to the Rectory, very intoxicatedly, and insisted on signing the register as little Onofre's joint godfathers. The priest had to let them, to avoid a scandal.

And guess what? In April they're all going to the Seville Fair at the invitation of Sita's new *novio*, who's a Chilean millionaire called Don Jacinto; I have met him. Don Jacinto is also lending Onofre and Marujita five million pesetas to start a much more luxurious Palma dance-house than 'The Blue Parrot'. He says 'That will teaching Don Isidoro not to insult poor beautiful dancing-girls who are positively saints!' It's going to be called 'Los Cinco Padrinos', which means 'The Five Godfathers', because Don Jacinto has added his name to the list too, for solidarity.

All the same, I can't say I trust him, somehow, and Marujita doesn't either; but we hope for the best.

Lots of Love,
Margaret

EVIDENCE OF AFFLUENCE

I f I do not know what degree of mutual confidence exists in the United States between income-tax official and private citizen, this is so because the question does not immediately concern me. I have never in my life been asked to fill out an American income-tax return; as a British non-resident I have all my American earnings painlessly taxed at source, and there the matter ends. In Great Britain, of which by an ingenious legal quirk I am 'deemed to be a resident, though permanently domiciled abroad', my earnings are also taxed at source; but I am at least allowed to employ an income-tax consultant, or rather a pair of them – Messrs Ribbons & Winder of Aquarium Road, Rhyl – in my defence. Every year they send me a form to fill in (we British fill in, not out, I don't know why) and discreetly advise me how, by clever albeit legal devices, to get a chunk of my forfeited earnings refunded. This year, however, they took twelve months to conclude their business, because the Bank of England ('Safe as the Bank of England!') admitted that it had lost certain documents relevant to my case – the .Government meanwhile enjoying an interest-free loan of my money. Unfair, surely, to Graves, who left his country only for his country's good?

Nevertheless, Mr Bloodsucker, as we British affectionately call the income-tax collector, is a decent man at heart and, not being himself responsible for the Schedule he is called upon to implement, does his best to mitigate its cruelty. Long ago, while a struggling poet, still domiciled as well as resident in Great Britain, I used to visit Mr Bloodsucker once a year, and actually looked forward to our confabulations. He would beam at me through his horn-rims and say: 'Now, don't forget to claim for the upkeep of your bicycle, young man – or the heating of your work-room, not to mention library subscriptions. And, I suppose, you take in some learned journals? You can recover a bit from that source. By the bye, are you sure you are not contributing in part to the support of an aged relative? Oh, and look here! This claim for postal and telegraphic expenses is remarkably low. Why not add another couple of pounds for good measure? Doubtless you have left something out.'

You see: in Britain the theory is (or at any rate was in those halcyon Twenties) that since the simple blue-jeaned or fray-cuffed citizen, as opposed to the clever-clever natty-suited businessman, seldom, if ever, tries to cheat the government, he should be discouraged from cheating himself. And my Mr Bloodsucker possessed great moral rectitude: if he found an anonymous note on his desk informing on Mr Ananias Doe or Mrs Sapphira Roe as unlawfully concealing taxable income, he always (I was told) would blush and tear it into a thousand fragments. To be brief, the British system of income-tax collection was not then, and is not now, fraught – have I ever used that word before in my life? Never, but here goes! – *fraught* with so much drama as that of certain Latin countries, where it is tacitly understood that only a fool or a foreigner will disclose more than a bare tenth of his net earnings. And where, also, the authorities have no effective means of discovering what these earnings are, since many a – I hesitate to say 'every' – sensible businessman, besides keeping at least two sets of books, running at least two secret bank accounts, and forgetting to record cash payments, has the collusive support of a large family and of the political party or racket to which he belongs. Income-tax sleuths in those countries are therefore forced to rely on what is called 'evidence of affluence', meaning the worldly style in which a man lives, and make a preliminary assessment of ten times the amount they hope to recover. Then battle is joined and victory goes to whichever side has displayed the greater strength of character.

Since 1954, I have become liable to Spanish income-tax and, although an honest English fool, take care to offer the minimum evidence of affluence. Indeed, while I occupied that Palma apartment, I found income-tax a splendid excuse for wearing old clothes, shaving every other day, dining at the humble fonda round the corner rather than at the neon-lighted *El Patio* or *El Cantábrico*, and living an obscure, almost anti-social, life. For Señor Chupasangre (Mr Bloodsucker's Majorcan counterpart) lurked behind the cash-desk of every expensive restaurant in Town, and behind the curtains of every night club as well. Moreover, if I had joined the Tennis Club and bought a shiny new car, a motor launch, or even an electric gramophone, Señor Chupasangre would have heard of it the next day through his very efficient intelligence service.

Well, I must stop talking about myself – there is no more threadbare subject in the world than a writer's finances – and get on with my story about the Sanchez family, whose apartment adjoined ours. Since Majorcans always talk at the top of their voices (I once dared ask why? and was told : 'lest anyone should think us either ill or frightened') and since the party-walls of Palma apartment-houses are extraordinarily thin, for the sake alike of economy and neighbourliness, I can describe in faithful detail a domestic scene which I did not actually witness. You think this impossible, and suggest that the french-windows of both apartments must have been wide open all the time? Permit me to sneer! Half an inch of sandstone, thickened to three-quarters by twin coats of plaster and whitewash does not provide adequate insulation even against a decently mumbled Sanchez rosary.

Don Cristóbal Sanchez, the smart young owner of a newly-established furniture factory, and his plump, brown-eyed, sallow-skinned young wife, Doña Aina, with incongruously beblonded hair and a heavy gold crucifix dangling on her bosom, always greeted us politely on the stairs, however often we might meet in the course of the day; they also borrowed from us with monotonous regularity methylated spirit, matches, bread, electric light bulbs, needles, thread, iodine, aspirins, and our step-ladder, and came calling at unreasonable hours, frequently when we were in bed, to ask whether they might use our telephone for a long-distance call to Barcelona. The family Sanchez owned a radio-set and a baby, both shockingly audible; but I persuaded Doña Aina not to turn on the radio during my work-hours, except on red-letter feast days (of which the Spanish calendar, to my Protestant way of thinking, contains far too many). The baby I could disregard : when other people's babies are teething, their wails are almost a pleasure to one who has suffered as much as I have from the sorrows of his own large family. Besides, teething babies do not cry in any tune, or use words intelligible enough to interrupt my inner voice and so destroy the rhythm of what I am writing.

Twelve years ago, before the Majorcan real-estate boom began, Aina's father, a scion of the Aragonese nobility who came over here in 1229 with King James the Conqueror and drove out the Moors, was forced to sell the family palace in Palma, and two heavily mortgaged country estates, to satisfy his deceased uncle's creditors. The prices which they realized were pitiful. Aina's father, however, managed to keep a row of fourteenth-century houses in the centre of Palma, which the Town Council subsequently commandeered and pulled down to make room for a new arcade lined with tourist shops. This brutal act did the poor fellow a lot of good, because under the Rent Restriction Law his tenants were paying him at a rate fixed in 1900, when the peseta was still a silver coin and a labourer's daily wage; it is now not worth two U.S. cents. The generous compensation awarded for the sites saved Aina's father from the poorhouse, and he even started speculating in new suburban building schemes; though not with much judgement, as will appear.

Aina, in the circumstances, was lucky to marry as well as she did. Don Cristóbal comes of respectable, if hardly resplendent, lineage; and has looks, industry, optimism and money to recommend him. Not that Aina had no previous offers; we heard from our maid's brother, who works in a fashionable El Terreno bar, that she was engaged for three years to her second cousin, Don Gregorio de la Torre Oscura y Parelada – whom we never met, but about whom Cristóbal teased Aina pretty often with loud guffaws of laughter. Cristóbal's major failing, it should be emphasized, was his self-satisfaction, complicated by an inability to keep his large, neatly-moustached mouth shut. We had overheard Doña Aina making some pretty caustic remarks on this trait.

Our maid's brother described for us the precise means by which Cristóbal contrived to detach Aina from Don Gregorio. Briefly, it was as follows. Owing to the impossiblity of forming new political parties under Franco's rule, Majorcan youth had found an alternative outlet for its intellectual energies: the ultra-religious group known as 'Mau-Mau'. Aina's parents were among its founders. Mau-Mau was ascetically ultra-Catholic, aghast at the present decadence of manners, and run somewhat on the catch-your-buddy principles of Moral Rearmament: with earnest parties called together amid delightful surroundings, and an active policy of infiltration into high society and the learned professions. Ordinary Catholics, such as our maid's brother, were offended by the Mau-Mau's custom of referring to the Deity as *Mi Amo*, 'my Master'; and the word 'Mau-Mau' stands, he told us, for *Mi Amo Unico, Mi Amo Universal*, 'My only Master, my Universal Master'.

Cristóbal Sanchez, it seems, joined the Mau-Mau and volunteered to act as the Group's secret watchman at the Club Náutico, our local yacht club, keeping tabs on not-too-trustworthy young Mau-Mau members there. His motive may only be guessed at, not roundly asserted. All we can say for sure is that though Don Gregorio had also joined the Group as a means of conciliating Aina's parents, his mind was not wholly bent on heavenly things. He used to get drunk at *Tito's* and *Larry's* and *Mam's*, kept disreputable company, preferred American jazz to the *Capella Clásica*, consorted at the *Granja Réus* with a Mexican divorcée, and in his cups used to sneer at Mau-Mau by making an irreverent single-letter change in one of the words that form its nickname – but our maid's brother would not disclose which. Cristóbal reported all this to Aina's father, as was his duty, and Don Gregorio found himself ignominiously expelled from the Group. Moreover, the Mau-Mau's *vigilante* squad, being authorized to take strong-arm action against such of their fellows as had fallen from Grace, waylaid him outside *Tito's* one night, pushed him into a taxi, drove him to a lonely building outside the town, and worked on him until dawn, with austere relish.

Aina, having already heard from a friend about the Mexican divorcée, shed no tears for Don Gregorio; he had nearly run through his inheritance, but refused to work and took her complaisance too much for granted – 'almost as if they had already married and put their honeymoon behind them'. She very sensibly switched to the more eligible Don Cristóbal. Having secured his law-degree, he was now embarking on a prosperous business career, kept an *esnipé* (or fourteen-foot sailing dinghy) at the Club Náutico, and also enjoyed conveying her on the pillion-seat of his motor-scooter to beauty spots not easily accessible by sea. After an apotheosistical scene in the Club Náutico – the sordid details of which I must withhold – Don Gregorio shook the dust of Palma (and very dusty it can be in the sirocco season) from his pointed shoes, and left for Madrid, where he had relatives. 'But listen to me well, you assassin, you pig,' he warned Cristóbal, 'the day will come when I shall return and settle accounts with you!'

And return he did. One hot morning in May, as I sat at my table patiently translating Lucan's *Pharsalia*, and begging my inner voice to disregard the gramophone across the street playing 'La Paloma', a very loud ring sounded through the wall of Cristóbal and Aina's unusually quiet apartment.

'A beggar,' I thought. 'Beggars always press the bell-push twice as hard as tradesmen or friends. In half-a-minute he'll be pushing at mine ...'

I waited, but no beggar appeared. Instead, Doña Aina hurried out to the Sanchez terrace, which is separated from ours by an iron railing. My work-room mirror showed her flattened against the house wall, clasping and unclasping her hands in obvious anxiety. Cristóbal, I guessed, had looked through the grilled spy-hole of the front-door and signalled for her to vanish; so I laid down my pen and listened.

Cristóbal was greeting the visitor in his high tenor voice with every indication of pleasure: 'Why, Gregorio, what a magnificent surprise! I thought you were still in Madrid. Welcome home!'

To my relief, I could distinguish an answering warmth in Gregorio's resonant baritone: 'It is indeed delightful to shake you by the hand, Cristóbal, after so long a time. I have been thinking of you often, remembering the trotting track, and the pigeon-shooting, and our *esnipé*-races across the harbour, and all the high times we had before ... in fact, before ...'

In the mirror I watched Doña Aina's face, alert and troubled, as Cristóbal replied: 'Gregorio, I honour your nobility of mind. That you deign to visit my house after the painful threats you uttered at the Club Náutico on that sad day, suggests that you have at last forgiven me for my great felicity. Aina is now not only my wife but has given birth to a precious little boy.'

An anxious moment, but Gregorio, it seemed, took the blow stoically enough. 'Well,' he said, 'your behaviour was a trifle violent, I must confess – when Aina and I had been courting for three years and made all our wedding preparations; but, of course, now that your theft has been legalized, and crowned with the registered birth of a new citizen, what can I do but felicitate you in truly Christian spirit? Not another word, man! Besides, Aina is by no means the only girl in Spain. In fact, though I do not mean to insult either of you by invidious comparisons, I have lately formed strong relations with (some might say) an even more intelligent and beautiful girl, of a better family also – if that were possible. We met at Seville during the Fair. As it happens, she also is a native of this city, and loves me madly.'

Ice having thus been broken, the two former rivals grew still more affectionate.

'My heartiest congratulations, dear friend!'

'Accepted with enthusiasm ... The only defect in this new situation is, however, the exaggerated wealth of my fiancée's family. It is a constant trouble to me.'

'Well, Aina's family do not suffer from *that* defect, at least. On the contrary, they come to me every second Monday, asking for material support.'

'Naturally! Aina was a prize that demanded handsome payment. But your furniture business flourishes, I understand?'

'Like a row of runner-beans: I am pretty well off now, thanks be to God and the tourist boom. Thirty-three new hotels, sixty new *residencias*, and eighty-four *pensiones* are building this winter! But, dear Gregorio, if your fiancée is so deeply attached to you, why should her family's wealth discommode you?'

'Don't pretend to be a fool, friend Cristóbal; clearly, they wish to assure themselves that their daughter will continue to live as she is accustomed to live – with servants, parties, visits, tennis, plentiful new clothes, an hour at the hairdresser's every day, and so forth. However, she's a match for that old egoist, her father. She threatens to enter a nunnery if she may not marry me. So he has given way, with bad grace. But first I must make a respectable quantity of money in my new job; that is his firm condition.'

'You really have a job, Gregorio? Love indeed works miracles!'

'Oh, not much of a job; hardly, indeed, one to boast about, or even mention in polite society. But it has certain possibilities.'

'Black market, I presume?'

'No, no: my future father-in-law, Don Mariano Colom y Bonapart, is so highly connected that he would never think of damaging his reputation by putting me into any dubious business.'

'No? I suppose that the fortune he made a few years ago, smuggling penicillin from Tangier to our hospitals – so-called penicillin that required an act of faith to make it work – has now been decently invested in those fantastic tourist novelties? He must be prospering.'

'Well, of course, nobody ever proved that he smuggled penicillin – a most charitable business, by the way – still less that it was ineffective when properly used. I have no doubt but that the doctors themselves adulterated their supplies to make them go further. At any rate, the case against him has been officially dropped ... Oh, yes, the novelties you mention are doing well enough, especially among conducted groups of Germans – best of all, the diverting little dog that cocks its leg. Don Mariano is now considering more austere lines for the English; he has consulted an English judge who is here on holiday.'

'But your job, Gregorio?'

'Forgive me, Cristóbal; I am ashamed. It is with one of the Ministries – too boring and distasteful to discuss.'

'Yet it carries its traditional perquisites?'

'Of course! Would Don Mariano have arranged it for me otherwise?'

'You seem a trifle gloomy, Gregorio. Will you drink a nipkin of brandy?'

'I don't drink, for the present. Don Mariano would not favour an alcoholic son-in-law. It will have to be orangeade, I fear.'

'Why not a Coca-Cola? I'll fetch you one from our electric refrigerator.'

'So you own a refrigerator, Cristóbal?'

'Thanks be to the Virgin! We are not among those who cool their butter in a pail let down the well!'

'It is very pleasant to hear of your increased earnings and domestic amelioration, dear Cristóbal. This refreshing Coca-Cola is conclusive evidence of prosperity ... Friends tell me that you gave a grand party the other day at the Hotel Nacional?'

'Ah, I wish you had been there! How the champagne corks popped! It was to celebrate the christening of our son.'

'That must have cost you a capital!'

'It did, and Aina's parents contributed not a single peseta of all the five thousand. I can speak freely to you – Aina is away at the moment, being fitted for an evening dress. By the bye, she still thinks very highly of you.'

To judge from the tightening of Doña Aina's lips, Cristóbal would pay for his remark as soon as Gregorio left. But she continued in hiding, though I could see that the sun's glare was bothering her. I quietly opened my french windows, went out and, with a polite smile, handed her a pair of sun-glasses through the railing. Doña Aina looked startled at this unexpected loan, but gratefully slipped them on.

Gregorio was saying: 'Your wife's opinion flatters me. And you could hardly expect much help from those Mau-Mau simpletons, her parents. They have suffered several financial reverses of late, or so I hear from my lawyers: particularly their need to compensate the former tenants of that new apartment-house. What an unfortunate investment it proved!'

'You are altogether right!' Cristóbal agreed. 'Your prospective father-in-law palmed it off on my actual father-in-law only just in time. I trust Don Mariano will not be sent to gaol when the Inquiry publishes its findings on the cause of the building's collapse.'

'Don Mariano in gaol!' laughed Gregorio. 'What a ridiculous

thought! No, no! The Inquiry has already been closed. You see, the plans were the City Architect's, and a City Architect is above suspicion; and if Don Dionisio Gomez, the building-contractor, economized in cement and used defective beams, how was Don Mariano to know? Don Dionisio emigrated to Venezuela, I understand, before Aina's father could sue him ...'

'Of course, that was a great blow to us. But, by the mercy of God, no one perished in the disaster, except the Ibizan widow without relatives; all the other tenants were away, watching the Corpus Cristi procession. As for the automobile in the garage below, which got smashed to pieces when the four apartments with their furniture fell on top of it – fortunately, that old museum-piece was Don Dionisio's own! In the circumstances, he will hardly dare claim compensation.'

'I agree, my dear Cristóbal. It is, as a matter of fact, about that automobile that I have heard an amusing story. You yourself sold it to Don Dionisio in 1953, as I recall?'

'Exactly; and very glad I was to rid myself of it, at so good a price, too. Not only were the brakes and the steering defective, but someone warned me just in time that, under the new income-tax system, possession of an automobile would be regarded as evidence of affluence. I acted at once ...'

'That was smart! But, Cristóbal, what about your other signs of affluence – the 5000-peseta christening party, that electric refrigerator, this vacuum cleaner, your honoured wife's evening dresses, the English baby-carriage in the hall, the financial help you are known to give your father-in-law? Don't you realize that these must inevitably catch the attention of Señor Chupasangre, the Chief Inspector?'

'Aina and I laugh at him. We pass for poor folk; I am careful to keep no automobile.'

'But Cristóbal, you do!'

'*I* keep an automobile? What joke is this?'

'I mean the one which got crushed by the deciduous apartments.'

'Idiot, I sold that to Don Dionisio four years ago!'

Gregorio said slowly and clearly: 'Yes, you sold it, but Don Dionisio never registered that change of ownership at the Town

Hall; consequently it remains in your name. As I see it, you are liable for income-tax during the whole of 1954, 1955, 1956 and 1957, at a high rate that is almost certain to be discussed between you and Señor Chupasangre.'

'The insect! How did you discover this trick?'

'I happened to consult the register at the Town Hall in the course of my business.'

'But, Gregorio, that is nonsense! The automobile has been Don Dionisio's, not mine, since 1953!'

'In the eyes of the Law it is still yours, pardon me. And Don Dionisio is not here to tell them otherwise.'

'Pooh!' blustered Cristóbal. 'Who says that I am liable to income-tax? I can show Señor Chupasangre my business accounts – the more pessimistic official ones, naturally – to prove that I do not qualify. If he asks me, I shall swear that the refrigerator and the vacuum cleaner were wedding presents, and that the English baby-carriage has been lent us by my sister. As for the party and Aina's evening dresses ...'

'Do you take Señor Chupasangre and his colleagues for fools?'
'Why not?'

But Doña Aina had already scented danger. I saw her involuntarily clap a hand over her own mouth, since she could not clap it over her husband's.

Gregorio protested: 'Cristóbal, dear friend, as I have been trying to tell you throughout this pleasant conversation, Aina is no longer anything to me, except your faithful wife and the mother of your little son; yet I owe to myself, and to my Ministry, the performance of a sacred duty. For, granted that I may be the fool you call me, this new job of mine ...'

'Gregorio! What are you saying, man?'

'... this new job, however distasteful it may be at times, carries with it (as you suggested) certain traditional perquisites. By your leave, I shall call again officially tomorrow. Meanwhile, my best regards to your distinguished wife! Tell her how enchanted I am that she still remembers my name.'

The door slammed. Gregorio's footsteps could be heard retreating unhurriedly down the stairs.

In the mirror, I saw Doña Aina stoop to pick up a sizeable

pot of pink geraniums. Would she drop it, *¡catacrok!*, on Gregorio's head as he emerged into the street?

But I should have known that this would not be Doña Aina's way. Instead, she flung wide open the french-window of her own apartment and stood for a moment with one foot advanced, the flower-pot poised low on her right palm, the left hand raised as though in a Falangist salute.

'Animal! Imbecile!' she cried, and let fly at Cristóbal with all her strength.

I stuffed a finger into each ear to drown the crash.

GOD GRANT YOUR HONOUR
MANY YEARS

I SLIT open the flimsy blue envelope and, pulling out an even flimsier typewritten slip, began to read without the least interest; but recoiled like the man in *Amos* who carelessly leans his hand on a wall and gets bitten by a serpent. The Spanish ran:

> With regard to a matter that should prove of interest to your Honour: please be good enough to appear in person at this Police Headquarters on any working day of the present month between the hours of 10 and 12. Business: to withdraw your Residence Permit. God grant your Honour many years!
>
> *Signed:* Emilio Something-or-other.
> *Stamped in purple*: The Police Head-
> quarters, Palma de Mallorca.

For two or three minutes I sat grinning cynically at the nasty thing. '*Para retirar la Autorización de Residencial*' Well, that was that!

Though often warned that in a totalitarian state anything might happen, without warning, without mercy, without sense, I had imagined it could never happen to me. I first came to Majorca, twenty-five years ago, during Primo de Rivera's dictatorship; and stayed on throughout the subsequent Republic. Then one fine summer's day in 1936 small bombs, and leaflets threatening larger bombs, began to fall on Palma; soldiers hauled down the Republican flag; unknown young men with rifles invaded our village of Binijiny and tried to shoot the Doctor by mistake for a Socialist politician; the boat service to Barcelona was suspended; coffee and sugar disappeared from the shops; all mail ceased; and one day the British Consul scrawled me a note:

Dear Robert,
This afternoon H.M.S. *Grenville* will evacuate British nationals: probably your last chance of leaving Spain in safety. Luggage limited to one handbag. Strongly advise your coming.

I.L.

I hastily packed my handbag with manuscripts, underclothes and a Londonish suit.

An hour later Kenneth, two other friends and I were heading for the port in the taxi which the Consul had considerately sent out to us. Thus we became wretched refugees, and wretched refugees we continued to be for ten years more until the Civil War had been fought to a bloody close, until the World War had broken out and run its long miserable course, and finally until the Franco Government, disencumbered of its obligations to the Axis, had found it possible to sanction our return. Reader, never become a refugee, if you can possibly avoid it, even for the sake of that eventual happy homecoming in an air-taxi, with a whole line of bristly village chins awaiting your fraternal salute. Stay where you are, kiss the rod and, if very hungry, eat grass or the bark off the trees. To live in furnished rooms and travel about from country to country – England, Switzerland, England, France, the States, England again – homesick and disorientated, seeking rest but finding none, is the Devil's own fate.

This brings the story up to 1946. I came back to Binijiny, and thanks to the loyalty of the natives found my house very much as I had left it. Certain ten-year-old Kilner jars of homemade green tomato pickle had matured wonderfully, and so had a pile of *Economists* and *Times Literary Supplements*. 'Happily ever after,' I promised myself. Then in 1947 Kenneth joined me again, and we resumed work together.

And now this! '*Para retirar la . . .*'

But why? I belong to no political organization, am not a *frémasón*, have always refused to write either against, or for, any particular form of Spanish Government, and if ever people ask me: 'What is it like on your island?' am careful to reply: 'It is not mine; it is theirs.' As a foreigner who must apply every two years for a renewal of his residence permit, I try to be the perfect guest: quiet, sober, neutral, appreciative and punctilious in money matters. Then of what crime could I be accused? Had someone perhaps taken exception to a historical novel of mine about Spanish colonization under Philip II? Or to the rockets I release every July 24th, which happens to be my birthday as well as the anniversary of the capture of Gibraltar? Had some cathe-

dral canon denounced me for having acted as Spanish-English
interpreter at a serio-comic meeting of solidarity between the
corn-fed Protestant choir of the U.S. aircraft-carrier *Midway* and
the bleak encatacombed Evangelical Church of Majorca? Where
could I find out? The police would doubtless refuse an explanation. What means had I of forcing them to say more than 'Security Reasons', which is about all that our own democratic Home
Office ever concedes?

Nobody had invited me to settle in Majorca; almost anyone
had a right to object to my continued presence there.

... So this was why they had brooded so long over my appli-
cation for renewing the damned permit!

My wife probably wouldn't much mind a change of house and
food and climate. But how could I break the news to Kenneth?
Although I should be sunk without him, he could scarcely be
expected to share my exile again; the poor fellow had hardly
enjoyed a day's happiness, I knew, during those ten long years.
And what if our long association put him on the black list too?
And just as he was buying that motor-cycle!

Yet why the hell should I take this lying down? After twenty-
five years – after all the sterling and dollars I had imported –
and my four children almost more Majorcan than the Majorcans! I'd hire a car, drive to Palma at once, visit the Chief of
Police and ask, very haughtily, who was responsible for what
was either a tactless practical joke or a cruel *atropellada*.
(*Atropellada*, in this sense, has no simple familiar English
equivalent, because it means deliberately running over someone
in the street.) Afterwards I'd ring up the British Embassy at
Madrid. And the Irish Embassy. And the American Embassy.
And ...

Here came the car. Poor Kenneth! Poor myself! Poor children! It would have to be England, I supposed. And London, I
supposed, though in my previous refugee days I had always
been plagued by abscesses and ulcers when I tried to live there.
My wife loves London, of course. But how could we find a house
large enough and cheap enough for us all? And what about
schools for the children? And a nurse for the baby? And who
would care for our cats in Binijiny?

I had forgotten that, this being a total fiesta in honour of San Sebastián, the Patron Saint of Palma, all offices would be closed. Nothing doing until the next day; meanwhile church bells rang, boot-blacks pestered me, Civil Guards sported their full-dress poached-egg head-dresses and stark white gloves, and the population drifted aimlessly about the streets in their Sunday best.

As I stood check-mated outside the Bar Fígaro, a dapper Spaniard greeted me and asked politely after my health, my family and my busy pen, remarking what a pity it was that so few of my books were available in Spanish and French translation. I couldn't place him. He was probably a shirtmaker, or a hotel receptionist, or a Tennis Club Committeeman, or a senior Post Office clerk, whom I would recognize at once in his proper setting. Awkward!

'Come, Don Roberto, let us take a coffee together!' I agreed miserably, suspecting that, like everyone else, he wanted to cross-examine me on contemporary English Literature. But, after all, why shouldn't I continue to humour these gentle, simple, hospitable people? It was their island, not mine. And the Bar Figaro has sentimental memories for me.

We sat down. I offered him my pouch of black tobacco and a packet of *Marfil* papers. He rolled cigarettes for us both, handed me mine to lick and stick, snapped his lighter for me, and said: 'Well, distinguished friend, may we expect your visit soon? I ventured to send you an official reminder only yesterday. When will you find time to withdraw your Residence Permit – *"para retirar la Autorización de Residencia"* – from our files? It has been waiting there, duly signed, since late October.'

In my gratitude I gave Don Emilio an hour's expert literary criticism of the works of such English *gran-novelistas* as Mohgum, Ootschley, Estrong and Oowohg, promising not only to visit him at the earliest opportunity with the necessary 1 peseta 55 céntimos stampage but to lend him a contraband Argentine edition of Lorca's *Poems*.

God grant him many years! What a sleepless night he saved me!

THE VISCOUNTESS AND THE
SHORT-HAIRED GIRL

TWENTY-FIVE years ago, Master Toni, the squat, bald, dark-eyed, muscular, smiling proprietor of our village garage, invited me to dinner on his Saint's Day. The fiesta of San Antonio, which falls on January 17th, is always marked in Majorcan villages by the priest's rather hilarious aspersion with holy water of as many asses, mules, sheep-dogs and motor-cars as his parishioners may care to bring along to the Church door; and by a bonfire, lighted on the previous evening, which around midnight has usually died down low enough for *buñuelos* – a sort of doughnut – to be fried over the embers. On this occasion, the fire being still alive after morning mass, Master Toni's wife Doña Isabel sent her children with shovels to salvage lumps of glowing charcoal for the brazier under our dinner table. The main dish was missel-thrushes stewed in cabbage-leaves, with snails, octopus and saffron rice. We also ate smoked ham; slices of out-sized radish; the first pickled black olives of the season; Minorcan sheep-cheese; fig-bread; ordinary bread; and plenty of Binisalem red wine. I remember the missel-thrushes, because a German lady had been enraged to see a pile of them heaped on the garage floor that morning. 'How dare you massacre our beautiful German songbirds?' she screamed.

'Señora,' Master Toni answered, 'your German songbirds are ill-educated; they come to steal the olives. Olives are our main source of wealth: olives, and figs – figs such as I often watched you steal from my trees as you went down the path by our house this last September.'

Missel-thrushes are caught by a method once known as 'bat-fowling' in England, but now, I believe, extinct there. Two men station themselves a few paces apart, in one of the broad alleys down which the thrushes fly from their roosts among evergreen oaks near the mountain top. The bat-fowlers stretch across the alley a length of fishing-net lashed to two very long canes, held upright. At dawn, the first coveys of thrushes, known as *tordos d'auba*, descend on the olive groves and find themselves entangled in the net. Both canes are simultaneously flung forward and downward, after which the bat-fowlers wring the necks of whatever birds have been caught underneath. At about eight o'clock down flies a smaller wave of thrushes, known as *tordos de gran dia*; then no more can be expected until the *tordos de vispear*, or evening thrushes. Bat-fowling is one of the few sports in which the villagers engage. A mountain terraced steeply all the way up from the sea provides no level space large enough for a football field, or even a tennis court; and since 1906, when a passing traveller had his eye knocked out by a sling-stone flung by young Mateo of the Painted House – he had mischievously aimed at the man's pipe – the ancient Balearic sling has been officially banned even for rabbit-hunting.

Anyhow, Master Toni, having made merry on the Eve of San Antonio, and eaten quantities of *buñuelos*, had returned home for a couple of hours' sleep, then started off at five o'clock to catch *tordos d'auba* for our dinner. But along came the sexton, in overcoat and slippers, to say that his sister, Maria the Spaghetti-maker, was desperately ill again and that the Doctor must be fetched at once from Sóller. So Master Toni climbed into his antiquated Studebaker; and by the time the Doctor had attended to Maria (on her death-bed these past fifteen years) and been driven back to Sóller, only the despised *tordos de gran dia* were left to hunt. Nevertheless, Master Toni and a certain Sentiá Dog-beadle, the village odd-job man, managed between them to bag two dozen – a remarkable catch that year. And very good they tasted.

Perhaps I should explain that Maria Spaghetti-maker had never made any spaghetti; it was her great-grandmother who plied the trade, but the nickname persisted in the female line. There is now a grown-up grand-daughter who holds it, though she only sews gloves. Similarly, the timorous and greedy Sentiá Dog-beadle inherited his nickname from an ancestor whose task had been to keep stray dogs from taking sanctuary on hot days in the cool of Palma Cathedral. 'Sentiá' is short for Sebastian. There are almost too many things which need explanation, once one begins to tell stories about our village.

After dinner, over the coffee and brandy, I found it easy to swear that I had never eaten so well, or so much, in all my life.

'Not even in Piccadilly, Don Roberto?' asked Master Toni shrewdly.

'Certainly not, I assure you!'

'Well, Damián the Coachman, Sentiá Dog-beadle and I ate pretty well there, during our famous stay at the Regent *Palacio* Hotel.'

'Why have you never told me of this visit to London?'

'I am a busy man, you are a busy man. I have saved up the long history of the Viscountess and the Short-haired Girl for this fiesta.'

Here then is Master Toni's story, as I wrote it down that same evening. Respecting his inability to manage an initial *St, Sc, Sp* or *Sm* without an anticipatory *e*, I prefixed one to all the proper names which demanded it. Let that *e* stay as a convenient reminder of the estory-teller's Espanishness.

THE VISCOUNTESS AND THE SHORT-HAIRED GIRL

It all began one day in August when two gentlemen, both wearing black coats and striped trousers – hardly suitable clothes for the weather, which was of a barbarous heat – drove up in a very fine taxi from Palma and stopped at my garage. The chauffeur, who knew me, asked whether they might have a private word in my ear. 'At the gentlemen's service,' I answered, 'unless they are trying to sell me something. I am excessively short of money this month.'

One of the gentlemen, who could speak Spanish, heard what I said. He was a little game-cock of a man, and had a habit of tilting his head on one side inquiringly, as poultry often do. From his black mushroom hat, I judged him to be less important than the other, who wore a black silk stove-pipe hat. 'Then let me congratulate you, Don Antonio,' he said. 'My friend here, Mr P. P. Jonés, will soon remedy your financial straits. If you listen to his proposal, he will fill your pockets with silver *duros*. My own name is Charley Estrutt, at your service.'

'He does not require me to violate the Law?' I asked.

Mr Estrutt translated this question to Mr Jonés, who resembled a large, well-cured ham. Mr Jonés shook his head violently, saying: 'On the contrary!' – a phrase which I understood, the word 'contrary' being identical in our Majorcan idiom, though we sound it differently.

I asked them both upstairs, to take a coffee. They accepted, and when we had emptied our cups I waited until they should come to the point, after all Mr Estrutt's compliments on the beauty and tranquillity of our village. When he continued silent, I said boldly: 'By your gold watch-chains and your reticence, gentlemen, I judge you to be lawyers; and your black clothes indicate that you are here on business, not on a vacation. The labels on your brief-cases say "London". Therefore, since this village has had the honour of welcoming only one compatriot of yours during the past twelve months, that is to say a certain young girl with hair cut short like a boy's, who stayed for a week in May at the Hotel Bonsol with a tall foreigner from God-knows-where, may I conclude that your business somehow concerns her?'

Mr Estrutt's face lighted up. He said: 'You are very intelligent, Don Antonio! That is almost precisely the case, though Señor Jonés alone is a lawyer. In effect, he represents the short-haired girl's disconsolate mother, recently widowed.'

I asked: 'And your profession, Señor? Would it be inconvenient to divulge it?'

Mr Estrutt smiled. 'No inconvenience at all,' he said. 'I used to be an inspector in our Metropolitan Police force. I am now retired, and have become·a private detective employed by rich people to conduct delicate inquiries. The remuneration is better.'

I went on: 'By the formality of Mr Jonés's appearance, he must be a lawyer of great importance?'

Mr Estrutt whistled. 'He never accepts less than fifty thousand pesetas a week for a case! The fact is that the disconsolate mother in question reeks of money. Her father was a multi-millionaire from Chile. I worked for the family once; an illegitimate son of his happened to be blackmailing him.'

I remarked: 'One recognizes your accent as South American.'

He blushed a little: 'Yes, yes,' he said, 'you Spaniards despise South Americans for their abuse of your ancient tongue.'

Since Mr Charley Estrutt seemed a pleasant enough man, for all the ridiculous black mushroom-hat balanced on his knee, I assured him that here in Majorca we speak an even coarser dialect of Spanish than the Chileans. Our talk proceeded in this inconclusive manner until Mr Jonés, who did not understand a word, looked at his big gold watch and made some observation to Mr Estrutt. Clearly, the moment had come to discuss business. I told myself: 'These people can pay well. I shall certainly not accept the first price they offer – for whatever it is that they require of me.'

Mr Estrutt now put forward his proposal. He explained that the short-haired girl, a minor, having run away from a French convent where she was being educated, had been brutally kidnapped by a Bulgarian artist. The pair had, with great difficulty, been traced to our village. The disconsolate Viscountess, her mother, wished to collect sufficient sworn evidence about the tragedy to incarcerate this Bulgarian heretic for life. Yet scandal must be avoided at all costs, and therefore the Spanish police had not been invited to assist. Well, if I and two friends of mine could testify before an English judge to the Bulgarian's having dragged the wretched girl to our Hotel Bonsol, and there committed an offence against her, the unfortunate entanglement could be legally proved, and the criminal punished.

Mr Jonés, so Mr Estrutt told me, knew that I had conveyed the couple in my taxi from the mole at Palma to the Hotel Bonsol; that a certain Sebastian Vivés (meaning Sentiá Dogbeadle) had carried their bags up to a bedroom at the said hotel; and that Damián Frau, meaning 'Damián the Coachman', the hotelkeeper, had brought them breakfast in bed, on a tray, the next morning. Mr Jonés hoped that we would kindly visit London in a month's time, to avenge the honour of a noble English house, more particularly because the disconsolate Viscountess was a very devout Catholic; he had heard of our Majorcan zeal for the sanctity of a Catholic home.

I replied: 'Speaking between ourselves, Mr Estrutt, the short-haired girl seemed to be in no way acting under duress; in fact, on our journey from Palma she was embracing and caressing the heretic – as I could not help seeing in my driving-mirror – with every appearance of genuine enjoyment.'

Imagine my surprise, when Mr Estrutt winked at me (but with the eye hidden from Mr Jonés) and answered: 'Don Antonio, in England our young girls have been completely demoralized by the excitements of the recent war. Moreover, the poor child may have feared that, unless she caressed him in public, he would ill-treat her most cruelly once they were alone.'

To be brief, the terms offered us three witnesses for a visit to London were twenty pesetas a day, besides travelling expenses, bed, board, laundry, wine, cigars, and anything else within reason that we might need, not omitting sight-seeing excursions; and another five hundred pesetas each, if we gave our evidence in a way that convinced the Judge. He also asked, would I be kind enough to repeat this offer to my friends, Don Sebastián and Don Damián?

I wanted to know how long we should be away, and Mr Estrutt estimated that we should be home again within three weeks. My reply was that we should answer yes or no after a night's reflection; but Mr Jonés urged us to sign a contract that same night. He intended to catch the Barcelona boat.

Well, I left the Englishmen at my house while I went to the Bonsol and took Damián for a little stroll. 'You are a knowledgeable man,' I said, 'and acquainted with the ways of the rich. I have been invited to visit London as witness in a kidnapping case. Now, for a commission of this sort, are twenty pesetas a day, all found, sufficient? I shall be away for about three weeks.'

Damián stopped, gazed at me in wonder, spat with emphasis, and said: 'Ka, man, you would be a fool to refuse! Myself, I would gladly go without pay – if only to escape from this dull hole and see grand civilization again.'

Damián, you must understand, had earned his nickname himself as coachman to the President of the Argentine Republic, and still remembered those days of glory. He added: 'But what, in the Devil's name, has the kidnapping case to do with you?'

'Patience, friend,' said I. 'First advise me whether the fee is correct in principle.'

He considered the matter. Then he spat again and said: 'In principle, Toni, you should insist upon thirty pesetas a day. The English, as a rule, allow fifty per cent for bargaining where Spaniards are concerned.'

'And five hundred pesetas on top of that!'

'A tidy sum, by God! I wish I had the chance to earn so much by a three weeks' holiday.'

'Then be joyful, Damián! You are invited too!'

He took this for a joke, but when he heard my story he threw his hat so high into the air that it sailed over the terrace, down the valley and into the torrent, and was not found again.

We went off together at once and acquainted Sentiá with his luck. As Sentiá was earning hardly five pesetas a day, a casual labourer's wage at that time, his eyes truly bulged with greed. Yet we had to pour a deal of *coñac* down his throat before we could persuade him to join us. Never having left the island in his life, Sentiá cherished a tremendous fear of being drowned by a tempest at sea. Finally, however, he agreed; and after Damián and I had won the extra ten pesetas a day from Mr Jonés, without a struggle, we took Sentiá along to the Mayor, who was the local Justice of the Peace, and persuaded him to witness the amended contract. In effect, we all signed the document, which had been prepared by a Spanish notary. Sentiá scrawled his name and rubric with a trembling hand, saying: 'God grant that this be not my death warrant!'

Nobody from our village had ever seen the shores of England, and it seemed a great thing for us three to be the first. Naturally, our wives did not favour the adventure, unless they could come too; is that not so, Isabel? But Mr Estrutt declared that such an arrangement would be most unwise, even if we cared to pay those extra passages and expenses out of what we should earn. Then Sentiá's wife created a scandal. She called us fools for not asking fifty pesetas a day, and a thousand at the close, Mr Jonés having agreed to our demand so readily. She knew in her heart, she shrieked, that I had been bribed by the Englishmen to keep the payment low. But Isabel here, and Damián's wife, Angela, told her to be silent, since the offer was a handsome one and the document had now been securely signed.

Nothing more. After promising to write frequently, and making our wives promise to behave themselves during our absence and keep the children in good order, we declared, hands on heart, that we should never have dreamed of leaving the village even for three weeks, were the preservation of a Catholic home not at stake. Indeed, the women of this island are hardly less zealous in this matter than Mr Estrutt suggested; and I doubt whether any of the three concerned would have let us go for the money alone. I learned later that, while we were away, Isabel here spent half her days in church, praying for my safety and for the spiritual consolation of the unhappy widow.

Well, you have made that journey more than once, Don Roberto, so it is nothing new to you, but for me it was tremendous once we had crossed the frontier into France! It seemed a miracle that within half a mile of country the aspect of so many things could suddenly change: the clothes, the language, the uniforms, the telegraph-poles, the colour of the mail-boxes, the very shape and taste of the bread!

Mr Estrutt had fetched us by taxi from the village in order to shepherd us through the customs, the passport inspections, and other troubles. He seemed a very different man, once he had emerged from the shadow of the serious Mr Jonés: being dressed now in a cream-coloured gaberdine suit, a hard straw-hat with a canary-yellow ribbon, and carrying a gold-headed cane. He also began to tell us jokes of the sort we call 'green'. He arrived at my house somewhat fatigued, having spent the previous night at the Bar Macarena. Perhaps you know the Macarena? If so, you will consider it no small feat that he escaped alive from those gipsies and even contrived to preserve his wallet, his pearl tie-pin, and his gold-headed cane. The Metropolitan Police must be a race of lions.

We embarked on the night-boat to Barcelona, and the tears streamed down our wives' faces as they waved us good-bye from the quay; and I confess that, for a moment, I wondered whether my decision had been a prudent one. As for Sentiá, he was in a lamentable condition, and Mr Estrutt made him swallow a tablet which rapidly put him to sleep.

As soon as we were clear of Palma harbour, Mr Estrutt invited Damián and me to join him in the Bar. Over a *coñac*, he said: 'Boys, presently I shall go to the cabin to restore my loss of sleep, but first let me be honest with you. That kidnapping story, you must understand, is a work of fantasy. The old Viscountess and I thought it out together as a means of convincing your wives that it was their duty to let you go. Moreover, we decided that we should say no word about it to Mr Jonés. Though an intelligent lawyer, he is insular and highly moral, and would never practise a little deception even to assist a good cause.'

'Well, then for God's sake tell us the truth at once!' Damián demanded fiercely.

'The truth,' he replied, 'is that this old witch of a Viscountess lost her husband, the Viscount, three months ago – he fell from the balcony of their bedroom at the Hotel Esplendido, Cannes, and perhaps it truly was an accident – who can say? But no matter! The widow is now enamoured of a retired officer in the King's Bodyguard; and this officer, whose profession is to direct a pack of foxhounds, possessses a large estate, but little money to maintain it – only a mountain of gambling debts. In fact, he is willing to marry the old trout, who is not bad-looking by candle light, if one places the candle well behind her and wears sunglasses. The sole bar to their union has been his young wife, an actress, who married him not long ago, thinking he was rich but, finding that he had cheated her, now considers herself free to take what consolation she can find in the company of others. Yet she carefully covers her tracks when she goes hunting – hunting men, not foxes, of course. She is good-looking, you agree?'

Since Mr Estrutt was clearly referring to the short-haired girl, Damián and I pronounced that, yes, she was a delicious morsel, though a little thin perhaps, and her eyes of too pallid a blue.

Mr Estrutt went on. 'So you see, boys, that your testimony will be most valuable to the Viscountess. If the foxhunting officer wins his decree of divorce from the short-haired girl, the Viscountess can then marry him, having paid all the expenses of the trial. Now, this is how I enter the story. Last May, the short-haired girl was invited to stay with her elder sister at Tossa on the Costa Brava; but when the Viscountess sent me there in July to make inquiries, I found that after a single morning at Tossa the girl had crossed over to Majorca at the side of the Bulgarian artist, whom she had met on the Paris train. I discreetly followed their tracks and obtained your names, without visiting your village, from a friendly corporal of Coastguards. With such information I went back to London, where Mr Jonés resolved to make the Viscountess pay a capital sum for his corroboration of my story. I should add that other acts of adultery are charged against the short-haired girl; but this is the only one which Mr Jonés at present dares to bring into Court. Well, boys, do you forgive me for the lies I told you?'

I laughed. 'Ka, man, it is all the same to Damián and me,' I said, 'so long as we are paid according to our contract.'

Mr Estrutt slapped my back and cried: 'I like your spirit, Toni, if I may call you that? And you must call me Charley, as everyone does who is anyone at all! Now, another thing. When you asked for those extra ten pesetas a day, I informed Mr Jonés that, being staunch Catholics, you were dead against the marriage of divorced persons, and must therefore obtain at least thirty pesetas in all before testifying in a matter that so little interested you. Now I have said enough; but I wager that we will enjoy a wonderful time in London. By the bye, you must not let my love-sick old baggage of a Viscountess know that I have given you the true story; and it would be well, surely, not to let the good Sentiá into our secret, either. It might unsettle his ideas about me.'

Then we refilled our glasses and toasted the Viscountess, the late Viscount, the short-haired girl, the foxhunting officer, Mr P. P. Jonés and the Judge, together with many other persons more remotely connected with the affair, in a multitude of *coñacs*. Mr Estrutt did not restore his loss of sleep during that particular night.

Despite our excesses we reached port safely, and later ate a grand meal at the Hotel *Palacio* of Barcelona, with lobster mayonnaise, French wines, and everything of the best. Sentiá Dog-beadle, feeling much embarrassed by the elegant ambience, opened his mouth only a little when he introduced food and kept his enormous red hands under the table while not using them. But Damián gloried in this brief return to the high life he had enjoyed at the Presidential Palace of Buenos Aires, and recounted more about his past than I should ever have believed, though we had known each other twenty years or longer.

After a night spent on a train with very narrow beds, we came to Paris and were taken in a taxi to the Gare du Nord. At once Mr Estrutt said: 'Boys, will you do me a great favour? I am off into the city. Please wait for me in the restaurant yonder, order what food and drink may be convenient, but be careful to enter into conversation with no one at all! My orders from the Viscountess are never to leave you out of my sight. I shall be back in time to catch our train.'

Damián asked: 'What is this great favour worth to us, Don Charley?'

He answered: 'If you protect me, Damián, I shall protect you. Is that not sufficient?'

Since Mr Estrutt had all the money and our tickets, his answer could not fail to satisfy Damián. Yet it was embarrassing that two Palma businessmen whom I knew by sight should enter the Station Restaurant and greet me. I gazed blankly at them and pretended to be German. I even turned to Damián, saying: *'Heute ist Sonntag!'* which was all the German I knew. Damián, who is quick-witted enough, shook his head and answered: *'Donnerwetter!'* which was all the German *he* knew. The two Palma men sat down at a table in the far corner, and from there stared at us. We three dared not talk to one another in our own language until they had gone out again. The food, by the way, was not good.

This was two o'clock. Our train to Calais would depart at six o'clock; but four o'clock had passed, and five, and half past five, and a quarter to six, and still there we sat. At ten minutes to six, Damián said: 'I like this very little. What can have happened to Mr Estrutt?'

'Patience!' said I. 'He's a good fellow and will keep his word.'

But Sentiá grew more and more nervous. He cried out that we should never have come: we have been decoyed to Paris for some business of the Devil, he said – to be sold in slavery to the Moors, it might· be. Had he not been plagued by a black foreboding on the day of the contract?

We made no reply. At last Damián stood up: 'Well,' he said, 'let us put on our overcoats and have everything ready. Mr Estrutt will, I have no doubt, appear mathematically at the last moment.'

Even as he spoke, Mr Estrutt burst into the restaurant, paid our small bill with a single large banknote, and rushed us off to the platform. We caught the Calais train with thirty seconds to spare.

'My God, that was close!' exclaimed Mr Estrutt, sinking into his seat. 'Nevertheless, I found what I went out to find!'

Damián asked: 'Was it a nice tender chicken?'

Mr Estrutt took the joke in good part. 'Alas, no,' he answered, 'this was serious business, not gastronomic pleasure. You shall hear about it one day. But I thank you very much for your great patience, boys! Now, what about a game of cards?' So we played *truc* until we reached Calais.

Contrary to all we had heard, the English Channel was as smooth as glass, and on the other side we found an altogether different country again, green and beautiful! Though it was already autumn, the sun shone without pause all the time we spent there. I cannot imagine why Spaniards call the English climate a bad one. At Dover, a huge Rolls-Royce limousine took us by road to London, in which we drove for hours, it seemed, through a wilderness of streets, and across the river *Tamesis*. Finally we came to Piccadilly Circus with its fantastic coloured signs, and its hurrying crowds. Close by stood the Regent *Palacio* Hotel, where a private suite awaited us on the first floor complete with two bathrooms, a dining-room, and every comfort in the world, including waiters to wait on us and a barber to shave us every day after breakfast!

Mr Estrutt was a humorous man. On the next morning he took Damián and me aside, and said: 'When the old hen enters to greet you, do not omit to condole with her on the fate of her

poor daughter. The more profuse your condolences, the more it
will disturb her conscience because of the kidnapping fiction;
and the less carefully will she examine our expense account.
Flatter her, too! I should have explained that we occupy this
private suite owing to her fear of your making contact with the
general public. I myself suggested that, were the short-haired
girl's lawyer to hear of your presence here, he would surely try
to impress the true story upon you; with the result that you
might not wish to testify. It is a situation very useful for us. We
shall play on these fears of hers, and enjoy a marvellous life
together; and I shall never (in theory) let you stray from my
sight.'

Scarcely had he spoken, when the Viscountess herself came
through the door, wearing a fur-coat of black sable-skins, a black
hat, and black gloves. She also kept a black-edged handkerchief
pressed to her black eyes. After welcoming us in fluent Spanish,
broken by many sobs, she thanked us from the bottom of a
mother's heart for our readiness to rescue her daughter from
that criminal Bulgarian heretic – whom the police, thanks be to
the Virgin of Guadalupe! now held in safe custody. Sentiá wept
too, and Damián assured her that he also had suffered a like
tragic sorrow – his own daughter having once been decoyed
away from home by an English Lord, ruined and cast aside like
an old glove. Damián, as you know, is childless; and can lie
without a tremor of his wicked face, which resembles carved
mahogany. This tale impressed even Mr Estrutt, who patted
Damián on the back and said in admiration: 'I wonder, Señor
Frau, that your heart ever permitted you to forgive the English
aristocracy. It must be ruled by a very pious spirit.'

A comedy, in short! For myself, I told the Viscountess that
only so great a distress as hers could have persuaded me to aban-
don my island, my wife and my children, and venture to this
unknown, this most terrifying city. The Viscountess, still occupied with her handkerchief, replied that only a Spaniard could
have spoken so nobly. She was no less devout a Catholic than I,
she declared, and God and the Virgin would bring the righteous
cause to triumph.

I spoke what came into my mind. 'The Bulgarian heretic

looked a veritable ruffian,' I said. 'Let us hope that they hang him high! Imagine any well-nurtured girl trusting herself to the beast! Yet that your poor daughter did so, must surely be a sign of her formidable innocence ... But what surprises me in this painful affair is how you, Señora Viscountess, can be her mother – you do not look half old enough!'

'I married very young,' she explained, drying her eyes again.

When she went away, we opened the windows in order to drive out the strong perfume of violets and sandalwood which she had left behind.

The trial was postponed for a fortnight, because of some legal complication; we should now be absent for another three weeks at least, but none of us cared a tassel. On Mr Estrutt's advice, however, we told Mr Jonés that our business would surely go to ruin in our absence, and that we should need fifty pesetas a day, and one thousand at the close. The Viscountess was delighted to meet our demands, and we were delighted to sign a new contract. Never in my life had I earned so much money for nothing at all!

Mr Estrutt, I should tell you, had that same enormous Rolls-Royce limousine at his disposal whenever we wished to take an outing. He showed us the principal sights of London: the Tower and the Tower Bridge, and the Historical Waxworks, and the Museum of Animals and Birds, and the Docks, and the wonderful Botanical Gardens where one enters a tropical palm-house and nearly dies of the heat! Also the Law Courts, where we would soon give evidence, and many other places; with *cinés* or music-halls nearly every evening.

Mr Estrutt also took us to visit his wives, first explaining to Sentiá that polygamy was customary among the Metropolitan Police force. Two of these wives lived in different parts of London – each occupying a small red brick house with a flower garden. We Majorcans sat in the sunny garden drinking beer and smoking cigarettes, while Mr Estrutt went upstairs to talk family affairs with his wife. Each wife also had a little boy, with whom we played, throwing a ball about on the lawn. We next met a third wife, who had a big house near Brighton. She seemed very rich, though not nearly so beautiful as the other

two. The rich one gave us whisky and cigars, while we Majorcans sat on the lawn and played with a poodle-dog. Mr Estrutt
afterwards showed us a new gold cigarette-lighter, his birthday
present from this lady. The fourth wife, however, who lived
many kilometres to the north of London, was old, ugly and ill-
tempered. To judge from her curt greeting to Mr Estrutt, she
must have been the head-wife. Or so Damián said, who had
seen similar behaviour in Moorish families while doing his military service at Melilla; the head-wife was invariably jealous and
spiteful.

One day Mr Estrutt took me aside and said: 'Toni, my
friend, I think we need a little change. I have no complaint to
make against the *Palacio*, but even the best hotel grows weari-
some after three weeks. Nor should I wish my old clothes-rack
of a Viscountess to think that I have forgotten the serious task
that she has imposed on me. Be prepared, therefore, to move at
midnight; but, as usual, not a word to Sentiá!'

That night, Sentiá retired at about eleven o'clock and was
soon snoring. Then Mr Estrutt telephoned the Viscountess,
speaking in tones of great seriousness. Damián and I heard her
frightened voice ring high through the apparatus. Mr Estrutt
answered: 'Yes, yes, yes, my lady!' several times. He told her,
I believe, that though a Spanish-speaking waiter had been bribed
by the short-haired girl's lawyer to provide us with the true
story, his own prompt appearance fortunately interrupted the
conversation as soon as it started. The Viscountess urgently
begged Mr Estrutt to remove us to another hotel at once.

We packed our bags and woke Sentiá. Damián said: 'Lad,
we are in great danger! The Bulgarian heretic has discovered
us. Pack for your life!'

The Rolls-Royce limousine was waiting at the hotel door
when we emerged. The Viscountess sat inside, very nervous,
and wearing a purple scarf pulled over her face so that she
might not be recognized. Mr Estrutt agreed that no time should
be lost, and the chauffeur drove off without delay. We purred
away at great velocity, but the Viscountess felt certain that
we were being pursued. She ordered the chauffeur to dodge
down side-streets at random, twisting and turning until we had

shaken off the pursuit. The chauffeur obeyed but, however wild his course, she continued to peer through the rear-window and cry: 'There it is!' The same car again!' Sentiá, sweating with terror, kept crossing himself and asking: 'Do you think they will kill us?'

After an hour of this foolishness we reached open country. The chauffeur backed the Rolls-Royce down a lane, and turned off its lights. We sat in the darkness for another hour, while a stream of cars raced by. When at last the Viscountess was confident that she had cheated our pursuers, we turned back by devious ways, and at two o'clock in the morning found a new private suite awaiting us in the Estrand *Palacio* Hotel (hardly a kilometre distant from the Regent *Palacio*) where, for secrecy, we were admitted by the service door. Strange, was it not, that each of the hotels we visited on our journey was named the *Palacio*? But poor Sentiá had died a hundred deaths that night!

We wrote home once every week to say we were well, that business prospered, and that we trusted all would end normally; adding those graceful concluding phrases which one learns at school. Our families replied in the same manner, though more religiously. Nothing of importance had happened to the village during our absence, except that a great thunderstorm had torn many branches from my olive grove, and caused the walls of three terraces to collapse.

One day Mr Estrutt asked me: 'My friend, do you still enjoy this life?'

I answered: 'Enormously! Only think! under this new contract I shall soon have gained enough money for the purchase of a fine American car; giving my old Studebaker in partial payment. A just reward for all my hard labours! But, Don Charley, in one thing you have deceived us!'

'How deceived you?' he asked with surprise.

'Well,' I answered, 'you have fed us nobly, you have given us good beds, good drinks, and admirable Havana cigars, you have taken us often to the *ciné* and the music-halls and once, even, to the Opera, besides showing us the famous sights of London ... But you have not ministered to other pressing needs of ours!

That is, as we say in Majorca, like asking children to view the confectioner's shop, but buying them no caramels. Though we are all good Catholics, none of us happens to be a monk.'

(How fortunate, Don Roberto, that at this particular stage of my story Isabel has gone off, to wash the dishes, I suppose, and feed the hens; otherwise I should have been forced to omit the subsequent incident. In any case, I must keep it short.)

Well, Mr Estrutt understood me before the words were well out of my mouth. 'If there is nothing else, my friend Toni, this can readily be arranged,' said he, 'but I had feared to make any suggestion that might offend your sensibilities. Not being members of the Metropolitan Police force, I thought you might consider yourselves less free in certain respects than I am. Very well, I shall at once telephone to an associate of mine who orders such matters. I promise that you will have no further cause to complain of having been deceived.'

He kept his word. That night after coffee, we heard a soft knocking at the door and in walked three beautiful smiling blondes, all wearing the tightest of silk dresses. Mr Estrutt at once made the necessary introductions, taking care to give us fictitious names. Then he uncorked a prodigiously large bottle of champagne and filled seven glasses. I quickly engaged the attention of the leading young lady; and Damián was not far behind me in securing the second. But Sentiá, who, as usual, had not been informed of the arrangement, sat perplexed and paralyzed, goggling like a great moribund fish, when he saw the two young ladies perch on our knees. The third had addressed herself to Mr Estrutt, who explained, however, that the shy gentleman in the corner was her chosen sweetheart; he himself would merely be our interpreter. Although disappointed, she flung herself on Sentiá with a fine pretence of enthusiasm. Sentiá leaped up, knocking over his chair, and retreated to the bathroom; but the determined girl thrust her foot between the door and the jamb, calling on Mr Estrutt for help. Mr Estrutt pushed the door open, and when she had entered, locked it behind her.

I shall say no more than that Damián and I needed no interpreter.... But, Lord, how ashamed of himself Sentiá was afterwards, and how we laughed! Of one thing we could be sure: once safely home again, he would never reveal one word of the proceedings, not even in the confessional!

The Viscountess came to visit us the next morning, with her usual tale of how God and the Virgin would uphold the right, and how greatly she appreciated our chivalrous defence of her Catholic home. Then, noticing suddenly how ill-at-ease Sentiá appeared to be, she laid a black-gloved hand on his shoulder to comfort him. 'My poor fellow,' she cried, 'you must miss your wife deeply!'

At that, Sentiá Dog-beadle wept like a little child. Fearful that he would make some foolish remark, I hastened to say: 'Yes, my lady, Sebastián here misses his Joana terribly, not having expected to be away so many weeks. Nor is he the only one of us who suffers. Don Damián and I are equally sensitive; but, for the sake of your unfortunate daughter, we try to suppress our misery.'

The Viscountess promised that we should never regret our visit, and charitably dabbed Sentiá's eyes with her scented black lace handkerchief. But even that did not console him!

Two days later, the divorce case began. Mr Estrutt sat with us in the Law Court and explained in a whisper who was who, and what was happening. The foxhunter had presented four or five charges of adultery in respect of the short-haired girl, but Mr Jonés and his squadron of lawyers chose from them only those two that seemed easiest to prove: namely, the affair with the Bulgarian artist at Damián's hotel, and an earlier affair in Paris with a rich Escottish manufacturer named Simon Macwilly. Mr Macwilly was married and, shocked to find himself cited as co-respondent in this case, had agreed to pay the short-haired girl's defence, so as to protect himself against the complaints of his wife.

It appears that an official of the British Embassy at Paris had lent Mr Macwilly his apartment during a temporary absence, and that the short-haired girl passed the night there with Mr Macwilly. This Embassy official, however, did not wish to be accused of pandering to his friend's vices, and when Mr Estrutt and Mr Jonés went to make inquiries of him, immediately sent his two servants away into the country, thus preventing them from becoming witnesses. The only relevant evidence could now come from a taxi-driver who had conducted the couple, with their bags, to the door of the apartment; and this would, perhaps, be found insufficient. Yet Mr Estrutt, by studying the calendar, reckoned that the short-haired girl must have spent another night somewhere in Paris, after vacating the Embassy official's apartment. Therefore, during our long wait at the Gare du Nord, he had persuaded his friends among the French Police to scrutinize the registers of certain hotels. Sure enough, they found a small hotel on the left bank of the *Sena* where Mr Macwilly had signed the register for himself and Mrs Macwilly on the night in question. The French hotelkeeper and his wife demanded an expense fee which Mr Jonés thought excessive, but which they refused to make less; to give the required evidence, they said, might injure their establishment's name for discretion. The Viscountess, however, would pay almost anything for this testimony, and an agreement was reached.

The charge of having committed adultery with Mr Macwilly was heard first. Now, on the previous afternoon the advocate, a King's Councillor, had explained to us just what questions he would ask, and how we should reply. This drama we rehearsed over and over again with the help of an interpreter; but Sentiá Dog-beadle proved so slow at learning his lesson that the advocate cried impatiently: 'Man, man, I hardly dare call you as a witness; for fear you may ruin our case! Your companions have far greater agility of mind.' We implored Sentiá to gather his wits, since three thousand pesetas hung on our satisfying the Judge; but he seemed like a lost man.

'You will be called next, boys!' Mr Estrutt warned us, as the first witness appeared and took the oath on a large Bible, which he kissed. Sentiá went whiter than a sheet at the warning, and began crossing himself like a madman. I felt uneasy myself, though with little cause, being now word-perfect in my lesson.

To be brief: the French hotelkeepers identified the short-haired girl, who was now wearing black in competition with the Viscountess, and swore to her presence at their establishment that night, in company with the fat, bald man who signed the register as Simon Macwilly. The couple had engaged two bedrooms with a communicating door, the key of which was on the short-haired girl's side.

When summoned to give evidence herself, the short-haired girl admitted having spent a night in that hotel, but strongly denied the charge of adultery. Mr Macwilly, she said, was liable to heart attacks and, as his only reliable friend in Paris, she had wished to be at hand to attend him if he were taken ill during the hours of darkness. Our advocate put it to her that misconduct had certainly taken place between them. She pretended to be outraged and cried: 'Misconduct, why, that is ridiculous! Mr Macwilly is an ancient man of sixty!'

It was a grave error in tactics. At once our advocate addressed the Judge (who was wearing an enormous wig, I did not ask why). Having observed the Judge's angry expression when the short-haired girl implied that, at sixty, a man is ancient and altogether spent, he said very shrewdly: 'My Lord, I shall call no more witnesses; but let my plea rest upon the evidence you have now heard.' For this Judge had not only just celebrated his sixtieth birthday: he had emphasized it by a third marriage!

Mr Estrutt had difficulty in repressing his joy when he heard these words spoken. He clapped Sentiá on the shoulder and whispered in his ear: 'My lad, you are saved!' Then he similarly told Damián and me: 'You also are saved. You will not be required to give evidence after all.'

Damián flew into a temper and asked in a loud voice: 'What of my thousand pesetas? I am being robbed. Why should I not give evidence?'

The Judge glared at Damián in great anger, calling for order in Court.

Mr Estrutt whispered: 'You madman, of course you will be paid!'

At that, Damián subsided, muttering.

We listened to the Judge's summing-up, and his decision that he could not believe the story told by this shameless young woman, and doubted whether anyone else present could believe it either. Then he praised our advocate for his great restraint in not pressing the second charge, and thus perhaps exposing the wretched woman as a common prostitute – since two proved charges of adultery, she must be aware, would under English Law earn her that disgraceful appellation!

In brief, he granted the divorce, and ordered the short-haired girl to pay all the legal costs of the case. Her advocate did not appeal from this decision, and so the case ended . . .

But that is not quite the end of my story. When the Judge and all the fashionable spectators had dispersed, there remained in Court only ourselves, the French hotelkeeper and his wife, several lawyers and their clerks, some ushers, the short-haired girl and the Viscountess. The costs of the case having been paid by Mr Macwilly's lawyers, the Viscountess came running up with eyes that shone like stars, and kissed us each in turn on both cheeks, including Mr Estrutt. She cried: 'God and the Virgin have listened to my prayers!'

It then amused me to say: 'Heartiest congratulations, my lady. Yet your poor daughter there seems quite overcome by distress. Perhaps she grieves for the fate of that Bulgarian heretic? Or could it be that she fears you will never forgive her?'

'Indeed, friend!' she cried. 'How stupid I am! I must make my peace with her at once.'

She hurried across to the short-haired girl, followed by Mr Estrutt, who was a most inquisitive man. He heard her say: 'My dear girl, you put up a very good fight, I must admit, and I do not wish to triumph over your misery, having suffered this sort of trouble myself once. What do you propose to do now?'

The short-haired girl smiled back at her faintly and replied: 'How can I tell? I have lost everything! Though Mr Macwilly has paid the costs of the case, his wife would never agree to a divorce, even if I consented to marry him, which I have no intention of doing. Boris is the man I love. Yet I have not a copper to call my own, and neither has Boris.'

The Viscountess kissed her on the forehead. 'My poor innocent,' she said, cooing like a pigeon. 'You should never have chosen an artist as your prospective husband, and really, were you not rather imprudent to tease the old Judge as you did? How much money would put you right with the world again?'

The short-haired girl thought for a moment. Then she said slowly: 'I fear I could hardly manage with less than ten thousand pounds. Boris and I might start some business with that, I suppose.'

'Let me make it twenty thousand!' cried the Viscountess in a burst of commiseration, producing her cheque-book and a gold fountain-pen. She signed the cheque then and there.

We Majorcans, too, profited from her generosity to the extent of still another thousand pesetas each; and six months later, we heard that she had married her foxhunter. On the very same day, but in a different city, the short-haired girl was united with the Bulgarian artist. They bought a *pensión* near San Sebastián, which is now very luxurious and always crowded; so Mr Estrutt recently informed me on a picture postcard. He wrote that his wife had accompanied him to San Sebastián for a holiday, and that he wished Damián Frau and I could have been present to share their fun. He did not specify which wife; but perhaps he had recently married a fifth, unknown to us, with the money that the Viscountess paid him.

You may wonder, as we all did, why the Viscountess, however fabulously rich, wasted so much money on the case when, by offering the short-haired girl twenty thousand pounds before the trial, she might have persuaded her not to defend the action. Well, the answer, supplied by Mr Estrutt, was that Mr P. P. Jonés advised against this course, which would have been a crime known as 'collusion', and therefore in conflict with his high moral principles. Besides, why should he deprive himself of an excessively profitable legal case? Again, the short-haired girl prided herself on having shown such prudence that no charge could possibly be proved against her; but she had not reckoned with a detective of the experience and perspicacity possessed by my friend, Mr Charley Estrutt!

A TOAST TO AVA GARDNER

In Spain, a married woman keeps her maiden name, but tacks on her husband's after a *de*. Thus, on marrying Wifredo Las Rocas, our Majorcan friend Rosa, born an Espinosa, became Rosa Espinosa de Las Rocas – a very happy combination. It means 'Lady Thorny Rose from the Rocks'. Rosa was much luckier than her maternal cousin Dolores Fuertes, who thoughtlessly married a lawyer named Tomás Barriga, and is now Dolores Fuertes de Barriga, or 'Violent Pains of the Stomach'. My wife and I first met Rosa at a Palma store. We were complaining bitterly, in English, of an age-old Majorcan superstition that the sun shines brightly throughout the year, and that consequently no trouble about drying clothes can ever imaginably arise. Majorcans provide no airing-closets in even their grandest houses, and scorn that old-fashioned English contrivance, the nursery towel-horse, which allows harassed mothers to keep abreast of their children's washing during long rainy spells. We had by now visited every furniture shop in Palma, searching for one, but been greeted only by shrugs and smiles.

Then Rosa piped up at my elbow, in beautiful clear English, with hardly a trace of a Spanish accent: 'Excuse me! I could not help overhearing your conversation. My husband Wifredo Las Rocas will, I am sure, be delighted to make you a towel-horse. He knows all about towel-horses. My dear old English nurse, the late Nanny Parker, brought a towel-horse with her when she came to us from the British Embassy at Madrid; but I'm afraid my elder sister in Saragossa has it now. If you care to come along with me ...'

Wifredo and his partner, Anibal Tulipán, worked in a large furniture factory on the outskirts of Palma. Though originally they owned fifty per cent each of the factory shares, the building got badly damaged by fire; so the Central Bank rebuilt and restocked it for them at the price of a controlling interest. Wifredo and Anibal were, in fact, reduced to mere employees of the Bank, subject to dismissal if they failed to show a profit – an uncomfortable position in times as difficult as those, for men so proud.

Anibal looked after supplies and sales; Wifredo, after design, production and personnel. They had been brothers-in-law, but the death of Wifredo's sister from an overdose of sleeping-pills, taken in protest against Anibal's too serious liaison with a dentist's receptionist, snapped the family tie; and if ever two men were temperamentally more unsuited to become partners, these were they. Anibal, who loved all things German, especially metaphysics, music and sauerkraut, closely resembled Goering in appearance, and had a truly Wagnerian ill-temper; often, when he felt cross, he would emulate Adolf Hitler by throwing himself on the floor and biting the carpet. Until the war ended victoriously for the Allies, Wifredo – tall, fair, and rangy – was careful to conceal his strongly anglophile tendencies. These had been excited some years previously when he first fell in love with Rosa and came under the posthumous spell of the celebrated Nanny Parker. Nanny Parker, on entering the Espinosa household, had brought with her a bound series of the *Illustrated London News*, dating from 1906 to 1925, and kept adding a fresh one every year. In 1936, the outbreak of the Spanish Civil War and Nanny Parker's death – under a fast car driven by a party of non-intervening Italian airmen, remember? – closed the series. But a constant study of these volumes had made Wifredo an expert in all things English for the thirty years that they covered.

When Rosa introduced us to Wifredo, and asked whether he could supply a nursery towel-horse, he agreed with enthusiasm, seeing in us a helpful source of information about all that had happened to the British race since the death of George V. The outcome was an almost breathtaking towel-horse, stout and capacious as a church, in solid mahogany, with fluted rails and brass knobs – and that at a period when mahogany was practically unobtainable on the island. Wifredo charged us only a nominal sum for this masterpiece, assuring us that the pleasure was entirely his.

Then Anibal heard about the towel-horse from the factory foreman, flew into one of his infernal rages, called Wifredo all sorts of gross names, and accused him of cheating the business, wasting valuable materials, delaying the execution of other orders, and allying himself with certain ancient and inveterate enemies of Spain. He even threatened to bring the ridiculous towel-horse to the notice of the Central Bank. Wifredo replied passionately that Great Britain was Spain's best customer and, after Spain, the noblest country in Europe. He also commented on Anibal's Teutonic lack of taste, humour and imagination, adding that he proposed to start immediate production, though on a rather less expensive model than the prototype, of no less than one hundred 'Nanniparkér' nursery towel-horses. Then followed some very pointed remarks, such as: 'The priest must have had a bad cold when he christened you "Anibal". He surely meant "Animal". You are indeed a fat, brutish, sophistical, Germanic beast, save for whose degraded adventures in the lowest haunts of Santa Catalina, my poor sister would still be alive today!'

A rough-house ensued. Wifredo was the stronger of the two; but at some stage or other of the Civil War, Anibal had attended a hard course in street-fighting, and learned all sorts of clever tricks from his SS volunteer-instructors. Both combatants were seriously injured.

The factory had not been running too well even before this. Worn-out but irreplaceable machinery; power cuts; timber shortages; new national fiestas commemorating the triumph of the Forces of Light, on each of which the management was obliged to reward the workmen with double pay for taking a patriotic vacation; trouble with the syndicates; decrees forbidding the dismissal of a single workman however inefficient, dishonest or redundant — all this had been bad enough; but a complete breach between the partners brought matters to a crisis. Wifredo and Anibal now obstinately pursued their own uncoordinated policies: Wifredo designing his furniture in a yet more provocative English style, Anibal starving him of suitable timber and making no attempt to sell whatever he might manage to make.

Realizing that the factory would soon go bankrupt unless someone intervened decisively, Rosa did so. She had the good sense to phone a certain Cathedral Canon: elder brother and

confessor of the man who stood with a whip above these war-
ring partners – the Central Bank Director himself. After explaining her predicament, Rosa begged the Canon to impose
peace by whatever means he thought best, short of ruining both
households. 'Very reverend Father,' she said, 'although it is true
that Don Anibal began this disgraceful quarrel by calling Wifredo gross names which no man of honour could accept, I must
admit that Wifredo's reply did nothing to ameliorate the situation. It is equally true that Don Anibal struck the first blow; yet
Wifredo failed to turn the other cheek. Now, however, he re-
pents of his un-Catholic attitude. It is no joke that every day, on
going to the factory, he must carefully remove his wrist-watch
and place it on a shelf, together with his spare reading glasses,
for fear that they may both be splintered in a fresh hand-to-hand
encounter.'

The Canon listened with encouraging snorts, and finally gave
his opinion. 'My daughter,' he said, 'I can see only one way out
of the trouble which you have so clearly presented. It is that
you and Don Anibal's wife must form a realistic alliance for
peace. Until your husbands can be persuaded to clasp hands in
friendship, you must insist, at least, on their jointly asking the
Bank to appoint a permanent arbiter who shall settle all disputes
between them. Such an arrangement should involve no great
expense: some retired military man of rectitude and discretion
will, I have no doubt, be pleased to undertake the task. Not for
a monetary remuneration but, let us say, for a daily allowance
of refreshments. Thereafter, your two husbands need not meet
except in this arbiter's presence; though the Bank will of course
desire them to accept all his decisions without question – as
football players accept those of the umpire, on pain of being
ordered off the field. If you can answer for your husband's agreement, let us arrange a meeting between yourself and Don Anibal's wife at my house tomorrow; there, with God's help, all will
be decently settled.'

The name of Anibal's new wife, the pretty ex-dental receptionist, was Gracia Joncosa de Tulipán. (Another floral combination of names: 'Reedy Grace of a Tulip'.) Gracia was a
tough girl and also, like Anibal, stubbornly anti-clerical. She

attended the meeting, but warned the Canon straight out that, since the initiative had clearly come from Rosa, Anibal would reject the plan of arbitration as energetically as if it had been proposed by the Kremlin itself.

This brought a frown to the Canon's roseate face. Yet he refrained from dredging up Gracia's reprehensible past, and merely begged her to imitate Rosa's truly Catholic spirit. 'Blessed are the peacemakers' he intoned, wagging a fat finger.

'Blessed are they indeed!' Gracia echoed, impressed against her will by the huge, cigar-scented study: its dark, forbidding bookcases, its dark, forbidding pictures of saints being flayed alive, being grilled over hot coals, or merely kneeling in ecstasy on a mountain crag surrounded by winged demons. 'But my Anibal,' she went on, 'will at once convince himself that such an arbiter was chosen by connivance between yourself and Don Wifredo as a means of ousting him from his post.'

The Canon replied smoothly: 'Dear daughter, your hot-tempered husband must have no fear. Assure him that I, a Canon of Palma Cathedral, solemnly guarantee to find an arbiter of such absolute rectitude and insight that he might well be a descendant of King Solomon himself. If, however, your husband refuses my assurances, I shall feel that the Church has been spurned, as well as the Bank, and will inform my brother of his obduracy.'

Gracia saw the red light. She cried: 'No, no, most reverend Father! Pray do not talk in that sense! Anibal is, at bottom, a peace-loving man, and entertains the highest esteem both for yourself and for your distinguished brother. Let me try to make him see reason.'

'You will do well to try, my daughter,' the Canon answered grimly; and so the interview ended.

Anibal threw another fit when Gracia delivered the Canon's message. 'It is a hold-up!' he is reported as exclaiming. 'Must I indeed hand over my wallet to these shameless gangsters with a truly Catholic smile?'

Yet there was no way out when the Bank Director offered as a possible arbiter the retired and much-decorated Colonel whom I shall call Don Hilario Tortugas. During the Rif War he had been shot on three separate occasions, through calf, knee and shoulder, finally losing all the fingers of his left hand in performing a deed of such terrific valour that it earned him the Grand Cross of San Fernando. For Anibal to challenge the integrity of so outstanding a hero would have made him ridiculous. Moreover, Don Hilario, bored by inactivity, had readily accepted the task, asking a daily honorarium no larger than two cups of coffee, a salami sandwich, a bottle of beer, and a Canary Islands cigar. The coffee must be scalding hot; that was his one stipulation.

The arrangement worked well enough. True, Don Hilario could claim only the most meagre knowledge of how a factory was run – an educational fault displayed in Spanish history by a long sequence of gallant, honourable, high-ranking Army officers who have found themselves charged with their country's economic fate. Nevertheless, experience in the command of men had sharpened his natural intuition as to whether people were telling him lies, truths, or half-truths; and, when disputes arose on technical points he decided them by a careful study of the partners' voices, faces, and demeanour, rather than of the documents laid before him. Thus he settled the vexed question of the 'Nanniparkér' towel-horses by arguing that though Wifredo would doubtless turn out a superbly professional product, if given the required materials, Anibal's lack of confidence in these novelties suggested the wisdom of postponing their manufacture. He also ruled: 'The factory should, however, bear the expense of creating the prototype, and of selling it at a minimal price to an influential foreign family by way of justifiable propaganda.'

Don Hilario's daily appearance at the factory did much to restore the morale of the workmen. They used to boast in the cafés: 'We have the famous Colonel Tortugas on our payroll – he who once ran his sword through seventeen Cabyls, one after the other, though wounded in a score of places. There's a fighter for you!' Yet Anibal found it difficult to swallow his resentment: 'Only imagine! That ancient military relic set over me as supervisor and spy!' He continued to make things as difficult as he could for Wifredo, by misrepresenting both the supply situation and the sales prospects; at the same time complaining to Don Hilario that Wifredo spoiled the workmen and showed an utter ignorance of modern furniture trends.

On Rosa's advice, Wifredo kept cool and behaved as Englishly as possible, in the hope of provoking Anibal to over-reach himself by some crude act that could not escape official censure. But he was secretly worried by Anibal's attempts at ingratiating himself with Don Hilario. For instance, when he gave Don Hilario a box of a hundred *Romeo y Julieta* cigars on his Name Day. Don Hilario, needless to record, firmly declined the gift, swearing that much as he enjoyed a good smoke, he could never allow himself to deviate one hair's breadth from his more than Draconian code, and must avoid even the suspicion of venality. Nevertheless, Wifredo saw him eye the box with badly disguised wistfulness.

From time to time, Wifredo offered Don Hilario a lift back to the centre of town in his boat-shaped 1922 Renault two-seater – Majorca is where good cars go to die, and they take unconscionably long about it – but Don Hilario always insisted on walking, even on wet days when his wounds troubled him. He would accept no more and no less than the daily two cups of sweet, scalding coffee, the Canary Islands cigar, the salami sandwich, and the bottle of beer stipulated in the contract. Once only, his conscience permitted him to borrow from Wifredo a couple of cigarette papers with which to roll his own cigarettes; but paid them back the very next day.

So much for the situation at the factory. Now for that of the 'influential foreign family'. We had an unexpected visit from Ava Gardner, a close friend of our Maryland friend Betty Sicre. Betty suggested that Ava should take a short holiday from the exhausting social life of Madrid to visit soporific and truly rural Majorca. There she could catch up on sleep, study Spanish grammar, swim daily, and consult me about how to finish her random education by a crash-course in English poetry. We had met Ava at Betty's house a few months before and found her great fun; afterwards she sent us a huge bouquet of red roses, an attention which my wife and I appreciated all the more because, as we already knew, Ava is not one to distribute idle favours. She was feeling lonely at this time, her elder sister having just gone back to the States, and would borrow each of Betty's four small sons in turn to keep her company at night. 'The other boys at the American School will think me a sissy,' the youngest but one had tearfully complained, 'if they find out that I sleep twice a week with Ava!'

At Palma's Son Bonet airport, she came rushing towards us across the tarmac: a startled deer, pursued by a hungry-looking wolf. When the wolf saw her suddenly engulfed in our large family – the children had played truant from school by telling their monks and nuns that an aunt was arriving from London – he slunk off slavering. But word flew from end to end of the airport that the famous Ava Gardner had finally come to Majorca; and crowds went milling around in search of the red carpet, the bouquets, and the press photographers. Meanwhile, we hurried Ava into our Land-Rover, and hauled her baggage off the airline truck. One film-struck enthusiast saw a woman who closely resembled his idol bandying nonsense with our children in the dusty car; he stopped, narrowed his eyes, and passed on – it could not, of course, be she. We made a clean getaway.

Ava explained that there had been two really troublesome Spanish wolves aboard the plane. The first, seated across the gangway, kept addressing her in an experimental sort of Italian, until she slammed shut the *Oxford Book of English Verse* (supplied by Betty for the poetry course) and said: 'If you *must* interrupt my reading, why don't you at least talk your own language?'

The wolf answered gallantly: 'Signorina, I decided to give myself the honour of employing your own musical tongue.'

Ava looked puzzled. 'You must have got things mixed,' she said. 'I happen to have married a Sicilian, but my Italian is even worse than yours.'

The wolf leered at her craftily. 'Do not think to deceive me! All our papers assure us that you are a true daughter of Naples.'

'Then they're lying. I was born and raised in North Carolina.'

A horrid doubt overtook the wolf. 'Then I am mistaken? You are *not* Sofia Loren?'

With a cry of indignation Ava leaped up and took refuge in a vacant seat forward, but found Wolf No. 2 waiting there to pounce. So she read the *Oxford Book of English Verse* in the washroom, from which she emerged when the plane had landed; only to find the wolf waiting for her with amorous yelps at the foot of the landing-steps. Female film stars, it seems, are bound by a strict code: they must never insult journalists or press photographers, never refuse to sign autographs (unless desperately pressed for time), and never either slug wolves with overnight bags or poke out their eyes with parasols.

Ava's plans for improving her Spanish grammar and catching-up on sleep did not come to much. There are too many places in Palma where gipsies strum at guitars and dance *flamenco* all night; and Ava can never resist *flamenco*. Besides, her first visit to Majorca attracted such immense attention that she was forced to change hotels four times in five days; but it fascinated us to bask for a while in the spotlight of her glory. Though far preferring, she said, a meal of shepherd's pie or sausage-and-mash at our Palma flat, she gallantly took us out once or twice to the lusher restaurants.

After dinner, in one of these, she asked me for her poetry lesson, and I told her that so few poems were worth reading, and so many were wrongly supposed to be worth reading, that she had better make sure she would not waste her time by this poetry course. Washing for gold could be very dull work. Then, changing the metaphor, I said that a clear, personal voice was better than all the technical skill and daring experimentation in the world – really good poetry always makes plain, immediate, personal sense, is never dull, and goes on making better sense the oftener one reads it. 'Poems are like people,' I said. 'There are not many authentic ones around.'

Questioned about the monstrous legendary self which towers above her, Ava told us that she does everything possible to get out from under, though the publicity-boys and the Press are always trying to clamp it even more tightly on her shoulders. Also, that she has never outgrown her early Hard-Shell Baptist conditioning on that North Carolina tobacco farm, with the eye of a wonderful father always on her; and still feels uncomfortably moral in most film-studios; it isn't what she does that has created her sultry reputation, but what she says. Sometimes she just can't control her tongue.

A photographer suddenly let off a flash-bulb at us, and Ava flashed back at him almost as startlingly in the fiercest language. But when he apologized at once, she half forgave him. The rest of our talk was punctuated by the waiter's handing a succession of autograph-books to Ava for signature; she obliged automatically with a fixed, sunny smile, not losing the thread of our conversation until one autograph-hunter, an over-stuffed sofa of a woman, plumped herself down next to me, leant across me, and said: 'Oh, dear Miss Gardner, I have seen *every single one* of your films! Now I wonder whether you would be so good as to give me your *personal* autograph for my seven-year-old grandchild. Her name is Wendy Solgotch Wallinger.'

Ava frowned. 'Is the Solgotch Wallinger strictly necessary?' she asked. 'And what am I supposed to write on?'

'Oh, I thought film stars always supply the paper!'

Ava frowned more deeply. Her comments on that paper shortage had better stay off record. They were quite enough to account for her sultry reputation. Nevertheless, loth to infringe the code further, she tore a corner off the menu, scribbled 'Wendy, with best wishes from Ava Gardner,' and waved Mrs Wallinger away with it.

Having found my *Collected Poems* at our apartment, Ava asked which of them to read first. This question embarrassed me, after what I had already told her. However, there was one, I said, which she might perhaps like to take personally; though it had been written long before we met. I marked the page for study when she went to bed that night – if she ever did.

> She speaks always in her own voice
> Even to strangers ...

and:

> She is wild and innocent, pledged to love
> Through all disaster ...

That was Ava to the life.

Meanwhile, at the furniture factory, Anibal had been consistently difficult. He accused Wifredo to Don Hilario of stirring up the workmen and alleging that the timber he supplied was so green, warped and knotted that it would serve only for making rustic seats and the like. Confronted with this charge, Wilfredo informed Don Hilario that he had made a factual statement, not a complaint: indeed, far from stirring the workmen up, he had encouraged them to hope that something at least could be made from the eccentric lumps of raw tree which were all that his partner could now buy.

When Don Hilario looked at him quizzically, Wifredo went to the workshop and returned with a particularly unattractive section of local pine, consisting almost wholly of large knots. He asked: 'Am I seriously expected to fulfil a municipal order for eighty class-room desks with timber of this quality? And what about my saw-blades?'

Don Hilario eyed the exhibit and ventured cautiously: 'Well, you might hammer out these knots and use the holes for securing the scholars' ink-wells; but I shall make it plain to Don Anibal that if you were to take this course, there would undoubtedly be many times more ink-wells than scholars.'

Seven o'clock struck, and Wifredo exclaimed: 'Pardon me, Don Hilario! The workmen have gone off, and so has my partner. I must lock up without delay. Since I am aware that any invitation to ride home in my battered car will be declined, let me wish you a respectful good night. There is a certain haste; my English friends, the intellectual Graves family, are honouring my house with a visit, and hope to bring Miss Ava Gardner.'

Don Hilario caught his breath and clutched at Wifredo's sleeve. 'Do you mean the veritable Ava Gardner?' he asked slowly. 'She ... is here, in Majorca?'

'Yes, the one inimitable Ava,' Wifredo answered easily. 'The Señores Graves assure me that she is as gracious and intelligent as she is beautiful.'

'"Gracious and intelligent" indeed! "Gracious and intelligent" is petty praise! For me, Ava Gardner is the greatest artist alive!'

*

Ava did not, as it happened, come to Wifredo's with us that evening. She had made a trip to the fine sandy beach of Camp de Mar; but, the weather being bitterly cold – it was just before the fearful February freeze-up of 1956 – she alone was hardy enough to swim. Several carloads of admirers stood watching, and a roar of admiration rose as she tripped down the hotel steps in her bright Italian bathing costume and dived into the tempestuous waves. Yet no would-be life-saver, we were told, jumped in after her; if only because Spaniards, though incurably romantic, are not altogether Quixotic. Later, Ava was whisked on to the Binisalem vineyards, where she spent so agreeable a time sampling our sole Majorcan vintage wine that we did not catch up with her again until midnight.

The next morning, Don Hilario drew Wifredo aside and said urgently: 'Friend, tell me about her!'

Hating to disappoint the Colonel, Wifredo answered: 'A phenomenon! So gentle, so beautiful, so humorous.'

Don Hilario sighed. 'Ah, Don Wifredo, your experience fills me with the greenest envy!' He added in a sudden rush: 'I have never, you know, accepted a gift or a favour from you, ever since I came to this factory. Not a cigarette, not a match, not a ride in your crazy automobile! However, I will say that, unlike your boorish partner, you always show the utmost consideration for my feelings in this respect, never making any move which might be open to malicious misinterpretation; and for that I honour you. Indeed, I honour you so highly, and so commend your correctness, that I feel emboldened to make a surprising request: one that you will, I am sure, recognize as being on a quite different level from the mundane round of industry in the ambience of which we daily meet. Don Wifredo, I am a lonely old man; all winter long my wounds ache; I have few pleasures. Well ... to be short, if you could, by any plea, prevail on your distinguished English friends to approach Miss Gardner ...'

Wifredo answered: 'Not another word, Don Hilario! And if anyone else in all Palma were to ask this of me – even the Director of the Central Bank, upon whose good will my livelihood depends – I should say: "Impossible!" But when the most courageous soldier of our race makes such a request, how dare I rebuff him? I trust that the matter can be arranged before Miss Gardner leaves the island early this afternoon.'

A few minutes later our phone rang. 'Robert,' Wifredo said excitedly, 'will you meet me at noon in the Café Mecca on a matter of the gravest importance? I cannot explain over the telephone.'

To my relief, Ava had read the marked poem and decided to accept it as a personal tribute; in fact, begged me to copy it out in long-hand and sign it for her.

'With great pleasure,' I said, 'if you'll do a trade. Ava, I want a print of your most supremely glamorous photograph, inscribed: "To the heroic Colonel Don Hilario Tortugas y Postres, with the heartfelt admiration of Ava Gardner." Let me write it down for you.'

'Is "heartfelt admiration" strictly necessary?'

'It's essential!'

I wrote out the poem for Ava in a fair hand, and soon after she had flown back to Madrid (with four crates of Binisalem wine among her luggage) a splendidly large signed photograph arrived, duly inscribed for the Colonel: a portrait, I was half-glad to see, of her exotic legend rather than of herself.

Rosa and Wifredo invited us to the most English dinner we had eaten in years: mulligatawny soup; roast beef with roast potatoes, Yorkshire pudding, a boiled cabbage; apple dumplings with cream; and (as Edward Lear has put it) 'no end of Stilton cheese'. Wifredo even produced a bottle of vintage port – how he got hold of either the Stilton or the port, beats me – and solemnly toasted Ava Gardner.

We all drank.

Then, in a voice thick with emotion, he announced: 'Dear friends, in consequence of Don Hilario's report to the Bank, delivered two days ago, I now have sole charge of the factory, being answerable to the Bank Director alone. Anibal has been bought out and dismissed; and I am empowered not only to arrange my own timber supplies, but to choose a new sales manager !'

We congratulated him riotously.

'That is not all,' he went on. 'The "Nanniparkér" Nursery Towel-horse now goes into immediate production, as well as a similar contrivance, suggested by dear Rosa, for hoisting wet linen to the kitchen ceiling by means of a cord and pulley. It will equally serve, in better weather, for hams, sausages, strings of red peppers, and ropes of onions. How original, and how very useful ! I propose to name it "The Ava Gardner Drying Rack". Each example will bear a beautiful coloured miniature of my benefactress, taken from the authentic photograph of her plunge into the sea at Camp de Mar. Do you consider that I need write to ask her permission?'

'She would consider it strictly unnecessary,' I answered, sipping my port, cracking my walnuts, and thinking: 'Dear Ava !'

THE LOST CHINESE

JAUME GELABERT was a heavily-built, ill-kempt, morose Majorcan lad of seventeen. His father had died in 1936 at the siege of Madrid, but on the losing side, and therefore without glory or a dependant's pension; his mother a few years later. He lived by himself in a dilapidated cottage near our village of Muleta, where he cultivated a few olive terraces and a lemon grove. On my way down for a swim from the rocks, three hundred feet below, I would cut through Jaume's land and, if we happened to meet, always offered him an American cigarette. He would then ask if I were taking a bathe, to which I answered either: 'You have divined my motive correctly,' or: 'Yes, doctors say it benefits the health.' Once I casually remarked that my blue jeans had grown too tight and, rather than throw them away, I wondered if they might come in handy for rough work. 'I could perhaps use them,' he answered, fingering the solid denim. To say 'thank you' would have been to accept charity and endanger our relationship; but next day he gave me a basket of cherries, with the excuse that his tree was loaded and that June cherries were not worth marketing. So we became good neighbours.

This was June 1952 – just before Willie Fedora appeared in Muleta and rented a cottage. The United States Government was paying Willie a modest disability grant, in recognition of 'an anxiety neurosis aggravated by war service in Korea', which supported him nicely until the tide of tourism sent prices rocketing. Brandy then cost a mere twelve pesetas a litre, not thirty-six as now; and brandy was his main expense.

Our small foreign colony, mostly painters, at first accepted Willie. But the tradition here is that instead of drinking, playing bridge, sun-bathing, and discussing one another's marital hazards, as at expensive resorts with more easily accessible beaches, foreigners *work*. We meet only in the evening around a café table, when our mail has arrived. Occasional parties are thrown, and sometimes we hire the village bus for a Sunday bullfight; otherwise we keep ourselves to ourselves. Willie disliked this unsociable way of life. He would come calling on trivial pretexts, after breakfast, just when we were about to start work, and always showed his independence by bringing along a four-litre straw-covered flask of cheap brandy – which he called 'my samovar' – slung from his shoulder. To shut the door in Willie's face would have been churlish; to encourage him, self-destructive. Usually, we slipped out by the back door and waited until he had gone off again.

Willie wrote plays; or, rather, he laboured at the same verse play for months and months, talking about it endlessly but making no progress. The hero of *Vercingetorix* (Willie himself disguised in a toga) was one of Julius Caesar's staff-captains in the Gallic War. Whenever Willie began his day's work on *Vercingetorix* he needed to down half a pint of brandy, because of the fearful load of guilt which he carried with him and which formed the theme of his Roman drama. Apparently towards the end of the Korean War, a senior officer had put Willie in charge of five hundred captured Chinese Communists but, when he later marched them to the pen, a bare three hundred were left. The remainder could neither have been murdered, nor committed suicide, nor escaped; yet they had disappeared. 'Disappeared into thin air!' he would repeat tragically, tilting the samovar. Any suggestion that these Chinamen had existed only on paper – a 3 scrawled in the heat of battle, we pointed out, might easily be read as a 5 – enraged Willie. 'Goddam it!' he would shout, pounding the table. 'I drew rations and blankets for five hundred. Laugh *that* off!'

Before long, we shut our doors against Willie. Let him finish his play, we said, rather than talk about it; and none of us felt responsible for his lost Chinese. Yet every night they haunted his dreams, and often he would catch glimpses of them skulking behind trees or barns even by day.

Now, it is an old custom at Muleta to support the Catholic China Missions, and on 'China Day' the school children paint their faces yellow, slant their eyebrows and dress themselves up in the Oriental clothes, of uncertain origin, which the Mother Superior of our Franciscan convent distributes from a long, deep, camphor-scented chest. They drive around in a tilt-cart and collect quite a lot of money; though who ultimately benefits from it remains a mystery, because (as I told the incredulous Mother Superior) no foreign missions have been tolerated in China for some years. Unfortunately, the young Chinese came tapping at Willie's cottage window one afternoon and scared him out of his wits. Accidentally smashing his samovar against a wine barrel as he stumbled into the café, Willie collapsed on the terrace. When he felt better, we recommended a Palma doctor. He groaned at us: 'You jump off a cliff! I'm through with you all. I'm going native.'

Willie did go native. To the surprise of Muleta, he and Jaume Gelabert struck up a friendship. Jaume, already branded as the son of a Red, had earned a reputation for violence at that year's *fiesta* of San Pedro, Muleta's patron saint. The Mayor's sharp-tongued son, who owned a motorcycle and led the *atlotes*, or village bucks, made Jaume his victim. 'Behold the Lord of La Coma!' Paco sneered. Jaume went pale. ' "Lord of La Coma" comes badly from you, Paco, you loud-mouthed wencher! Your own uncle robbed my widowed mother of her share in the estate, and the whole village knew it, though they were too cowardly to protest.' Paco then extemporized a *copeo*, a satiric verse of the sort current on San Pedro's Day:

> The Lord of La Coma he lives in disgrace:
> He never eats crayfish nor washes his face!

A group of *atlotes* took up the chorus, dancing in a ring around Jaume:

> Ho, ho, that's how we go —
> He never eats crayfish nor washes his face!

Jaume pulled a stake from the baker's fence and ran amok, felling Paco and a couple of other *atlotes* before he was disarmed by Civil Guards and shoved without ceremony into the village lock-up. The Justice of the Peace, Paco's father, bound Jaume over after a stern caution. At Muleta, no decent man ever uses force: all fighting is done either with the tongue or with money.

The two social outcasts became such close friends that it

spared us further responsibility for Willie's health. He had decided to learn Majorcan from Jaume. This old language, not unlike Provençal, is in domestic use throughout the island, though discountenanced by the Government. Willie had a natural linguistic gift, and within three months could chatter fluent Majorcan — the sole foreigner in Muleta (except my children, who went to school there) who ever achieved the feat. Willie gratefully insisted on teaching Jaume how to write plays, having once majored in dramatic composition at a Midwestern university, and meanwhile laid *Vercingetorix* aside. By the spring, Jaume had finished *The Indulgent Mother*, a Majorcan comedy based on the life of his great-aunt Catalina. In return he had made Willie eat solid food, such as bean porridge and *pa'mb'oli*, and drink more red wine than brandy. Jaume did not question Willie's account of those lost Chinese, but argued that the command of five hundred prisoners must have been too great a burden for so young a soldier as Willie; and that omniscient God had doubtless performed a miracle and cut down their numbers. 'Suppose someone were to give me five hundred sheep !' he said. 'How would I manage them all single-handed? One hundred, yes; two hundred, yes; three hundred, perhaps; five hundred would be excessive.'

'But, if so, why do these yellow devils continue to haunt me?'

'Because they are heathen and blaspheme God ! Pay no attention ! And if they ever plague you, eat rather than drink !'

In 1953, Muleta suffered a financial crisis. Foul weather ruined the olive prospects, blighted the fruit blossom, and sent numerous terraces rumbling down. Moreover, Dom Enrique, our parish priest, had ordered a new altar and rebuilt the chancel at extravagant cost; while neglecting the church roof, part of which fell in after a stormy night. One consequence was that the village could not afford to hire the Palma Repertory Troupe for their usual San Pedro's Day performance. But Dom Enrique heard about Jaume's play, read it, and promised to raise a cast from the *Acción Católica* girls and their *novios* : if Willie would stage-manage the show, and Jaume devote its takings to the Roof Fund.

This plan naturally met with a good deal of opposition among

the village elders: Willie, now nicknamed 'Don Coñac', and
Jaume the violent Red, seemed most unsuitable playwrights.
Dom Enrique, however, had felt a certain sympathy for Jaume's
use of the stake, and also noted the happy improvement in
Willie's health under Jaume's care. He preached a strong sermon
against the self-righteous and the uncharitable and, having got
his way, cleverly cast Paco as the juvenile lead. Nevertheless, to
avoid any possible scandal, he laid it down that rehearsals must
follow strict rules of propriety: the girls' mothers should either
attend or send proxies. He himself would always be present.

The Indulgent Mother, which combined the ridiculous with
the pathetic, in a style exploited by Menander, Terence, Plautus
and other ancient masters, was an unqualified success. Although
no effort of Willie's or Dom Enrique's, as joint stage-managers,
could keep the cast from turning their backs on the audience,
gagging, mumbling, hamming, missing their cues, and giggling
helplessly at dramatic moments, the Roof Fund benefited by
fifteen hundred pesetas; and a raffle for a German wrist-watch
(left on the beach two years previously) brought in another eight
hundred. The *Baleares* printed a paragraph on the remarkable
young playwright, Don Jaime Gelabert, below the heading:
'Solemn Parochial Mass at Muleta; Grandiose Popular Events.'
Paco and his *novia*, the heroine, also secured a niche in the news.

Meanwhile Willie, whom the *Baleares* unfortunately named
'Don Guillermo Coñac, the transatlantic theatrician', had celebrated Jaume's debut a little too well, singing Negro spirituals in
the village streets until long after midnight. When at last he fell
insensible, Paco and the other *atlotes* pulled off his clothes and
laid him naked on a vault in the churchyard, with the samovar
under his head. He was there discovered by a troop of black-
veiled old *beatas*, or religious women, on the way to early Mass –
an appalling scandal! Jaume had gone straight home, after the
final curtain, to escape congratulations. In the morning, however, he pieced the story together from village gossip, caught
Paco outside the café and threw him into the Torrent, where
he broke an ankle. This time, Jaume would have been tried in
the capital for attempted homicide, had Willie not intervened.
'Punish Jaume,' he warned the Mayor, 'and you will force me to

sue your son. I have witnesses who can testify to his shameless behaviour, and the United States Government is behind me.'

Jaume and I remained on good terms. I told him: 'Jaume, in my view you acted correctly. No true friend could have done less under such provocation.'

Winter and spring went swiftly by, and another San Pedro's Day was on us. Willie visited Dom Enrique at the Rectory and offered to stage-manage a new play of Jaume's: *The Difficult Husband*. He did not arrive drunk but (as they say in Ireland) 'having drink taken', and when he announced that this comedy had merits which would one day make it world famous, Dom Enrique could hardly be blamed for excusing himself. A deceased widow, the Lady of La Coma, had just left the Church a small fortune, on the strength of which his parishioners trusted him to re-engage the Palma Repertory Troupe as in previous years.

Bad news further aggravated this setback. Jaume, due for the draft, had counted on being sent to an anti-aircraft battery, three miles away, from where he could get frequent leave; in fact, the Battery commander had promised to arrange the matter. But something went wrong – Paco's father may have spoken a word in the Captain's ear – and Jaume was ordered to Spanish Morocco.

Willie, with streaming eyes, promised to irrigate the lemon grove, plough around the olive trees, plant the beans when the weather broke, and wait patiently for Jaume's return. But two hundred phantom Chinese took advantage of his loneliness to prowl among the trees and tap at the kitchen window. Willie's samovar filled and emptied, filled and emptied four or five times a week; he neglected the lemon grove, seldom bothered with meals, and locked the cottage door against all callers: at all costs he must finish an English translation of *The Difficult Husband*. I met him one morning in the postman's house, where he was mailing a package to the States. He looked so thin and lost that, on meeting the Mayor, I suggested he should take some action. 'But what would you have me do?' cried the Mayor. 'He is committing no crime. If he is ill, let him consult the Doctor!' That afternoon, Willie saw Toni Coll digging a refuse pit below the cottage: convinced that this was to be his own grave, he sought sanctuary in the church organ-loft, drank himself silly, and was not discovered for twenty-four hours. Dom Enrique and his mother carried him to the Rectory, where they nursed him until the American Embassy could arrange his transfer to the States. At New York, a veterans' reception committee met Willie, and he was sent to a Pittsburgh army hospital. On New Year's Day, 1955, he broke his neck falling out of a window, apparently pursued by Chinese oppressors. I felt bad about him.

If Muleta expected to hear no more about Jaume's comedy, Muleta erred. Just before the rockets soared up in honour of San Pedro two years later, Mercurio the postman (who also acts as our telegraphist) tugged at my sleeve. 'Don Roberto,' he said, 'I have a telegram here from New York for a certain William Schenectady. Do you know the individual? It came here three days ago, and none of your friends recognize the name. Could he be some transitory tourist?'

'No: this is for our unfortunate Don Coñac,' I told him. In Spain only the middle name counts, being the patronymic, and Willie's passport had read 'William Schenectady Fedora'.

'A sad story,' sighed Mercurio. 'How can telegrams benefit the dead, who are unable even to sign a receipt? And there is no means of forwarding the message ...'

'I'll sign, since that's what worries you,' I said. 'Probably it contains birthday greetings from some old aunt, who has remained ignorant of his fate. If so, I'll tear it up.'

After the fun was over, I remembered the cable. It ran:

WILLIAM SCHENECTADY FEDORA: MULETA: MAJORCA: SPAIN

MAGNIFICENT BRAVO BRAVO BRAVO STOP DIFICTUL HUSBAN
SENSACIONAL FUST THE PLOY NEEDED ON BIRDWAY WIT
NEUMANN DIRECION HARPVICKE IN THE LED STOP AIR-
MALLING CONTRACT STOP PROPOSE FOLOV UP WIT PRESONAL
VISIT SO ONEST KINDLY REPLAY STOP REGARDS

EVERETT SAMSTAG EMPIRE STAT ENTERPRIXES NEW YORK

I frowned. My neighbour Len Simkin was always talking about Sammy Samstag, the Broadway impresario, and had even promised Willie to interest him in *Vercingetorix*; but somehow this cable did not seem like a joke. Who would waste ten dollars on kidding a dead man? Yet, if it wasn't a joke, why did Samstag send no prepaid reply coupon?

I tackled Mercurio, who admitted that such a form had, as it happened, come with the cable for Don Coñac; adding: 'But since Don Coñac is no more, perhaps some other foreigner may care to dispatch a telegram with its help.'

So I cabled Samstag:

INTERESTED IN YOUR INTEREST STOP WILL ADVISE AUTHOR OF DIFFICULT HUSBAND CURRENTLY ON SAFARI TO GRANT OPTION IF FINANCIALLY COMMENSURATE WITH YOUR TRIPLE BRAVO STOP REGARDS

To explain that Willie was no longer available, and that the job of protecting Jaume fell to me, would have exceeded the prepaid allowance, so I signed 'Fedora'. 'Currently on safari' was cablese for 'at present trailing his rifle through North Africa, but will be back next week', and sounded far more opulent.

At the café, I met Len, a young-old fabricator of abstract mobiles. He had once briefly taken a very small part in an off-Broadway play, but was Muleta's sole contact with the Great White Way. 'A pity poor Willie's dead,' I said, when Len had finished his scathing comments on last night's performance by the Palma Repertory Troupe. 'He might have got you a speaking part in this new Broadway play. Willie always admired your delivery.'

'I don't get the joke,' Len grumbled. 'That wack gave me the creeps! One of those "creative artists" who create chaos. A few drinks from the old samovar, and I could *see* those goddamned Chinese! I bet they infiltrated into his coffin, and pulled the lid down after them.'

'If you take my front-page news like that, Len,' I told him, 'you'll not be offered even a walk-on!'

'Still, I don't get it ...'

'Well, you will – as soon as Sammy Samstag turns up here

toting an enormous box of Havanas, and you're left in a corner smoking your foul *Peninsulares*.'

'Neumann directing? Harwicke in the lead as Vercinge-torix?'

'No, the title isn't *Vercingetorix*. It's *The Difficult Husband*. Otherwise you've guessed right.'

'You're very fonny, don't you, Mister?' Len stalked away, then wheeled angrily, and came out with a splendid curtain line: 'In my opinion, jokes about dead Americans stink!'

When Jaume stepped from the Palma-Muleta bus, looking bigger and more morose than ever, no one rolled out the red carpet. That evening I found him alone in his cottage, cooking a bean and blood-pudding stew over the wood fire; and accepted an invitation to share it. Jaume asked for details on Willie's death, and wept to hear about the open window.

'He was a brother to me,' he choked. 'So magnanimous, so thoughtful! And since he could not manage this little property by himself, I had asked Toni Coll to tend the trees, and go half-shares in the lemons and oil. Toni has just paid me two thousand pesetas. We are not friends, but he would have lost face with the village by neglecting my land while I was doing my service. He even repaired the terrace that fell before my departure.'

I had brought along a bottle of red Binisalem wine, to cele-brate Samstag's cable.

'Poor Willie, how wildly enthusiastic he would have been,' Jaume sighed, when I read it to him. 'And how he would have drunk and sung! This comes too late. Willie always wanted me to enjoy the success that his frailties prevented him from attaining.'

'May he rest in peace!'

'I had no great theatrical ambition,' Jaume continued, after a pause. 'Willie forced me to write first *The Indulgent Mother*, and then *The Difficult Husband*.'

'Did they take you long?'

'*The Indulgent Mother*, yes. Over the second I did not need to rack my brains. It was a gift.'

'Yet Señor Samstag, a most important person, finds the result magnificent. That is certainly a triumph. You have a copy of the play?'

'Only in Majorcan.'

'Do you realize, Jaume, what will happen if *The Difficult Husband* pleases Broadway?'

'Might they pay me?'

'Pay you, man? Of course! With perhaps five per cent of the gross takings, which might mean fifty thousand dollars a week. Say it ran for a couple of years, you'd amass ... let me work it out – well, some two hundred and fifty thousand dollars.'

'That means nothing to me. What part of a peseta is a dollar?'

'Listen: if things go well, you may earn *twelve million pesetas* ... And even if the play proved a dead failure, you'd get two hundred thousand, merely by selling Señor Samstag the right to stage it!'

'Your talk of millions confuses me. I would have accepted five hundred pesetas for the job.'

'But you would equally accept twelve million?'

'Are these people mad?'

'No, they are clever businessmen.'

'You make fun of me, Don Roberto!'

'I do not.'

'Then, at least, you exaggerate? What I want to know is whether this telegram will help me to buy a donkey and re-tile my roof.'

'I can promise you an avalanche of donkeys!'

Two days later the contract came, addressed to Willie. Its thirty pages covered all possible contingencies of mutual and reciprocal fraud on the part of author and producer, as foreseen by the vigilant Dramatists Guild of the Authors League of America; and dealt with such rich minor topics as Second Class Touring Rights, Tabloid Versions, Concert Tour Versions, Foreign Language Performances, and the sale of dolls or other toys based on characters in the play ...

I was leafing through the document on the café terrace that afternoon, when Len entered. 'There's a man at my place,' he

gasped excitedly, 'name of Bill Truscott, who says he's Willie's
agent! Bill and I were at Columbia together. Nice guy. He
seems sort of puzzled to find no Willie ... See here: could it
be that you weren't kidding me about his Broadway show the
other day?'

'I never kid. Got no sense of humour.'

'Is that so? Well, anyhow, I told Bill you might be able to
help him. Come along!'

Bill Truscott, a gaunt Bostonian, welcomed us effusively. 'I
sent *The Difficult Husband* to Samstag's office ten days ago,' he
said, 'and a spy I keep there sent word that the old s.o.b. was
jumping my claim. Doesn't like agents, favours the direct approach. But let's get this straight: is Fedora really dead? My spy
swears that he cabled Samstag from this place.'

'Correct. He's dead. Yet he promised to meet Samstag and
discuss this document' – I tapped the contract – 'which maybe
you'd better have a look at. Tell me, do you speak Spanish?
Jaume Gelabert has no English or French.'

'Gelabert? Who's Gelabert? Never heard of him.'

'Author of *The Difficult Husband*. Fedora's only the translator.'

'Only the translator – are you sure? How extremely tense!
That changes everything. I took it for Fedora's own work ...
What sort of a guy is this Gelabert? Any previous stage
successes?'

'He made a hit with *The Indulgent Mother*,' I said, kicking
Len under the table. 'He's a simple soul – you might call him a
recluse.'

'Know of any arrangement between Fedora and Gelabert as to
the translator's fee?'

'I can't think that they made one. Fedora drank, and did the
job by way of a favour to Gelabert, who had been caring for
him. ... Are you worried about your commission?'

'*Am* I worried? However, Gelabert will need an agent, and,
after all, Fedora sent the play to my office. Len will vouch for
me, won't you, Len?'

'I'm sure he will, Mr Truscott,' I said, 'and you'll vouch for
him. Len needs some vouching for.'

'I'm on my knees, Don Roberto,' Len whined, grovelling gracefully.

I let him grovel awhile, and asked Truscott: 'But didn't Fedora acknowledge Gelabert's authorship in a covering letter?'

'He did, I remember, mention a local genius who had defended him against some Chinese and was now setting off to fight the Moors, while he himself guarded the lemon grove – and would I please try enclosed play on Samstag; but that's as far as it went, except for some passages in a crazy foreign language, full of x's and y's.'

'I gather the letter has disappeared?'

Truscott nodded gloomily.

'In fact, you can't prove yourself to be Fedora's agent, let alone Gelabert's?'

No reply. I pocketed the contract and rolled myself a cigarette, taking an unnecessarily long time about it. At last I said: 'Maybe Gelabert would appoint you his agent; but he's a difficult man to handle. Better leave all the talking to me.'

'That's very nice of you ... I surely appreciate it. I suppose you've seen a copy of *The Difficult Husband*?'

'Not yet.'

'Which makes two of us! You see: after reading Fedora's crazy letter, I tossed the typescript, unexamined, to my secretary Ethel May, who, for all that she was the dumbest operator on Thirty-eighth Street, had beautiful legs and neat habits. Hated to throw away anything, though – even gift appeals. She filed it under "Try Mr Samstag". Ethel May got married and quit. Then, one day, I came down with the grippe, and that same evening Sam wanted a script in a hurry – some piece by a well-known author of mine. I called Ethel May's replacement from my sickbed and croaked: "Send off the Samstag script at once! Special messenger." The poor scared chick didn't want to confess that she'd no notion what the hell I was talking about. She chirped: "Certainly, Chief!" and went away to search the files. As a matter of fact, said script was still in my brief case – grippe plays hell with a guy's memory. Scratching around, the chick comes across *The Difficult Husband*, and sends Sam that. A stroke of genius! – I must give her a raise. But Sam is short on ethics. He bypassed my office and cabled the defunct Fedora, hoping he'd sign along the dotted line, and remember too late that he should have got my expert advice on what's bound to be the trickiest of contracts. If ever there was a thieving dog !'

'Yes,' I said, '*if* Fedora had been the author, and *if* you'd been his agent, you'd have a right to complain. But, let's face it, you've no standing at all. So calm down ! I suggest we call on Gelabert. He can probably supply supper.'

Night had fallen windily, after a day of unseasonable showers; and the path to Jaume's cottage is no easy one at the best of times. The ground was clayey and full of puddles; water cascaded from the trees. I lent Truscott a flashlight; but twice he tripped over an olive root and fell. He reached the cottage (kitchen, stable, well, single bedroom) in poor shape. I gave Jaume a brief outline of the situation, and we were soon sharing his *pa'mb'oli*: which means slices of bread dunked in unrefined olive oil, rubbed with a half tomato and sprinkled with salt. Raw onion, bitter olives, and a glass of red wine greatly improved the dish. *Pa'mb'oli* was something of a test for Truscott, but he passed it all right, apart from letting oil drip on his muddied trousers.

He asked me to compliment Jaume on 'this snug little shack. Say that I envy him. Say that we city folk often forget what real dyed-in-the-wool *natural* life can be !' Then he talked business. 'Please tell our host that he's been sent no more than a basic contract. I'm surprised at the size of the advance, though : three thousand on signature, and two thousand more on the first night ! Sam must think he's on to a good thing. Nevertheless, my long experience as a dramatic agent tells me that we can easily improve these terms, besides demanding a number of special arrangements. Fedora is dead; or we could fiction him into the contract as the author. Unlike Gelabert, he was a non-resident American citizen, and therefore non-liable to any tax at all on the property. Maybe we can still fiction it that way ...'

'What is he saying?' asked Jaume.

'He wants to act as your agent in dealing with Señor Samstag, whom he doesn't trust. The rest of his speech is of no interest.'

'Why should I trust this gentleman more than he trusts the other?'

'Because Willie chose Señor Truscott as his agent, and Samstag got the play from him.'

Jaume solemnly held out his hand to Truscott.

'You were Willie's friend?' he asked. I translated.

'He was a very valued client of mine.' But when Truscott produced an agency agreement from his brief case, I gave Jaume a warning glance.

Jaume nodded. 'I sign only what I can read and understand,' he said. 'My poor mother lost her share of the La Coma inheritance by trusting a lawyer who threw long words at her. Let us find a reliable notary public in the capital.'

Truscott protested: 'I'm not representing Gelabert until I'm sure of my commission.'

'Quit that!' I said sharply. 'You're dealing with a peasant who can't be either bullied or coaxed.'

A cable came from Samstag: he was arriving by Swissair next day. Mercurio asked Len, who happened to be in the postman's house, why so many prodigal telegrams were flying to and fro. Len answered: 'They mean immense wealth for young Gelabert. His comedy, though rejected by Dom Enrique two years ago, is to be staged in New York.'

'That moral standards are higher here than in New York does not surprise me,' Mercurio observed. 'Yet dollars are dollars, and Jaume can now laugh at us all, whatever the demerits of his play.'

Len brought the cable to my house, where he embarrassed me by paying an old debt of two hundred pesetas (which I had forgotten), in the hope that I might deal him into the Broadway game. 'I don't need much ... just an itty-bitty part,' he pleaded.

Why dash his hopes? Pocketing the two hundred pesetas, I said that his friend Bill would surely recommend him to Samstag.

News of Jaume's good fortune ran through the village two or three times, each time gaining in extravagance. The final version made Samstag a millionnaire second cousin from Venezuela who, reading the *Baleares* account of *The Indulgent Mother*, had appointed him his heir. I asked Jaume to say no more than that he was considering the American offer: it might yet prove unacceptable.

Truscott and I met Samstag's plane at Palma airport. Spying Truscott among the crowd, he darted forward with scant respect for the Civil Guard who was shepherding the new arrivals through Customs, and grabbed his hand. 'By all that's holy, Bill,' he cried, 'I'm glad to see you. This solves our great mystery! So that anonymous package emanated from you, did it?'

'Yes, it did, Sammy,' said Truscott, 'and, like all packages I've ever sent you, it was marked all over with my office stamp.'

'Why, yes, my secretary did guess it might be yours, and called you at once – but you were sick, and I couldn't get confirm –'

The Civil Guard then unslung his rifle and used the barrel-end to prod Samstag, a small, dark roly-poly of a man, back into line. Finally he emerged with his baggage and guessed that I was Mr William Fedora. When Truscott undeceived him, he grew noticeably colder towards me; but the two were soon as thick as thieves, and no less suspicious of each other. Climbing into our taxi, Samstag lighted a large cigar, and turned away from me; so I asserted myself as a principal in the business. 'I can use one of those,' I said, stretching out a finger and thumb.

Startled, Samstag offered me his case. 'Take a couple,' he begged.

I took five, smelt and pinched them all, rejected three. 'Don't mind me, boys!' I said through a fragrant cloud of smoke. 'You haggle about the special arrangements. I'll manage the rest.'

At this reminder of our compact, Truscott hastily enlarged on the strong hold I had on Señor Gelabert, assuring Samstag that without me he would get nowhere. Samstag gave him a non-committal 'Oh yes?' and then back to his discussion of out-of-town performances prior to a possible London *première*. Just before we sighted the village round the bend of our road, I tapped Samstag on the arm: 'Look here, Sam, what told you that *The Difficult Husband* was God's gift to Broadway?'

'Not *what*, but *who*?' he answered cheerfully. 'It was Sharon, of course! Sharon always knows. She said: "Pappy, believe me, this is going to be the hottest ticket in town." So I cabled Fedora, and flew. She's only fourteen, my Sharon, and still studying at Saint Teresa's. You should see her grades: lousy isn't the word! And yet she always *knows* ... Takes a script, sniffs it, reads three lines here, four there; spends a couple of minutes on Act Two; skips to the final curtain ... Then' – Samstag lowered his voice and ended in a grave whisper – 'then she goddamwell *pronounces*!'

'So you haven't read the script either? That makes three of us. What about having a look at it after supper? Or, to save time and eyesight, we might have Len Simkin – another Thespian chum of yours, Sam – read it aloud to us?'

'If you insist. Perhaps Señor Gelabert has a copy. I haven't brought one myself – came here for business, not to hear a dramatic reading.'

In fact, nobody had a script. But that did not prevent Samstag and Truscott from arguing Special Arrangements together at the village inn all the rest of the day, until everything seemed sewed up. The meeting with Señor Gelabert, they congratulated themselves, would be a mere formality.

Hair slicked, shoes well brushed, Jaume arrived at our rendezvous in his Sunday best, and showed impressive *sang-froid*. Early cares, ill luck, and the tough barrack life at Melilla had made a man of him. After profuse congratulations, which Jaume shrugged off, Samstag sent for the village taxi and invited us both to dinner in Palma. Len, to his disappointment, was left behind. We chose *Aqui Estamos*, Majorca's most select restaurant, where Samstag kept slapping Jaume's shoulders and crying '¡*Amigo!*', varied with '¡*Magnifico!*', and asking me to translate Sharon's appreciative comments on the play, one of which was: 'The name part couldn't be more like you, Pappy!' ('¡*El papel titular corresponde precisamente contigo, Papaito!*') At this Jaume, now full of crayfish, asparagus, roast turkey, wild strawberries and champagne, smiled for the first time that evening. We wound up around 3 a.m. drinking more and worse champagne to the sound of *flamenco* in a gipsy night club. Truscott and Samstag, who were flying back together at 8 a.m., had let themselves go properly; their good-byes could not have been warmer.

However, Jaume had stood by his guns: declining to commit himself until he could read the amended contract and get it approved by a reliable notary. Nor would he anticipate his good fortune by the purchase of so much as a pig, let alone an ass.

When Truscott finally sent me the document, Len offered his expert advice gratis – he knew all about Broadway contracts, and could tell at a glance whether anything were wrong. 'Maybe Bill and Sammy did a crooked deal together,' he suggested. 'Of course, he's an old friend of mine, but in show business ...'

Shaking Len off, I took the contract to Jaume's cottage. 'A letter from Señor Samstag is attached,' I told him. 'Shall I read it first, or shall I first translate this document?'

'The document first, if you please.'

I read: 'Whereas the Author, a member of the Dramatists Guild of the Authors League of America Inc. (hereinafter called the "Guild") has been preparing the book of a certain play or other literary property now entitled *The Difficult Husband*. And whereas the Producer etc., etc., desires to produce the said play in the United States and Canada, etc., etc. ... Now therefore, in consideration of the premises and the mutual promises and covenants herein contained and other good and valuable considerations, it is agreed:

'FIRST: The Author hereby a) warrants that he is the author of the said play and has a right to enter into this agreement –'

Jaume interrupted: 'But I am not a member of this Guild!'

'Never mind, you can apply for membership.'

'And if they won't accept a foreigner?'

'Don't worry! Señor Truscott will fix you up. Let's get on: "The Author b) agrees that on compliance with this contract –"'

'Maybe, Don Roberto, you should translate the letter first.'

'Very well, then. ... It says here that Señor Samstag greatly enjoyed his visit to Majorca, and is delighted that we all see eye to eye, and that it only remains for you to sign the attached instrument, your agent, Señor Truscott, having agreed with him on the terms.

'Then, wait a bit ... then the tone of the letter changes. While still considering the play to be superb, Señor Samstag suggests certain radical changes in the treatment. It is by no means good theatre yet, he writes. The Difficult Husband, for instance, remains too static a character; his actions are predictable, and so is the eventual victory of his wife. In a sophisticated play, the leading man's character must develop; and this development must be substantiated by brisk dialogue. Here, the Husband should grow gradually less difficult, more *human*, as the action advances. Also, he should be granted an occasional small victory over his wife...'

Jaume's eyes were smouldering. 'He says that, does he, the imbecile?'

I tried to smooth him down. 'After all, show-business people are apt to understand the market. They study it year in, year out.'

'Read on!'

'He insists that the scene where the couple quarrel about household accounts must be changed. Let the husband, instead, teach his wife how to manage something else, something *visible* – say, a television set or a garbage disposer. "In the theatre we want to *see* things," he writes. "Then, when the wife wins his permission to take a long cruise and pretends that she has gone, but stays ashore to save household money – this is most unconvincing! Let her go for her health, really go, and fall in love with a handsome adventurer on the ship! Her husband can get comically jealous at the beginning of the Third Act –"'

'Stop!' Jaume roared. 'Why does this fellow first telegraph that my play is magnificent, and now want to change it altogether, though offering me the same immense sum of money?'

'Patience, Jaume! He cabled "Bravo!" because he hadn't read your play. Now he writes the reverse because he still hasn't read it. Knowing you to be inexperienced, he naturally entrusts *The Difficult Husband* to his assistants, who are expert play-doctors. The suggestions you so dislike emanate from these play-doctors. If you will not rewrite the play, that task necessarily falls to them, or to somone working under their direction.'

'Then it will no longer be mine?'

'Oh yes, it will be! You're protected by the contract. Your name will flash out in red, green, and yellow neon lights from the front of the theatre, and you will get the big money. Play-doctors get no more than their salaries. They can't *write* plays; they can only rewrite them.'

'Willie would never have agreed!'

'Are you sure?'

'Willie would not have changed a single word! He had a stubborn nature.'

'Well, I admit that this letter sounds nonsense – not that I've read *The Difficult Husband* ... But you are faced by a clear choice. Either fight for every word of your play, and be lucky if you keep one in ten; or else refuse to sign the contract.'

'Enough, enough, Don Roberto! My mind is made up. The devil take this contract! If Señor Samstag's assistants care to re-write my play, very good! Let them spin a coin to decide who shall be the author. I will sell *The Difficult Husband* outright, making no conditions whatsoever, except that Señor Samstag must pay me a sum down, in pesetas, and – *pff!* – that's it! ... What might he pay?'

I told him: 'Fortunately it's not a case of buying your *name*: he's only buying your story. Since the Señorita Samstag believes in it so strongly, he might be good for ten thousand dollars – around half a million pesetas. That's nothing for a producer like Samstag.'

Jaume said slowly: 'Not having yet signed my agreement with Señor Truscott, I am still my own master. Let us telegraph Señor Samstag that, if he flies here again, a new one-page contract will be awaiting him at the notary's.'

'And Señor Truscott?'

'For three hundred thousand I can become the Lord of La Coma, which is in the market now; so, since Señor Truscott envies me this cottage, he may have it and welcome. I will add a terrace or two, to round off the property. As for the lemon grove and olives, which are worth far more, they are yours, Don Roberto.'

'Many thanks, Jaume; but I want nothing but your friend-ship. We should dispatch your message at once.'

Three days later Samstag flew in, delighted not to find Bill Truscott about. 'Agents create unnecessary complications between friends, don't you think?' he asked us. A one-page contract in legal Spanish was easily agreed upon, and Samstag had arranged for the necessary pesetas. They went straight into an account which Jaume opened at the Bank of Spain.

As we drove home from Palma, Jaume said the last word on the subject: 'What can be done with a man who complains that a play is dramatically bad before he even reads it? *The Difficult Husband*, as many Majorcans know, though perhaps few Americans, enjoyed a remarkable success at the *Cine Moderno* some years ago. My poor mother took me there. The film ran for three whole weeks. Only an imbecile would wish to change its plot. It was called – what was it called? – ah, now I remember: "*La Vida con Papa*." How does one say that in English, Don Roberto?'

SHE LANDED YESTERDAY

AFTER collecting the family mail at five o'clock one Friday afternoon, in Majorca, where I live, I stopped by at the village café, and found everyone disturbed and excited. I asked what was wrong. 'The Count of Deia is dead,' Catalina told me, from behind the bar. She and her husband, as proprietors of the café, know all the news. I could see that she had been crying.

'But I met him only a few hours ago!' I exclaimed. 'He seemed in perfect health and full of jokes, though perhaps rather sad ones.'

'Where was that, Don Roberto?'

'On the path near the Ass Rock.'

'At what time?'

'Just after the midday Angelus.'

'Then you must have been the last man to see him alive. What did he say?'

'He asked me for a cigarette. I told him that I had no blond tobacco, only black. "All the better," he said. "I do not enjoy smoking straw." I handed him my old seal-skin pouch and a packet of cigarette papers. We sat down together on a rock. He rolled a cigarette, and I offered matches, but he excused himself and used a small burning glass to light his cigarette. He said that this was a more economical procedure, and besides the sun was his friend.'

'Did he make any other remark?' Catalina asked.

'That the sun was indeed his only friend now.'

'The poor gentleman!'

'I had wine in my basket and gave him a drink. He took a sip, and then considerately wiped the mouth of the flask with a clean handkerchief. After discussing a Latin poet admired by both of us we shook hands, whereupon he went up the hill, hoping that I would soon pay him a visit.'

'He was found in the Ass Rock reservoir, at three o'clock – may his soul find peace! Don Julián hurried there, followed by the doctor, who tried artificial respiration. The Count had tied a heavy stone to his feet, but Don Julián, who is a very good priest, always ready to give sinners the benefit of every doubt, insisted that this had been an ill-advised means of reaching the reservoir bottom in search of a fallen coin or some other small object. In effect, that the poor gentleman was the victim of an accident. He pointed out that the Count's gold watch and pocketbook had been placed for security on the wall. Then, although the doctor at last pronounced him dead, Don Julián would not believe it. He bent over the Count, asking him to make a sincere act of repentance. No reply came, but Don Julián says that the Count's face expressed humble assent, and that he therefore felt justified in giving him absolution. The deceased will be buried tomorrow, with the customary rites, the judge having now signed a certificate of accidental death.'

'A great solace for the Count's family,' I said.

'For what remains of it. He has a nonagenarian aunt in Madrid, and a second cousin, a nun, cloistered at Cartagena. The seven-hundred-year-old title is at last extinct.'

'There will be an all-night vigil at his house?'

'Yes, Don Roberto. My husband and I hope to see you there presently.'

How much did I know about the Count, after a casual acquaintance of four or five months? Not very much, really. He was what is called a character. My mother always warned me against becoming a character. I remember that when I once asked her the meaning of 'a character', she said, 'Like people who feed birds in public gardens, and usually have two or three perched on their heads.' But the Count would never have done anything so obvious and vulgar as that. Vultures, in a cemetery, perhaps. He was a neat, ugly little man of fifty, always dressed in the same grey fustian jacket and trousers, with a French hunting waistcoat, and his hirsute but well-manicured hands were, as a rule, fidgeting at the links of a thick gold watch chain. He never wore a hat, and his bald head was lavishly freckled. A humorous contempt for the world showed in the curl of his nostrils, and the anger smouldering behind his black eyes attracted me; most Majorcans are childishly stolid and complaisant. The Count talked a beautiful Castilian and a still more beautiful Majorcan. Our island aristocracy converse in *Mallorquina aulica*, a courtly dialect of their own, close to Provençal, and distinguished by numerous thirteenth-century forms that have disappeared from *Mallorquina plebeia*, the language of commoners. I gathered that the Count was recently widowed and had no children. I knew that he was an admirable Latin scholar, and an authority on the late-medieval Peasants' Revolt; he talked of publishing a monograph on Christopher Columbus, to prove him a Majorcan outlaw who had fled to Genoa after his family estates were confiscated at the collapse of the Revolt. The Count lived alone, attended by a valet, at Ca'n Deia – a tall sixteenth-century house, adjoining the church, which had his coat of arms carved above the lintel. Except for an occasional game of *truc* at the café, with the mayor, the schoolmaster, and the doctor, he took almost no part in village life. Women and children seemed to be scared of him, though I could not understand why, since he never raised his voice nor made a scene.

Every villager of consequence went to pay his last respects that evening. The Count ranked as a local man, because he owned Ca'n Deia; but the family seat was the Palacio Deia, at Palma, and until he settled among us, only six months before his death, Ca'n Deia had stood empty for generations, though it was opened and ritually whitewashed once a year, at Easter. The furniture, pictures, and china suggested the early eighteen-thirties as the period of its last tenancy. According to the sacristan, who preserved ancient village traditions, one of the Count's collateral ancestors – 'one afflicted with most informal habits' – was then guarded there by a couple of servants, to save his family the embarrassment of keeping him at home, or the disgrace of confining him in a madhouse. The sacristan explained that the unfortunate young fellow had had to be sewn into his clothes to prevent him from removing them in public, especially at Mass. 'He came here during the Carlist Wars,' he once told me, 'in the very year when a famine reduced the village to eating locust beans. It was he who contrived those silhouettes hanging on the passage walls. Are they not curious?'

The silhouettes were intricate cut-outs, made of white paper: a palm tree, hunting scenes, pipe-smoking gallants in extravagant costume, heraldic designs, enormous doves, flowers, mermaids, and unicorns, all crazily juxtaposed on a background of blue sugar-loaf paper, but formalized by plain gilt frames.

The dead Count lay upstairs, among white roses and Madonna lilies, wearing court dress adorned with splendid orders. The flower scent nearly drowned the smell of camphor, and carefully placed rose petals hid, I discovered later, the more conspicuous holes (moths? mice?) in the black velvet of his suit – there had been no occasion for him to wear court dress since Alfonso XIII's abdication, more than twenty years before. The Count's face had been decently made up by the midwife, and everyone agreed that he looked as peaceful as a child: she had not disguised the characteristic half-smile at the corner of his mouth.

When I went in, a memory made my own mouth twitch sympathetically '¡O Señor muerto!' I muttered. It was a joke that the Count had told me himself, about a village theatrical show he had once seen. A faithful page, discovering the murdered body of his liege lord, should have cried out, in desperation '¡O Señor! ¡Muerto está! ¡Tarde llegamos!' ('O my lord! You are dead! We have come too late!') But the actor had learned his part from a prompt script without accents or punctuation, so he tripped onto the stage and gaily exclaimed, '¡O Señor muerto, esta tarde llegamos!' 'Oh, Mr Corpse, we are coming this evening!')

Downstairs, in the stone-flagged parlour, we mourners occupied a long line of low, corded chairs, such as almost every Majorcan family keeps for baptisms, funerals, weddings, and first communions. But these had been borrowed from the sacristan's house, next door; Ca'n Deia contained only huge seignorial armchairs in faded red velvet and tall black leather ones with octagonal brass studs. Black coffee and biscuits were served, and a box of cigars lay open on the two-inch-thick tabletop. As the last man to have seen the Count alive, I had to tell my story several times. For the sake of good manners, I embellished it by recalling his comments on the unstinted hospitality that the village worthies had shown him — the devout priest, the correct justice of the peace, the learned schoolmaster, the indefatigable doctor. But one genuine and most enigmatic remark of the Count's I kept to myself, for fear it might perhaps hurt someone's feelings. He had thrown the words over his shoulder as he turned toward the reservoir. 'She landed yesterday, you see. Not far from here. That is why I must leave you.'

Our solemn gathering grew somewhat cozier at eleven o'clock, when the electric light dimmed and recovered three times, as a sign that half an hour later it would be cut off for the night. At this signal, most of the villagers took their leave. Those of us who remained drew up our chairs in a circle around the table, and the Count's burly Majorcan valet, our host, lit long ecclesiastical tapers stuck in pewter candlesticks. Two bottles of brandy, and another of *anís*, appeared on a tray, and we soon started talking freely. There were seven of us: Guillermo, the valet; the schoolmaster, who had literary pretensions; the emaciated sacristan; Maria, the midwife; Don Tomás Fons y Pons, the Count's family lawyer, whom I had not met before; Catalina's husband, who drives our village bus as well as owning the café; and myself.

'An ideally constituted party,' said the schoolmaster, beaming. 'More in number than the Graces, and less in number than the Muses.'

'But,' said the sacristan, 'precisely equal in number with those who sufficiently honour the memory of the deceased gentleman upstairs to keep an all-night vigil for him!'

'I have seen no member of the nobility about the village,' said Catalina's husband, 'though news of his accident must have reached the capital hours ago.'

The lawyer stroked his white moustache, hemmed, and explained: 'Many are out of town, the rest are attending the Italian opera. But we can expect representatives of all the great families at tomorrow's funeral service. They cannot well omit this act of courtesy to one who was not only the senior nobleman of Majorca but also hereditary pomander-bearer to His Majesty the King of Spain.'

'The hypocrites, how they disliked my master!' the valet burst out. 'His father fell in love with a beautiful peasant girl from Costitx at the Martinmas pig-killing, and had the good sense to marry her, instead of seducing the poor innocent and flinging a hundred-peseta note in her lap, as any of them would have done. She was a woman of great character, was the old Countess, and pious to a fault. Those degenerates pretended to scorn our Count as the offspring of a misalliance, yet they envied him his learning, his courage, his independence of spirit! None of them but would have been better for a few spoonfuls of wholesome peasant blood in his veins. The old Countess died when my master was five years old, and he adored her memory; indeed, some say that it was the unfortunate nobleman's ruin.'

'Come, man!' Maria, the midwife, challenged him. 'How can adoration for a mother's memory ruin anyone?'

Guillermo appealed to the lawyer. 'Don Tomás, correct me if I am wrong, but this is the story as told in the servants' quarters, and we are sticklers for accuracy.'

'Tell it your own way, Guillermo,' said the lawyer.

'Well,' the valet continued, 'Don Ignacio, the Count's only brother, two years his junior, drove a fast car down the La Puebla road. Rain had fallen, and the tarmac was slippery with mud from the potato carts. He had his wife beside him, and both were killed instantly when they skidded and hit a tree. Their graceful, green-eyed, thirteen-year-old daughter, Doña Acebo, came under my master's guardianship – she had no suitable aunts or other relatives on either side of the family – and since he was a bachelor, this embarrassed him a little. But he accepted his responsibility, and, finding the child sadly ignorant, though not lacking in intelligence or humour, removed her from the convent school where she had studied, and became her tutor. They lived in the Palacio Deia. He taught Doña Acebo history, heraldry, geography, botany, French, and Latin. She soon dropped her school friends, because none of them had the same interests or enjoyed the same liberty as herself, and my master kept her out of Palma society – "Lest she should turn into a profligate modern woman," as he said. Only three hours a day she studied, yet they were worth thirty hours at a convent, for he taught like an angel, and work was more like play to them. The family chaplain, of course, attended to her religious needs. My master took Doña Acebo everywhere with him – to theatres, concerts, bullfights, cockfights, free-style wrestling matches – but both enjoyed far more the entertainments of their own devising. They were formidable jokesters, and would leave the palace at all hours, disguised as gipsies, or drunks, or pedlars, or peasants, and have a thousand droll adventures in the bystreets of Palma.'

'Give us an example,' said the schoolmaster. ' "A thousand droll adventures" is no way to tell a story !'

'Well, they once competed as to who could first earn fifty pesetas from a stranger by barefaced fraud. I was the timekeeper. My master, wearing a cloth cap, a false beard, and spectacles, visited a second-hand bookstall, where he paid five pesetas for a volume on apiculture. He then added a zero to the figure on the flyleaf, wrapped the book in a sheet of brown paper, slipped into a café to find a newspaper, and went through the obituary notices on the second page of *La Ultima Hora*. Discovering that a certain Don Fulano de Tal, an importer of uralite piping, had died only two streets away, he took the book to his house, and inquired for Don Fulano. "Alas, he is dead !" sobbed the widow. "Alas, and doubly alas !" echoed the Count. "Don Fulano, a valued friend of mine, ordered this volume a week ago, and I have just managed to procure it in Barcelona." He was turning sorrowfully away when the widow asked leave to inspect the book. "Ah, a practical treatise on beekeeping," she said tenderly. "My poor angel must, after all, have contemplated the tranquil country life that I so often urged upon him, begging him to sell his business in good time. How right I was, for an overworked heart carried him off. I must buy this as a memento of his affection. How much did it cost you?" My master showed her the price on the flyleaf, and mentioned another five pesetas of postal charges. In the circumstances, he was prepared to forgo his commission, and the widow let him do so, thanking him for his nobility of heart. That game took less than half an hour, but Doña Acebo had already won the contest. She sold two out-of-date twenty-five-peseta raffle tickets for an automobile to some

German tourists and was home before my watch marked five minutes.'

'Proceed with your story, man!' said Maria, the midwife. 'You mentioned the Count's ruinous love for his dead mother.'

'I am coming to that. The innocent comradeship between the Count and Doña Acebo could not last forever, because, as she grew older and plumper, she came to bear such a close resemblance to the portrait of her grandmother, the old Countess, whose Christian name she inherited, that they might have been twins. In short, when she reached the age of fifteen, my master fell in love with her, much to his alarm and confusion. What should he do? The two had become so deeply attached to each other, from living alone in the great palace, with only the chaplain and us servants as chorus to their prolonged comedy, that it seemed most cruel to send her away. But would it not be worse if she stayed? After much heart-searching, and with the chaplain's dubious approval, he decided to marry her. Of course, though marriage between uncle and niece can be sanctioned by the Church, out of respect for a well-known gospel precedent, such unions are extremely rare. Here in this village, if an uncle were to show a niece undue tenderness, conches would be blown all night around his house, and filth left on the doorstep. But to a Count of Deia all things within reason are permitted, for did not his ancestors play a distinguished part in restraining the Majorcan clergy from allegiance to the anti-popes at Avignon? Nevertheless, it was a costly and troublesome procedure, even for my master, to secure a dispensation from the Vatican; to begin with, the Bishop of Palma had to supply a covering letter, explaining the peculiar nature of the case, and the Bishop raised technical difficulties.'

'Enough, Guillermo!' interrupted the lawyer. 'Leave the intricacies of canon law to canons, and stick to the facts! The Count of Deia and Doña Acebo were married, and it proved no happy marriage.'

'That is the truth,' the valet agreed. 'At first, Doña Acebo, who was still only sixteen years old, treated the wedding as another of their wild, scandalous jokes, and one that would give her an enviable social status, so they went off on their honeymoon to San Sebastián in the highest spirits. Then, finding that she was seriously expected to become her uncle's wife, in fact as well as name, and to present him with an heir, she felt a certain distaste and even, it may be, moral scruples, though their union had been fully legitimized.'

'I heard some talk of that,' said the midwife, keeping a straight face. 'She rejected his caresses, but in a most affectionate manner.'

' "Affectionate" is right, Doña Maria,' the valet answered, no less gravely. 'The Count was very ticklish, and whenever he attempted any more than avuncular endearments, she would tickle him in the ribs until he nearly died from laughter and annoyance.'

The lawyer interrupted again. 'A tragic tale! The exasperated Count, aware that he had made a serious error, but determined to teach his Countess a lesson, sued for an annulment – which proved as troublesome and costly to obtain as the marriage licence – without her consent or knowledge. One fine morning, she awoke to find the wedding ring absent from her finger, and when she raised a hue and cry, Margalida the housemaid informed her, as she had been instructed, that she no longer had any need of the trinket.'

'Doña Acebo resented this joke so bitterly,' said the valet, nodding his head up and down for emphasis, 'that the couple never resumed their former carefree play, and soon she ran off with a young Colombian band leader, whom she had encountered at Tito's Bar. From every city they visited, to comply with his engagements, she would send the Count picture postcards of lovers – some sentimental, some grossly comic, and all in the lowest popular taste. The Count grew increasingly morose, and took to his bed, seeing nobody. When at last he regained his health, we found him altered and the prey to a compulsion for strange games. If we attended Mass in Santa Eulalia church, for instance, where patterns of alternate white and dark-red marble squares line the pavement, he would experience great difficulty in approaching the altar steps; there were always holy women kneeling in prayer on the red marble squares he felt he had to tread upon. "Excuse me, good woman," he would mutter. "Would you mind moving twenty centimetres to the right?" They would look up in great vexation, but he always got his way. The Mass priest would blanch when he saw him, because the Count, once he had gained the steps, would wring his hands and utter a low moan of "Oo-oo!" at the slightest mispronunciation or grammatic error in Latin.'

'I watched him once for a half an hour at the Palm Sunday Fair,' put in Catalina's husband, 'some three months after Doña Acebo's departure. He was leaning over the counter of the shooting gallery, and behind him waited a queue of little boys, whom he made stand to attention, like soldiers. Having fired a few preliminary shots to gauge the precise twist in his rifle barrel, he bought an enormous stack of counters and shot with monotonous insistence at the same iron plate. "Crack!" "Crack!" "Crack!" At each hit, a door would fly open, and out came a doll, dressed as a waitress, with a tray in her hands, and on it a miniature bottle of so-called *vermut*. He would beckon for the bottle, uncork it, pour the contents down the throat of the foremost boy, send him back to the end of the queue, and resume his marksmanship. The proprietor shouted curses at him, but could do nothing else.'

'Why did he leave the palace?' asked the sacristan. 'Was it to avoid unhappy memories of his marriage?'

'Perhaps,' said the valet. 'But he announced that he had taken refuge from the enemy, here in the mountains. When I inquired what enemy, he answered, "Those who smoke blond tobacco; those who strew our quiet Majorcan beaches with pink, peeling human flesh; those who roar round the island in foreign cars ten metres long; those who prefer aluminium to earthenware, and plastics to glass; those who demolish the old quarters of Palma and erect travel agencies, souvenir shops, and tall, barrack-like hotels on the ruins; those who keep their radios bawling incessantly along the street at siesta time; those who swill Caca-Loco and bottled beer!" The last straw came with the closing of the Café Figaro, which everyone of character in Palma used to frequent and the conversion of its premises into palatial offices for Messrs Thomas Cook & Son. He had sat there most mornings, at a corner table, playing dominoes with the Cat-stewer –'

'Who was that?' I asked.

Both the schoolmaster and Catalina's husband wanted to tell me about the Cat-stewer, but the sacristan held the floor. It appears that this well-known figure had been cook to the old Bishop of Palma, who died, and the new Bishop made the mistake of criticizing one of his sauces. Though he kept silent, his pride was wounded, and at a banquet to which the new Bishop invited the Captain-General and his staff, he served up a delicious rabbit ragout. When called into the dining room to receive extravagant compliments, he said, 'Yes, beyond all doubt I am the best cook in Majorca! I can make stewed alley cat taste like the tenderest rabbit. And now, My Lord Bishop, I have finished, and wish you and your guests a very good night!' He threw his tall chef's hat on the floor, and marched out in glory. After that, he drifted around Palma picking up cigarette butts dropped by tourists, and accepting coffees from Palma folk who admired his spirit. He never cooked another meal. In the severe shortage of cooks caused by the building of too many hotels, the Cat-stewer was wooed with enormous offers – up to a hundred thousand pesetas a year – for his culinary services. He only spat for an answer.

'What did the Count do about his persecution by the ex-Countess's postcards?' I asked.

It was an embarrassing question. Three of my fellow-mourners stirred uncomfortably in their chairs, but kept silent, warned by the lawyer's frown.

Maria, the midwife, took pity on me. 'The Count had peasant blood, Don Roberto. It is known that, in his chagrin, he consulted a wise woman at Andraitx. Nothing can be said for certain as to the advice she gave him. At all events, the persecution ended when Doña Acebo died, early last year.'

'How did she die, Doña Maria?'

'By drowning, also. The new liner in which she and her young band leader were travelling from Brazil to the Argentine struck a rock and foundered.'

Don Tomás hastily changed the subject. 'The Count had the kindest heart,' he babbled. 'One day, plagued by his neurotic compulsion, he tried to pass from one end of San Miguel Street to the other while dodging alternately to the right and left of persons who approached. This made him perform a hazardous dance, because it was a busy Saturday morning, with the farmers, as usual, crowding the streets and the tables outside the Café Suiza. Along roared a Vespa motor scooter; the Count dashed across its path, trying to pass it on his right. The scooter struck his foot, the rider fell off, and the machine fell, though its engine continued to throb where it lay overturned by the side-walk. A baker's boy astride a bicycle, balancing a huge tray of pastries on his head, ran into the Vespa, and all the pastries were spilled. "Young man," cried the Count to the Vespa rider, who was nursing a bruised elbow, "how dare you take your dangerous machine down San Miguel Street on a Saturday morning?" A blind woman lottery vender, seated on the curb, felt her skirts lifted by the wind of the Vespa's exhaust, and let out a scream. The Count immediately paid the baker's boy, and then consoled the old creature, kissed her hand, bought five lottery tickets and tore them up – having a soul above money – and guided her into the Suiza, where she rapidly downed several brandies. The baker's boy collected the pastries, dusted them on his trousers, restacked them on the tray, and rode on, the richer by a hundred pesetas. The deceased had his faults, as who had not, but will we ever look upon his like again?'

We sat talking and drinking until five o'clock, and then prepared to depart. We went upstairs for a last farewell, before leaving the Count to the companionship of his best friend, who was already gilding the mountain-tops. 'The Spanish taste for black velvet,' observed the schoolmaster sententiously, eyeing the Count's court dress, 'is often thought to reflect the gloomy side of our national character. That is an error. Our ancestors gloried in the indigo plant, which alone afforded them a fast sable dye to contrast with the brilliant white of their linen cuffs and ruffs. Spanish black velvet never turned rusty or green. Guillermo did well in choosing those lilies and roses to set it off. Our friend's darkest moods were always enlivened by vivid flashes of the purest white.'

•

The funeral Masses for the Count took place at ten o'clock, and every noble house in Palma sent representatives. Our village square was crowded with their sleek American and Italian cars. The visitors kept together in a tight, silent bunch, and made me feel a peasant of peasants. Throughout the service, which the Bishop himself conducted, with the aid of several subsidiary priests, including Don Julián, I was puzzling to myself: 'She landed yesterday, you see. Not far from here. That is why I must leave you.' *Who* had landed that Thursday? Where? 'She' could not have been Doña Acebo, and it was generally agreed that no other woman had figured in the Count's adult life. Maria, the midwife, had hinted at a recourse to witchcraft, but since witchcraft is a subject that Majorcans never discuss with foreigners, I concluded that it would be wiser to let the problem lie.

The next day, as it happened, Jack and Gloria Stonegate – Jack is a shrewd North of England retired businessman, and Gloria is a genius at repairing antique china – had asked my wife and me to lunch with them at Paguera, which is a few miles from Andraitx. Paguera has the sunniest climate in Majorca, which means, of course, insufficient rain, and therefore a perpetual water shortage. But against that you may set a fine, sandy beach, pine forests, and swimming as early as March.

'Anything new happened here since last time?' I asked Jack, over drinks.

'Nothing much, old boy, except two motor-bike accidents, one death by drowning, a kerosene shortage, a fight between some Dutchmen in the grocery store, and a coffin washed up on the islet three days ago.'

'The coffin sounds the most interesting.'

'It certainly was! It contained a carved wooden doll, about three feet long – obviously a portrait of someone real – wearing a bridal robe and veil. What do you make of *that*? Round her shoulders she wore a miniature postbag, striped with the Spanish colours, and in the bag we found an assortment of rather stupid amatory picture postcards from all over the place – Tangier, Honolulu, Blackpool, Atlantic City, Copenhagen. The name and address of the person who had received them all had been carefully scraped away with a razor, and there was no message on any of them – only the signature "A".'

'How big was the coffin?'

'Life-size. It must have been a long time in the water. I got a good look at the cards. The latest one came from Rio de Janeiro, postmarked eighteen months ago. A yard or two of frayed rope hung from a handle of the coffin. Evidently it had been weighted down by stones – the lead lining wasn't quite heavy enough to keep it on the bottom – but it must have broken loose in the big storm last week. The Guardias and the priest were examining it as I wandered up. The priest seemed shocked to the core, and even the Guardias were upset. What do you make of that story, old boy?'

'Oh, just a practical joke,' I reassured Jack. 'Some Majorcans will go to any length for a laugh – you'd be surprised!'

'I call it a damned macabre form of humour,' Jack grumbled. 'But then, I'm English.'

Please do not ask whether, in my opinion, Doña Acebo's death by drowning was just a coincidence. Be content with facts. The coffined doll must be accepted as valid evidence that the Count, with a witch's assistance, tried to procure Doña Acebo's death by magical means. Unofficially, my fellow-villagers do not doubt that he succeeded. They condemn his action as un-Catholic, of course, but the provocation was enormous, and how else could a Count of Deia, with a peasant mother, have been expected to act? Officially, they agree with the priest: it was a sad coincidence. Officially, so do I.

THE WHITAKER NEGROES

HAUNTINGS, whether in waking life or dream, are emotionally so powerful, yet can be so rarely ascribed to any exterior agency, that they are now by common consent allotted to the morbid pathologist for investigation – not, as once, to the priest or augur. A number of hauntings 'yield to treatment', as the saying is. The great Dr Henry Head told me once about a patient of his who was haunted by a tall dark man, always standing on the bedside mat. Head diagnosed a trauma in the patient's brain, of which the tall dark man was a projection, and proved his case by moving the bed slowly around; the tall dark man swung with it in a semi-circle until he ended on a veranda just outside the french window. An operation removed him altogether. And I read in an American medical paper the other day of a man who, as a result of advanced syphilis, was haunted by thousands of women every night; after he had been given extract of snake-root they were reduced to the manageable number of one.

There are also occasional hauntings which most psychologists would tend to dimiss as fantasies or, however grotesque, as symbols of some inner conflict; but which deserve to be accepted at their face value and placed in the correct historical context. Let me describe a persistent haunting from my own case-history. I am glad to say that it did not originate in my ghost-ridden childhood and is therefore easier to assess, though I cannot claim to have been in good mental and physical health at the time; on the contrary, I was suffering from vivid nightmares and hallucinations of the First World War, in which I had fought. Shells used to burst on my bed at night, by day I would throw myself flat on my face if a car backfired, and every rose garden smelt terrifyingly of phosgene gas. However, I felt a good deal better now that the War seemed to be over: an armistice had been signed, and the Germans were not expected to renew the struggle.

January 1919 found me back again with the Royal Welch Fusilier reserve battalion, at Limerick; where twenty years before my grandfather had been the last Bishop of the Established Protestant Church of Ireland. Limerick was now a stronghold of Sinn Fein, King George Street had become O'Connell Street, and when our soldiers took a stroll out of barracks they never went singly and were recommended to carry entrenching-tool handles in answer to the local shillelaghs. This return as a foreign enemy to the city with which my family had been connected for over two hundred years would have been far more painful but for old Reilly, an antique-dealer, who lived near the newly-renamed Sarsfield Bridge. Reilly remembered my father and three of my uncles, and gave me fine oratorical accounts of my Aunt Augusta Caroline's prowess in the hunting field, and of the tremendous scenes at my grandfather's wake – at which his colleague, the Catholic Bishop, had made attendance compulsory in tribute to his eminence as a Gaelic scholar and archaeologist. I bought several things from Reilly: Irish silver, prints, and a century-old pair of white, elbow-length Limerick gloves, left by the last of the Misses Rafferty and so finely made (from chicken-skin, he told me) that they folded into a brass-hinged walnut shell.

The shop smelt of dry rot and mice, but I would have gone there to chat more often, had it not been for a nightmarish picture hanging in the shop entrance: a male portrait brightly painted on glass. The sitter's age was indeterminate, his skin glossy-white, his eyes Mongolian, their look imbecile; he had two crooked dog-teeth, a narrow chin, and a billy-cock hat squashed low over his forehead. To add to the horror, some humorist had provided the creature with a dudeen pipe, painted on the front of the glass, from which a wisp of smoke was curling. Reilly said that the picture had come from the heirs of a potato-famine emigrant who had returned with a bag of dollars to die comfortably of drink in his native city. Why this face haunted and frightened me so much I could not explain; but it used to recur in my imagination for years, especially when I had fever. I told myself that if I ever saw a midnight ghost – as opposed to midday ghosts, which had been common enough phenomena during the later, neurasthenic stages of the War, and less frightening than pathetic – it would look exactly like that.

In the spring of 1951, when Reilly had been thirty years in his grave, Julia Fiennes visited me in Majorca. She was an American: Irish-Italian on her father's side, New Orleans-French on her mother's; a textile designer by profession; young, tall, good-looking, reckless and romantic. She had come 'to take a look at Europe before it blows up'. When we first met, a shock passed between her and me of the sort usually explained in pseudo-philosophic terms as 'We must have met in a previous incarnation.' Psychologists postulate 'compatible emotion-groups'. I am content to call it 'Snap!' Indeed, as it proved, Julia and I could converse in a joking verbal shorthand, which meant little to anyone else, but for us expressed a range of experience so complex that we could never have translated it into everyday language. An embarrassing, if exhilarating discovery, because this rapport between us, strong as it was, proved inappropriate both to her course of life and mine. We wanted nothing from each other except a humorously affectionate acknowledgement of the strength of the link; thirty-three years separated us; we belonged to different civilizations; I was perfectly happy in my own life, and she was set on going on and on until she came to a comfortable stop in either contentment or exhaustion; which she has since done.

With Beryl, to whom I am married, I enjoy the less spectacular but more relevant rapport that comes of having all friends in common, four children, and no secrets from each other. The only eccentric form which our rapport takes is that sometimes, if I am working on some teasing historical problem and go to bed before I reach a solution, its elements may intrude not into my dream but into hers. The classic instance was when she woke up one morning, thoroughly annoyed by the absurdity of her nightmare: 'A crowd of hags were swinging from the branches of a large tree in our olive grove and chopping off the ends with kitchen knives. And a horde of filthy gipsy children were waiting below to catch them ...' I apologized to Beryl. I had been working on textual problems in the New Testament, and established the relation between *Matthew* xviii, 20 and *Isaiah* xvii, 6 which ran: 'As the gleaning of an olive-tree: two or three berries at the top of the topmost branch'; and of this with

Deuteronomy xxiv, 20 : 'When thou bearest thine olive-trees thou shalt not go over the boughs again : the gleanings shall be for the stranger, the fatherless and the widow.' I went to bed wondering idly how the fatherless and the widow managed to glean those inaccessible olives, if no able-bodied stranger happened to be about.

'Well, now you know !' Beryl answered crossly.

Once when Julia and I were taking a walk down a dark road not far from the sea, and exchanging our usual nonsense, I suddenly asked her to tell me something really frightening. She checked her pace, clutched my arm and said : 'I ought to have told you, Robert, days ago. It happened when I was staying with my grandmother in New Orleans, the one who had the topaz locket and eyes like yours. I guess I must have been twelve years old, and used to ride off to school on my bicycle about half a mile away. One summer evening I thought I'd come home by a different route, through a complicated criss of cross-streets. I'd never tried it before. Soon I lost my way and found myself in a dead-end, with a square patio behind a rusty iron gate, belonging to an old French mansion overgrown with creepers. The shutters were green too. It was a beautifully cool, damp place in that heat. And as I stood with my hand on the latch, I looked up, and there at an attic window I saw a face ... It grinned and rapped on the glass with its leprous-white fingers and beckoned to me ...'

By Julia's description it was the identical face that had been painted on glass in Mr Reilly's shop. When I told her about it, we broke into a run of perfect terror, hurrying towards the nearest bright light.

I thought it over afterwards. Perhaps Julia had become aware of my long-buried fear, which then became confused in her imagination with childhood memories of New Orleans; and it stood out so vividly that she really believed that she had seen the face grinning at her. She mentioned no pipe; but then the pipe could be discounted as extraneous.

After supper, an American called Hank, a New York banker's son, burst into the house, in a state of semi-collapse. Since he came of age Hank had fallen down on every job found for him by his father, and now drifted about Europe as a remittance-man. He wanted to write, though without an inkling of how to begin, and was more than a bore about his problems. Hank told me once: 'The night before I sailed my father said a very cruel thing to me. He said: "Hank, you're a good watch, but there's a part missing somewhere." ' As a regular time-piece Hank was certainly a dead loss; and the place of the missing part had been filled by an erratic ancillary movement which by-passed time altogether. For instance, a few days before this, Hank had begun to jabber hysterically about a terrifying earth-quake, and wondered whether the world were coming to an end. Next morning the papers mentioned a very limited earth-quake in Southern Spain, which had swung pictures on walls, dislodged cornices from half a dozen buildings in a small town, and made several girls in the telephone exchange faint for terror. Now, Hank could hardly have felt the distant shock, although Majorca is said to form part of a range, mostly sub-merged, which continues south-westward to the mainland; but he had certainly caught the emotion of the frightened telephone girls.

'What's new, Hank?' I asked coldly.

'I've had a most horrible experience,' he gasped. 'Give me a drink, will you? I took a car to Sóller this afternoon. The heel had come off my walking shoe and I wanted to get it fixed. You know Bennasar the shoemaker, off the market square? I was just about to go in when I happened to look through the window ...'

Julia and I glanced at each other. We both knew what Hank was going to say. And he said it: 'I saw a frightful face ...'

That made us feel more scared than ever.

Soon afterwards Julia went off on a rambling tour through France, Austria and Italy, and next year revisited Majorca with her mother. That was September 1952. She found me collaborat-ing in a film-script with Will Price. Will comes from Mississippi; but New Orleans is one of his family's stamping grounds, so he and Mrs Fiennes were soon discussing third and fourth cousins. One day as we all sat outside a café, Julia happened to

mention Hank. 'Who's Hank?' the others wanted to know. We
explained, and Julia repeated the story of the New Orleans face.
Her mother gasped and shook her roughly: 'Darling, why in
Heaven's name didn't you tell me about it at the time?'

'I was terrified.'

'I believe you're making it up from something I told you,
sweetie. I saw the same face myself before you were born – *and*
the rusty iron gate – *and* the creepers and the shutters. '

'You never told me anything of the sort. Besides, I saw it myself. I don't have other people's visions. You mustn't confuse me
with Hank.'

It occurred to me: 'Probably her mother had the vision, or
whatever it was, first. And then Julia as a child must have heard
her telling the story to somebody, and incorporated it in her own
private nightmare world.'

But Will eased back in his chair and, turning to Mrs Fiennes,
asked in the playful Southern accent that they were using:
'Honey, did you ever hear them up there in the old attic, sloshing water all over the place?'

None of us understood what he meant.

That night, when we were sitting about, drinking *coñac*, Will
raised his voice: 'Ladies and gentlemen, may I have your permission to spin a yarn?'

'Why, of course.'

Will started: 'A good many years ago my father's law firm,
Price & Price, acted for the mortgagees of a bankrupt property
in Mississippi. Money was not forthcoming, so my father consented to take his fees in real estate – about eighty acres of almost
worthless land at Pond near Fort Adams. Fort Adams was once
a prosperous river port for the cotton country east of the River;
the town itself was perched on the high bluffs which overhang
the water hereabouts. But the River suddenly chose to change
course five miles to the west and left Fort Adams with a wide
frontage of swamp, so that all trade moved along to Natchez
and Baton Rouge, which were still ports. These bluffs form the
edge of a three-hundred-mile line of hills raised, they say, by
prehistoric dust storms blowing in from the Great Plains, and
cut up by streams and swamps. There used to be dozens of rich

plantations in the hills, but when the River deserted Fort Adams they were abandoned and allowed to revert to jungle.

'A victim of this catastrophe was Pond, a village that had got its name from the cattle-pond which its leading citizen, old man Lemnowitz, dug and surrounded with two-storey frame stores and warehouses. It used to be a tough job to fetch cotton over the hills from the plantations in the interior. The bales were loaded on enormous, sixteen-wheeled wagons drawn by from six to ten yoke oxen. Teamsters and planters would camp at Pond before making the final drive up-hill to Fort Adams. Old man Lemnowitz hired them extra oxen for the effort, and carried on a thriving trade in supplies of all sorts which he had hauled up from the River in the off-season.

'There were still traces of ancient wealth near Pond when I visited it – ruins of the ante-bellum mansions and slave-quarters, with huge, twisted vines writhing up through the floors – and at Pond itself Lemnowitz's warehouse, formerly a sort of Macy's, was still in business under the same name. But only one corner was now occupied : by a small, not very elegant, store that sold tobacco, notions, staples and calico. It also called itself the Pond Post Office.

'The rest of Pond was jungle. My mother had come down there to see whether Price & Price owned any camellias; because sometimes these old planters collected rare flowers, and camellias could still be found growing wild in their deserted gardens. No ! No orchids in that area, but camellias had been imported from all over the world, including even the Chinese mountains where they originally belonged. I was there to keep my mother company and check the land lines. Well, I went to buy a pack of cigarettes in the Lemnowitz store, and before I could get my change, a Thing walked in..

'It was undoubtedly human, in a weird way – walked upright and had the correct number of limbs. It even strode up to the counter and held out a dime for a can of snuff. But for the rest ... The face was a glazed greenish white, with four fangs that crossed over the lips, and a protruding underlip. It had dark-brown hair, dripping with wet, under a black felt hat – the sort that gave the po' white trash from Georgia their nickname of "wool-hats". Long arms ending in gauntlets – the local work-gloves of canvas and leather with stiff cuffs – which hung below its knees as it walked. Muddy "overhawls", leather brogans called "clod-hoppers", and a stink as if fifty cess-pools had been opened simultaneously. I said nothing, except perhaps "Oh !" What would any of you have said in the circumstances? Imagine the dark cavern of a mouldering warehouse behind you, with acres of empty shelves lost in the gloom, and then in It comes through the door with the blazing sun behind it. When It vanished again, I ran to the window to make sure that my mother had not fainted, and then tip-toed back to the counter. *"What was that?"* "Why, that was only a Whitaker Negro," Mr Lemnowitz said casually. "Never seen one before?" He seemed to be enjoying the situation.'

As Will told the story my old terrors came alive again. 'Well, what was it really?' I croaked.

'I guess it was just a Whitaker Negro,' said Will. 'Later, I decided to check up on my sanity. Mr Lemnowitz told me that for a couple of nickels Boy Whitaker, who was only a half-Whitaker, would guide me to where his folk lived. And he did. There are, or were, several families of Whitaker Negroes near Pond, tucked away in the jungle swamps where nobody ever ventures, not even the Sanitary Inspector. You have to understand the geography of these hills and reckon with their amazing verdancy and complete lack of vistas. One can march in a straight line up and down hills and over swamps for scores of miles without seeing a self-respecting horizon. The jungle is so thick in places that whole families have grown up and died within a mile of neighbours whose existence they didn't even suspect; and we Mississippians are noted for our gregariousness. I don't know how I ever reached the place myself, because I was working to windward and the stench spread for half a mile around the place. I nearly threw up even before I arrived. They live tax-free and aren't mentioned in the census, and don't of course have to send their kids to school, still less get drafted for military service. The kids live in wallows under their huts, which are built on piles: apparently they don't come out much until they're fourteen years old or so – can't stand the sun. A good documentary sequence could be taken of a sow and her litter wallowing in the slime with a bunch of young Whitaker monsters: you could title it *Symbiosis* – which is what we call a "fo'bit" word.

'The adults make a sort of living by raising hogs and chickens: enough to keep them in snuff and brogans and gauntlets and other necessities. The hair proved to be mostly spanish-moss clapped wet on the head to keep it cool – it comes grey-green and goes dark when you soak it; but their real hair is also long, brown and wavy, not kinky in the usual negroid style. The brogans and gauntlets were filled with water. You see, they have no sweat-glands – that's their trouble. It's a hereditary condition and their skin needs to be kept wet all the while, or they die. They're Negroes; but said to be mixed with Choctaw Indian, also perhaps a strain of Chickasaw and Natchez.'

Someone asked: 'Didn't the snuff get a bit *damp*, Will?'

Will answered blandly: 'No, sir, it did not! Snuff is "dipped" not snuffed, in those parts. It's sold in cans about an inch and a half high. The lid of the can is used to dip a little snuff into the buccal pouch – which is another "fo'bit" word meaning the hollow under your nether lip, excuse me for showing off.'

Most of the *coñac*-drinkers grinned incredulously, but Will turned to me: 'Did you ever hear of Turtle Folk? That's what they call whites afflicted by the same disease. There are quite a few cases up and down the Mississippi – Natchez, Vicksburg, Yazoo City, Baton Rouge – kept a close secret, though. Once I was in a house at Natchez where they kept a turtle-man in the attic, and I heard him sloshing water about overhead. That was what Julia must have seen in New Orleans, and Mrs Fiennes before her. And I guess what you saw in Limerick was a portrait of a turtle-man brought back from the South as a curiosity.'

We asked Will: 'How did they get there? And why are they called "Whitaker Negroes"?'

He answered: 'I was coming to that. Around 1810, or so the story goes, a big planter named George Whitaker grew disgusted with his labour problems. He was an intelligent, wide-eyed, gullible New Englander, with Christian leanings, who wanted to reform the South and incidentally get even richer than he already was. He disliked the business of buying slaves and breeding them like cattle – with the result, he said, that they had no traditions, no morals, and no discipline but what could be instilled into them by fear. Ideally, he thought, a planter should be able to take a long vacation, like a European landlord, and come back to find work proceeding smoothly under coloured overseers – only petty crimes to punish, and the crops properly harvested. He argued that if the early slave-traders had kept families and clans together under their African chiefs, the labour problem would not have existed. Then it occurred to him: "Why not experiment?" And he went down to New Orleans, where he interviewed the famous pirate Jean Lafitte. "Sir," he said, "I wish you to visit Africa on my behalf and bring me back a whole tribe of Negroes. Two hundred is the figure I aim at, but a hundred would do. I'll pay you two hundred dollars a head: men, women and children. But mind, it must be a whole tribe, not samples from a score of them, or I don't buy."

'George was a serious man, and Jean Lafitte decided to take his offer. He sailed to the Gold Coast with his brother Pierre on the next tide and there, almost at once, as luck would have it, surprised a whole tribe on the march. The Negroes had been expelled from somewhere in the interior, and being in a pretty poor way, offered no resistance. The Lafittes got two hundred of them aboard, made ingenious arrangements for their welfare on the voyage, and brought across alive one hundred and fifty – smuggled them through Fort Adams and the Bayou St John until Pond came in sight. This constituted, you see, fraudulent evasion of the 1808 Federal embargo on the importation of slaves; so two hundred dollars a head was not an unreasonable price, considering the risk. But think of it in terms of modern money! Well, Mr Lemnowitz told me, at Pond, that when George Whitaker saw the livestock that the Lafittes had brought back from Africa, and realized they were now his responsibility – though because of their constitution, of no more use as field workers than the bayou alligators – he turned deathly white. He paid Jean Lafitte without a word; then he went home, made out his will, bequeathing the bulk of his land to the then "Territory of Mississippi" – after which he and his young wife jumped into the River, hand in hand, and were not seen again.

'Someone took over the plantation, but allowed the Whitakers to remain in a swamp and make out as best as they could. And they hung on there long after the Whitaker mansion was swallowed up by the jungle. Their "forty" is tax-free and inviolable because the original deed of gift represented taxes paid in perpetuity. About fifteen years ago a Whitaker went crazy – they are none of them very bright – and hit the trail for he didn't know where. He travelled from swamp to swamp, living off the land, and eventually reached the town of Woodville which is not very far away as the crow flies, but a thousand miles as the jungle grows. The good people of Woodville, who normally publish an extra of their local paper only when a war is declared or a President assassinated, hurried one through the press with the banner headline: "MAN FROM MARS!" because the poor wretch was half-dead and couldn't explain himself, and all the horses in the town were bolting, and the women screaming their heads off.'

'And the Choctaw blood?'

'The Choctaws and Chickasaws were the local Indians, who obligingly moved away from the neighbourhood to make room for cotton. I was told that a few rogue males stayed behind in the swamps, mostly pox-cases, and intermarried with the Whitaker Negroes for want of other women.'

'Did your mother find any camellias?'

Will, detecting a hint of irony in the innocent question, answered: 'Thank you, ma'am. She got a lapful.'

Then he turned to me again. 'Do you know anyone on *Time* magazine?'

'Only the editor,' I said. 'I happened to rent Tom Matthews a house here in 1931, while he was still a book reviewer.'

'Then ask him to send you a copy of a piece about Turtle Folk published that year.'

'I certainly will.'

And in due course of time Tom sent me the medical column of *Time*, December 14th, 1931, and this is what I read:

TURTLE FOLK

At Houston, Miss., a Mrs C. keeps a tub of water in her back yard for an extraordinary purpose. It is a ducking tub for her five-year-old son. Every time he feels uncomfortable he jumps in, clothes and all. Mrs C. does not scold. For that is the only way the boy can keep comfortable. He lacks sweat glands, which in normal people dissipate two to three quarts of cooling perspiration every day.

Mrs C. has another son, an infant, who likewise lacks sweat glands. He is too young to go ducking himself. So she dowses him from time to time with scuppers of water. Neither child can sleep unless his night clothes and mattress are wet. They take daytime naps in their damp cellar, with moist sacks for pillows.

Nearby at Vardaman, Miss., are two farmer brothers similarly affected. Each works alternate half days. While one plows the other soaks himself in a creek. Every once in a while the worker saunters to the creek for a cool dowsing. The brothers have a sister who dunks herself in the cistern back of their house.

They have a sweatless neighbour woman who must also wet herself for comfort.

At Vicksburg, Miss., there is a seventh of these folk who, like turtles, must periodically submerge themselves. The Vicksburg case is a 12-year-old boy, handled by Dr Guy Jarrett. The others are cases of Dr Ralph Bowen of Memphis.

Dr Bowen last week had on hand a medical report concerning the phenomenon. The seven suffer from 'hereditary ectodermal dysplasia of the anhydrotic type'. That is, they lack sweat glands, and the lack is hereditary. However, the seven Mississippi cases are related only as indicated above. This suggests that the failing is not so uncommon as heretofore believed (only 23 cases have been reported in medical literature). The ailment must often escape medical attention. Along with the lack of sweat glands goes a lack of teeth. None of the seven Mississippi cases has more than two teeth.

Tom also sent me a typescript from *Time*'s research files:

From ANDREWS' DISEASES OF THE SKIN
Hereditary ectodermal dysplasia

There are numerous anomalies of the epidermis and appendages due to faulty evolution of the epiblastic layer of the blastoderm. The term 'ectodermal defect' has been limited to those conditions arising from incomplete development of the epidermis or its appendages,

or its absence in circumscribed areas, thus excluding the kerato-
dermias and the nevi. Atrichosis congenitalis with or without
deformities of the nails and teeth is common, and is accompanied at
times by nevi and other congenital anomalies. Congenital absence
or malformation of the nails and teeth is also of frequent occurrence,
and in circumscribed areas it is not out of the ordinary to find that
the sebaceous and sweat glands are absent or impaired. In restricted
areas there may be a complete absence of the epidermis and appendages at birth. It is more rare to encounter cases of extensive
deformation or complete absence of all, or nearly all, of the cutaneous
structures originating from the epiderm, to which group the term
'congenital ectodermal defect' is given. Guilford, an American dentist, was the first to report a case of this kind. The appearance of
these patients is typical and conspicuous, as they have a facies that
is suggestive of congenital syphilis. The skin is hairless, dry, white,
smooth, and glossy. The teeth are entirely absent or there may be a
few present, but the development is always defective.

There are dystrophic disturbances in the nails. The scalp hair is
sparse and of a fine soft texture. The cheek bones are high and wide,
whereas the lower half of the face is narrow. The supraorbital ridges
are prominent; the nasal bridge is depressed, forming a 'saddle-back
nose'. The tip of the nose is small and upturned, while the nostrils
are large and conspicuous. The eyebrows are scanty, none being
present on the outer two thirds. The eyes slant upwards, producing
a Mongolian facies. At the buccal commissures radiating furrows,
'pseudorhagades', are present, and on the cheeks there are telangiec-
tases and small papules simulating milium and adenoma sebaceum.
The lips are thickened, the upper one being particularly protrusive.

The patient studied by Dr MacKee and myself never sweated. He
was uncomfortable during hot weather due to elevation of body
temperature and was unable to play baseball and running games
with other boys of his age, because of great fatigue induced by such
exertions. These symptoms resemble those in other cases reported in
the literature, and not uncommonly the subjects find it necessary
during the summer to have pails of water thrown over them if they
are to keep comfortable.

The affection is familial, generally affecting males, and seems to
be due to an injury during the third month of uterine life. Some of
these patients are mentally deficient, but the majority of them
have normal mentality because the anlage of the nervous system is
distinct from the cutaneous ectoderm long before the injury occurs.
MacKay and Davidson report 4 cases occurring respectively in a

woman, aged thirty-four years, and her two sons and one daughter, aged six, eleven, and thirteen years. A comprehensive article with good references on this subject has been written by Gordon and Jamieson.

I was now in a position to review the story from the beginning. In 1919, I had been neurotic, as a result of having spent thirteen months in the trenches under continuous bombardment, and had begun to 'see things' in France even before a fragment of eight-inch shell went clean through my right lung and knocked me out. Limerick was a dead-alive city haunted by family ghosts, and the glass picture focused my morbid fears of the past and future – yes, it must have been the portrait of a turtle-man brought back to Ireland from the Southern States.

Julia and I: because of the unusually close rapport between us, partly explained by her Irish blood, it was not surprising that we should be scared by the same sort of face. Will had testified that the original was highly terrifying to any but a physician who could look coldly at it and characterize it as a *facies*. ('When am a face not a face, Massa Bones?' 'When it's a *facies*.') And why should Julia's mother not have stumbled across the same old house in New Orleans, and seen the same turtle-man peering through the attic window twelve years previously?

Hank: no natural sympathy existed between him and me, or between him and Julia. But he did have a remarkable receptivity for the emotions of people at a distance, and the trick of converting them into waking visions of his own. Clearly, he had subjectivized the fright which Julia and I conveyed to each other into something horrible that he had himself seen at Sóller. I need hardly add that Señor Bennasar keeps no tank in his patio for dunking turtle-folk in.

Will Price: he had a keen dramatic sense, but I found him far more accurate than most of my friends about names, dates and facts, and could not disbelieve his story. That is to say, I could accept what he saw with his own eyes. And what Mr Lemnowitz told him about George Whitaker and the Lafitte brothers was, Will himself confessed, 'shrouded in local myth'. On principle I suspect any legend about the Lafittes, as I do any legend about Paul Revere, Paul Jones, or Paul Bunyan. Besides, what connexion could there be between the Whitaker Negroes and the white Turtle Folk who occur spasmodically on the Lower Mississippi? Nobody had suggested that sophisticated white women of Natchez, Vicksburg, Vardaman, Baton Rouge, Yazoo City and New Orleans ever paid clandestine visits to Pond in search of a new sexual *frisson*. It therefore seems probable that if the Lafittes did indeed smuggle a shipload of Negroes to Pond, these were healthy enough when they arrived, but proved susceptible to the turtle-disease, which is endemic to the Mississippi; and because of inbreeding it became hereditary among them. The families affected were disowned by their masters but permitted to camp on the swampy fringes of the Whitaker estate, after George dragged his wife with him into the River – which he probably did, if at all, for some simple, domestic reason. And because high cheek-bones and a weak growth of hair are characteristic of the turtle-folk *facies* – which resembles that of the congenital syphilitic – there seems to be no reason for bringing the pox-stricken Choctaws and Chickasaws into the story either.

But what about the numerous coincidences which hold the story together? Julia, her mother, Will, Hank, and myself had all been frightened, directly or indirectly, by the same rare phenomenon; and we met accidentally in Deyá, a village of four hundred inhabitants commendably unknown to history, which lies three or four thousand miles away from Pond, an even smaller place, to the geographical existence of which only Will among us could testify. Moreover, Tom Matthews who clarified the phenomenon (scientifically at least) for all of us – both Julia and her mother were immensely relieved to know that it was a real face after all – had also been living at Deyá when the *Time* article appeared. But these coincidences do not amount to much, perhaps, and would never have come to light had not the Whitaker *facies* been so unforgettably frightening. (It occurs to me as I write that the real explanation of the Glamis Monster – the reputedly 'Undying Thing' which used to peer out from one of the attic windows at Glamis Castle – may have been hereditary ectodermal dysplasia in the Bowes-Lyon family, hushed up because one of its victims was heir to the earldom.) Finally, I suspect myself of having exaggerated the telepathic sympathy between Julia and myself. Did the face she described so vividly superimpose itself, perhaps, on the fading memory of the one I had seen in Mr Reilly's antique shop? My imagination is not that of a natural liar, because my Protestant conscience restrains me from inventing complete fictions; but I am Irishman enough to coax stories into a better shape than I found them.

This is not yet all. In 1954, I broadcast a short summary of the foregoing story for the B.B.C. As a result, a doctor wrote to tell me that he once had under observation, in a Liverpool hospital, a white child suffering from this rare disease; but that occasional sponging was sufficient relief for its discomfort, except in unusually hot weather. Another letter came from Mrs Otto Lobstein, an Englishwoman who was going off some months later with her husband for a tour of the Southern States, and proposed to check up on the Whitaker Negroes. 'Where did you say that they lived?' she wrote.

I provided the necessary map-references, not really expecting to hear from Mrs Lobstein again; but in due process of time she sent me a letter and a photograph. The photograph showed a Mississippi finger-post pointing south to Woodville, north to Pinckneyville, east to Pond and Fort Adams; and the fine condition of the three roads suggested that prosperity had returned to the neighbourhood since Will Price's visit there more than twenty years previously. This was the letter, which I have been kindly allowed to print here.

New Orleans,
February 1st, 1955.

Dear Robert Graves,

We spent an interesting day tracking down the Whitaker-negroes, after camping for a night in the Mississippi woods – a wretched night because this was the hardest frost of the winter. But the early morning sun was startlingly warm and the fields beautiful; no wind blew and thin, erect strings of smoke came from the small shacks along the road.

Pond is not on the map, so we took the road to Fort Adams until we came to a very lovely old plantation home, where one Rip White directed us to the Whitaker plantation. But he was far more anxious to tell us about his own house, which 'had been granted to Henry

Stewart, son of Mary Queen of Scots about 180 years ago'. Henry
was 'a contender to the Throne', so they shipped him off to America,
where he was given this plantation of 2,200 acres to keep him
quiet and occupied. The house did have a royal air, but I was a
little troubled by the discrepancy in date between Mary Queen of
Scots and King George III, and between the names Stewart and
Stuart!

When we reached the plantation, we met Mr Whitaker, the owner,
who was going somewhere in a hurry, but told us that the old mansion some way back in the fields had been demolished a few years
before. (Its place was now taken by a large, hard-looking, unromantic
modern bungalow.) He also told us that the land had been split up
at the same time between the various Whitaker sons – which didn't
seem to coincide with Will Price's story that the land had been
deeded to the State, unless perhaps a brother of the man who committed suicide had contested the deed of gift and won it back. Anyhow, Mr Whitaker advised us to ask Mrs Ray about the story; she
had raised all the Whitaker whites for two or three generations.

Dear old Mrs Ray gave us interesting recollections of what her
mother and father had told her as a child: how, when the overseer
had whipped a slave over a log for not picking enough cotton, the
rest would creep out of the plantation after dark and go into a 'holler'
– bending their heads low down so as not to be heard, they would
sing and pray for freedom. But she had no stories about Whitaker-
negroes.

At Woodville, a small town on the way to Pond, we visited the
Court House to look for records of the original George Whitaker.
There we found an intelligent official, Mr Leek, who had actually
met some of the Whitaker-negroes, when he helped them to fill up
questionnaires during the Second World War. He told us that they
were dying out fast. In winter, he said, they wore ordinary clothes;
in summer, heavy underclothes soaked in water. The Court House
records, however, did not show that any Whitaker land had been
deeded to the State since 1804, when they began. Mr Leek's explanation of why the Whitaker-negroes were so called was that the first
sufferer had 'Whitaker' as his Christian name.

At last we reached Pond. Pond Post Office is a big, barn-like
structure which, as in the days of trading-posts, carries everything
and deals in sacks of flour and rolls of cotton; the large, serene pond
mentioned by Will Price lay at the foot of the hill. Mr Carroll Smith,
the postmaster in succession to Mr Lemnowitz, sold us some safety-
pins. He was small and silver-haired, with sensitive brown eyes. At

first he showed a certain reticence when we questioned him, but gradually shed it. He confirmed that very few Whitaker-negroes are left, and said that they lived on the plantations, not in the swamps. Nowadays, only one member of a family of five or six children would inherit the disease. Occasionally a Whitaker-negro visited the Post Office, which was always an unpleasant experience, because the glandular excretions emitted through his mouth conveyed an appalling odour of decay. Mr Smith had never heard the story of George Whitaker's suicide and believed, with Mr Leek, that the original sufferer was an immigrant negro from Virginia. He suggested that we should visit a Mr McGeehee in Pinckneyville, the nearest village, who had a couple of Whitaker-negroes working for him. He would say no more on the subject, after that, though we talked for some time about share-cropping. So we drove on.

Mr McGeehee's plantation was very English, with a tree-lined driveway running through park-like meadows (where Herefords and Red Devons grazed) to a big, unpretentious house. Mr McGeehee himself was most hospitable; so was his mother, a gentle old lady, looking like a pressed flower. We chatted politely in the spacious drawing-room about farming and children and plantation houses; but both the McGeehees remained emphatic that we must not meet the two Whitaker-negroes working for them. Mr McGeehee, very rightly, felt responsible for his employees and said that too many sightseers had come to stare at the pair recently, which made them sensitive. So my husband and I did not press the point; and, in any case, we felt the point slipping away from us. A group of people with a strange history, living in odd conditions and with a bizarre inheritance, are one thing; and a few sufferers from skin disease, who happen to have been born into normal families, are quite another.

In the 1930s, apparently, Will Price found them living in a group, and this was natural because they are not popular with the other negroes, for obvious reasons; and he must have gone there in the summer, when their distinctive habits were more conspicuous. As for the story of their origin, it seems probable that Mr Lemnowitz heard it from some source, now lost, which was as untrustworthy as that of Rip White's legend about 'Henry Stewart, the Contender to the Throne'.

A novel feature of the countryside which may interest you is that plantation owners have begun to import Brahmini cattle – instead of orchids – from the Far East. These withstand heat and drought better than other breeds, and make good store cattle; I saw many of them grazing in the fields – silky-grey in colour, with huge horned heads. The bulls were humped like camels, and added a richness to the Pond landscape.

Yours sincerely,
Anna Lobstein

This calm and practical travelogue has dispelled my haunting nightmare for ever. Terror gives way to pity; the pirates Jean and Pierre Lafitte, together with the rogue Choctaws and Chickasaws, are banished to the realms of macabre legend. Only the hospitable Mr McGeehee and his gentle old mother, who resembles a pressed flower, are left on the stage; in charge of two sensitive sufferers from hereditary ectodermal dysplasia of the anhydrotic type, whose principal purpose in life is to herd silky-grey Brahmini cattle in lush parkland – a far more agreeable example of *symbiosis* than the one reported by Will Price.

FOR THE BEST IN PAPERBACKS, LOOK FOR THE

In every corner of the world, on every subject under the sun, Penguin represents quality and variety – the very best in publishing today.

For complete information about books available from Penguin – including Pelicans, Puffins, Peregrines and Penguin Classics – and how to order them, write to us at the appropriate address below. Please note that for copyright reasons the selection of books varies from country to country.

In the United Kingdom: Please write to *Dept E.P., Penguin Books Ltd, Harmondsworth, Middlesex, UB7 0DA*

In the United States: Please write to *Dept BA, Penguin, 299 Murray Hill Parkway, East Rutherford, New Jersey 07073*

In Canada: Please write to *Penguin Books Canada Ltd, 2801 John Street, Markham, Ontario L3R 1B4*

In Australia: Please write to the *Marketing Department, Penguin Books Australia Ltd, P.O. Box 257, Ringwood, Victoria 3134*

In New Zealand: Please write to the *Marketing Department, Penguin Books (NZ) Ltd, Private Bag, Takapuna, Auckland 9*

In India: Please write to *Penguin Overseas Ltd, 706 Eros Apartments, 56 Nehru Place, New Delhi, 110019*

In Holland: Please write to *Penguin Books Nederland B.V., Postbus 195, NL–1380AD Weesp, Netherlands*

In Germany: Please write to *Penguin Books Ltd, Friedrichstrasse 10–12, D–6000 Frankfurt Main 1, Federal Republic of Germany*

In Spain: Please write to *Longman Penguin España, Calle San Nicolas 15, E–28013 Madrid, Spain*

In France: Please write to *Penguin Books Ltd, 39 Rue de Montmorency, F-75003, Paris, France*

In Japan: Please write to *Longman Penguin Japan Co Ltd, Yamaguchi Building, 2–12–9 Kanda Jimbocho, Chiyoda-Ku, Tokyo 101, Japan*

ROBERT GRAVES

—

I, CLAUDIUS

Robert Graves's magnificent reconstruction of the grandeur and folly and vileness of early Imperial Rome is one of the most distinguished historical novels of this generation. Its setting varies from a Roman palace to a desert in Tripoli, a dark German forest, a garden at Pompeii, a camp in the Balkans, the Sibyl's cavern at Cumae, and a cliff-top on the island of Rhodes. The action is strange, tragic, and ludicrous, for Rome knows herself under a long-standing curse – the curse of the gods with whom she broke faith when she destroyed Carthage – and has lost all moral self-control. Treachery, incest, black magic, and unnatural vice flourish. Insane cruelties are committed. And through it all moves the strange, lovable figure of Claudius himself, despised, neglected, and apparently ineffective, but destined in the end to become Emperor against his will.

CLAUDIUS THE GOD

In this book Claudius continues his historical memoirs, bringing the story from his own acclamation as Emperor at the death of his terrible nephew, Caligula, to his assassination in the year 54. Quite as much as his age, Claudius comes to life in these pages – Claudius, who survived the violent reigns of four earlier Caesars, who remained Emperor for fourteen years, and who yet was thought by his contemporaries to be a fool.

COUNT BELISARIUS

The Sixth Century was not a peaceful one for the Roman Empire. Invaders threatened on all frontiers; Huns, Vandals, Goths, Saracens, Moors, Persians. But they grew to fear and respect the name of Belisarius, horseman, archer, swordsman and military commander of incredible skill and daring. Belisarius led the Imperial armies wherever the Emperor Justinian sent him; to the Eastern Frontier on the Euphrates, across the Mediterranean to Carthage, and to Rome.

In his palace at Constantinople, Justinian plotted and intrigued, dominated by his wife Theodora whose spies were everywhere. Justinian hated Belisarius for his success, his nobility and his universal popularity. But Belisarius was the one man who could save the Empire . . .

ROBERT GRAVES

—

THE GREEK MYTHS
(in two volumes)

Not for over a century, since Smith's *Dictionary of Classical Mythology* first appeared, has the attempt been made to provide for the English reader a complete 'mythology', in the sense of a retelling in modern terms of the Greek tales of gods and heroes. In the two volumes of this book Robert Graves, whose combination of classical scholarship and anthropological competence has already been so brilliantly demonstrated in *The Golden Fleece*, *The White Goddess*, and his novels, supplies the need. In nearly two hundred sections, it covers the Creation myths, the legends of the birth and lives of the great Olympians, the Theseus, Oedipus, and Heracles cycles, the Argonaut voyage, the tale of Troy, and much else.

All the scattered elements of each myth have been assembled into a harmonious narrative, and many variants are recorded which may help to determine its ritual or historical meaning. Full references to the classical sources, and copious indexes, make the book as valuable to the scholar as to the general reader; and a full commentary to each myth explains and interprets the classical version in the light of today's archaeological and anthropological knowledge.

GOODBYE TO ALL THAT

Robert Graves's famous account of his life at Charterhouse School and as a young officer in the First World War.

'It is a permanently valuable work of literary art, and indispensable for the historian either of the First World War or of modern English poetry. . . . Apart, however, from its exceptional value as a war document, this book has also the interest of being one of the most candid self-portraits of a poet, warts and all, ever painted. The sketches of friends of Mr Graves, like T. E. Lawrence, are beautifully vivid' – *The Times Literary Supplement*

'From the moment of its first appearance an established classic' – John Wain in the *Observer*